# The price of Betrayal . . .

Devlin's world narrowed until all his focus was bent on the small circles of metal that bound his wrists. The left manacle showed no signs of budging, but the one on his maimed right hand had begun, ever so slightly, to yield. He never thought that he would be grateful to Duke Gerhard, but the duel that had cost Devlin two of his fingers also meant that his right hand was narrower than his left.

Something his captors had overlooked. No doubt they thought him helpless. For all he knew he had been their captive for weeks, instead of mere days or hours. There was no way to be certain how far he had been taken. Nor what was happening in Kingsholm.

The thought spurred him to renewed efforts, and he twisted his right hand slightly and pulled. The muscles in his arm trembled with strain as the blood-slicked manacle slipped a bare fraction. It was working, though far too slowly for his tastes. He took a deep breath, counted to three, and strained again.

Patience and cunning would set him free, and then he would show these folk the folly of underestimating the Chosen One . . .

# Devlin's Justice

## THE SWORD OF CHANGE • BOOK III

# Patricia Bray

**BANTAM BOOKS**

DEVLIN'S JUSTICE
A Bantam Spectra Book / April 2004

Published by Bantam Dell
A Division of Random House, Inc.
New York, New York

ISBN 0-553-58477-4

Manufactured in the United States of America
Published simultaneously in Canada

OPM  10  9  8  7  6  5  4  3  2

For Mrs. Margaret Hudnall, who taught creative writing at Northwest Catholic High School, and told me that I had the talent to be a writer.

I was listening.

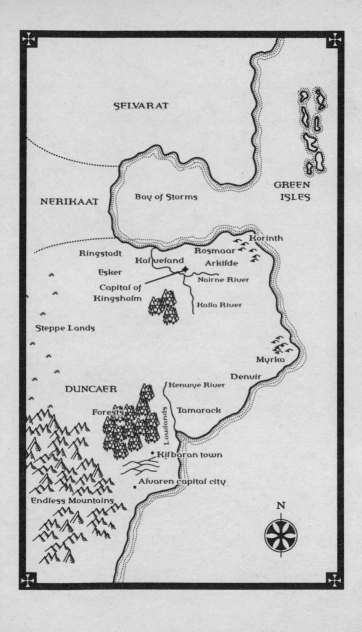

# One

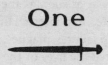

KING OLAFUR SURREPTITIOUSLY RUBBED HIS damp palms against the sleeves of his silken robe. A lesser man might have shown his impatience by fidgeting, or given in to the urge to pace, but Olafur was beyond such temptations. The blood of great rulers flowed in his veins. Thorvald, his father, had conquered Duncaer and expanded the reach of the empire from sea to sea. Olaven, his grandsire, had brought glory to Jorsk as the hub of a trading empire. And his great-grandsire was King Axel, whose brilliant diplomacy had enabled him to forge an alliance with Emperor Jeoffroi of Selvarat, ending two hundred years of enmity between their peoples. And King Axel's skill at diplomacy had been equaled by his prowess as a war leader, for the combined might of Selvarat and Jorsk had crushed the Nerikaat alliance that had threatened both their realms.

His forebears had left him a mighty kingdom, along with the responsibility to preserve it. Since his father's death, Olafur had done what he could, in the face of nearly insurmountable odds. But Axel had faced only one enemy—and the Nerikaat alliance, for all their vicious-ness, had been an honorable foe who attacked openly. By contrast Olafur had been fighting a series of faceless ene-mies who melted away as soon as they were confronted. Border raiders, pirates, and internal unrest had bedeviled him, along with crop failures, plagues, and a host of mon-sters that had claimed the lives of the Chosen Ones with depressing regularity.

Olafur knew that no other man could have held the Kingdom together so long. But even he could only do so much. Help must be had, if the Kingdom was to survive. It was time to call upon the ancient alliance once more and ask Selvarat to honor its promise of friendship and mutual aid.

His eyes swept the receiving room, ensuring that all was in readiness. On his left side stood Lady Ingeleth, the leader of the King's Council. Ranged beside her were a half dozen high-ranking nobles, carefully chosen so that each region had a representative. If this had been a formal reception in the great throne room, his entire court would have been in attendance. But a mere ambassador did not rate such an honor, regardless of the importance of his mission.

Standing on his right side was Marshal Erild Olvarrson, who now led the Royal Army in the absence of the Chosen One. While the Marshal would never com-mand the strong devotion that Devlin inspired in his fol-lowers, his loyalty to the throne was unquestioned. As was his obedience.

And while no one could question the Chosen One's loyalty to his oaths, Devlin had yet to learn the value of political compromise. He continued to see matters in the most simplistic terms. It was for the best that Devlin's journey to Duncaer had taken longer than expected. His presence here would only complicate matters.

Not to mention that it would give Olafur great pleasure to be the one who ensured the security of his kingdom. He and he alone would be hailed as the savior of his people. Devlin's heroics and his strange ideas about the place of the common people would be forgotten.

Once the Kingdom had returned to normalcy, Olafur would see about making other changes in his court. Devlin had served ably as Chosen One, and such he would remain until his inevitable death. But it might be time to appoint another as General of the Royal Army. Olvarrson, perhaps, or another scion of a noble family who owed him a favor.

But those were considerations for another day. Now he must focus all his energies on meeting the ambassador and the negotiations that would take place in the days to come. Only in his private thoughts would he admit how relieved he had been when word was brought that Count Magaharan and his party had arrived in the city. He had expected them for some time, as the ice on the Kalla River had been clear for nearly a month. But it would not do to give any hint of his impatience, so in a show of politeness, Olafur had given instructions that they be welcomed and shown to their quarters to refresh themselves after their long journey.

Having given them a chance to bathe and dress in their court finery, he could welcome his guests. A nervous man might have resorted to a formal diplomatic reception, trying to overawe his visitors. But Olafur was too subtle for such tactics. He did not need to wear a heavy crown or be seated upon the royal throne in order to demonstrate his power. Instead he could greet the ambassador as a friend, setting the tone for the discussions to come. He would treat with the Count as an equal, not as a beggar. Misfortune might have plagued Jorsk in these last years, but he was still the ruler of a powerful kingdom. The aid he sought had been paid for tenfold by the blood Axel's forces had shed on behalf of the common alliance.

Indeed the last letter he had received from Empress Thania had been a carefully worded assurance that she was prepared to assist Jorsk in defending itself against the foreign aggressors. Now with the return of her ambassador, he could negotiate what form that aid should take. Devlin, along with the barons of the coastal provinces, insisted troops were needed to stave off a possible invasion. He argued that last year's landings in Korinth had been but a feint, and that their enemies would strike Korinth in force before the summer was over.

A few of the army officers shared Devlin's views, but Olafur himself was not convinced that they faced a land invasion. In his opinion the sea raiders from the Green Isles were as much a threat as any possible invasion. The raiders destroyed coastal villages, but they also wreaked havoc on the shipping that was the lifeblood of the Kingdom. A few well-armed ships from the Selvarat navy might be worth more than a regiment of soldiers.

He wondered just how generous Thania was prepared to be. His earlier requests had fallen on deaf ears, but it seemed last summer's aborted landing in Korinth, and the events surrounding Duke Gerhard's execution, had convinced her that Jorsk was indeed in need of assistance. It chafed to be put in the position of supplicant, but he reminded himself that the aid he asked for was no more than his rightful due, promised by long-standing treaties and paid for by years of mutual alliance. If Selvarat had been the one to fall into danger, he himself would have done no less.

Still he knew better than to suppose that the help would come without a price. Treaty or no, there was always a cost. He would have to rely upon his own cunning and skill at diplomacy to ensure that the price of salvation did not beggar his kingdom.

His musings were cut short as two guards swung open the doors, then clicked their heels and bowed their heads in respect.

Count Magaharan was the first to enter. Tall and lean, he had an ascetic look, even in his brightly colored court robes, more suited to a scholar than a veteran courtier. The Count had been Selvarat's ambassador to Jorsk for the past two years, and he appeared completely at his ease as he strode into the receiving room.

Following Count Magaharan was his aide Jenna, a young woman who called herself a commoner, though rumor claimed she was a bastard offspring of the royal house. Behind her were two men whom he immediately dismissed as minor functionaries by the plainness of their dress.

Then, just as the guards were getting ready to close the doors, a fourth man stepped through, trailing so far behind the others that it was not immediately clear that he was a member of the ambassador's party.

Perhaps he had deliberately chosen to make an unconventional entrance. Olafur's eyes narrowed as he studied the newcomer. The man was plainly dressed, his court robe showing only a narrow band of silver brocade, but he carried himself with utter confidence. As he approached the others, Olafur noticed that the Count's aide stepped aside so the newcomer could take her place.

The ambassador bowed deeply, extending his right hand in a flourishing sweep. His companions followed suit.

"Count Magaharan, it is a pleasure to welcome you and your companions, and to offer you the hospitality of my court."

The ambassador drew himself erect. "On behalf of myself, and in the name of the Empress Thania, whom I have the honor to serve, I thank you for your courtesy. The Empress sends her greetings to her friend Olafur of Jorsk, along with her wishes for your continued health and the prosperity of your kingdom."

"Empress Thania is gracious indeed, and we count ourselves fortunate in her friendship," Olafur replied.

"May I present my companions? You already know my aide Jenna, and this is Vachel of the house of Burrel, and Guy from the house of Saltair."

As they were named, Vachel and Guy each stepped forward a pace and made their bows, which Olafur acknowledged with a polite nod. Burrel and Saltair were midrank houses in Selvarat, and this confirmed his impression that the two were mere advisors. Worth keeping an eye on, but they would defer to Magaharan in all matters of importance.

"And this, Your Majesty, is Karel of Maurant."

"Your Majesty," the late arrival said, with a deep bow and an even more elaborate hand flourish than Magaharan had made. His manners showed that he had traveled little outside his own land, for while this might be the fashion in Selvarat, here such a display might be taken as mockery.

Although new to diplomacy he might be, the man was not one to be taken lightly. Maurant was not just any noble house, it was the house of Prince Arnaud, the royal consort of Empress Thania. And while he could not quite remember the intricacies of the imperial family tree, it would be wise to err on the side of caution. Simply because no title had been claimed did not mean that this Karel was without rank.

"Lord Karel, I welcome you to my court," Olafur said. "I would make known to you my chief councilor, Lady Ingeleth, and Marshal Olvarrson of the Royal Army."

Karel acknowledged the introductions with studious politeness. As Lady Ingeleth introduced the remaining Jorskian nobles to the ambassador's party, King Olafur took the opportunity to study their visitors. He thought he saw a certain resemblance between Karel and Jenna, in the shape of their noses and their unusually small ears, which gave further credence to his belief that Karel was a member of the royal family.

Olafur had been disappointed when his equerry had reported that there was no senior military officer among the ambassador's party. If the Empress intended to honor the treaty, then surely she would have sent along a general or a marshal at the very least, someone who could discuss the makeup and disposition of the Selvarat forces and how they could aid in the defense of Jorsk. But perhaps his disappointment had been premature. Sending a member of the royal family, however distant his connection to the Prince, must be taken as a sign of favor.

Whatever their intentions were, he would have to wait.

He knew better than to expect that Count Magaharan would immediately reveal the messages he had been entrusted with. There were certain rituals to be observed. And it would not do to give the impression of desperation. Need, yes, but desperation would be taken as a sign of weakness and exploited accordingly.

"A feast has been prepared in your honor," King Olafur said. Though *feast* was perhaps too strong a word, since the royal kitchens only had hours to prepare for their guests. Still, whatever was served was bound to be better than journey fare. And he had ordered the remaining Myrkan red brought up from the cellars, so there would be no cause for complaint there. "If you would join us?" Olafur asked.

"It would be our pleasure," Count Magaharan replied.

Captain Drakken buckled the scabbard of her sword over her dress tunic, then tugged at the hem of her uniform until it hung straight. Seldom used in the winter months, a musty odor arose from the garment and she made a mental note to have words with the servant who oversaw her quarters. With the court about to commence its annual session, she could not afford to find her dress uniforms moth-eaten or rotted from neglect. King Olafur was known to be a stickler about such things, and her place in court was tenuous enough without incurring his wrath over such a trifle.

He was also insistent on punctuality. A glance at the sand clock showed that she needed to leave soon if she was to be on time for the dinner honoring the Selvarat ambassador. But she did not want to leave before Lieutenant Embeth had made her report.

Just as she had resolved that she could wait no longer, there was a sharp knock and the door to her quarters swung open before she could respond.

"Captain, your pardon." Lieutenant Embeth paused to gasp for breath. Her face was flushed and she was panting.

"Wait. Breathe," Captain Drakken said. There was no sense in listening to a report made incomprehensible from lack of breath.

"Report," she ordered, when Embeth had gained control of herself.

"Captain Drakken," Lieutenant Embeth drew herself to attention. "As you know, Ambassador Magaharan and his party arrived by ship just before the noon hour. They were met by a royal equerry who escorted them to the palace. In addition to the ambassador, there was his aide Jenna, two noblemen named Vachel and Guy, and a man called either Karel or Charles whose status I could not confirm. He was accorded his own chamber, so he may be another aide."

Strange that Count Magaharan would have brought not one but two aides, along with a pair of advisors who had never visited Jorsk before, but then again this was no usual visit. Drakken knew full well that King Olafur was hoping for a renewal of the ancient alliance and for Selvarat to supply troops to defend Jorsk's borders. The dinner tonight would serve to introduce the ambassador's party to the court, but it would do no harm to check also with Solveig, to see if she knew anything of their visitors.

"There were also four clerks, a priest, a half dozen servants, and the ambassador's personal honor guard."

"Is that all?"

"That is the party that arrived at the palace. But we kept watch on the ship that carried the ambassador, and at dusk six persons left the ship and took rooms in the old city. They were dressed as sailors but they had the gait of landsmen, and at least one of them was wearing a sword under her cloak."

"Soldiers," Captain Drakken said. "Or mercenaries."

"So I suspected. I stayed long enough to confirm the report, then ordered a watch kept on the inn where they were staying."

"You did well. Make sure the watchers know to be discreet, and that they are to make a daily report of what these people do and whom they meet. If they see anything suspicious, they are to notify me without delay."

"Understood, Captain."

She dismissed Embeth with a nod, and the lieutenant saluted before making her departure.

A glance at the sand clock showed that she would have to make haste to avoid a late entrance at the dinner. Instead Captain Drakken crossed over to her desk and unrolled a parchment scroll that showed a map of the Kingdom. Along the Southern Road was a small spot, so faint that it might be mistaken for a flaw in the parchment. But in truth it was the latest position of the Chosen One, as she had verified by checking with the soul stone in the temple only that morning. He had made good time since leaving Duncaer, but in the last days his pace had slowed. By her reckoning Devlin was at least a fortnight away from Kingsholm. She glared at the map, but all her wishing could not make the leagues any shorter, and with an angry curse she rolled up the map.

Devlin had been gone too long. He should have been back over a month ago, but his errand in Duncaer had taken longer than expected. Now he was returning, presumably bearing the Sword of Light, but they could not wait another two weeks for him. They needed him here in the capital. Now.

The court was beginning its spring session. The ambassador from Selvarat had arrived, bringing with him the Empress Thania's response to King Olafur's request for military assistance. Intelligence had indicated that the Empress would respond favorably, but intelligence could be wrong. And even if she sent troops, it would take skill to deploy them to the maximum advantage.

Now was the time when decisions would be made that would secure the Kingdom's safety, or see it fracture under the competing pressures from within and without. It was a time for bold leadership, but such was noticeably lacking. Devlin's few friends at court had no influence with either King Olafur or his council. Marshal Olvarrson was neither a strategist nor a leader. He would do as King Olafur instructed, heedless of the long-term consequences.

Captain Drakken knew that many were expecting great things from the Selvarat alliance, but she herself was wary of strangers offering gifts. Ancient treaties or no, if Empress Thania was prepared to have her soldiers shed blood on Jorsk's behalf, then it was safe to reason that she was expecting to receive something of equal value in return. Depending on what concessions the Selvarats might win out of King Olafur, the cure might well prove worse than the disease.

And if politics were not enough for Drakken to worry

about, she also had six mysterious strangers who would have to be closely watched. Not to mention that she had yet to discover who had sent the assassins after Devlin last fall. For all she knew their paymaster might well be among those nobles who were even now arriving in the city for the spring council.

There were plots among plots, and very few people whom she could trust. For the past months she had done what she needed to do to ensure that Kingsholm would be ready for Devlin's return. She had held her tongue, taking care that she gave the King no cause to relieve her of her command. But now she could no longer afford inaction. She owed it to herself, and to those whom she served, to make her opinions known. And she knew Devlin's other friends, including Lord Rikard and Solveig of Esker would be facing similar dilemmas.

Only Devlin's voice could balance the conservative forces of the court. She prayed to the Gods that his errand had been successful. If Devlin returned bearing the Sword of Light, it would be impossible for King Olafur and the courtiers to ignore him.

"Hurry back," she said aloud. "We cannot hold on much longer."

King Olafur led the way into the great dining hall, with Count Magaharan at his side. The rest of the party followed, and from the corner of his eye he saw Lady Ingeleth speaking to Lord Rikard. Rikard, who had been intended to sit on the main dais, found his way to a seat at the head of the center table along with Vachel and Guy, while Lady Ingeleth escorted Lord Karel to a place at the dais.

The main doors were opened and the rest of the court filed in, along with the members of the ambassador's retinue who had been too lowly to be presented to the King, but were too important to be consigned to the servants' hall. Only a third of the tables had been set, for with winter just ended, most of his nobles were only just beginning to make the long journey to court. Still, there were enough courtiers who had wintered over in the capital to make for a lively gathering.

Conversation at dinner was general, as he had known it would be. Affairs of state were too delicate a matter to be discussed in such a public setting. Instead they spoke of trivialities. Count Magaharan described his journey on the newest ship in the imperial fleet, and how it was so comfortable one could scarcely believe they were on a ship instead of dry land. Olafur, whose own memories of sailing ships included misery and wretched discomfort, kept his doubts to himself.

For his part he spoke little, content to let Lady Ingeleth play the role of hostess—a part she was well suited for. Knowing the ambassador's love of culture, Lady Ingeleth reported that a new poet had come into favor at the court over the winter, and offered to arrange a private performance for the ambassador and his party.

Such trifles kept them occupied until the last course had been removed and the final toast had been drunk. King Olafur dismissed the diners, and then invited Count Magaharan and Lord Karel to join him in his private chambers. Lady Ingeleth and Marshal Olvarrson accompanied them.

He waited with seemingly endless patience as the party settled themselves, and the servants served glasses of ice wine and citrine. At his signal the servants placed the pitchers on the sideboard, then took their leave, bowing low as they closed the doors behind them.

Ambassador Magaharan lost no time in coming to the point. "Empress Thania has sent a letter of greeting that I will give to your secretary. But I am authorized to tell you the gist of her message, which is that she honors the alliance between our peoples and has sent troops from our armies to assist in the protection of Jorsk."

Olafur nodded gravely, though he felt nearly dizzy with relief. This was no more than he had expected, and indeed the last letter from Selvarat received before the winter ice locked the harbor had strongly hinted that such aid would be forthcoming. But much could change in three months' time, and only now did he realize how much he had feared that she would have found some reason to refuse his request.

"When friends stand together there is none can divide them," Olafur said. "As it was in the time of Axel and Jeoffroi, so shall it be with Empress Thania and myself. Just as our enemies are your enemies, we pledge that your enemies will be ours as well."

It was a speech that he had rehearsed for days, yet had never quite been sure that he would have the opportunity to deliver.

Marshal Olvarrson cleared his throat, drawing all eyes to him. "If I may, Your Majesty," he said. "Count Magaharan, did I hear you say that the Empress had already sent the troops? Are they on their way even now?"

"Better than that, they have already landed," Count

Magaharan replied with a small smile. "Two hundred horsemen and a thousand foot soldiers have already disembarked on the coast of Korinth. Our ship accompanied the transports and witnessed their landing. By now they have secured the whole of the province."

Lady Ingeleth's eyebrows rose. "This is indeed unexpected," she said.

It was more than unexpected. It was presumptuous, to say the least. True, Thania had been generous in the number of troops she sent, but he should have been consulted before they were deployed.

"I appreciate the Empress Thania's loan of her troops, but I had expected to be informed before they set sail. My commanders will want to make best use of them," King Olafur said. His pride was stung by the high-handed way in which this had been done, but he could not afford to offend those who represented the Empress. He needed those soldiers.

"Of course, but such consultations would take time, and the Empress wished to send her aid with all possible speed," Count Magaharan said. "She did not want you to be caught unprepared, if there should be an invasion this spring. We knew of your concern over Korinth from our discussions last fall, and felt it was best to send the troops where they were needed without delay."

He allowed himself to be somewhat mollified. Help that came too late was no help at all, and the journey between Selvarat and Jorsk could take several weeks, depending on the weather. Having asked for help to be sent with all speed, he should not quarrel if his allies had used their own judgment about the method of fulfilling his request.

"And now that we have arrived, we can discuss the disposition of the next wave of forces with you and Marshal Olvarrson," Lord Karel added. "Our general staff recommended that our troops be used to secure the eastern provinces, which are the closest to Selvarat. You could then use your own units to secure your northwestern border. But . . . this is just a proposal. Naturally you will want your advisors to review these plans and see if you agree with our suggestions."

"Naturally," he echoed.

Marshal Olvarrson rubbed his chin thoughtfully. "I would have to see the plans, but there is sense in what he proposes. Major Mikkelson has been complaining for months that if an attack came, he could not hold the east coast on his own."

Mikkelson. Now there was a man who was nearly as much trouble as his mentor Devlin. Mikkelson had pleaded that the troops be released from their central garrisons, not seeming to realize that trouble was just as likely to come from the west as the east.

"It seems you have thought of everything," Lady Ingeleth said dryly. From the tone of her voice Olafur knew that she was not pleased. "And what precisely do you expect from us in return?"

"The Empress seeks a pledge of friendship. And a gift to seal the alliance."

Olafur had a strong suspicion that he knew what the gift was to be. He had had months to resign himself to this, though he had not yet told Ragenilda of her probable fate. Fortunately she was a biddable girl and would do as she was told.

It was a shame that he had only the one child. Ragenilda would rule Jorsk after him, and whoever she married would be the father of the next king or queen. Still, it was a small price to pay if it meant ensuring there was a kingdom for her to inherit.

"My daughter Princess Ragenilda is young—"

"Not too young to be pledged," Lord Karel interrupted. Lady Ingeleth hissed at this breach of court etiquette.

"Prince Nathan is just turned sixteen and would be a fitting match for your daughter, when the time comes. But Ragenilda's future is a matter for another day," Karel continued.

"Then what is it you want?" Olafur asked.

"The Chosen One," Lord Karel replied. "We want Devlin of Duncaer."

# Two

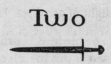

KRONNA'S MILL WAS TOO INSIGNIFICANT TO be listed on Devlin's maps—scarcely more than a village, if a prosperous one. Deep in the interior of Jorsk it showed few signs of the troubles that afflicted the outlands. In addition to the mill from which it had taken its name, there were a handful of well-kept shops and a large inn that offered the promise of shelter from the icy rain. Though it was only midday, Devlin called a halt, despite Didrik's protests.

The inn-wife took one look at the shivering party and shooed them into the common room, where she coaxed the smoldering fire into a roaring blaze. Wet cloaks were hung to dry, while their hands were soon wrapped around mugs of hot kava. Muscles that ached from the cold began to relax as their blood warmed.

Saskia grimaced at the taste of the kava, then gulped down the contents of her mug in three quick swallows. "Flames, I don't know how you drink this stuff. What happened to decent tea?"

"We ran out a week ago, if you remember," Devlin said

mildly. "I doubt the merchants here will have any, but you can ask."

Saskia shook her head. "I would not trust these Jorskians to know aught of good tea. They're as like to sell me bitter weed. I'll wait till we're in Kingsholm and I can find one of our own folk."

Saskia had led the honor guard that had escorted Devlin and his companions from Alvaren to the Jorskian border. When they reached the border town of Kilbaran, the peacekeepers had turned back. All of them except Saskia, who had declared that her orders were to see Devlin safely returned to Kingsholm. He had tried to dissuade her, but his words had fallen on deaf ears.

He did not believe that Chief Mychal had ordered her to accompany him all the way to Kingsholm, and wondered why she had decided to leave Duncaer and embark on this long journey. Did she see this as a duty that she owed her lost comrade Cerrie? Or was her interest more personal? He had not missed the growing friendship between her and Lieutenant Didrik.

Whatever her reasons, he had not protested. Though their journey so far had been untroubled, an extra sword arm could prove useful. Especially given that one of their party was already hurt.

He looked over at Didrik, who clutched his mug in hands that trembled despite his best efforts to control them. Didrik's complexion was gray with exhaustion, but he held himself erect as if refusing to admit that there was anything wrong.

Stephen finished his kava and set his mug on the nearest table before reaching for his cloak. "I'll go get the saddlebags. If we hang our blankets by the fire, they'll be dry by the time we finish eating and are ready to ride on."

"A good thought, but we are not riding on today," Devlin said. "The inn-wife has ordered our baggage brought to our rooms. If you go into the kitchen, she'll show you where they are."

Stephen's eyes flickered in Didrik's direction, then his gaze returned to Devlin's face, nodding almost imperceptibly. "Of course. It's too miserable a day to travel. I'll take care of things," he said.

"No," Didrik growled, but it was a weak sound. "You'll not stop on my account. I can ride."

"I know that," Devlin answered. Didrik could ride, and he would, right up until the moment it killed him. "We're not stopping for you. We're stopping because these damn cobblestones are slick with ice. I cannot risk another horse going down. This time someone might be seriously injured, then where would we be?"

A fortnight ago Didrik's horse had slipped as they were descending a narrow switchback, and the others had watched in helpless horror as the horse began to fall. Didrik had managed to kick himself free from the stirrups, and thus avoid being crushed by his mount. But his tumble down the hillside had snapped several ribs, undoing the work of those who had healed him in Duncaer.

The accident could have befallen any of them. It was the Gods' own luck that it had been Didrik who happened to be in the lead as they began their descent. Another might have suffered mere bruises and discomfort, but Didrik had been vulnerable—as his newly healed ribs had been no match for the strain.

At least Didrik had lived. His mount had snapped a

foreleg, and Devlin had put the beast out of its misery. They had done what they could for Didrik, binding his ribs and taking turns walking while Didrik rode, until they reached the next village where a suitable mount could be procured.

The delay had chafed Devlin, though he knew it was unavoidable. Since that time he had done his best to take things slowly, fighting the maddening pull of the Geas, which urged him to return to Kingsholm with all haste. But despite shortened days of journeying, and ensuring that Didrik did no unnecessary labor, Didrik was growing weaker, not stronger. He could not keep up the pace much longer.

And yet what choice did they have? Even now, there was a part of Devlin's mind that pulled him toward Kingsholm, reminding him that if he rode hard, he could be there in less than a fortnight. Were he to listen to its call, he would leave here at once, setting off without friends or protection, heedless of anything except the need to fulfill his oath and return the Sword of Light to Kingsholm.

He stretched his right hand out and touched the scabbard of the sword, feeling strangely comforted as he did so. Since he had reclaimed the sword, it had seldom been more than a few feet away from him. It was as if the sword were a part of him, or perhaps a part of the Geas that ruled him. Even when the sword was out of his sight, he always knew precisely where it was.

Indeed it was hard to remember that there had been a time when he had not held this sword, not valued it for the superb weapon it was. That there had been a time when he had once been a craftsman, renowned for the jewelry he created, who had seen only the beauty of the sword's crafting. But the past three years had changed him, and with or without the fabled sword, no one would ever mistake him for anything other than a warrior.

He wondered how the King and court would react to his return. They knew that he was on his way; the wretched soul stone would have told them as much, as it faithfully tracked every league of his travels. But did they think him returning in triumph? Or in failure? They had dispatched him on a fool's errand, sending him to seek a sword that had been lost in battle nearly fifty years ago. It had been a brilliant plan, for it had taken Devlin far away from the one place he could have influenced the course of events in Jorsk. In Kingsholm Devlin was not just the Chosen One, he was also a King's councilor and the General of the Royal Army. While he was at court he could use his power and influence to challenge the conservative council—hold King Olafur to his promise to seek true reform.

His few friends at court might be hopeful, but perhaps it was better that the rest of the court think him returning to report his failure. They could use this pretext to strip Devlin of his post as Chosen One and the titles he had earned. Disgraced, he would be no threat to anyone.

They would never expect that Devlin had done the impossible and found the lost sword. The common people would see his success as proof that he had indeed been chosen by the Gods—as uncomfortable as that idea made him feel. And Devlin would become too powerful for the court to ignore. So if his enemies even suspected he might have the sword, they would try to destroy him before he reached Kingsholm.

That his journey had passed untroubled so far spoke much about their probable contempt for his abilities.

The door to the common room swung open, and the inn-wife entered, followed by an elderly man.

"Sir, this is Jonam, the healer I spoke of," Kasja said.

Jonam might have been a strong man in his day, but his broad shoulders were stooped with age, and what hair he had left was the color of pewter. He wore no torc, but slung across one shoulder was a well-worn leather pack marked with the sigil of Lady Geyra, the patron of healers.

"The inn-wife tells me that you are a true healer," Devlin said.

"I was a healer of the second rank," Jonam replied. "I served at the temple in Skarnes for nearly fifty years, but when my power waned, I returned to where I had lived as a boy."

Even the smallest of villages had someone who served as bonesetter or herbalist, but true healers were rare. While a few of Lady Geyra's servants wandered the roads, most were to be found in city temples or attached to a noble's household. Finding a healer of the second rank, even one who no longer practiced his craft, was an unexpected gift, and the reason why Devlin had chosen to spend the night in this place.

"My companion is in need of your services," Devlin said.

"No I am not," Didrik insisted, but then a fit of coughing gave the lie to his words.

"What harm can it do?" Stephen said. "We are here, and the healer is here, so why not speak with him?"

Didrik shook his head. "I just need to catch my breath is all."

One could almost believe him, if you did not notice his fever-bright eyes, or how his right arm was wrapped around his ribs to ease their pain.

"This is not a choice," Devlin said. "Mistress Kasja, if you would be so kind as to show Didrik and the healer to a chamber?"

The inn-wife nodded. "Of course. If you would come with me?"

Saskia rose to follow, but Didrik waved her back. After a moment she returned to her seat.

The inn-wife and her son came in, bearing bowls of hot soup and a platter of freshly baked bread. A hot midday meal was an unaccustomed luxury for the travelers, and Devlin gave himself over to its appreciation. For the moment at least, he refused to think of what would happen if the healer could not help Didrik.

The soup was strange, with a watery broth rather than the thick cream Saskia was accustomed to. Floating amidst the generous chunks of chicken were strange lumps of dough. Tentatively she bit one, and found that it was filled with mashed tubers. Still, for all its strangeness, the soup was warm, and Saskia eagerly devoured one bowl, then a second.

Her companions were quiet, apart from murmured requests to pass the bread. Devlin's silence came as no surprise. Never talkative to begin with, he had grown increasingly withdrawn since Didrik's accident. Stephen's restraint was a different matter, for on an ordinary day the minstrel was like to chatter about anything and nothing. But perhaps Devlin's silence was infectious, or perhaps it was merely that Stephen's thoughts, like Saskia's, were with their friend.

A true warrior, Didrik had not once complained about the pain of his broken ribs, or asked that his companions slow their pace to accommodate his weakness. He bore his injuries with a grim stoicism that impressed Saskia. But will alone could only do so much, and she feared that he had reached the end of his endurance.

When the healer reentered the room, he was alone. It was not a good sign.

"What say you?" Devlin asked.

"He has the lung sickness," Jonam replied.

It was what she had expected, yet still she flinched at the news. In Duncaer the lung sickness was often fatal, although usually it claimed the very old or the very young.

"Can you help him?" Devlin asked.

Jonam shrugged. "Ten years ago I could have cured him in an afternoon. Now all I can offer are potions to ease him through the sickness, but even those he refuses to take."

"Can he travel? There are healers aplenty in Kingsholm," Stephen asked.

"Travel?" Saskia was incredulous. What could Stephen be thinking?

"He needs rest, and a chance for the medicine to purge the poison from his lungs. You are lucky that he lived this long. If he continues to travel, he will be dead within days," Jonam said bluntly.

"Didrik is going nowhere," Devlin declared. "Jonam,

come with me and tell me what must be done for him. I will see that he takes the medicines you have prepared."

Saskia waited until they had left the room before she whirled to face Stephen.

"Travel? You would have Didrik ride? You heard what the healer said."

Stephen held up both hands. "Peace," he said. "I had to know what he would say. Didrik would have asked the same question in my place."

"His foolishness does not excuse your own. He is ill, and not in his right mind. You need to think clearly."

"I am thinking clearly," Stephen said. "Devlin cannot stay here. Not for long. Didrik knows it, as do I."

"Why not?" She knew that Devlin had enemies who might be pursuing him, and a stationary quarry was easier to find than a moving one. But they had taken due precautions once they reached Jorsk, exchanging their uniforms for plainer garb and being careful not to identify themselves. No one would think it odd that they stayed at the inn while Didrik recuperated. And if they kept careful watch, they would be as safe here as on the road. Perhaps safer, for the place at least had defensible walls.

"Devlin *cannot* stay here," Stephen repeated. He looked around the common room, as if to ensure that they were alone. "His control is far greater than it was, but even his will is no match for the Geas. He may be able to delay a few hours, or even a day, but longer than that and he must leave."

Saskia felt her frustration rise. "What is this Geas you speak of? He is under orders to return, but is he not also your champion? What is so urgent that he must give over all common sense and risk the life of his friend?"

Stephen sat heavily down on a bench, and after a moment she did the same.

"As Chosen One, Devlin was bespelled—"

"I know of that," Saskia said hastily, making the hand gesture to avert ill luck. "Chief Mychal told me of his misfortune."

"Then you understand that he has no choice."

She understood nothing. She had traveled with Stephen for weeks, but suddenly it was as if a stranger looked at her over the table.

"The wizard cured Devlin. Mychal told me of this."

"Ismenia was able to free Devlin from the mind-sorcery, but she could not break the Geas spell," Stephen said, shocking her by naming a wizard aloud. "When he became Chosen One, Devlin swore an oath to serve faithfully until death. The Geas will hold him to that oath, regardless of personal cost. He is bound to return the sword to Kingsholm, and that is what he must do. Each delay will chip away at his will, until he can think of nothing but his duty. He will stay as long as he is able; but in the end he will leave, with or without us."

His blunt words sent a chill through her, and for a moment she wished that she had returned to Duncaer with the others. Even the smallest of children knew better than to mix their affairs with that of a wizard, and yet these Jorskians freely submitted themselves to such powers.

"You trusted him so little that you bespelled him? What honor is there in that?"

"All the Chosen Ones are bound by the Geas. It has been that way since the time of King Olaven."

"And Devlin agreed to it?" It had taken a leap of faith for her to imagine that Cerrie's gentle husband had transformed himself into a warrior. But this sorcery went against everything their people believed. Devlin must have been tricked. Surely he could not willingly have accepted such chains upon his soul.

"At the time I don't think he expected to live long enough for it to matter. And now he cannot undo what has been done. Even the mage who cast the spell does not have the power to lift it. Devlin has found a way to control it, after a fashion, but his duty comes before all else. Those who would befriend him need to understand that."

Saskia shook her head in denial. She did not wish to be Devlin's friend. Cerrie had been her friend. They had trained together, served together in the peacekeepers, and when Cerrie had married the gentle metalsmith, Saskia had borne witness. But now Cerrie was dead, and few traces remained of the man who had once been her husband. Still—for the sake of her old friend—Saskia had vowed to protect Devlin. She had sworn to see him safely delivered to Kingsholm, where his comrades could keep watch over him. She needed no spell to tell her her duty. But once she had completed her task, she would take her leave of these people and their strange ways.

She turned her thoughts back to the matter at hand. "But what does this spell have to do with the matter? Would he really leave us behind? He has been gone for months. How can a few more days matter?"

Stephen shrugged. "I know only what he has said, that he needs to be in Kingsholm before the spring session of court begins. He will stay as long as he can, but then—"

"We will ford that stream when we come to it," she said

firmly. Surely Stephen was exaggerating the influence of the Geas. Devlin had proven himself a wise man, far too cunning to charge off blindly, no matter what his friends thought.

Devlin returned to the common room with the news that Didrik had finally taken the medicines prepared for him and fallen asleep. The healer Jonam left with the promise that he would return after sunset to check on his patient.

There being no other travelers, the inn was quiet, though Saskia had learned enough of Jorskian ways to understand that the common room would be crowded after sunset, with local folks come to drink watered wines and ease the aches of a day spent clearing muddy fields for planting. Still, it was empty for now, and they used that to their advantage, emptying their packs and spreading their spare clothing to dry.

Devlin checked each of his weapons, ensuring that their wrappings had held true and that they had taken no damage from the rain. He then did the same for Didrik's gear. And though Saskia could see no flaw in the lieutenant's blades, Devlin was not satisfied. He oiled and sharpened each of them in turn.

Mistress Kasja came in, and her eyebrows rose at the sight of the weaponry spread across the tables of her common room. Then she took one look at the linens hanging by the fire and promptly gathered them up for the washing they so desperately needed.

Saskia wondered what the inn-wife thought of her strange guests, and how long it would be before she guessed the truth. Caerfolk were rare in this land, and she and Devlin would be remarked upon wherever they went. To the inn-wife they had told the same tale they had used since crossing into Jorsk: Stephen was Lord Kollinar's understeward and had been granted leave to return home after three years of service with Lord Kollinar in Duncaer. Didrik was likewise in the governor's employ, bearing messages between the governor and his native estates in Jorsk. Devlin and Saskia were mercenaries, hired to escort Stephen and Didrik on their journey.

It was a plausible tale, but it would not hold up in close quarters. Not for long. Neither Stephen nor Didrik was an actor, and any who watched them would note that they deferred to Devlin, even when they appeared to be ignoring him. And while there was sufficient unrest in Jorsk to warrant an armed escort, even an inexperienced eye could see the difference between an escort and a war party. Devlin did not travel as if he thought there might be trouble. He traveled as if he knew that there would be trouble and he had armed himself and his followers accordingly.

The longer they stayed, the greater the chance that they would be discovered. All it would take was a few careless words. Devlin might be a common name in Duncaer, but in Jorsk there was only one Devlin of Duncaer—the Chosen One. Discovery would mean all their efforts had been for naught.

If Devlin shared her concerns, he gave no sign of it. She observed him carefully but he did not appear unduly worried. Nor did he appear to be a man laboring under a sorcerous compulsion, and she comforted herself with the thought that Stephen must have exaggerated the effects of the spell.

When he had finished caring for their blades, Devlin repacked their gear and stored it in the second of the two rooms that had been allotted to them. Then he put his cloak back on and went out, saying he wanted to check on the condition of their horses and inspect their tack.

Stephen left soon thereafter, to visit the local shopkeepers and replenish their supplies. He continued to behave as if they might need to resume their journey at a moment's notice. But there was no harm in his errand, and he promised to buy tea for her if there was any to be found.

She put on her now dry cloak and went out to the stables to help Devlin; but he waved her off, seemingly content to care for the horses by himself. Saskia knew better than to wander around the village and call attention to herself, so she returned to the inn and accepted a mug of citrine from the inn-wife before going to see Didrik.

He was sleeping, propped up on pillows to ease the strain on his lungs. She could hear a faint wheeze with each exhalation, and the hair on his temples was soaked with sweat. He looked worse now than he had before the healer's treatments. She reached out to check on his fever.

Her hand had barely brushed his cheek before her wrist was caught in a crushing grip. She did not try to pull away, instead waiting as Didrik opened his eyes and blinked away the confusion of his drugged sleep. She could tell the moment he recognized her, for his grip relaxed.

"Saskia," he said.

She nodded and gently disentangled her hand from his. "I did not mean to disturb you."

"It is good that you did," Didrik replied. He levered

himself up with his arms, as if to rise. Saskia leaned over and pushed his shoulders firmly down on the pillows. He struggled for a moment, glaring at her, then lay still.

"What do you need?" she asked.

"I need you to promise me something. Swear to me that you will not leave Devlin unprotected. Swear that you will not let him leave here on his own."

First Stephen and now Didrik. They seemed convinced that Devlin was a madman, immune to all reason and logic. Stephen's warning she had put down to an overactive imagination, but if Didrik was concerned . . .

"Devlin is going nowhere. Neither are you. We will stay here till you are fit to travel, then the four of us will journey on to Kingsholm. Just as we had planned."

Didrik shook his head. "Damned healer and his potions have made me sicker, not better. I am too weak to travel like this, but Devlin cannot tarry for my sake." Fever-bright eyes pleaded with her. "You must do this for me. Guard him with your life. He needs someone to protect him, even against himself. Once he is in Kingsholm, you may safely trust him to the City Guard. But till then he is not to be left alone. Not for even an hour. Do you understand?"

She did not understand. But even as she hesitated, she could see that Didrik was becoming agitated, and that would do him no good.

"Swear to me that you will protect him," he repeated. "Or I will rise from this bed and do it myself."

"Peace," she said. "Rest easy. I have already sworn to see Devlin safely in Kingsholm, and I will not forsake my oath. When he leaves here I will go with him. You have my word on it, as a warrior."

She had to repeat her promise twice before it sank in. Reassured that he had not failed in his duty, Didrik fell back asleep, and this time he did not wake even when she straightened his blankets.

She wanted to dismiss Didrik's concerns as the product of a feverish mind. But when she left his chamber, she crossed the hall to the room allotted to her and repacked her gear in her saddlebags, ensuring that she would be ready to leave on a moment's notice. Just in case.

# Three

DEVLIN KNEW HE COULD WAIT NO LONGER. IT
was time to leave. After three days under the care of the
healer Jonam, Didrik was finally beginning to show signs
of improvement. The sickly gray had left his complexion,
and his breath no longer rattled quite so deeply in his
lungs. But he was still very weak, and it would be many
days before he was fit enough to travel.

Days that Devlin did not have. Each day, from the moment he awoke until the hour when he finally fell into a
restless sleep, there was but a single thought that consumed
him. He must fulfill his duty and return to Kingsholm. It
had taken all of his willpower to delay this long, to ensure
that Didrik would survive. Now he must leave.

Which presented him with another dilemma. Didrik
was his friend, and it went against everything that Devlin
believed in to leave him here alone, in the care of
strangers. Yet it was too risky for Devlin to travel to the
capital on his own. Last fall assassins had dogged his footsteps, and he had no reason to expect that his enemies had
resigned themselves to his return. Didrik would be safe

enough at the inn, while Devlin could need the help of both Stephen and Saskia to overcome any obstacles he might face.

Devlin paced the length of the tiny chamber he had been given. He had retreated here earlier because his impatience had made him foul-tempered. He glanced toward the foot of the bed and confirmed that his gear was fully packed, for experience had taught him he might have to make a hasty departure. He knew that Saskia and Stephen would also be ready to leave the moment he gave them the word. All that remained was to inform his companions and saddle their horses.

Didrik was a warrior. He would understand.

Devlin felt the tension in his shoulders ease as he realized that he had made his decision. A glance through the narrow window revealed that it would soon be dark. Too late to resume the journey, but they could leave at first light. Both they and the horses had benefited from their days of rest, and without the burden of an injured companion, they could ride hard and make up for some of the time they had lost.

He decided he would inform Didrik first, and then tell the others to make their preparations. But as he opened the door, he saw Mistress Kasja standing in the hall, her fist raised as if she was about to knock. Devlin took a hasty step back.

"Your pardon, sir," she said. "I was just coming to fetch you."

"Is anything amiss?"

"Yes, I mean no, that is, err, my lord," she stammered. Devlin took a deep breath and waited for the woman to calm herself. He had never suspected her of a nervous temperament.

"Yes?" he prompted.

"There is a company of armsmen downstairs, sent by Baron Martell. They say they have a message for the Chosen One. . . ." Her voice trailed off, as she peered at Devlin quizzically, apparently unable to reconcile the legendary Chosen One with the humble traveler who had been her guest for these past days.

It was not her fault that she confused the office with the man. He wondered how she would have treated him if he had arrived wearing his dress uniform.

"Then you had best take me to them," Devlin said. He took down the sword belt that hung on the wall and buckled it around his waist. It never hurt to be prepared.

"Of course, my lord." She bobbed a hasty curtsy, then turned and led the way.

He could hear voices raised in conversation as they approached. Saskia was waiting at the doorway, and as he entered the common room, she took up a position on his right side. There were only a half dozen armsmen in the room, but they were fully armed and seemed to fill the space with their presence. Despite their uniforms he knew this might well be a trap, so he rested his right hand on the hilt of the Sword of Light.

"Who is in charge?" he asked.

A tall man stepped forward and bowed low. "My Lord Chosen One, I am Pers Sundgren, commander of Baron Martell's armsmen."

The rest of the attachment drew themselves to attention and saluted.

Devlin responded with a nod. He did not remove his hand from his sword.

From the corner of his eye he saw Saskia's left arm twitch and knew she had released a throwing knife into her hand, ready for a quick release should the situation turn ugly.

"What is your errand with me?"

"King Olafur sent a messenger bird to the baron, instructing him to send out armsmen to find you and to speed your swift return to the royal court. We have been seeking you for the past three days."

Devlin wracked his brains trying to remember what he knew of Baron Martell. The baron's holdings were small, but his title was an old one. He had met the man during the last court session, but his overall impression was that the baron was firmly committed to the middle ground. A young man with an old man's politics, favoring neither Devlin's supporters nor his conservative opponents.

A man trusted by both sides, his loyalty should be unquestioned. Then again, traitors did not declare themselves openly. Martell's public neutrality might well be a shield for more nefarious activities. Though if he had wished Devlin dead, it was far more likely that he would have tried to ambush him on the road.

Commander Sundgren reached into his belt pouch. "I was entrusted with a personal message for you," he said, withdrawing a small scroll.

Devlin took the scroll with his left hand and broke the wax seal with his thumbnail. He knew at least one other person had read the message, since messages carried by bird were written in tiny letters on long strips of paper. Most likely Baron Martell and his scribe already knew whatever message King Olafur had sent to him. He hoped they could hold their tongues.

"Chosen One. Empress Thania honors alliance. Your presence required in council. Return at once. Olafur, King of Jorsk."

Devlin read the message thrice before he allowed himself to believe. This was good news. Indeed, it was beyond all hope. If the Empress of Selvarat was prepared to send troops to help defend Jorsk, then the odds had just tipped in their favor. Such an alliance might well deter the invasion that Devlin had long feared. And if their enemies were foolish enough to attack anyway, Devlin would now have the strength to crush them.

More than ever he was needed in Kingsholm. It was clear that events were unfolding swiftly, and he needed to be in a position to influence their outcome rather than trying to undo what others had already agreed to— though it boded well that King Olafur had urged his swift return. Perhaps the King had paid more heed to Devlin's advice than he had realized at the time. Or perhaps the new alliance was just one of the changes that had been wrought in the politics of the Kingdom during the long months of Devlin's absence.

"Horses are saddled outside, and my troops and I are ready to escort you," Commander Sundgren said.

His eagerness was commendable, if misplaced. The weather had warmed, so the roads were no longer icy, but they were still slick from the morning's rain, and the sun was rapidly setting. Traveling at night on such roads was the act of a fool.

"Then unsaddle the horses and arrange with the inn-wife to find rooms for your troop. We'll leave at first light."

"I'll inform the others," Saskia said. "We will be ready."

"You will stay here, with Didrik," Devlin replied.

"I am going with you."

Devlin turned to face her. "There is no need."

"If you leave anyone behind, let it be Stephen. He is your friend, but I have sworn to be your sword arm," Saskia said, in the tongue of their people. "I promised Didrik that I would see you safely to your King."

He should have expected as much. Didrik was Devlin's aide, sworn to obey his orders; but Didrik had made it clear that his first duty was to ensure Devlin's safety. It seemed he had enlisted Saskia in his cause.

Stephen was a friend, and a proven fighter who had shed blood on Devlin's behalf; but he lacked the hard edges and killing instinct that Saskia possessed. She, like Didrik, was a warrior trained. If this was a trap, she might spot it even before he could, and he had no doubt that she would acquit herself well in any battle.

"I accept your pledge," he said in their own tongue.

The commander frowned, clearly unhappy that they had chosen to exclude him from their debate.

"Saskia will ride with us," Devlin said, dropping back into the common tongue of Jorsk. Stephen would not be pleased to be left behind, but someone had to ensure that Didrik stayed until he was healed, even if that meant tying him to the bed.

"Chosen One, there is no need for this foreigner to accompany us. My men and I have sworn to protect you with our lives," Commander Sundgren said.

"Saskia hails from the same city where I was born,"

Devlin said, watching the commander flush red as he realized his mistake. "And she, too, has sworn an oath. Let us hope for an uneventful journey where neither of you is forced to put yourself to the test."

"Of course, my lord Chosen One."

Devlin sighed. It was going to be a long journey.

They left early the next morning, just as the stars were beginning to fade. The roads were still wet from last night's rain, but it had not been cold enough for the ground to freeze. Devlin took this as a sign that their journey would be swift.

Indeed they set a fast pace, far faster than Devlin could have traveled on his own. When he had received the King's message, Baron Martell had done more than simply send out riders to search for Devlin. He had also arranged to have post horses waiting at key towns along the route. Devlin and his escort changed mounts nearly every day. When there were no post horses available, Commander Sundgren requisitioned the best horses the villagers had to offer—whether they willed it or no.

Such was within his rights as the baron's man, and indeed as Chosen One Devlin could have done the same. But he was too much the peasant to be comfortable with such tactics. For every mount that was taken, Devlin made sure that the owner knew that he would be able to reclaim his horse at the next posting station, and gave him coin for his trouble.

If he found Devlin's concern unusual, Commander Sundgren said nothing. Indeed the commander hardly ever spoke to Devlin unless the needs of the journey dictated it. He treated Devlin with the utmost formality, always referring to him as "My lord," or "Chosen One" despite Devlin's protests. Such rigid propriety was suited for the royal court, but hardly proper for a small band of riders.

The troops that accompanied them followed Sundgren's lead. They did not speak to Devlin unless he asked them a question, and their replies were as brief as possible. They offered no opinions of their own, instead deferring to the wisdom of their commander. It was a far cry from what he was accustomed to. Even the Royal Army, with its officer corps drawn from the nobility, did not stand on ceremony to such an extent.

Saskia took her role as his protector with due seriousness, and was seldom more than a few steps away from his side. Despite her actions, Commander Sundgren and his troops did their best to pretend that she was invisible. She was not called on to take a watch, nor did the commander ever ask her to ride ahead to ensure the road was clear. That suited Devlin well enough. Saskia, at least, he knew he could trust.

But however strange he found Sundgren's manner, he could not quarrel with the results. Their journey was swift, and without incident. Nine days after they had left Kronna's Mill, Devlin saw the torchlit walls of Kingsholm looming ahead in the darkness.

One of the troopers had ridden ahead, and she was waiting for them at the junction where the great road they traveled split into three. From here one could ride either to the east or the west, along the first of the great ring roads that encircled the city. If they rode straight on, it would take them through the outlying villages, then into the city through the southern gate. But Sundgren turned his horse to the left.

"Wait," Devlin ordered, drawing his horse to a halt.

"My lord, I was instructed to bring you to the city by way of the western gate," Sundgren explained.

Devlin raised his eyebrows. This was the first he had heard of any such order.

"And are there any other instructions that you have failed to share with me?" He kept his voice low, but he knew Sundgren heard the implied threat. Their journey so far had been without incident, but that did not mean that he trusted the commander. Anything could happen, and Devlin would not count himself safe until he stood within the palace walls.

Commander Sundgren drew himself to even more rigid attention, if such a thing was possible. "It is past sundown, my lord," he said. His face was expressionless as he pointed out the obvious. "The other gates will be barred shut at this hour, but the postern in the western gate is always open for messengers."

"Of course," Devlin said. He should have realized that himself, but fatigue and his overriding need to reach Kingsholm had blinded him to the practicalities of entering a guarded city after dark. The southern gate was closer, but it would take time to unbar the wooden doors and raise the massive metal gate.

Devlin nodded to the commander and kneed his horse to a walk. After a moment, the others fell in behind him.

Two city guards stood watch outside the West Gate, and though Devlin did not recognize them, they clearly knew who he was, for they began to open the postern gate as soon as they caught sight of the travelers.

The gate was narrow and Devlin fought the urge to duck as he passed underneath the stone archway. On the other side he was greeted by a woman wearing the shoulder cord of a corporal. Her face was unfamiliar to him, but she was too old to be a new recruit. It seemed the City Guard had begun recruiting experienced armsmen, which boded well for the changes that had taken place in his absence.

The corporal waited until the travelers had passed through the gate and the postern door was shut behind them. Then she saluted, saying, "Chosen One, I have been instructed to bring you and your companions directly to the palace. The King is expecting you."

"At this hour?" It was nearly midnight. Despite the urgent summons, the best he had hoped for was an audience with King Olafur in the morning.

"I have my orders," she said.

Devlin drew himself erect in his saddle and rubbed his face, trying to shake off his exhaustion. His very bones ached, and he had scarcely slept in the past few days. It was no comfort to know that his companions were equally tired. Commander Sundgren and the rest could seek their beds, secure in the knowledge that they had done their duty. But Devlin would need all his wits about him, if he was to speak with the King.

His right hand gripped the hilt of the Sword of Light, and he felt renewed strength at the tangible proof that he had succeeded in his quest. Devlin was the Chosen One. Mere tiredness would not be allowed to distract him.

"Lead on," he instructed.

# Four

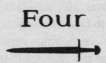

CAPTAIN DRAKKEN TUGGED AT A BLANKET FOLD
that had somehow gotten trapped under her right side.
Finally, she managed to straighten the blanket to her satisfaction, but the lumpiness of the mattress seemed to
mock her efforts to become comfortable, and with a sigh
she rolled over onto her back and opened her eyes.

The banked fire in the grate provided only the faintest
illumination, letting her glimpse the forms of dark objects against the slightly lighter walls. But she did not need
to see. The room was as familiar to her as her own quarters. She could not count the number of nights that she
had spent on that very same cot, in the small room tucked
behind her offices in the Guard Hall. It was a place where
she could rest when the demands of her schedule caught
up with her—catching a few hours' sleep after days of al-
ternating twelve-hour watches with scant four-hour
breaks. Since her youth she had been able to sleep whenever and wherever she found herself, but for once her
long training had deserted her.

It was a shocking lapse of discipline in one who had

been a guard for over a quarter century. She was no raw recruit, too impatient to sleep on the first night before an engagement. She was Captain Morwenna Drakken, who had chased criminals, faced down assassins, and once challenged an angry mob of looters with only her partner to guard her back. And since becoming Captain, she had survived a hundred tricky council meetings and the worst that her political enemies could throw at her. She knew full well the value of having all her wits about her, and once Devlin arrived it was likely that there would be long days and nights ahead for them both.

Despite that, she could not find it in herself to sleep. Five months ago, Devlin had left Kingsholm on his quest. He had carried all their hopes with them, but now, at long last, he was mere hours from the city. He should arrive sometime today, and if he indeed carried the Sword of Light, his presence would turn the city on its ear.

She was too old to behave so foolishly, she thought, even as she rose from the cot. Crossing over to the fireplace, she stirred up the fire, adding a handful of kindling, then lit a thin scrap that she used to light the lamps.

She opened the narrow wardrobe that held her spare uniform and dressed herself swiftly. Sleep was a lost cause, and if she were to be wakeful, she might as well do something, rather than lying in the dark fretting.

It took only a few moments to make herself ready. Leaving the sleep chamber, she walked through her office, then into the corridor. As she descended the stairs to the ground floor, the watch bells sounded, indicating that it was two hours before dawn.

The sentry outside the office saluted as Captain

Drakken drew near, then opened the door. As she stepped inside, Lieutenant Ansgar quickly rose to his feet.

If he was surprised to see his Captain appear in the middle of his shift, Ansgar gave no sign. "Captain, all is well in the city."

It was the routine report.

"And the gate sentries?"

"They have their orders. They are to report the Chosen One's arrival at once and offer him any assistance he may require. I will brief the next shift of sentries personally, before they take their posts."

"Good."

She had visited the Royal Chapel yesterday at noon, where the glowing soul stone gave proof that Devlin was nearing the city. She had done what she could to prepare for his coming. The guards would inform her when he arrived, though it was likely that Devlin would seek out the King first, to report on the success or failure of his quest. Only then would he be free to seek out his friends.

"I hope this return is calmer than the last," Drakken mused.

"Captain?" Lieutenant Ansgar's voice rose in question.

"The last time Devlin returned from a quest, his first act was to challenge Duke Gerhard to a duel. Let us hope this time he receives a warmer welcome."

"As you say." Ansgar's features were once again a blank mask.

The man had no sense of humor, but that was hardly news. Ansgar was nearly an agemate, having joined the guard only two years after Drakken. A stolid, unimaginative man, his years of experience and faultless service had finally elevated him to the rank of sergeant.

Left to her own, she would never have chosen him as one of her lieutenants, but then Hemfrid had been killed by his lover, a man who promptly took his own life. And King Olafur, who had never interfered in the Guard before, took the opportunity to select Ansgar for promotion. It was the King's way of reminding her that she served at his pleasure and that he was the ultimate authority in Kingsholm.

Drakken, though angry at the usurping of her traditional authority, had not argued against the King's decision. Seemingly pleased by her acquiescence, the King had thrown her a bone, allowing her to recruit fifty new guards. Placing Ansgar in charge of their recruitment cost her nothing but pride.

The newly expanded Guard was just one of the changes that Devlin would find when he returned to Kingsholm. She wondered what he would make of the presence of the Selvarat delegation and their new military alliance. Time alone would tell.

Satisfied that she had done all she could for the moment, Captain Drakken left Lieutenant Ansgar and the nearly deserted Guard Hall and began an impromptu tour of inspection. As she emerged from the darkness, the sentries at the first guard tower challenged her, barring her path with lowered spears until she gave the night's password. Only then did they allow her to step forward into the light. Such diligence pleased her, though she knew better than to praise the guards for merely doing their duty.

She climbed the steps to the battlements and made the long circuit around the high walls that enclosed the palace compound. It was a good time for a surprise inspection, as the end of a long shift approached, when fatigue and boredom were likely to have taken their toll. But newcomers and veterans alike proved themselves alert and watchful. One guard greeted Drakken by name, rather than waiting for the challenge and response, thus earning herself a week's stint of extra duties. But that was a minor failing, and overall Drakken was satisfied by what she found.

The sun had risen by the time she had finished her inspection, and she witnessed the changing of the duty shifts. Then she went down to the courtyard and watched those who were taking part in the morning drills. She paid close attention to the newest recruits. One in particular showed great skill with the sword, while a deceptively slender man had proven himself so apt at unarmed combat that Sergeant Lukas had already made him an instructor.

She watched for over an hour, moving among the ranks of those practicing, paying close attention to the newest members of the Guard. It was not enough to put names with faces. She had to know their skills as well as their weaknesses, though the latter were fewer than she expected. Indeed, for the first time in living memory, most of the new recruits were not raw novices but experienced fighters. The King's edict had drawn experienced provincial armsmen to the capital, as well as veterans who—for one reason or another—had given up their calling. Caravan guards; soldiers who had quit the army after their ten years only to find that the world outside was a hard place for someone without a trade; even a sailor who had lost his taste for the sea. Captain Drakken had been allowed to recruit from among them before the rest were evaluated by Marshal Olvarrson's command, and those who measured up assigned to one of the newly formed squads sent up to reinforce the Nerikaat border.

Recruiting experienced fighters meant that she did not have to waste months training these newcomers to tell one end of the sword from another. But fighting skills alone were not enough to make one a guard. Enforcing the law and keeping the peace in the city was a skill that only time could teach, and each newcomer was always paired with an experienced guard while on duty.

Perhaps sensing her restless energy, Sergeant Lukas invited Captain Drakken to help demonstrate the correct techniques to use when a guard with a short sword found himself facing an opponent with a long sword. She stripped off her tunic, and after a few preliminary stretches to warm her muscles, accepted a short sword and faced off against Sergeant Henrik.

Their first bout was done in slow time, each move executed to the beat of a drum that Lukas used to keep time. Years of training paid off as she and Henrik held each position for several heartbeats, while Lukas provided a running commentary. Only the most disciplined of fighters could demonstrate in this mode, for it required both extraordinary muscle strength and the control to execute each move precisely on the beat.

The second bout was done at half time. Still slow enough that even an inexperienced eye could follow their movements, but less of a strain to muscles, and Lukas's commentary was more rapid, simply naming the moves. "Spin. Low feint. High. Block, retreat. Lunge."

By design, that bout too ended in a draw. They repeated

the exercise, with Drakken wielding the long sword while Henrik held the short sword of a guard.

Drakken rolled each shoulder in turn, stretching the arm muscles that had grown taut. Henrik did the same, and then he grinned at her.

"Quick time?" he asked.

"Why not?" It had been far too long since she practiced against a skilled opponent.

"Everyone rise and take two paces back," Lukas ordered, and the circle of students around them widened, giving them room to fight.

She and Henrik raised their swords in salute. His sword was only partly lowered, as Henrik lunged forward, seeking to strike the first blow. Drakken had been expecting such a move, and she danced away to her left. She slashed his right arm with a blow that would have drawn blood if the sword had been steel, but after a short exchange of parries, it was Henrik whose sword point rested on her abdomen.

"Hold," she called, acknowledging the hit.

Henrik froze, and then withdrew his sword. She nodded, in acknowledgment of his victory, then turned in a slow circle, looking at the students. A few of them appeared appreciative, but most appeared stunned, for the match had taken less than a hundred heartbeats.

"What did I do wrong?" she asked.

There was no answer.

"Anyone?"

One of the new recruits raised his hand, and she nodded at him to speak.

"You won the match," the recruit insisted. "If your

sword had been steel, your first strike would have disabled Henrik's sword arm. He would have dropped his sword."

"Mayhap," she conceded. "But maybe no. Henrik is a tough fighter. He would be bloodied, yes, but he judged the blow glancing, true?"

"Yes, Captain," Henrik confirmed. "Though I'll have a bruise to show for my troubles."

In such a practice match it was up to each participant to determine whether or not he or she had received a disabling wound. Younger fighters would often overestimate their endurance and refuse to concede that they had been injured in a practice match; but she knew Henrik well enough to know that he was an honorable opponent. She had known from the moment she struck that it was a mere slash, and Henrik had agreed with her.

"So, again, what did I do wrong?"

"You were focused on a high strike, and let Henrik get under your guard," Oluva said, after glancing around and seeing that no one else was willing to say what should have been obvious.

Captain Drakken nodded. "Precisely. I was thinking as a duelist. A short sword lacks range, but it is more maneuverable than a long sword. I'd deliberately left an opening for Henrik to take a high strike hoping to disarm him, but he ignored the trap and went for a gut strike instead."

And if they had been fighting with steel swords, she would have been mortally wounded. Henrik would not have escaped unscathed, but he would have lived to fight another day.

"Let us try this again," Drakken said.

She handily won the next bout, and in the third she managed to disarm Henrik using a move she had learned from a Selvarat officer. She demonstrated the move twice in slow time, and then demonstrated how to counter it.

Mopping the sweat from her face with a towel, she watched for a few moments as Lukas lined the guards up in two rows facing each other and had them practice the maneuver they had just seen. Then, with a final word to Lukas, she took her leave.

She had done well, she reflected, holding her own against a fighter who was barely half her age. Her aching ribs and the rising bruise on the back of her thigh proved that Henrik had not held any of his blows out of respect for her rank or age.

The bells chimed the noon hour as Captain Drakken left the courtyard, intending to return to the Guard Hall to wash up and make herself presentable in case the King summoned his council to hear Devlin's report. As she reached the hall, she saw Solveig of Esker descending the steps.

"Captain Drakken, what good fortune. I was just looking for you," Solveig said.

"How may I serve?" Captain Drakken asked. In public they maintained the facade that she and Solveig were mere acquaintances, and Captain Drakken was careful to treat Solveig with the formal respect due to one who would someday hold the title of Baroness. Only a trusted few knew that Solveig and Drakken were both among the inner circle of Devlin's advisors.

Solveig waited until Captain Drakken had caught up to her. "What news of Devlin and his quest?" she asked, in low tones. "I expected him to wait upon the King, but was surprised that not even my own brother saw fit to bring me news."

So she was not the only one who had grown impatient.

"There is no news yet, though I expect to hear of his arrival shortly. And I am certain Stephen will seek you out as soon as he may."

Solveig's eyes widened, and she clutched Drakken's forearm. "But you are mistaken. Devlin is already in the city. He returned last night."

Drakken swallowed hard. "Come," she ordered, leading the way up the stairs into the Guard Hall. She did not speak another word until they had reached the sanctity of her own office and shut the door firmly behind them.

"What do you mean Devlin has returned?"

It could not be possible. He could not have entered the city without passing through one of the gates, and the guards would surely have informed her. Solveig must be mistaken.

"Lord Rikard and I had agreed to meet last night at the Royal Temple, to trade gossip."

Captain Drakken nodded. They knew that Solveig's and Rikard's public encounters were closely watched. But with the court in session, there were numerous diversions offered each evening, and no one found it odd that a noble would be returning to the palace long after sunset. If they took a path that led them past the unfashionable Royal Temple, well such was not suspicious in and of itself. And the deserted temple was a perfect place for a clandestine meeting, given Brother Arni's tacit approval.

"It took me longer than I expected to take my leave from Lady Vendela's ball. When I arrived, I found Rikard had been there for some time. We could see that the soul stone had reached Kingsholm, and Brother Arni had begun offering prayers of thanks for the Chosen One's safe return," Solveig continued.

"And that was at midnight?"

"I arrived after midnight, but Brother Arni said the stone had changed color an hour before."

Perhaps Brother Arni was mistaken, though she had never heard of the soul stone spell failing. And he had no motive to lie about what he had seen. The priest was a man of sincere faith, who lived to serve the seven Gods and the Chosen One, their anointed representative.

But if Devlin had been in the city for twelve hours now, then where was he? And why hadn't she heard anything?

"I returned to my chambers, but there was no word. The servants had no news, so I expected that Devlin had decided to wait until morning before seeking out the King. But as the morning passed, I became impatient. I knew he would seek you out, so I came here. But you haven't seen him, have you?"

Captain Drakken shook her head. "Nor have I had any word that he arrived. It makes no sense that he would hide himself from his friends."

"But surely someone must have seen them—the guards who let them in the gate, the sentries at the palace, the stablemen who took their horses . . . They did not simply fall from the sky."

And Didrik, at least, would not have let twelve hours pass without reporting to her. Something was gravely wrong.

"I do not know what is happening, but I will find out," Captain Drakken promised.

"What can I do?"

"Return to the palace. Make yourself visible. Listen for

any gossip, but do not let on what you know. If you hear anything, send word to me. And above all, do not wander off alone. I'll assign one of my guards to watch you."

"You think I may be threatened?" Solveig's voice was incredulous. "Why?"

Drakken did not know what to think, but her instincts were telling her that there was grave danger. Until she knew the shape of the threat, it was best to err on the side of caution.

"Right now there are four people who know that Devlin has returned. You, Rikard, Brother Arni, and now me. Rikard has his own armsmen and the priest should be safe. But until we know why Devlin's return has been kept secret, you should be on your guard. It may be nothing, but better safe than sorry."

# Five

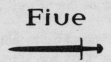

DIDRIK GAVE A SIGH OF RELIEF AS THE ROAD widened and he caught his first clear view of Kingsholm. The high walls were gray and forbidding, meant to discourage potential attackers, but to him they were a welcome sight. These were his walls, and this was his city. He knew every yard of the long walls, and every one of the streets and alleyways. Blindfolded he could be set down in any part of the city and instantly know where he was using just his hearing and sense of smell. The city had its dangers, but those were things he understood. And there, at least, he had a reputation of his own that made him formidable. Not to mention the full weight of the Guard behind him.

He felt as if he were coming off a duty shift that had lasted months, not mere hours. The long trip to Duncaer had demanded his constant vigilance. And even the return had been tense, though the presence of Saskia and her sword arm had been a welcome addition to their party. Jorsk was his homeland, but there were those among his fellow countrymen who wished Devlin ill, and it had been Didrik's responsibility to keep him safe. A charge he had failed when he foolishly allowed himself to become injured. Instead of watching over Devlin, he had become a burden.

He understood why Devlin had left him behind, though he had chafed mightily during the week that the healer had kept him in bed. And even when they resumed their journey, Stephen had insisted on a slow pace, coddling Didrik as if he were a cripple. Didrik had protested, but allowed himself to be overruled when it became clear that he did not have the strength for a full day of riding. Still, he had grown stronger with each day, and they had agreed to press on in hopes of reaching Kingsholm by sundown.

He urged his horse to a faster pace, ignoring the curses of the few pedestrians who had to scurry away or risk being stepped on. Had he been in a proper uniform they would have yielded at once, but the hardships of the journey were reflected in his garb. He wore a dark blue cloak that had been gifted him in Duncaer over his much-abused uniform. Stephen had acquired plain but serviceable clothes for them both in Kronna's Mill, which they had worn for the past fortnight. But Didrik's pride insisted that he appear in his uniform when he made his report to Captain Drakken.

At last he was forced to slow, when their way was blocked by a knot of people. The southern gate was only partially open, forcing those entering and leaving to file through a narrow gap that was flanked by a pair of guards. Didrik waited their turn with some impatience.

"I'm for a hot bath, a fresh-cooked meal, then I'll sleep for a week," Stephen declared.

It was a tempting vision, but Didrik had his duty. He had to seek out Devlin and inform him of his return. Then once Devlin released him, he would have to make his report to Captain Drakken. It would be many hours before he would be free to seek out his own quarters.

"You'll be at the Singing Fish? Or staying with your sister at the palace?" Didrik asked. It was possible that Devlin might wish to speak with Stephen, though unlikely.

"At the Fish," Stephen replied. "Solveig would insist on hearing every detail. Time enough to see her on the morrow."

At last they reached the front of the queue.

"Anders Kronborn, you wretched sod, what are you doing here?" Oluva called out.

Didrik, who had opened his mouth to greet her, closed it firmly. Her left hand was resting on her sword belt with two fingers pointed down, the hand sign for caution.

He looked over at the other guard, but the man was a stranger to him. Too old to be a novice, yet what else could he be? The leather of his sword harness was unworn, and his cloak unstained by weather or the exigencies of service in the poorer quarters.

Was it her comrade Oluva did not trust? Or the possibility of spies in the crowd? What was going on?

"It's been a long time. I never thought you'd have the nerve to show your face," Oluva continued.

"A man has a right to go where he pleases," he said, scratching his chest with his left hand, as he signaled *explain*.

Stephen, for once, was silent, and he gave thanks for the minstrel's quick wits.

"I can't believe you kept your old uniform. Captain

Drakken isn't going to be happy to see you. We may be taking on newcomers, but there's no room for a man who cheats his bunkmates." Oluva's hand made the signal for an unknown enemy.

Didrik shrugged, as if he were well used to such insults. Anders Kronborn had been thrown out of the Guard four years ago, after he had been repeatedly caught cheating in a game of dice. The first offense had earned him a stint in the guardhouse. The second offense had earned him ten lashes. Growing wiser, he had taken his games from the Guard quarters to the taverns, where his luck had finally run out. Caught cheating, his fellow gamesters had been for summary justice, but before they could carry out their sentence, Captain Drakken had intervened, dismissing him from the Guard and banning him from the city.

As an alias, it was a good choice, but he itched to find out why Oluva had felt such a deception necessary.

"That bitch Drakken may not want me, but there's plenty of work for a man who can handle a sword," Didrik declared.

"And who's this?" Oluva asked, jerking her thumb toward Stephen.

"My cousin Jesper. My aunt asked me to ride herd over him, to keep him out of trouble in the city." Didrik smirked.

"Setting a wolf to guard the lamb. Well, it's none of my concern. Stay out of trouble and stay away from the palace." Her eyes caught his and held his gaze. "You have no friends there, understand?"

Oluva made the handing for betrayal.

Didrik swallowed hard, not needing to feign his sudden fear. "I understand."

"Enough chatter," the unknown guard said. "Ride on, then, you're holding up these honest citizens."

Didrik nodded, not trusting himself to speak. He forced himself to ride off slowly, still slouched in the saddle, as if he was indeed the rogue he had claimed to be.

"What was that all about?" Stephen asked.

"Not now," he growled. Not here. Not until he could find somewhere safe. And then he had to figure out what to do next.

His thoughts whirled around and around, but they kept coming back to Oluva's grim face as she flashed that last sign. Betrayal.

It was his worst fear, come to life.


He could feel Stephen's gaze boring holes into his back as he turned down the street that led toward the old quarter of the city.

Oluva had warned him away from the palace, and for now he would trust her judgment. But what had she meant by betrayal? Drakken was still Captain; her words had made that clear. If the palace was no longer safe, then why not? If there were traitors in the Guard, surely Drakken could set that to rights. More puzzling still, who was the target? Didrik? Stephen? Both of them? What possible threat could there be?

And where was Devlin in all this? A part of him longed to go back to the gate and shake Oluva until she gave him the answers he needed, flames take the consequences. If the new guard took objection to his tactics, Didrik could defend himself. But he knew that such was foolishness. He was not a raw guard, still flushed with the impetuousness of youth. He was a sober lieutenant of nearly thirty winters. Personal aide to the Chosen One. Oluva had warned him to caution, and cautious he would be, until he knew more of the situation in Kingsholm. Then, and only then, would he act.

Stephen suggested they lodge at the Singing Fish, but Didrik rejected that immediately. Stephen was too well known there. If someone was looking for them, it would be one of the first places they checked. Nor could Didrik turn to his own parents, who were bound to be watched as well. Neither of them could afford to go anywhere their faces were likely to be known.

A short distance from the gate, they left their horses at a livery stable. The owner, a woman of enormous girth called Selma the Fat, took one look at the shabby travelers and offered to sell the horses for them and split the proceeds. Didrik, his cloak drawn close to conceal his uniform, agreed.

He fully expected to be cheated by Selma, but that was all to the good. Selma would have no reason to mention just which two travelers had left the horses with her.

From there they made their way to a tavern along the river, though tavern was perhaps too fine a name for a place that could hold a mere dozen drunken sailors. But he knew there was an old storeroom, where the owner sometimes let folks down on their luck sleep. And indeed the serving boy reported that the room was empty, and he pocketed Didrik's coppers without giving them a second glance.

As soon as the door swung shut behind them, Stephen's patience ran out.

"What is going on?" Stephen demanded. "Why did

Oluva call you by another name? And why can't we go to the palace?"

Didrik dropped his saddlebags on the floor and looked around. There was a long bench against one wall and a tattered blanket hanging from a peg near a fire grate that looked like no fire had burned there for months. There was no pallet, nor any wood for a fire. Barely two paces across, and four paces long, the room was likely the safest place in Kingsholm. For now.

Taking off his blue cloak, he hung it on a peg. Then Didrik knelt down by his saddlebags and pulled out the set of plain clothes. He placed them on the bench, then sat down.

"What's wrong?" Stephen asked.

Didrik reached back and untied the leather cord that held his warrior's braid. He began to comb his fingers through the long hair, separating it.

"I don't know," Didrik confessed. "Oluva gave me the hand signs for danger and betrayal."

"And she warned you against the palace?"

"Yes."

"She said you had no friends there." Stephen's voice was flat, as if with only a mild curiosity.

Didrik nodded. He gathered his hair with his left hand, then reached down and removed the dagger from his belt. With a firm stroke he began to saw through the hair that had been allowed to grow since he was first named a warrior.

"In the name of the Seven, what are you doing?" Stephen asked.

"We need information. If I leave this place looking like

a guard, it is only a matter of time before they find me. But if they see a mercenary, I may be able to slip by."

With a final jerk of his knife, he cut the remaining strands of his hair. He looked for a moment at the length held in his left hand, then tossed it in the fire grate. They would have to burn it.

Replacing the dagger in his belt, he tied the short strands that remained back in a simple tail, in the style of a mercenary or caravan guard. His head felt strangely light and he turned it from side to side, wondering how long it would take him to become accustomed to it.

"They may not be looking for me," Stephen said. "I could go."

"Or you could be the one in danger. Besides, you don't know who to talk to."

"And you do?"

"Maybe." If his luck held. If the city had not changed beyond all recognition in the months of his absence. If old loyalties still held true.

"But what about Devlin?"

"I don't know."

Devlin should have arrived in the city over a fortnight ago. He'd had a full escort from Baron Martell, not to mention Saskia at his side. And if the Chosen One had been attacked, surely the news of it would have been on the lips of every person that Didrik and Stephen had encountered in their travels.

Had Devlin arrived in the city only to be dispatched on another errand? Had his duty called him elsewhere before he could meet with the King? What had caused Oluva to give the sign for betrayal?

Had Devlin somehow been betrayed? But that was

unthinkable. Devlin had the Sword of Light, after all. Proof that he was the chosen champion of the Gods.

There must be some other mischief afoot.

"Trust me. I will find a way to get word to Captain Drakken. She will know what is to be done next."

"And you are certain it is not Drakken herself that Oluva was warning you against?"

Didrik shook his head in instant denial. The thought had occurred to him, but only for a moment, then he had felt ashamed of his disloyalty. Drakken was his Captain, and she had proven herself worthy a hundred times over. He could no more doubt her than he could doubt the strength of Kingsholm's walls, or the skill of his own sword arm.

"The Captain is loyal. I will stake my life on it."

"It is more than your life at risk. It is all of ours," Stephen pointed out. "Tread cautiously."

"I will," Didrik promised.

The hum of conversation mixed with the clatter of utensils against pewter plates as the guards consumed their noon meal. As Captain Drakken entered the hall those closest to the door put down their forks and prepared to rise, but she waved them back to their seats.

A few called greetings that she acknowledged as she wound her way through the long tables to the small square table by the window where the seniors customarily sat. As she expected, she found Lieutenants Ansgar and Embeth there, both about to start their shifts, along with Sergeants Henrik and Niclas.

Embeth, perhaps sensing what was to come, hastily

crammed the last of her bread into her mouth and washed it down with citrine. Ansgar was far more correct, pushing his plate away and rising to his feet.

"Sorry to disturb your meal, Lieutenant Embeth, but I have an errand for you before you start your shift. Lady Vendela wrote to complain that the sentries assigned to watch the council chamber have been insolent and lax in their duty." Captain Drakken reached into her belt pouch and withdrew a small scroll. "Here is her complaint. I need you to speak with her to find out the details. If there is any substance to her complaint, I want those involved disciplined immediately, understood?"

Embeth took the scroll and rose to her feet. "Understood, Captain," she said, with a quick salute. "My report will be on your desk by the end of this shift."

"Good." Captain Drakken turned her attention to her next victim. "Ansgar, you're with me. The family of Goodwoman Katje Linsale held a banquet for her two nights ago, and half of the guests became ill, including the goodwoman herself. She is now claiming the wine was poisoned, but it seems more likely that it was merely tainted. Either way, I want to get to the bottom of this before panic sets in. If the wine was tainted, then there may be other contaminated barrels, and we'd best find them before it sickens anyone else."

"And if it was poison?" Lieutenant Ansgar asked.

"If it's poison, then the goodwoman's relatives are to be brought in for questioning. We'll find out which one of them was unwilling to wait for their inheritance."

Ansgar gave a thin smile. She'd noticed over the years that he bore a resentment against wealthy merchants, perhaps because his family had been street vendors, barely more than beggars themselves. His attitude was never enough to interfere with his duty, but he was always cheerful when the opportunity came to bring one of the mighty to justice. It was just this character trait that she was counting on.

"Let us go. I've already informed Lieutenant Nevyn that he has the watch until your return."

She had not raised her voice, but she knew that those at the tables around them had heard her instructions. Many of the diners watched as she left, with Ansgar at her heels. Her skin crawled, for she knew that not all of those eyes were friendly. Or loyal.

And it would be foolish to assume that it was only the Guard that was interested in her movements. As they left the palace, her street sense told her that other eyes were watching. She hoped Ansgar's presence would lull them into a sense of complacency. Had it been Embeth by her side, some might have wondered what errand drew the Captain and her most senior lieutenant into the city. But as senior it was Embeth's duty to deal with the contretemps at the court, and thus Ansgar was her logical deputy for the investigation of the attempted poisoning.

All according to routine, as if it were any other day. She wondered if she was fooling anyone with her pretense.

As they made their way through the streets of Kingsholm, she listened with half an ear as the normally reserved Lieutenant Ansgar offered his suggestions on the best way to interrogate Goodwoman Linsale and her household. He had a clear, logical plan, and despite her doubts about his loyalties, she was impressed at the thoughtfulness with which he approached the problem.

Had there really been an attempted poisoning, Ansgar's

methods would quite likely have identified the villain. But when they reached the merchant's house, they found Goodwoman Linsale full of apologies for having troubled them. The healers had traced the illness to an undercook who had been hired to help with the banquet. The undercook had recently been ill, and though recovered had been warned by the healers that he could not work as a cook for at least a fortnight. He had ignored their orders, and the contagion that he carried within him had been passed to the guests.

Lieutenant Ansgar was visibly deflated by this prosaic explanation, and demanded to know why the goodwoman hadn't informed the Guard. The goodwoman replied that she had sent a letter only that morning, which would no doubt be waiting for them when they returned.

She apologized again for wasting their time. Captain Drakken, after grumbling for form's sake, finally accepted her apologies.

"These merchants think we have nothing better to do with our time," Lieutenant Ansgar grumbled as the servants escorted from the house. "Next time she calls for help, we will not be so quick to come running."

Captain Drakken nodded. "If we'd waited another hour, we could have saved ourselves the errand. You will likely find her scroll on the watch desk when you return to the Guard Hall."

In fact she knew the scroll was there, for she had placed it on the desk herself. After first reading it, then resealing it carefully with wax. It had been just the excuse to leave the palace that she had been searching for all morning.

"You should return to the hall. Nevyn's already two hours into your shift, and he's back on again tonight."

"And you?"

"I will go speak with the healers," Captain Drakken said. "I don't like it that this cook was allowed out to ply his trade while still contagious. There must be a way to keep this from happening again."

She dismissed Ansgar with a nod and turned west, in the direction of the Healers' Guild. Ansgar hesitated a moment, then began walking back toward the palace. Drakken took a winding path through the streets, turning sharply twice, until she was convinced that she was not being followed. Then and only then did she allow her footsteps to turn in the direction of the river docks. It was time to find Devlin.

# Six

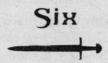

THE UNNAMED TAVERN WAS ONLY A FEW YARDS from the docks used by the fishermen to unload their cargo, and the smell of rotting fish mingled with the odor of raw sewage. Here, in the poorer quarters, the underground sewers had not been repaired in years, and as she walked down the alley the mud squelched suspiciously under her boots. And it was only spring. Come the heat of summer, this part of the city would be near unbearable.

Criminals disdained the area, able to afford better lodgings elsewhere. Only the poorest came here, or those who had worked the docks so long that they were immune to the stench. Few would think to look for one of the guards here.

In her quarter century of service, Captain Drakken had become familiar with every part of the city, and since becoming Captain she had made it a point to walk each of the patrol routes at least once a season. But routine patrols stopped at the docks. Only chance had brought the unnamed tavern to her attention, when Didrik was investigating a pair of sea captains who had taken to forcibly recruiting sailors. That investigation had been five years ago, and there should be nothing to connect this place to her. Which argued that the message she had received was indeed from Didrik.

She paused, glancing up and down the alley, but there was no one in sight. Even the feral cats scorned the place for better pickings elsewhere. In the daylight it was easy to see that the former storeroom had been tacked onto the tavern as an afterthought. The tavern was made of oak that dated back to better days, but the addition was made of lumber scavenged from packing crates and driftwood. The boards did not fully meet, and it would be a cold place in which to lodge.

She hesitated a moment. If the message was genuine, then on the other side of the door were those she had desperately sought for the past weeks. And if the message was a trap, then she would have delivered herself neatly into her enemies' hands, providing all the proof they needed that the Captain of the Guard was ignoring the orders of King and council.

Either way she would have her answers.

Prudently she loosened her sword in its scabbard before rapping thrice on the door.

The door opened a crack, revealing the minstrel's tense features. He nodded as he recognized her, then stepped back and opened the door wide to reveal Didrik standing beside him, his sword pointed at the door, ready to repel an attack.

At his gesture, Drakken entered the dark room, keeping a firm grip on the hilt of her sword.

Didrik waited until the door swung shut behind her before lowering his weapon. "You were not followed?"

"No," she said. Her eyes swept the tiny room, but the two men were its only occupants.

"It is good to see you," Stephen said.

She nodded, but her attention was elsewhere. "Where is Devlin? He should not be roaming the city alone."

"What do you mean? My message was to you, not Devlin. Unless you invited him to join us here?"

His words destroyed the small hope that she had carried within her ever since receiving Didrik's message. After days of private mourning for her friends, Didrik's message had seemed a gift from the Gods. After all, if Didrik was alive, then surely Devlin was with him. Despite all evidence that proved otherwise.

It seemed her darkest fears had indeed proven true.

"I haven't seen Devlin since he left the city on his quest," Drakken said.

Didrik's face paled and he took a few steps back, sitting down heavily on the bench as if his legs could no longer hold him.

"Devlin rode ahead, with a full escort of Baron Martell's armsmen. He should have returned over a fortnight ago," he insisted.

"There has been no sign of him. Nor of his escort," Drakken said. "The baron himself arrived in the capital just two days ago. But there was no mention of the Chosen One."

"What does this mean?" Stephen asked.

Captain Drakken crossed the narrow room, and took a seat on the bench not far from Didrik. Even in the dim light, she could see that his face was drawn, and he had lost more than a few pounds. Injured, ill, or perhaps both she surmised.

Stephen had seemingly fared better. If the hardships of the journey had aged him, it was an improvement. No one now would look at him and mistake him for a boy. She hoped he had grown in wisdom as well, for the news she had to share would lay a heavy burden on both men. Now was the time for reason, not for the impetuous folly of youth.

"What of Devlin?" Didrik asked.

"I'd hoped he was with you, though logic told me else-wise," Captain Drakken said softly. "But in truth, I believe he is dead. Murdered on the very night he returned to the city."

Stephen protested, insisting that Devlin must be alive. Didrik kept silent, though she could see that he, too, clung to the hope that she was somehow mistaken. She could not blame them. It seemed a cruel trick of fate that had struck Devlin down just at the moment he was poised to return in triumph. Devlin had been killed in the one place where he should have been safe.

Didrik's face grew grim as she recounted her tale. How the soul stone had told of Devlin's return, but she could find no one who had seen him. Frantic searching had re-vealed no sign of Devlin, until a frightened maid came to Drakken with a tale of the new carpet on the floor of the King's private audience chamber. When she'd rolled up the new carpet to sweep, she'd found a strange stain un-derneath.

"Being a dedicated worker, she brought a bucket and scrubbing rag to clean the marble floor. But when water hit the stain, it turned red and smelled like blood. Fright-ened, she replaced the carpet and came to me with the tale."

"What did the King say?" Didrik's voice was rough.

"The King no longer speaks directly with me," she said. Indeed her position at court grew more perilous every day. "After some discussion the Royal Steward agreed to let me inspect the room. He explained that the carpet had been replaced because it had been stained when a chamberman dropped a bottle of Myrkan red. I checked the floor, but it had been scrubbed with lime. You can see the outline of a stain, but whether it was made by wine or blood no one can tell. The maid apologized for her foolishness and the waste of my time."

"And was she a young girl, given to flights of fancy?"

"She had served at the palace for nigh unto thirty years. After the incident she quit her post and was said to have joined her family. I hoped to speak with her once she was free of the palace walls, but have been unable to find any trace of her, or of this so-called family."

The maid was not the first of those to go missing. Two of the guards who had been on duty the night of Devlin's return had failed to report to the barracks after their shift had ended. She had used their disappearance as an excuse to search the city, but so far her efforts had yielded nothing.

"But what of the soul stone? Surely that will tell us where Devlin may be found," Stephen said.

"Robbers broke into the Royal Temple on the day after Devlin returned. They stole the gold vessels, and the silken robes worn by Brother Arni on the high feast days. The mosaic was chipped, as if someone had taken the soul stone, but there were also traces of dust on the floor below," she said.

When the Chosen One died, the soul stone crumbled into dust. In itself it had no value, so there was no reason for the mosaic to have been vandalized. Not unless someone was trying to conceal the evidence that Devlin had been killed.

Common thieves should not have been able to enter and leave the palace compound without being discovered, which argued that they had had help from someone inside the palace. Perhaps from some of the guards that she commanded.

Didrik had reached the same realization. "There is a traitor in the Guard."

She gave a bitter laugh. "A traitor? There may be dozens. There are few left that I can trust. Embeth. Lukas. Oluva. It is not just the new recruits; many of the veterans appear to have divided loyalties. Even Lieutenant Ansgar is suspect, for he is the one who commanded the watch on the night Devlin was to return."

Didrik blinked in disbelief. "Ansgar? When did he become a lieutenant?"

"When his predecessor was killed. King Olafur recommended promoting Ansgar, and I was forced to agree."

At the time, Ansgar had seemed a safe political choice. An unimaginative man, but one who would scrupulously follow every regulation. She had not thought he had it in him to turn traitor.

Yet Ansgar had been the one to approve the change of the watch schedule, allowing two new recruits to man the western gate, despite her standing orders that the novices were always to be paired with a veteran. When questioned, Ansgar had explained that the guard originally scheduled for the watch had taken ill, and he had simply assigned the first person he could find to cover her watch. He had not realized that he had assigned two novices together until she had called his attention to it, at which point he had profusely apologized.

A simple, reasonable explanation. Ordinarily she would have thought no more of it. Except for the fact that the mix-up had occurred on the night she believed Devlin to have entered the city. So had it been an honest mistake? Or was Ansgar playing a deeper game?

Her suspicions were enough to make her fear for the future of Jorsk, and of the people she served. But that was all she had so far. Suspicions and coincidences. She needed tangible evidence if she was to back up her claims.

It was no light thing to accuse a king of murder.

"I do not believe Devlin has been killed," Stephen said. It was at least the third time he had made that claim. "Not until you bring me proof. Show me his body and that of Saskia. Only then will I believe."

"Saskia?"

"A peacekeeper from Duncaer," Didrik explained. "She led the unit that escorted Devlin to the border of Jorsk, and when her troop turned back, she insisted on making the rest of the journey. She was a fierce fighter, and she vowed to guard Devlin with her life, which is why Stephen stayed behind with me."

His eyes were haunted, and she knew he was wondering if matters would have turned out differently if he had accompanied Devlin instead of entrusting his safety to others. Much the same thoughts had run through her mind. If she had been on duty the night Devlin returned, if she had been at the gate to greet him, would Olafur have still dared have him killed? Would she have sensed the trap in time to protect him? Or would she have become merely another of those who disappeared?

"This Saskia, can you describe her?" she asked.

Didrik nodded. "Tall, perhaps two fingers taller than I, with a wiry build. Short black hair, close-cropped, and blue eyes."

Damn.

"A body matching that description was pulled from the river two days after Devlin's return. She'd been knifed and the body stripped, so we took it as a robbery. None of the Caerfolk seemed to know her, but at the time I suspected they were simply protecting their own."

"Was there a scar on her right thigh? A healed slash from a sword, about two hand spans in length?" Didrik asked.

She nodded.

Didrik's shoulders slumped. "Then that was her," he said.

"This doesn't prove Devlin is dead," Stephen said. "It could have been Saskia's blood that was found on the chamber floor."

On the contrary, Saskia's death seemed proof that Drakken was right. There was no reason to kill Devlin's escort, unless it was to prevent her from bearing witness against the conspirators.

"We need to find Baron Martell's men. The commander called himself Sundgren. Pers Sundgren," Didrik said. "Find him, and we'll find the truth of what happened when Devlin and Saskia arrived in Kingsholm."

"Would you recognize him by sight?"

"I would," Stephen said.

"Then it is you we must protect. Both of you. The council has given orders that you two are to be brought in for questioning. If you are taken, it would be far too easy for you to disappear."

Once she would have sworn that she knew everything that went on in the palace, from the top of the battlements to the deepest cellars. Now she knew better. It was quite possible that Stephen and Didrik could be arrested by guards acting on secret orders, and she would be none the wiser.

Last week her search for Devlin had taken her to the cellars that ran below the oldest part of the palace, where the old kings had once kept their enemies in cramped cells far from the eyes and ears of the court. The cells had not been used in living memory, so it was no surprise to find them empty. But it was a surprise to find that the rusting lock had recently been replaced, and there were fresh torches in the wall sconces, ready to be lit.

The King was preparing, but for what she did not know.

"But what should we do? We cannot hide here for long. And I will not stand idly by," Didrik said.

"You should be safe for a few days, at least. Let me try to find what happened to Martell's armsmen. And I will speak to Solveig and Rikard, see what they advise. For now, you can help most by staying out of sight."

She rose to her feet, conscious that she had already lingered longer than she intended.

"But wait," Stephen protested.

"I cannot. I have stayed too long already. I cannot afford to raise suspicions. Not now."

It was growing late and she had yet to visit the healers' hall. Just in case Ansgar checked on her story.


Stephen picked up the nearly flat waterskin and shook it thoughtfully, but heard only the faintest sloshing sound.

They would need more water soon. Removing the cap, he took a few mouthfuls, then offered it to Didrik.

"Water?" he prompted, when Didrik made no move to take it.

Didrik shook his head. Except for that tiny movement, he might have been a statue. Or a corpse.

Since Captain Drakken had left, Didrik had neither moved nor spoken. Stephen had tried to speak with him but grew tired of talking to the empty air.

Stephen knew that Didrik was grieving over the news of Saskia's death. The two of them had grown close during the journey. Closer than Stephen had realized at the time, for how else had Didrik been able to describe Saskia's scar?

Didrik had lost a friend, and a comrade. No doubt he was thinking that if he had been the one to accompany Devlin, then it might well have been Didrik's body that was found in the river. Saskia may have given her life to protect Devlin.

Such grief was to be respected. Stephen grieved for Saskia as well, but he would not let it paralyze him. Didrik and Captain Drakken might have given up all hope, but Stephen knew better. Devlin was still alive. He had to be. The Gods would not have led Devlin to the Sword of Light unless they intended for him to wield it.

Devlin might be injured. Imprisoned. Or off on a quest—one so secret that he had been ordered not to confide in Captain Drakken. It was up to his friends to find him, and offer him their aid. No doubt he would laugh if he knew that they were instead sitting passively in Kingsholm, mourning his supposed death.

"I am going out," Stephen declared.

"No."

"We cannot simply stay here. We need water." He shook the nearly empty waterskin in Didrik's face, then threw it into the corner of the tiny room. "We need food as well. But more than both we need information."

"You heard what Captain Drakken said—"

"Captain Drakken is wrong. Even if you believe Devlin is dead, there is nothing to be gained by sitting here in the dark, pitying ourselves." Stephen was proud that his voice did not shake. "You want to know the truth of what happened to Devlin? You will never find it by staring at these filthy walls."

He kicked the bench with the toe of his boot and it began to sag alarmingly.

"I am leaving," Stephen declared. He took his cloak down from the peg and swung it around his shoulders.

"No," Didrik said, rising and grabbing Stephen by the shoulders. "You will not. If anyone goes, it should be me."

His shoulders ached from the force of Didrik's grip, but Stephen stood firm, glaring up at him. "You cannot stop me," he insisted.

"I will tie you to the bench if I need to," Didrik said, giving him a shake as if he were a recalcitrant child.

Stephen grew angry. Who was Didrik to order him about in such a way? Stephen was not one of the Guard, nor was he Didrik's brother. He was a free man, capable of making his own decisions.

"If you leave here, you will be imprisoned or dead before sunset," Didrik declared.

"Keeping me safe will not bring Devlin back," Stephen said. "Nor will it make up for your failure to protect Devlin."

Didrik flinched and pushed Stephen away.

Stephen staggered before regaining his balance. "I did not mean . . ." he began, searching for words to apologize for the unforgivable.

"You cannot hate me any more than I hate myself," Didrik said. "I know where the fault lies."

"I should not have said it. I do not blame you, no more than I blame myself. But the past is past. We cannot change it. We can only seize the present and do everything in our power to find Devlin. Wherever he is, he will need our help."

"And if he is dead, I have sworn to bring his killers to justice."

Didrik's grim fatalism put a damper on Stephen's natural optimism. *Devlin is alive, he has to be alive*, he thought, trying to drown out the small voice that whispered that Didrik and Drakken might be right.

"So what do you intend to do?"

"I have contacts of my own. People who look at me and see Stephen the minstrel. They may have heard things that Captain Drakken has not."

Didrik nodded. "Be careful. I will make my own inquiries. Nifra proved herself loyal when she carried the message to Drakken. She may be able to tell me who else is to be trusted."

It was not much of a plan. But it was all they had.

"Good luck," Stephen said.

"And be careful," Didrik cautioned. "You are no use to anyone dead."

"Neither are you."

# Seven

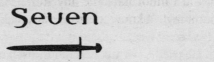

SLOWLY THE DREAM IMAGE OF CERRIE'S FACE faded away, and Devlin awoke to misery. His entire body ached, from his throbbing head to his frostbitten feet. Worst of all was his side, which had been torn open by the banecat's claws. He took a deep breath, and the stabbing pain of his ribs made him immediately regret the action.

How long had he lain here? He tried to think, but his mind was a jumble of confusion. Had it been only yesterday that he fought the banecats? Or had he lain here for days, dying by inches from the wounds he had received in battle? And who was the strange brown-haired foreigner who appeared in his dreams? The man was a Selvarat by his features, yet why would such a one inhabit Devlin's dreams? Even more puzzling, why would Cerrie appear to drive him off?

Cerrie. His wife's name gave him pause. He had avenged the murder of his family, but he felt no elation. Not even a grim satisfaction in having fulfilled his oath. Instead he felt a nagging unease, as if he had left a job half-done.

There was something wrong. Something more than fever addled his wits.

Devlin opened his eyes. It was dark, but not the darkness of the cave he remembered. Gone, too, was the numbing cold. And the floor was rocking back and forth. He was moving.

He tried to sit up, bracing himself on his arms. But his arms moved only a short distance before they were caught, held tight by cold metal fastened around his wrists. He tugged his legs, and found they too were chained.

His head fell back against the floor and he groaned.

Almost at once, the rocking motion stopped. Inborn caution made him close his eyes, as he heard the faint sound of voices. There was a rustling sound, perhaps a leather flap being pushed aside?

The floor dipped beneath him under the weight of another body, and he smelled the burning lamp oil even before the light struck his face. Devlin held himself still.

"Is he awake?" a man's voice called from outside. There was something very familiar about that voice.

Devlin whimpered softly, and twitched his limbs as if trying to roll over.

"No, just dreaming," said his observer. This was a woman speaking, with a strong accent that he could not place. From Nerikaat perhaps?

The lamplight left his face, and the wagon bounced slightly as the woman climbed out. He opened his eyes the barest fraction, and saw that he was indeed lying on the floor of a small wagon. Curved ribs overhead supported a leather covering, which was open at one end. The woman pulled the leather flap closed behind her, but not before he confirmed that it was night.

"We'd best prepare another dose just the same," the woman said. "Won't be long before he wakes."

"I don't like this," her companion replied. "The menas root is losing its effectiveness. Each time it holds him for a shorter period. And we are still days away from our rendezvous."

"We'll do what we must. If the drug no longer works, we'll simply keep him chained. Or hit him over the head again, if that's what it takes." The woman's voice was unconcerned as her fingers worked busily to tie the laces that held the leather flap shut.

"Fine for you to say. You're not the one who will have to explain to the Prince why his prize is damaged," the man grumbled. Then his voice drifted off as the wagon lurched into motion again.

His final words triggered an avalanche of memories. Devlin knew that voice. Karel of Selvarat. He had been present in the King's private receiving room when Devlin had been brought before King Olafur.

Ambassador Magaharan had been there too, along with Marshal Olvarrson and his aide.

From the moment he had entered the chamber, Devlin had felt uneasy. It had been past midnight, after all, an unusual hour for the King to be in council with his advisors. And the presence of the Selvarat ambassador had seemed odd. Regardless of the new alliance between their countries, surely the King would wish to hear Devlin's report in private.

But instead Devlin found himself in a room filled with foreigners, and those who had vigorously opposed him. Saskia's presence at his back gave him an obscure feeling of comfort, as did the presence of a pair of guards.

He remembered that King Olafur had frowned when Devlin revealed that he had returned with the Sword of Light. He had asked to examine the weapon, and Devlin had withdrawn the sword from its scabbard with an odd reluctance. The King took it from him, praising his accomplishment, then placed the sword on a table where others could admire it.

The King had suggested a toast to Devlin and personally handed him a wine cup. Devlin had taken it, only to be warned by his ring that the wine was drugged. He called out a warning to the King and stepped forward, only to be struck down from behind.

The last thing he could remember was hearing Saskia cry out.

She, too, had been taken or killed.

Even his drug-addled wits could see the obvious conclusion. He had been betrayed. King Olafur had not summoned Devlin to return because he wished to consult with the Chosen One. Instead he had lured Devlin into a trap, then handed him over to the waiting Selvarats.

There was no other explanation for his predicament. He had been struck down in the very presence of the King, then somehow smuggled from the palace. Chained like a prisoner or slave, he was being delivered as a gift to a foreign prince.

He wondered how many days he had passed in his drugged stupor. Reason said that he was still in Jorsk, for the Selvarats could just as easily have loaded him on a ship if they intended to take him to their homeland.

He did not know what they planned for him, nor did he intend to lie there passively waiting to find out. For once the Geas and his own will were in accord. He must escape. Whatever it took. The Chosen One was too powerful a weapon to be delivered into the hands of their enemies.

Slowly, so as not to rattle the chains, Devlin pulled his arms taut against their manacles and then released them. He repeated the movement as the metal began to cut into his flesh. The pain occupied but a distant corner of his mind as his duty consumed him. He would escape. And then he would have his revenge upon those who had betrayed him.

Stephen shifted his grip on the chest he carried, sliding his right arm underneath so it took more of the weight. His arms ached with the strain, and he found himself wishing that he had chosen a smaller item. But a smaller package would not have served his purposes. He needed an object that was small enough that one man could bear it, yet heavy enough that the palace servants would be content to let him deliver it himself.

That is if he wasn't recognized and arrested as soon as he reached the palace. He knew he was taking a great risk, but he could see no other way. It had been over a week since he and Didrik had returned to Kingsholm, and they were still no closer to finding Devlin.

He and Didrik had pursued their separate inquiries, much to Captain Drakken's displeasure. In his careful outings Stephen had found the mood of the city to be unsettling. On the surface, all were celebrating the end of winter and the long-sought alliance with Selvarat, which promised the return of peace and prosperity. But the celebrations were lackluster, and the public smiles faded away in private.

Some of his friends had refused to speak to him, their eyes passing over him as if he were a stranger. Those few to whom he did talk were worried. The King's most vocal critics had gone silent or disappeared. Some had been arrested for sedition, while others fled into hiding.

The Chosen One was seldom mentioned, and when he was, his name was cursed. It cost Stephen every ounce of control he possessed not to protest the first time he was told that Devlin had abandoned the people of Jorsk. By the tenth time he heard it, he had grown numb.

Didrik, too, had grown frustrated by their lack of progress. He had spent three days watching Baron Martell's residence, only to confirm that Pers Sundgren was not within. Recklessly he'd followed some of the Baron's armsmen to a tavern and engaged them in conversation. He'd confirmed that the Baron did indeed have a Commander Sundgren who was currently back at the Baron's seat. But his questions had raised their suspicions, and Didrik had been lucky to make his escape.

He knew that the others had grown discouraged. Didrik had even gone so far as to search the old cemetery, looking for fresh unmarked graves. He had returned to their room covered in dirt and smelling of death.

Captain Drakken had instituted a river patrol, ostensibly searching for smugglers; but he knew that she, too, was looking for a body. Devlin's body.

Only Stephen held firmly to the belief that Devlin was still alive, though his optimism waned with each day that passed without news.

As Stephen approached the palace gate, the two guards

on duty drew themselves to attention. He had purposely chosen the busiest gate, hoping to blend in with the others who passed through, but ill luck was with him, for the gate was strangely deserted, and there was no one to take the guards' attention away from him.

"Halt," one commanded. "State your business."

His stomach felt queasy, and he hoped fervently that none of his nervousness showed on his face. The guard who had spoken was a stranger to him, but his companion was one Stephen knew well: Private Thornke, a decent fiddler, who had often accompanied Stephen on those occasions that he entertained the guards. Stephen had covered his hair with a woolen hat and wore common clothes, but such a disguise would not fool one who knew him well.

"Silks for Lady Vendela. From Merchant Tansey," Stephen said, holding the chest before him.

"Put it down and open it up," the first guard commanded.

Stephen set the box on the ground, kneeling down beside it, then undid the clasps. He raised the lid, revealing the top layer of crimson silk. It had been all he could afford, and underneath the silk he had piled common muslin. The chest was worth far more than the price of the goods inside, but the guards had no way of knowing that.

The first guard reached down and extended one hand.

"Stop!" Stephen said indignantly, mimicking the high pitched tones of a trader he knew. "Your hands are unclean, and that silk is worth more than you earn in a season. If you ruin it Lady Vendela will have both our hides."

The guard hastily withdrew his hand. Lady Vendela's temper was well known.

"Summon a chamberman to bring the chest to Lady Vendela," the guard said.

"No," Thornke replied.

Stephen held his breath as Thornke's eyes widened in apparent recognition.

"No," Thornke repeated. "If he's so concerned about the silks, let him lug it up to Lady Vendela's rooms. The labor will be good for him."

His chest eased at the unexpected reprieve.

"Do you know the way?" Thornke asked.

Stephen picked up the chest and rose to his feet. Despite his burden, he made a half bow. "Yes, sirs."

"Go then, and be quick about your business," the first guard ordered. "Tradesmen are not allowed in the palace after sunset."

Stephen nodded. He walked slowly past the guards, though his instincts screamed at him to run. He muttered fervent thanks to Lord Kanjti that it had been Thornke who recognized him, and not another. Thornke had kept his secret, whether out of friendship or loyalty to Drakken. If it had been anyone else, they might well have chosen to obey their standing orders and arrest Stephen for questioning.

He hoped that his luck would hold, as he made his way across the courtyard and into the palace. He passed another pair of guards and several servants, but no one paid attention to him, as he kept the chest raised before him and his head bowed low.

Lady Vendela was not in her chambers, but her maid accepted the chest and promised to convey Merchant

Tansey's compliments to her mistress. No doubt Lady Vendela would be surprised when she opened the box to find that it held a mere yard of silk. The merchant would be equally surprised at Lady Vendela's complaints. But by the time they realized they had been hoaxed, Stephen would be long gone.

As he exited Lady Vendela's chamber he turned left and made his way to the very end of the corridor and up one flight of stairs. Luck was with him, for there was no one about as he made his way to the third door on the left. He drew a deep breath and knocked.

There was no answer. He paused for a moment, then knocked again.

This time the door swung open.

"Yes?" Solveig asked. Then her eyes widened as she recognized him. She grabbed his arm and pulled him into the room, shutting the door swiftly behind him.

"Stephen, you bloody great fool," she said. But her disparaging words were belied by the fierce embrace in which she held him.

Stephen wrapped his arms around his sister, giving himself up to the reassurance of her touch. For a moment he wished with all his heart that he was once again a small boy, that his eldest sister could make everything right.

She clung to him for several heartbeats, then finally she released him, but she kept hold of his hands.

"You look terrible," she said.

"I am pleased to see you as well."

"You should not have come here. Didn't Captain Drakken warn you?"

"Yes." Stephen's mouth twisted in a grimace. "Captain

Drakken gave me her orders, and Didrik forbade me as well. But I had to see you."

"You took a great risk. The guards have orders to bring you before the King's Council for questioning."

"I know."

Captain Drakken had shared a copy of the decree with them. It had not named Stephen or Didrik as traitors. Instead the orders directed that the two were to report to the King's Council with all haste upon their return to Kingsholm, and that any member of the Guard or army who encountered them was to take them prisoner if they refused to come under their own volition. And without Captain Drakken's warning, reporting to the council is precisely what Stephen would have done. And then they might well have become two more of the missing.

"Come, sit a moment, and let me take in the sight of you. Can I offer you wine? Citrine?"

"Wine," Stephen said absently. He paced around the sitting room before taking a seat by the cold hearth. Solveig filled two glasses with pale wine and handed one to him.

"May the Gods watch over you," she said, raising her glass in salute. It was an oddly solemn toast for what should have been a joyful reunion.

"May they watch over us all," Stephen said, raising his own glass before taking a sip. The wine was sweet for his taste, but far finer than anything he had drunk in the past weeks. He took a hefty swallow before setting it aside.

"What news have you?" he asked.

Solveig sat in the chair opposite his. She looked older than he remembered, her face drawn, and though she was not yet thirty, there were traces of white amid the gold of her hair.

"I have told Captain Drakken all I know," Solveig said. "There is no news of Devlin's fate. Indeed no one speaks his name anymore. At least not where the King or his spies may be listening."

"Do you believe he is dead?"

He held his breath, waiting for her answer.

Solveig hesitated for a moment, then shook her head. "I pray that he is not, but surely he would have found some way to get a message to us if he was alive."

He released his pent-up breath in a heavy sigh. It was not the reassurance he had hoped for.

"Devlin may not know that the soul stone was taken," Stephen argued. "He may assume that we know full well where he is."

"I hope you are right." She glanced up at the sand clock over the mantel, then rose to her feet. "I cannot stay much longer. There is a court dinner this evening, and I dare not stay away."

"How is the mood of the court these days?"

"Grim," Solveig said.

He tossed back the rest of his wine and stood up, following his sister as she entered her bedroom. Solveig peered at her reflection in the mirror over the dressing table, then opened her jewelry case, rifling through it till she found a pair of pearl earrings. She put them on, then nodded, apparently satisfied by what she saw.

"I thought the court would be rejoicing," Stephen observed. "Empress Thania has honored the alliance, we have troops from Selvarat protecting the northern coast against invaders, and with our own army reinforcing the border with Nerikaat, it seems the threat is over."

Solveig nodded. "So one would think. King Olafur has gotten what he wanted, but it has not made him happy. Instead, he seems possessed, a man starting at shadows. He sees conspiracies and threats against him everywhere. Those who question his judgment find themselves banished to the countryside, if they are lucky, or detained on suspicion of treason. Even Lady Ingeleth was nearly undone when she questioned the arrest of Lord Branstock. Only her fervent apologies to the King allowed her to keep herself out of the dungeon."

Lady Ingeleth was one of the most respected members of the court, and a firm supporter of the King. If she was not safe, then no one was.

A sudden fear gripped him. "What of you? It is well known that you were friends with Devlin. Are friends," he hastily corrected himself.

Solveig smiled reassuringly. "These past weeks I have publicly distanced myself from Rikard, and from Devlin's most vocal supporters. I find it best to remind everyone that our mother was born in Selvarat. They do not welcome me to their councils, but neither have I fallen under suspicion."

"Yet," Stephen said. "I think it would be best if you retired to join Father and Mother in Esker."

Her hand reached over to cup his face. "Shall I be less brave than you? There is no warrant for my arrest. And as for Mother, she is still in Selvarat. Madrene has married the youngest son of Count Bayard, and Mother elected to stay and help Madrene settle in her new home."

"Madrene? Married?" It was not possible. She would

never marry, not without the blessing of their father. It was not possible that she had chosen to make her life in that foreign land. At the very least, she should have brought her new husband home to Esker, to be presented to the family.

"Was it a love match?" he asked. As the fourth of the Baron's five children, Madrene had the luxury of choosing her own partner. Unlike Solveig, who carried the burden of being their father's heir, Madrene had no need to marry for political gain.

Solveig's next words shocked him to the core.

"Knowing Madrene, she was bound and gagged through the ceremony. The marriage was a sham. Mother's letter to me was all politeness, but it held the code words for danger. I believe that she and Madrene are hostages in Selvarat."

"I don't understand," Stephen said. Nothing made sense to him anymore.

"Neither do I. It is a mosaic with most of the pieces missing. But I fancy I can see the vague outline of the picture, and it is an ugly one indeed."

In a world where the Chosen One might be murdered within the very walls of the palace, any treachery might well be possible.

"What do you intend to do?" he asked her.

"Watch. Listen. Learn what I can, and wait for opportunity to present itself. And you?"

"I have sworn to find Devlin," Stephen said. "He would do the same for me."

Solveig picked up a lace shawl and wrapped it around her shoulders. "I must leave now, and you should go as well. I have reason to believe that my rooms are searched when I am absent."

Of course. "I will see you again," he said.

"Take no unnecessary risks. Captain Drakken is watched, but if you get a message to Master Osvald at the healers' hall, he will pass it on to Brother Arni, who will give it to me. I have become quite pious of late, and find much comfort in my devotions."

Stephen gave his sister a quick embrace. Every instinct told him that she was not safe here and that he should urge her to leave. But she could no more ignore her duty than he could his.

"Be safe," he said, though the words seemed inadequate.

"You as well," she cautioned. "And trust yourself. I know you will find him."

She opened the door and stepped into the corridor, looking both ways before motioning him to join her.

"Tell your master that I expect fair service," she said, pitching her voice loudly in case there were hidden ears. "The silver set is a gift to celebrate my sister's wedding, and the engraving must be done properly. I will not tolerate another mistake."

"Understood, my lady. I am certain you will be pleased with the final result."

"For your sake I hope so," Solveig said.

He bowed low and watched as she made her way down the corridor, toward the main staircase that led to the central part of the palace. Only when she had disappeared from view did he retrace his steps to the narrow servants' stairs and make his own departure.

The guards on duty had changed, but no one paid him

any heed as Stephen joined a group of similarly dressed laborers who were departing the palace. Still, he did not relax until he had turned off the central avenue and the palace walls were no longer visible.

He wondered why Captain Drakken had not mentioned that Lady Gemma and her daughter were being held hostage in Selvarat. Perhaps Solveig had held that news close, deeming it only suitable for family members to hear. Or perhaps Captain Drakken had feared that Stephen would do something rash.

He wondered how his father had reacted to the news. Lord Brynjolf had a temper and was devoted to his wife. Upon reflection, Stephen was surprised that his father hadn't already set sail for Selvarat, determined to take his family home by force if necessary.

But surely Solveig would have told him if that was the case. Indeed, now that he had left, there were dozens of questions that he wished he had thought to ask her. It hardly seemed fair that he had risked so much for only those few stolen moments.

Yet what he had learned from Solveig only made him more determined to find Devlin. He would rescue Devlin from whatever evil had befallen him, and Devlin would help him rescue his family.

# Eight

DEVLIN'S WORLD NARROWED UNTIL ALL HIS focus was bent on the small circles of metal that bound his wrists. The left manacle showed no signs of budging, but the one on his maimed right hand had begun, ever so slightly, to yield. He never thought that he would be grateful to Duke Gerhard, but the duel that had cost Devlin two of his fingers also meant that his right hand was narrower than his left.

Something his captors had overlooked. No doubt they thought him helpless. For all he knew he had been their captive for weeks, instead of mere days or hours. There was no way to be certain how far he had been taken. Nor what was happening in Kingsholm.

The thought spurred him to renewed efforts, and he twisted his right hand slightly and pulled. The muscles in his arm trembled with strain as the blood-slicked manacle slipped a bare fraction. It was working, though far too slowly for his tastes. He took a deep breath, counted to three, and strained again.

So lost was he in his efforts that it came as a shock

when light streamed into the wagon. He blinked, then tilted his head back, and looked straight into the face of a woman. She wore a necklace of bone teeth, in the manner of the sea folk from the Green Isles, over the brown tunic of a mercenary or fighter.

"He's awake," she called, her gaze not leaving his face. It was the same voice he had heard before.

As slowly as he could, he drew his right wrist close to his side, hoping that she would not think to check the security of his bindings.

"*Ni?*" he muttered in his own tongue. It was not hard to feign confusion. What was one of the sea raiders doing with a noble from Selvarat?

He let his eyes go wide and unfocused, as if staring through his captor. He kept his gaze fixed even as she crawled in the wagon beside him, giving silent thanks that she had taken position on his left, so she would not see his attempts to free himself.

Through the sliver of the open flap he could see a campfire and the vague outlines of several people around it. They must have been stopped here for some time, while he had continued his struggles, oblivious to what was going on around him.

A second form appeared in the opening. Karel of Selvarat.

"He's waking sooner and sooner each time," Karel said.

"Aye but he's not in his proper wits," the woman replied. She pushed Devlin's cheek with her hand, and his head lolled to the right. "See?"

A part of Devlin urged him to defiance, to let these folk know just what he thought of them. But reason told him that there was nothing to be gained by such an act. Patience and cunning would set him free, and then he would show them the folly of underestimating the Chosen One.

The woman's hand caught his jaw and turned his head back. He resisted a little as she opened his jaw, but allowed himself to be overpowered as if he were still under the influence of the drug.

Now it was time to trust in his luck. Karel held a small bowl to Devlin's lips and began to pour the contents inside. The liquid smelled sickly sweet but tasted foul, and he gagged slightly. With her free hand the woman pinched his nostrils shut and Devlin was forced to swallow. Karel tipped the bowl up, ensuring it was completely empty. Next the woman pushed Devlin's jaw closed, and covered his mouth. Then she released his nostrils, allowing him to breathe. Her movements had a practiced air, as if she and Karel had repeated the same maneuver dozens of times.

Which might indeed be the truth. Devlin fought off panic as he could feel the drug spreading through him, bringing with it a strange lethargy. He let his eyes drift shut and relaxed all of his muscles, leaving himself completely vulnerable.

He counted a hundred heartbeats before the woman released him, apparently satisfied that he would not reject the drug. "That should keep him quiet," she said.

"I pray you are right. I increased the dose of menas root, though at this rate we may have to buy new supplies. I've never seen someone so resistant to its powers." Karel's voice faded as he climbed out of the wagon.

"You worry too much," the woman replied. "We'll pass through a good-sized town tomorrow, no? We should be able to get what you need there."

With a final pat on Devlin's cheek, she climbed out of the wagon.

"Have another dose ready, for when we feed him at dawn," she said. "We'll try smaller doses, more often. Keep him too dazed to know what is happening."

"He'll sober up soon enough when he meets the Prince," Karel said.

The woman gave an unpleasant laugh. "I'm sure the Prince will live up to his reputation. Still I wonder what it is about this man that makes him so important? He's only one man, and Jorsk has other generals who can take his place."

"I don't ask those questions, and if you are wise, neither should you," Karel said. "All I know is that this Devlin is the key to the conquest of Jorsk. Deliver him safely to the Prince, and we will both be rewarded well."

"For what you're paying me, I'd hand over my own parents. And throw in my last set of shipmates as a parting gift," the woman said cheerfully.

Their voices faded as they moved away from the wagon. Devlin waited several agonizing moments to be certain that they were gone. Then he turned his head to the left and began to vomit.

It was awkward, for he could barely raise his head as he forced his body to rid itself of that foul concoction. At last, when he was coughing nothing but bloody bile, he let his head fall back to the wooden floor.

He took several deep breaths, trying his best to ignore the foul stench. But his thoughts were still befuddled by the drugs that stubbornly remained within him.

Angrily, he flexed his right hand, and then squeezed his three fingers tightly together as he began pulling at the manacle once again. Escape. He had to escape. This chance might never come again, and from what he had heard, it was more urgent than ever. This prince, whoever he was, believed that Devlin was the key to destroying Jorsk. As Chosen One, he could not let that happen. He would free himself, or he would die trying.

She was not a coward. Nor was she a traitor. She was an honorable woman doing everything within her power to fulfill her oaths and protect the people of Kingsholm. Prudence was not the same as cowardice, and being cautious did not make one disloyal.

Captain Drakken knew all those things to be true, but as she entered the banquet hall and caught sight of the King and his cronies seated on the main dais, chatting as if they had not a care in the world, she felt a sudden wave of self-loathing. Only long habit enabled her to salute the King and weave her way through the crowded tables to take her customary seat at the foot of the center table.

The King frowned, though whether it was at her tardiness or because she was in disfavor, it was difficult to know. Drakken exchanged greetings with those already seated, while a server set a trencher of fish in front of her. So they were on the second course already. It was no wonder the King was annoyed.

She pretended an absorption in her food, while her eyes scanned the room. The court was in session, so nearly every seat was filled, the tables so crowded together that the servers had to carry the platters of food high over their heads as they passed between them.

Solveig was there, engaged in an animated discussion

with Jenna, the aide to Ambassador Magaharan. In the past weeks Solveig had publicly distanced herself from Devlin's supporters, though it was difficult to tell if anyone believed her change of heart. The reformers who had supported the Chosen One and his radical ideas now clung to each other defiantly, and their disfavor was shown by having them placed as far from the dais as possible. She strained her eyes to see across the hall, and there at a table near the servant's door she saw Lord Rikard, but Lady Falda's seat was empty. Drakken's stomach clenched even as she told herself that it was most likely that Lady Falda had been too unwell to attend. She was an elderly woman who had complained of feeling poorly of late.

Still she must be gravely ill or foolhardy beyond belief to have missed the weekly court dinner. Olafur liked to have his courtiers where he could see them. Absence was taken as a sign of disrespect, and these days it was likely that the King would conclude that any missing courtier was plotting against him.

Of course there was another reason for someone to be absent. At least a dozen members of the court were no longer to be seen. Some, like Lord Branstock, had been arrested, but many had simply vanished. Few were brave enough to ask questions as it became apparent that the dungeons below the palace were once again being used.

Her stomach churned, and the fish was but half-eaten when the server cleared it away and replaced it with roasted fowl and the last of the winter vegetables. The fowl was tough and the vegetables stringy, but it was better food than most in Kingsholm had, and she forced herself to overcome her distaste for the company and eat a healthy portion.

She heard a young girl's laughter and looked at the dais to see Princess Ragenilda smiling at Count Magaharan. The Princess was in formal court garb, and wore a sapphire necklace and matching earrings. The outfit made her look much older than the mere eleven years she had to her claim.

The jewelry had been a gift from the Selvarat ambassador, a man who was much to be seen these days. He appeared everywhere with the King, regularly dining with the royal family as if he were a close relation or one of the King's chief councilors. His open interest in the Princess did not bode well for the girl nor for her future.

Drakken's gaze traveled down the dais to King Olafur, watching as the King beckoned the server to refill his wine cup. *Murderer*, she thought, and she quickly averted her gaze lest he could read the accusation on her face.

A true hero would not sit here, choking down the King's bounty. It did not matter whether the King had wielded the knife himself, or if he had merely ordered it done. He had still killed a man who had pledged his life to defend the kingdom against all perils. He had killed the Chosen One, and with that act shown his scorn for both the Gods and the people whose loyalty he commanded.

It had been many years since she had believed in the legend of the Chosen One. Believed that the Gods chose one person as their anointed champion, and gifted that person with the courage and skill needed to defend the Kingdom. Devlin had changed that. He had made her believe again, as if she were a child listening to legends told by the fire. Made her believe that a man with courage and conviction could do extraordinary things.

If Devlin were here, he would not hesitate. He would

challenge King Olafur in front of the court, secure in the strength of his own convictions and that the power of his calling would sustain him.

A part of her wished that she was able to take that simple path. Proclaim King Olafur's foul deed to the world and call upon the court to see that justice was done. Give over living a lie and free herself from her oaths of loyalty to a man she now despised.

It would be brave, but foolhardy, and she knew better than to expect the King to respond to her allegations. He would order her arrested and, save for a small handful of loyal guards, no one would lift a finger in protest. Her claims would be dismissed as the ravings of a lunatic. It was a swift way to get herself killed, but it would accomplish little else.

Drakken needed proof. Proof that Devlin was dead, proof that the King had ordered his assassination. Only then could she seek out allies in the court. If enough of them stood together, they might be able to bring down Olafur.

But even that strategy had its risks. Ragenilda was but a child, and unfit to take the crown. A Regent would need to be appointed, and while the courtiers might unite to depose Olafur, it was impossible that they would agree on who should serve as Regent. The result could well be civil war, at a time when the Kingdom stood in grave danger. Possible invaders aside, the Selvarat alliance carried as much risk as it did reward, or so Solveig had often cautioned her.

Where did her duty lie? Captain Drakken had sworn loyalty to the King, but she had also sworn to serve the cause of justice. Was it better to have a corrupt king reigning over a united kingdom? Or was it her duty to see justice done, regardless of the cost? She could serve the King or the cause of justice, but she could not do both. One of her oaths would have to be broken.

She threw the half-gnawed fowl leg back on her plate with a snarl of disgust.

"The chicken is not to your taste?" Troop Captain Karlson asked. He leaned across the table and gave a conspiratorial smile. "I find it tough going as well."

The troop captain was Marshal Olvarrson's chief aide, and she knew that anything she said would be reported first to the Marshal, then find its way to the King's ears. These days even the most innocent of remarks could be construed as treasonous.

Captain Drakken grimaced a bit and made a show of rubbing her lower jaw.

"Bad tooth," she explained. "Cracked it on a nut this week. The apothecary gave me a salve, but it does damn all to help."

Karlson leaned back in his chair, having lost interest in her. "My sympathies," he said, his eyes already wandering past her to see if any of the other diners were worthy of his attention.

"In fact, I think I had best depart, for I cannot bear to chew another morsel," Captain Drakken said, rising to her feet. She nodded in the general direction of the head of the table. "I leave the rest of the meal to those who can enjoy it."

The double meaning of her words passed unnoticed by her fellow diners, who barely acknowledged her leaving.

Only when she had left the hall did she breathe a sigh

of relief. Her stomach still churned from the tension of having to pretend that all was well. She did not know how much longer she could endure the strain. Another few evenings like this one, and her temper was bound to snap.

Time passed. Hours, or perhaps minutes that merely felt like hours. Devlin's world had narrowed to a few inches of metal as he strained to free himself. Nothing else mattered—not the searing pain of his abused wrists, nor the ache in his chest that told of cracked ribs. Not even the foul stench of his own vomit could distract him.

Enough of the drugs remained in his blood that his mind was clouded, and his thoughts wandered through scenes from his past. He was in Duncaer, dying from wounds received when he had killed the murderous banecats. He was in the great palace of Jorsk, blood dripping from his maimed hand as he stood over the corpse of the traitor Gerhard. Stephen offered encouragement, even as the lake monster crushed Devlin between its mighty jaws. Captain Drakken appeared, angry that Devlin had failed to report. She began to lecture him on duty, but her image faded and was replaced by that of the King.

The sight of King Olafur spurred Devlin's anger, though he could no longer remember why. Indeed, he no longer knew where he was, or what had happened to him. Weakened by captivity, he might have fallen into a drugged stupor, but the Geas would not let him rest. One message was burned into his mind. Escape. Nothing else mattered.

He pulled with every bit of strength left to him, but still

it was a shock when his right hand slipped free. In the darkness he could not see how badly he had damaged it, but when he flexed his fingers they responded to his orders.

He rolled to his left and used his right hand to explore the manacle that encircled his left wrist. It was slippery with blood from his struggles, but unlike the other it was properly fastened. He would not be able to slip it off. He might be able to pick the lock, if he could find a bit of metal, but that would take time, and his abused right hand was unlikely to be dexterous enough for the effort. His arm traced the length of the chain until he found where it was fastened to the floor of the wagon. It was a simple ring bolt, hammered into the wagon floor. His fingers traced the base of the bolt, and found that his struggles had partially lifted it away from the wood.

He looped the free chain around his right arm and pulled with all the strength of both arms. His arms shook, and he panted with the effort. His head swam, and he blinked as stars appeared in front of his eyes. Still he continued to pull, and with a screech of metal the ring bolt loosened and came free.

He lay back, panting, waiting for the alarm to be raised. But no one called out, and he realized that no one had heard his struggles. They must be sleeping or careless indeed.

He wrapped the short chain around his left arm, careful not to clink metal against metal. He could use the chain as a weapon, if needed. Raising himself to a sitting position, he bent forward and investigated the bindings on his leg. There were two shackles, connected to a central chain. Unlike the manacles on his wrists, these had no lock, and it was only a moment's work to undo them.

Now he had to make his escape. The prospect of freedom brought clarity to his thoughts, and he took stock of his situation. He was in an encampment surrounded by an unknown number of guards, some of whom he might have to fight. He had neither food nor water, nor did he know where he was, or whether the locals were likely to be well disposed toward the Chosen One. He had no cloak, no boots, and his only weapon was a length of chain with an iron bolt on the end. Even if he was successful in making his escape, without knowing where he was, he might flee toward his enemies rather than away from them.

Still, he had no choice. He remembered Lord Karel telling the female mercenary that Devlin was the key to destroying Jorsk. And as Chosen One, it was his duty to preserve Jorsk. Regardless of the cost. Better that he die in an attempt to win his freedom than risk being used against the people he had sworn to protect.

His brief glimpse outside the wagon had shown that the flap faced a central campfire, so he crawled to the opposite end. Here the leather covering was held in place by wooden pegs. He removed the pegs, then lifted the leather up a small bit and peered out.

The gray light of pre-dawn lit their surroundings, revealing them to be in a clearing bordered by fir trees. He could be anywhere in Northern Jorsk, or even Nerikaat for that matter. They would expect him to break south, so he would head north for a while and search for landmarks.

In his limited field of vision he saw no one, nor could he hear anyone moving. Prudence suggested that he wait and choose the right moment, but there was no time. It would be dawn soon, and the camp would be stirring. And his captors would be returning to the wagon to administer his next dose of drugs.

Devlin lifted the covering, swung his legs over the side, and slipped to the ground. His knees buckled, and he had to grasp the side of the wagon to keep himself from falling. His legs cramped with the ache of returning circulation, and he wondered again just how long he had been held captive, drugged and oblivious to his fate.

In the distance he heard a voice call out a greeting, and he knew he had to move. He pushed himself away from the wagon and began a shambling run toward the tree line.

He had gone no more than a few paces when the alarm was raised. "Alert! Ware!" a voice called out.

Others began to raise the cry, speaking in a tongue he did not recognize.

He urged his weakened body to greater speed, but not even his will could sustain him, and he stumbled and fell to one knee. When he rose back to his feet, he found himself surrounded.

There were at least a half-dozen of them, a motley group whose mixed features proclaimed them a mercenary band. Some were half-dressed, but there was no mistaking the intensity of their purpose, nor the meaning of their drawn swords.

He turned slowly in a circle, but there was no gap, and indeed new arrivals swelled their ranks until he was fenced in by cold steel. They made no move to attack, merely content to hold him at bay.

"Kneel down and raise your hands and you will not be hurt," a man said, in heavily accented trade tongue.

Devlin shook his head. "No."

From behind him he heard Lord Karel call out, in a language that Devlin did not recognize.

"I swear upon my honor that you will come to no harm," Lord Karel said.

Devlin turned to face his captor.

"I swear upon the honor of my house," Lord Karel repeated.

A trusting man might have believed him. But Devlin knew better than to put his faith in a noble's honor.

"And what of your prince? Does your word bind him as well?" Devlin asked.

Karel frowned angrily. He opened his mouth, but Devlin had no interest in whatever lies he was about to say. Instead, he whirled to his left, releasing the ring bolt so the chain swung in a wide arc. The mercenaries closest to him took an instinctive step back as Devlin charged.

With more luck than skill he caught the sword of the nearest mercenary in the chain, and with a sharp tug disarmed him. But there was no time to reach down and grab the sword. As they closed ranks, he saw that some of the mercenaries were carrying cudgels instead of swords, a sign that they meant to take him alive and not risk killing him.

But alive did not mean unharmed, and he felt a slash across the back of his left leg. It was a mere slice, as was the next. Then he was amongst the fighters. Blows rained down on him from all sides as he took the ring bolt in his right hand and looped it around the neck of a woman who had carelessly gotten within arm's reach. He pulled with all his strength and heard her neck crack. The sudden deadweight dragged his arms downward as he struggled to free himself from her corpse. He staggered as he felt a weight on his back, and an arm looped around his own neck. His opponent began to squeeze and Devlin's vision grew dim. His lungs burned for air, but even as he fell to his knees, the pressure around his neck grew. He was dying, and as he fell into the darkness he felt a brief surge of satisfaction.

He had done his duty. They would not be able to use him. Then the darkness consumed him.

# Nine

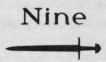

ALL HEADS TURNED AS THE COUNCIL CHAM-
ber doors swung open, but it was only Councilor Arnulf,
sweating and out of breath as he made his way to his customary seat at the long table.

"The summons came as a surprise," he paused to pant.
"I was in the old city, with, a, err, a friend. Thought I'd be
late."

Lord Sygmund, who was seated next to Councilor
Arnulf, muttered a sympathetic phrase. Then, once again,
the council room fell silent. In years past, the wrangling
had begun as soon as the chamber doors were opened
and King Olafur had often had to call his unruly advisors
to order. Today in the changed mood of the court, words
were rationed carefully and no one wanted to give even
the appearance of disrespect. No doubt each person present was wondering at the reason why they had been
hastily summoned, but no one would voice their
thoughts aloud.

Not even the empty chair at the foot of the table, newly
added since their last meeting, was enough to draw their

comments, though more than one let their gaze linger upon it as they waited.

Some of the councilors fidgeted, but Captain Drakken kept her calm, mentally reviewing each of the one hundred and twenty-two standing regulations that governed the guard. She had gotten to regulation thirty-three concerning the punishment for one caught in dereliction of duties when the doors again swung open.

With the others she rose to her feet as King Olafur entered the room, trailed by the Selvarat ambassador and Baron Martell. The nobles bowed, while Drakken and Marshal Olvarrson offered their salutes. The King acknowledged them with a wave of his hand then took his seat. The Selvarat ambassador took the seat to his right.

As the councilors sat back down, Baron Martell made his way to the empty chair at the foot of the table. Now she knew who it was for, but not why. There should be no reason for the Baron to attend the council. Not unless he had a grievance to air or evidence to offer, and even then custom dictated that he remain standing throughout his testimony.

"I summoned you today so you may be the first to hear of the changes that will be taking place. Changes that will strengthen and secure our kingdom, preserving the inheritance entrusted to me by my forebears, ensuring that it is passed along for generations to come," King Olafur began.

For a man who was informing the council of what should have been good news, he looked uncommonly grim.

"But first, I have unfortunate news to share," he continued, as if reading her thoughts. "Devlin of Duncaer was killed a fortnight ago."

King Olafur looked directly at her, and Captain Drakken did her best to appear shocked. And indeed she was startled, if only by the timing of the announcement.

"How? Where?" Lord Rikard asked, drawing the King's attention away from her.

Lady Ingeleth raised her eyebrows at this breach of etiquette. One did not interrupt the King. Ever.

But if Olafur was angry, he gave no sign.

"He was journeying to Kalveland, or so we believe, when he was set upon by a band of robbers. A traveling merchant found his body and notified the local magistrate." King Olafur shook his head sorrowfully. "We will never know why he chose not to return to Kingsholm, nor what duty called him north. But we are confident that Devlin was a loyal servant and remained true even in death."

It was skillfully done, for in praising Devlin he had also damned him. Many on the council were not Devlin's friends, and they would be quick to seize upon the implication that Devlin had turned rogue and deserted his duty.

"You will wish to hold a funeral service," she heard herself say. "A tribute to one who served you so loyally and well."

It had been at least a decade since anyone mourned the loss of one of the Chosen Ones. But Devlin had been different, a return to the heroes of old. And if Stephen and Didrik were to be believed, he had even wielded the Sword of Light, however briefly. Though this sign of the Gods' favor had not been enough to save his life.

"I am certain the priest will do what is fitting," King Olafur replied.

Captain Drakken continued to press, even though she knew such a course of action was folly. "Brother Arni can also oversee the next choosing ceremony. There are many who will be anxious to follow the path that Devlin laid out and serve as the next Chosen One."

She herself would endure the trial, if no worthier candidate could be found.

"There will be no new Chosen One named," King Olafur said. "Indeed, if Devlin's life has taught us one thing, it was the folly of placing all our hopes and fears upon the shoulders of a single champion. No one could live up to that burden."

"Many times I heard Devlin lament our custom, saying that we ought to defend ourselves rather than relying upon the Chosen One," Lady Ingeleth observed. "He urged us to seek strength in numbers and forge new alliances."

The King nodded and favored Lady Ingeleth with a small smile. "Precisely."

Captain Drakken ground her teeth. She, too, had heard Devlin grumble about the custom of the Chosen One. He'd once said that a Jorskian would watch his house burn while waiting for rescue rather than grabbing a water bucket to fight on his own. There was some truth in Devlin's words. The people had grown too used to depending upon someone else's strength rather than looking to themselves.

But Devlin would not have advocated leaving the people helpless. And that was just what they would be. There would be no one to stand up to the King, no one to oppose his tyranny. No doubt that was the very reason why Devlin had been murdered. Devlin would not have stood idly by while the King ran roughshod over his people. One by one, all those who opposed the King were being eliminated. She knew it was only a matter of time before the King decided to deal with her.

"With the passing of the Chosen One, his council seat falls vacant. I have asked Baron Martell to join our deliberations, and he has graciously consented."

The Baron rose from his seat and bowed in the King's direction. "It is my honor to serve, Your Majesty," he said.

So this was the price of murder. There was no longer any doubt in her mind that Martell had been involved in Devlin's death. A council seat in return for an assassination. She knew that there were many who would consider it a fair trade.

She turned her gaze on Lord Rikard, who squirmed uncomfortably under the regard of his fellow councilors. Most had grudgingly tolerated Rikard's presence, and few would be saddened by his absence. As the lone representative of the troubled borderlands, even when he held his tongue his very presence served as a reminder to the other councilors that all was not well in Jorsk. On the other hand Martell was the scion of an old house, from the conservative inland provinces. He would speak no controversy.

"All are agreed on naming Baron Martell the newest member of this honored council?" King Olafur asked. The question was for form's sake only. Traditionally the councilors could oppose the King's choice, but they had not done so in years.

The King was lucky that she did not have a vote, so she

merely observed as each councilor cast their vote in turn. There were no dissensions.

As chief councilor, it fell to Lady Ingeleth to cast the final vote. "Baron Martell, I welcome you to our ranks," she said.

Drakken had expected no less. Lady Ingeleth had worked hard to regain the King's favor after her defense of Lord Branstock had put her own neck at risk. The countess was too canny a politician to make another such mistake.

"And now we come to the matter of our kingdom and its future. Earlier this spring Empress Thania and I renewed the vows of alliance, and the empress graciously sent her troops to defend our eastern provinces. We are grateful indeed for their presence, for the troubles in the region were even greater than we had been led to believe. Fortunately, our allies have not flinched from this challenge, and have expanded their offer of support. I have asked Ambassador Magaharan to explain the new arrangement."

The King looked even grimmer than he had when he was recounting the news of Devlin's death. She wondered just what it was that he had had to trade away for this additional support. Princess Ragenilda was already destined for a Selvarat consort, so what else did the King have to offer? They would beggar themselves to pay for this largesse.

"It is my honor to speak before this council, and to share the terms of Empress Thania's alliance with your most gracious majesty, Olafur son of Thorvald. Privileged indeed are those who live under his wise rule," Count Magaharan began.

Such empty flattery was the currency of the court, but

long years of exposure did not make it any easier to bear. Captain Drakken waited impatiently as Ambassador Magaharan and King Olafur expressed their mutual admiration.

Finally, the ambassador got to the heart of the matter. "Our navy patrols your coastline, and our troops watch the shores," the ambassador said. "But what good does it do to guard the door of the house if the thieves are already inside? The disorder in the provinces comes from within your borders as well. Realizing the sternest measures were called for, the field commander summoned reinforcements, who have now taken control and brought peace to these once troubled lands."

She noticed he was careful not to name the field commander. Indeed, the exact makeup of the forces and how many troops had arrived were a closely guarded secret, and Marshal Olvarrson had firmly refused to discuss details with her. He had unbent enough to tell her that Karel of Maurant, who had accompanied the ambassador to Kingsholm, had been dispatched to the east to serve as liaison with the local troops. But beyond that she had heard nothing.

"How many troops have arrived?" Lord Sygmund asked.

The ambassador waved a hand. "I do not concern myself with the details, but I am assured that they are sufficient to ensure the peace."

Was that a battalion? A regiment? Whatever the answer, she'd wager her last copper that the ambassador knew the precise number of soldiers in the field, and where they were assigned.

"Would the ambassador care to elaborate on what he

meant by saying the provinces were under his protection?" Lady Ingeleth asked.

It was King Olafur who answered.

"We have established a special zone called the Selvarat Protectorate," King Olafur said. "It extends east from the Southern Road, from Rosmaar down to Myrka. Those provinces within the protectorate will now take their guidance from Prince Arnaud, whom Empress Thania has named as governor of the new protectorate. The Prince and his advisors will ensure order and tranquillity, freeing our attention for other matters."

Drakken's jaw dropped in shock, and she heard others mutter startled exclamations.

"King Olafur remains the sovereign ruler of these territories," Count Magaharan explained. "Our role is merely that of advisors."

But few would question this so-called advice, not when it came backed with the weight of an army.

She shook her head fiercely to clear her thoughts. Now she understood why the King appeared so grim. He had just bargained away a third of his kingdom, a region that contained the most fertile farmlands. He was naive to think the Selvarats would let him keep the rest. Once they had secured their hold on the eastern provinces, they would take over the rest of the Kingdom.

What fools they had been. They had been duped, welcoming the Selvarats as saviors, when in fact they were the vanguard of an invasion force. Only now with hindsight could she see what should have been clear from the beginning.

"What of our armies in the east?" Councilor Arnulf asked. It was an unusually bold move for him, but then she remembered that one of his daughters served as a troop captain under Major Mikkelson.

"The army has returned to the garrison in Kallarne, freeing up units to strengthen the northwestern border," Marshal Olvarrson said.

Arnulf nodded, seeming content with this answer.

Lord Rikard rose to his feet. "Will no one else speak against this folly? The Selvarats are not protectors, they are thieves who have just stolen our richest lands. Are we going to give them up without a fight?"

"Lord Rikard is overwrought," Captain Drakken said, rising herself. It had been too much to hope that Rikard could keep his mouth shut. His homeland of Myrka was one of the provinces the King had just bargained away. But there was nothing to be gained by challenging the King in this forum.

"If I am angered, then it is a righteous wrath," Rikard said. "I will stand alone if I must, but I will not be silent in the face of cowardice and treason. The King has betrayed us. He has betrayed us all."

She winced at the damning words. Lord Rikard fairly shook with anger, but none would meet his gaze.

"Guards," King Olafur called.

The council door opened, and the two guards stepped inside, ceremonial spears held at attention.

"Rikard has uttered treason and defiled this august gathering with his presence. Arrest him."

The guards looked at her, and in that moment she had to make her choice.

"Obey your King," she ordered, her voice harsh. "Arrest him."

"Coward," Rikard hissed as the guards led him away. And this time she knew the epithet was meant for her.

Stephen shifted the heavy curtain to one side and peered at the small crowd that had gathered in the Royal Temple. A stone pillar blocked part of his view and he opened the curtain a fraction wider.

"Stop," Didrik hissed. "You'll call attention to us. No one is supposed to be here, remember?"

Stephen nodded and let the curtain fall closed again, confining his view to the narrow gap where it didn't quite meet the wall. The small chamber where Brother Arni changed into his ceremonial robes was a tight fit for the two of them, but Stephen had insisted on witnessing the ceremony, and Didrik had insisted on accompanying him to make sure that he did nothing foolish.

Brother Arni called out, imploring the Gods for their blessings, then led the assembled worshipers in the prayer for the dead.

"I don't know why I agreed to this," Didrik whispered.

"No one will think to look for us here," Stephen replied. "And what better place for us to meet with Captain Drakken and Solveig? They are watched each time they leave the palace, but no one looked twice at us when we entered."

"We may not be as lucky when we try to leave," Didrik retorted. "And—"

As the congregation fell silent, Didrik closed his mouth over whatever he had been intending to say.

Brother Arni addressed the Gods, recounting to them Devlin's virtues and commending his spirit to the care of

Lord Haakon. Stephen shivered at the ill omen. Surely it was the worst of luck to invoke Haakon's care for a man who was not dead.

Not that anyone was listening to Stephen. Didrik, Drakken, Solveig, even the pious Brother Arni were all convinced that Devlin was deceased. As were those who had assembled this day to mourn his passing. It was a strange gathering, for the King was conspicuously absent, despite his public proclamation of mourning. Many courtiers had stayed away as well, rather than risk the King's wrath. So it was a surprise to see Lady Ingeleth standing in the front row, along with Captain Drakken. Lady Falda was there as well, her two daughters holding her propped up between them. She must have risen from her sickbed to be there, for Lady Falda had the look of someone who would soon make her own peace with Haakon.

As General of the Royal Army, Devlin was entitled to a full military honor guard, but only Marshal Olvarrson and his aide were there to represent the Royal Army, standing carefully apart from the other mourners.

That was not to say that the chapel was empty. The courtiers might have stayed away, but there were plenty of others to take their places. Among the front ranks he recognized Merchant Tyrvald, the Royal Armorer Master Timo, Mistress Alanna of the healers. Other faces were blocked from his view, but he noted that many wore dark green, the dress uniform of the guards.

As the service drew on, the worshipers prayed fervently to the Gods for their mercy, and he wondered who it was they were praying for. Did they seek mercy for Devlin's spirit? Or were they here to mourn the passing of the

Kingdom they had once known? In just a few weeks, the Selvarat diplomats had done what generations of their armies had failed to do: conquer Jorsk. Two hundred years ago they had invaded only to be beaten back, in a bloody defeat. This time the Jorskians had welcomed them as brothers, throwing open the doors and inviting them in.

It was tempting to wonder if Devlin could have done anything to stop it from happening. If he had been here when the Selvarat alliance was announced, would he have been the one to question their sudden willingness to help? When the troops landed on the eastern shores, would Devlin have given orders that Major Mikkelson withdraw from the garrisons? Or would he have advocated caution, seeing the risks inherent in turning power over to a foreign army that acknowledged no leader but their own?

If Devlin had spent the winter in Kingsholm, matters might have turned out differently. And yet at the crucial moments, Devlin had been hundreds of leagues away, searching for the Sword of Light. Stephen did not understand it. None of it made sense. He believed with all his heart that Devlin was the chosen champion of the Gods, sent by them to defend Jorsk. And yet at the moment of its greatest peril, Devlin was nowhere to be found.

It was tempting to believe that Devlin had gone off on his own, but even driven by the madness of the Geas, Devlin would know that one man could not hope to defeat an army. If his duty had called him east, Devlin would have found a way to get word to his friends. Yet each day that passed without news seemed proof that Devlin had not left of his own free will.

Which left only two other possibilities. Devlin was a

prisoner, or he was dead. And the latter Stephen refused to believe.

"More," Captain Drakken said, thrusting her goblet in Didrik's general direction.

He frowned, but lifted the wine bottle and poured her another generous measure.

She took a deep drink, then lifted the goblet to study it critically. The mismatched silver goblets were a poor replacement for the golden vessels that had been stolen when the temple was ransacked. But the sacrificial wine, at least, was first-rate. Aged Myrkan red, which was rarer than blood in the capital in recent days. It seemed the Gods believed in keeping the best for themselves.

It was a pitiful band that gathered in the storeroom beneath the Royal Temple. Stephen and Didrik, who had shown their foolhardiness by sneaking into the palace grounds, the one place they were sure to be recognized. And Solveig, who had held her tears in public but wept for Devlin as she embraced her brother. Now she sat next to him and murmured to him reassuringly. From the set of his jaw Stephen was not pleased by what she had to say.

No doubt Solveig was trying to convince Stephen that it was time to accept Devlin's death. But that Stephen stubbornly refused to do.

Some might admire his faith, but Drakken was irritated by his foolishness. All reason, all logic told her that Devlin was dead. She did not need to see his corpse. King Olafur would never have risked being caught in an obvious lie. He would not have announced Devlin's death unless he was absolutely certain that Devlin had been killed.

She took another gulp of wine and smiled grimly to herself. Perhaps Stephen would form a new cult, that of the Chosen One who would one day return. He would compose songs and tell tales of Devlin's great deeds and infect others with his belief that a great champion would one day return to save them.

She had no such illusions. Devlin was dead, Rikard imprisoned and Devlin's other supporters driven into hiding. The Kingdom was crumbling around them and her own future was bleak. That she would be killed was a certainty. Her only choice was whether she would wait for the King to accuse her of treason, or if she would deliberately court danger, choosing the time and manner of her death.

She gulped the rest of her wine and slid the empty goblet across the floor. It rolled and came to a rest by Didrik's foot. He gave her a hard look, then righted the goblet and filled it with the last of the wine. Carefully, he handed it back to her, then without being prompted snagged another wine bottle from the shelf behind his back.

She had not been drunk in over twenty years, not since her days as a novice guard. But this one night, she was going to make an exception.

The stone floor was cold beneath her legs, and not even the finest wine could disperse the chill in her blood. Her bones ached, a reminder that she was getting old. Too old for such foolishness, too old to be huddled on the floor of a storeroom, meeting here in secret because they had no place else.

"You should go to Esker. All of you," she announced.

"But—" Stephen began.

"You should go. Tomorrow would not be too soon,"

she said, interrupting what was sure to be another diatribe on how Stephen needed to stay here to continue the search for Devlin.

"Why Esker?" Solveig asked.

There was a woman with some intelligence. "We have lost the east and the heartlands will be next. The northwestern territories may yet survive, if they start preparing now. Your father is a strong leader, and he has the support of his neighbors. If they band together, and if you can convince the army troops stationed there to take their orders from your father, then there is a chance that you can hold the territories. A slim chance, but better than the odds of staying here."

Didrik shook his head. "I will not abandon you, nor my sworn duty. I am still an officer of the Guard."

"There is nothing you can do here. You will be dead as soon as you are recognized. It's time to think of your future. All of you. Grieve for what we have lost, but save what you still can."

"And what of you? Will you come with us?"

She shook her head. "My place is here. There are things I have left to do. I will join you when I can."

The last was a lie. There was but one final duty remaining to her. To stand as witness to the truth and to proclaim King Olafur guilty of the murder of Devlin of Duncaer. She would make her statement in full view of the court, knowing that she would then be arrested for treason.

She knew what would happen next. She would be tortured, by members of the Guard she had once commanded. Then she would be executed. But she would die with her honor intact, having fulfilled her oath to serve justice. And perhaps some of the courtiers would hear her words and would begin to doubt Olafur. If enough of them opposed his course of action, there might be time yet to steer the Kingdom away from disaster.

She shifted position, resting her left arm on the bundle by her side.

"What is that?" Stephen asked. It was an obvious attempt to change the conversation.

She patted the bundle absently.

"Devlin's effects," she said. "A chamberwoman gave them to me after the service. There wasn't much, but she thought that one of his friends should have them."

Stephen rose to his knees and crawled the few paces that separated them. He reached for the bundle, and after a moment she released it to him.

The bundle was wrapped in a woolen blanket, no doubt taken from Devlin's bed. It was a long, thin package, belted in three places with leather cords. Stephen undid the cords and unrolled the blanket. Inside were revealed a few trinkets, the clothes that Devlin wore when he was not wearing his uniform. And one item that she had recognized by touch without needing to unwrap the blanket. Devlin's great axe.

"His axe," Stephen said, as if the others might not have recognized the weapon.

"We see that," she replied tartly.

"Now we finally have proof that Devlin was in the palace," Didrik said. "This is what we have been searching for."

Did they think her blind? She had known at once what it was she held. The marvel was that the king's cronies had overlooked such an important bit of evidence. Not that she could use it. Not now.

"And what shall we do with this axe? You and Stephen are the only two people who can swear that Devlin had the axe with him when he traveled to Duncaer. And you are already under suspicion. You'd be arrested before you could give testimony."

"But—" Stephen said.

"It is evidence enough for me. But no magistrate will hear you."

Stephen had been Devlin's closest friend. She would not let him throw his life away on a foolish gesture. Didrik, too, did not deserve such poor payment for his loyal service. It would be up to her to make the accusation. She was the commander of the Guard and ultimately responsible for all that went on within Kingsholm's walls.

She heard low voices and the soft scrape of a sandal against the stone stairs. She scrambled to her feet and drew her sword.

"Peace, I have brought you a friend," Brother Arni announced. He stepped aside and held up a lantern to reveal the features of Master Dreng.

She would not have called the mage a friend, but neither did she count him among her enemies. With a nod to the priest, she sheathed her sword.

"I must return to my vigil," Brother Arni said, and he turned to make his way up the stairs and back to the temple.

It was customary that the priest of the temple spend the entire night in prayer for the soul of the Chosen One. It was a sign of how far she had fallen that she used him as a watchdog, perverting his pious vigil to ensure that they could meet in safety.

"Dreng, have you come to gloat? To tell us that you finally collected your wager?" she asked.

Dreng shook his head. "Believe what you will, but this time I wagered on Devlin's safe return."

"Then come, and have a drink with us. Didrik, find him an altar cup."

"No," Dreng said. "I came to the temple to pay my respects, and to offer you my services. I am fortunate that Brother Arni told me where you could be found."

"What can you do for us? Can you banish the enemy from the coast? Can you cast a spell upon King Olafur to make him see reason? Can you raise a man from the dead?" She spat the words out, even as she knew that her anger was not for Dreng alone.

"No. But I can help with disguises, and cast illusions to cover the tracks of those who would wish to make their escape."

It was a fair offer, and more than she had expected. Dreng had nothing to gain and everything to lose by helping them.

Didrik had found an odd-shaped vessel that looked like it might hold one of the fat candles used on feast days. He filled it with wine and handed it to Master Dreng before refilling everyone else's goblet. At this pace, they would be too drunk to stand well before the dawn.

"A toast in memory of a brave man," Master Dreng said, lifting his cup.

She raised her glass in salute, then took a hearty swallow with the others.

"There is one thing more you can do," Didrik said.

"You still know the spells for the Choosing Ceremony. We can name a new Chosen One. Tonight."

She had wondered what form Didrik's madness would take. She opened her mouth to protest, but Master Dreng was even quicker.

"No, I cannot do that. The spells are done in the King's name, and the King has abolished the post. I can no longer be certain that the spells would work. In all likelihood I would simply kill the candidate."

"And what good would it be to be named Chosen One? Without the Sword of Light, you would be denounced as an impostor and sent to meet Devlin's fate," she added.

No one challenged her pronouncement. She lowered herself back down to the ground, and after a moment the others followed her, Master Dreng perching awkwardly on the bottom step. He set his wine off to one side, a marked contrast from his behavior in years past.

Stephen picked up the axe and cradled it in his lap. He removed the cover that guarded the blade and traced the engraved pattern with his thumb. "Devlin once asked me a favor," he said, in a voice so soft that she had to lean forward to hear him. "The night before his duel with Gerhard. He made me promise that if he died that I would destroy this axe. He said it was cursed."

It was an odd thing to say, especially since the axe had been one of Devlin's most closely guarded possessions. But then again, many of Devlin's customs had been strange to her.

She reached out her hand. "I will see to it that it is destroyed," she said. After she had used it as evidence.

Stephen gripped it even tighter. "Devlin believed that his soul was bound up in the forging of this axe," he said.

He turned his gaze to Master Dreng. "The soul stone is gone, but we still have this axe. If Devlin is indeed alive, you should be able to feel it."

"And if the mage feels nothing?" she asked.

"Then I will have proof that he is dead. And I will go to Esker. Not because you asked, but because I promised my father that I would return to help him when Devlin died."

Stephen stood up and walked the few paces that separated him from Master Dreng. With visible reluctance Dreng accepted the axe.

"I have never heard of a living soul being bound in a weapon before," Dreng said.

"But you can still try," Stephen challenged him. "You owe him that much."

Master Dreng laid the axe across his knees. The others gathered around, watching as the mage lifted his hands over the axe. He closed his eyes for a few moments, and when he opened them, all trace of doubt was gone from his face.

"I invoke Egil, the Forge God, who presided over your making," he said. "In his name I command you. Give over to us your secrets and tell us of the one who made you. Share with us the news of his fate."

Master Dreng gripped the handle of the axe with both hands. "In the name of Egil I command you," he repeated.

His hands began to glow, as if illuminated from within. The light traveled up the handle of the axe, until it reached the steel blade, which began to pulse slowly with a reddish light, as if it were fresh from the forge.

Stephen reached over and touched the axe blade. Rather than complaining of the heat, the minstrel smiled.

She touched the axe blade herself, and realized that it was cool to the touch.

"What does this mean?" she asked.

The mage shook his head. "I would not have believed this if I had not seen it," he said. "A soul, tied to metal. There is no feel of magic as there is with the soul stone spell, and yet, somehow, the tie is there."

"But what does it mean?"

Master Dreng blinked at her angry tone. "It means Devlin is alive."

# Ten

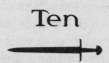

DEVLIN SLEPT, BUT HIS REST WAS PLAGUED BY nightmares. King Olafur mocked him, laughing as a faceless soldier ran Devlin through with a sword. He lay on the ground of the training yard, straining to reach a bucket of water that sat just out of his reach. A column of Guard recruits stepped over his body with barely a glance as they made their way to the practice field. As he lay, his skin shriveling from fever, Sergeant Lukas appeared. He paused by Devlin's side. "Thirsty, are you?" he said. Then he kicked over the bucket.

Tears ran down Devlin's face as he watched the water sink into the muddy ground. Yet even as he cried, he knew there was something wrong. He blinked his eyes furiously, and his vision swam. No longer was he in the courtyard, instead he was staring up at a sliver of blue sky, surrounded by leafy green trees. A face swam into view, and Devlin tried to speak, but his tongue was thick and clumsy. He tried to raise his arm, and was shocked when it did not respond. He could not even feel his limbs.

*I am dying,* he thought. And then he fell into confusion once more.

He could not tell night from day, nor waking from the fever dreams. He no longer knew who he was or what had happened to him. There was only one thing he was certain of. He was being held prisoner and he had to escape. He struggled with the mindless rage of a trapped animal, but his dulled wits were no match for his captors.

Time passed—how long he did not know. But then there came a day when he awoke, in full possession of his wits.

He was Devlin of Duncaer, called the Chosen One. He had been betrayed into the hands of his enemies, who had drugged him into insensibility. He remembered waking and his ill-fated escape attempt. Beyond that was nothing, save dark images that might have been truth or feverish imaginings.

He held himself still, trying to preserve what advantage he could. Slowly, stealthily, he took stock. There was a lingering ache in his wrists, but none of the pain he had expected. Gone, too, were the terrible thirst and hunger that had featured so prominently in his nightmares.

He lay not on the floor of a jolting wagon but on the soft surface of a bed. The scent of herbs filled the air, and he heard the sound of someone pouring liquid out of a pitcher.

"You can stop the pretense," a man's voice said. "I know you are awake."

Devlin opened his eyes. He glanced swiftly around and saw that he was in a large chamber that would not have looked out of place in a noble's house. The walls were hung with silk and the floor was of inlaid wood, but it was strangely bare of furniture. There was only the bed he lay in, a carved wooden chair by the fireplace, and a long table that held a pitcher, several small jars, and a brazier filled with ashes.

There were three windows, each covered by a lattice of iron bars. A pair of well-armed mercenaries flanked the door, while a man wearing a plain woolen robe stood by the table. The man picked up the clay cup he had been filling and brought it over to Devlin.

Devlin levered himself upright. His arms shook with weakness, but held his weight. He glanced at his captors, noting that in addition to belted swords, each held a heavy iron hammer. A strange weapon, but effective. Even if his legs would bear his weight, the chance that he could surprise and overpower the two was slim.

As the man held out the clay cup, Devlin saw that he was wearing the silver torc of a healer. But any reassurance of his profession was countered by the presence of the armed guards.

"Drink," the man urged.

"No," Devlin said, testing his voice and pleased to find that it worked.

"It is redfruit juice, nothing more," the man said. "If you tolerate this, we will see about getting proper food for you."

Devlin closed his lips tightly and shrugged. He would not let them drug him again.

"Stubborn ox," the man exclaimed. He raised the cup to his lips, and downed the contents in several noisy swallows. "Satisfied?"

Devlin watched as the man went back to the table and refilled the cup. This time when it was held out to him, he accepted.

His stomach had awoken, and it complained bitterly of long privation. At some point he would have to eat or drink, if only to keep his strength up. Besides, he reasoned, it was unlikely that they intended to keep him a drugged captive forever.

Devlin took a cautious sip. It tasted like redfruit juice. As he turned the cup in his hand, he was surprised to see that he was still wearing the ring of the Chosen One. The ring's stone remained dark, signifying that the liquid was safe to drink. With a shrug of his shoulders, he finished the contents.

"Who are you? And why have you brought me here?" Devlin said.

"I am Master Justin. As to why you are here, I cannot say. My orders were to heal you, and that I have done."

"Where am I?" Devlin asked, swinging his feet to one side of the bed.

"You are in—"

"No," one of the mercenaries interrupted.

Devlin looked at the speaker. He thought he recognized the man and his partner as being among those who had thwarted his escape attempt, but it was hard to be certain. The two wore the short tunic and leather pants customary among hired soldiers in Jorsk, while their elaborately braided brown hair called to mind the few sea folk he had seen. The healer, on the other hand, spoke as one who had spent years within Kingsholm's walls, and his features marked him as one born and bred within Jorsk.

And he had not forgotten that it was Karel of Selvarat who seemed to be giving the orders. It was a strange alliance that brought such disparate folk together.

The door opened and a nobleman entered, followed by Karel and the female who had helped drug Devlin during the journey.

Devlin rose to his feet, grasping the headboard for balance.

"You have done your work well," the stranger said.

"I kept my promise," Master Justin said.

Karel cleared his throat.

"I have kept my promise, Your Highness," Master Justin repeated, stressing the honorific. His attempt at civility was belied by the anger in his voice.

Interesting. So he was not pleased to be working for this prince. Such hatred might well prove to be a lever for Devlin to exploit.

"You may leave us and one of the guards outside will take you to see your family. When you have satisfied yourself that they are well, return to your quarters."

"But—" Justin protested.

"I may have use for you later, if my new guest proves uncooperative. You remember the terms of our bargain. You will be free to go when I have no use for either of you."

Master Justin muttered under his breath as he gathered up his supplies. Then he made his retreat.

"So you are the mysterious prince who holds Karel's leash," Devlin said.

Karel's face darkened, but his master only smiled. "Chosen One, I am pleased to see you living up to your reputation for brashness," he said.

The Prince's gaze measured him, as if Devlin were a piece of bloodstock he had just acquired. Devlin returned the regard with all the insolence he could muster. The

Prince was a lean man, lacking the heavy muscles of a warrior or laborer. Even his face was thin, the flesh stretched taut over angular features. His long, dark brown hair was gathered in the back in the Selvarat style, and a golden circlet sat on his brow, indicating he was of royal blood. He wore a long outer robe of pale green over a dark silken shirt and linen trews. He did not appear to be armed, but that did not make him any less dangerous.

Devlin tightened his grip on the bed post. He told himself it was his weakness that made him feel chilled, but he could not deny that there was something cold about the Prince's gaze. And surely it was a trick of the light that made his dark eyes appear flat and lifeless?

"Sit, sit," the Prince said. "It would be a shame to undo Master Justin's hard work."

The Prince took a seat in the carved wooden chair, and Devlin sank down on the bed.

"I am Prince Arnaud," he said. "I am pleased finally to meet one of the Chosen Ones."

Devlin was glad that he was sitting down. He had guessed that his captor was a prince of Selvarat. His dress and appearance had indicated as much. But Selvarat had numerous princes, since even second cousins of the reigning sovereigns were entitled to style themselves as royalty.

But there was only one Royal Consort, and he went by the name of Arnaud. His presence in Jorsk was a shock, if indeed Devlin was still within the borders of Jorsk.

Nothing made sense. He knew the King had resented Devlin's influence and power, but why choose such a strange way of ridding himself of a rival? What deal had Olafur struck with the Selvarats? Had Olafur used them to dispose of an inconvenient enemy? Or had the Selvarats sought Devlin out for their own nefarious reasons?

"If you wanted to meet me, you could have come to Kingsholm. There was no need for all this," Devlin said. He did not understand what was going on, but he would not let his captor see his confusion.

"I doubt I would be welcome there. Not today, although one day I will call it home," Arnaud said. "And you will be the key to my victory."

Devlin's heart quickened. First Karel, and now Prince Arnaud. He did not know what they wanted with him, but he could not allow them to use him. His left hand clenched in a fist.

"The guards have orders to break your arms and legs if you so much as move in their direction," the Prince said. "They will not kill you, but they will ensure that you are crippled. Do you understand me?"

Devlin gave a quick nod. The Geas insisted that he had to flee his enemies, but it was quieted beneath the voice of reason. He could risk death, since his death would prevent him from being used against Jorsk. But he could not risk being crippled, left helpless in their power. Better to be patient. In time he would find a way out of this trap.

The Prince turned his gaze on Karel. "See? Even the Chosen One is not immune to reason. Which brings me to the matter of your failures," he said.

Karel blanched, while the female mercenary swallowed nervously.

"Guards," Prince Arnaud called. Two soldiers came in. Unlike the others, these wore the uniform of Selvarat regulars. One stood behind Karel, and the other behind the woman. Karel began to shake.

"Cousin, I did my best. The spells did not work, and he fought us at every turn. Even with the drugs we could barely control him—"

Prince Arnaud waved his hand. "I have heard your excuses before. You were given a simple task and you botched it. Another two days of traveling and the Chosen One would have been beyond even Master Justin's skills," he said.

"I was only following orders," the woman stammered.

"Indeed," the Prince said. He rose to his feet and stood in front of her. Devlin held his breath, wondering would happen next.

The Prince nodded to one of the soldiers. Swiftly he looped a cord around the woman's neck and yanked it back. She reached up, her hands scrabbling uselessly for purchase, but he placed his knee in her back, and there was a sharp crack as he snapped her neck.

Her head lolled to one side as the soldier released the cord. Then, grabbing the limp body under her arms, he began to drag her away.

The juice Devlin had drunk rose in his gorge and he fought the urge to vomit. He would not have hesitated to kill the woman in a fair battle, but this was cold-blooded murder.

Karel trembled, but he did not move from his place. Arnaud stood in front of him for a long moment. "Cousin, what shall I do with you?" he asked.

"I am your loyal servant," Karel said. "I only wish to serve you."

Prince Arnaud smiled. "And so you shall," he said, leaning forward to kiss Karel on the forehead.

Karel stammered his thanks. He was still expressing his

gratitude when Prince Arnaud gave the signal, and the soldier looped the strangling cord around Karel's neck. He took longer to die than the woman, or perhaps it merely seemed so to Devlin, who forced himself not to turn away. There was no merciful neck crack, just a slow, painful struggle, as Karel's features contorted, turning first pale, then red. At last his limbs ceased twitching, and he, too, was dragged away.

Prince Arnaud then turned toward Devlin, who flinched involuntarily. "Karel got his wish. He gave his life as an example. I do think it is best to make things clear from the start. There must be no doubt as to the seriousness of my purpose."

Devlin looked long and hard into the face of evil. A monster with the manners of a prince, who had ordered the execution of his kin upon a whim. It was frightening to imagine what would happen if Jorsk fell under this man's rule. As Chosen One, it would be up to Devlin to prevent that from happening. At any price.

Prince Arnaud resumed his seat, arranging his robe carefully around him. "Now let us discuss your future," he said.

They came for her during the middle of the night watch. Drakken came awake at once, but from the grim look on Lieutenant Embeth's face, she knew this was no ordinary crisis.

"What is it?" Captain Drakken asked, as she rolled to her feet.

Embeth had not come alone. Lieutenant Ansgar was

with her, and Sergeant Henrik hovered just inside the door.

"We have orders to arrest you for treason," Lieutenant Ansgar explained.

Drakken shot a look at Lieutenant Embeth, who met her gaze steadily. She had expected Embeth, but the presence of the others were a surprise. And the plans they had put in place were for days from now. Something must have happened.

"You must have gone straight to the King," Drakken said.

"I did," Embeth replied, lifting her jaw. "I, at least, know the meaning of the oaths I swore."

She felt a moment of unease. Was Embeth simply mouthing these words for the benefit of these others? Or had she indeed changed her mind and decided to place her oaths to the King above her loyalty to her Captain?

Either way, there was nothing Drakken could do but play along and hope that she had not misplaced her trust.

"I always knew you were ambitious, but now I know you for a fool as well," Drakken said, for the benefit of their audience. "You will not like how the King rewards loyal service."

"Enough," Lieutenant Ansgar said, stepping toward her. Both hands gripped his sword belt, as if to still them. "We are not here to debate. You will come with us."

"Like this?" she asked, gesturing to her bare feet and the linen shift she wore to sleep in.

It was hard to tell in the darkness, but she thought Ansgar might have flushed. "Get dressed, but be quick about it," he said.

Drakken took a step toward her wardrobe.

"No. Stay where you are." Embeth turned to Lieutenant Ansgar. "She might have a weapon in there," she explained.

"What do you suggest?" Ansgar asked. By rights Embeth was his senior, having served as lieutenant for these half dozen years. For all his newfound favor with the King, it seemed the habits of discipline still held.

"Henrik, find the Capt—," Embeth stumbled. "Find Drakken some clothes to wear. Nothing fancy, and search everything for concealed weapons."

Henrik pawed through her neatly folded uniforms and came up with leather pants, a linen shirt, and a pair of thick woolen socks. The latter was a kindness that she expected to have need of soon. Three pairs of eyes watched her as she stripped off her shirt and donned her uniform. Boots were searched, then offered. It would have been humiliating if she were not so furious.

"Hands," Embeth ordered.

Drakken held out her hands, which were manacled before her. Then Henrik draped a cloak over her shoulders. He fussed until it hung just so, and for a moment she was touched by his care. Then she realized he was simply making sure that it hid her bound arms from any casual gaze.

"You will come with us and you will not call out or make any attempt to escape. Your cohort is already in custody," Lieutenant Embeth said. "There is no need to confuse the other guards who have not yet learned of your treachery."

They feared a riot if her guards saw her being led away in chains. A year ago they might have been right. Now she did not know what would happen. If even a veteran like

Henrik would not lift a finger in her defense, then she did not know who would aid her.

Though it was hard to blame Henrik for his behavior. He was following orders, and the oath that he had sworn to serve the King. He had not seen what she had seen, nor did he know what she knew. Indeed, there was a part of her that envied his ignorance and the comfort that was to be found in blind obedience.

Lieutenant Ansgar led the way. Outside of her quarters were a dozen guards waiting to serve as her escort. Newcomers and troublemakers, there was nary a friendly face among them. Some smirked when they saw her. They formed a strange procession as she was led past the guardhouse where prisoners were normally housed and into the palace through a narrow door by the kitchen. Down through the wine cellar they went, down a narrow winding staircase, until they reached the lowest level and the newly refurbished dungeon.

She was led past four cells that were empty, but whose filthy straw showed signs of recent habitation. The fifth cell held a figure lying on the floor, who lifted his head as the torchlit procession went by. Rikard.

Drakken was thrust into the very next cell. At Embeth's gesture she held out her hands, and the manacles were released.

"The King has ordered you put to the question," Lieutenant Embeth said. "A wise woman would recognize defeat and confess her crimes."

"A wise woman would know better than to serve a stinking worm like Olafur," Drakken replied.

The blow that snapped her head back came as no

surprise. Staggering on her feet, she watched as the cell door was closed on her.

Booted footsteps echoed as they made their way out of the dungeon, no doubt eager to report their success to the King.

She dropped to her knees. The cell was small with a narrow door, and only a single torch had been left to illuminate the corridor outside. When the torch burned out, they would be left in darkness.

"Cap'n, is dat you?" a slurred voice asked.

"Oluva?"

"Aye," Oluva said. Her voice came from the cell just beyond Drakken's.

"Are you hurt?"

"Only pride," Oluva said fiercely.

"So, how the mighty have fallen," Lord Rikard called out. She could hear the rustling of straw as he moved in his cell. "Even your cowardice could not save your hide. How does it feel to be called traitor?"

Drakken ignored him. She sank to the floor on her hands and knees in the center of the cell and began a careful spiral search, gently sifting the straw. It was a tedious task, and an unpleasant one too, for she was clearly not the first to occupy this cell. She wondered what had happened to the other prisoners. It was too much to hope that they had been set free. But if Olafur were conducting secret executions, surely she would have heard at least a whisper of it.

Rikard rained abuse on her, as she continued her task. Finally, on her eleventh circuit, her left hand closed around a piece of cold steel. She picked it up, and reverently traced the shape with her fingertips.

Now she had but to wait.

Rikard finally fell silent when neither she nor Oluva would rise to his baiting. Drakken counted cadence in her mind, imagining a line of new recruits being put through their paces. After she was certain a full hour had passed, she rose to her feet.

She slipped the key into the newly oiled lock, and it turned soundlessly. Pushing the door open, she padded her way over to Oluva's cell and unlocked that door. Oluva's face was swollen with fresh bruises but her grin was undimmed as she stepped into the corridor.

Rikard's eyes widened as the two stood in front of his cell, backlit by the flame from the failing torch.

"What?"

Captain Drakken held her finger to her lips, commanding him to silence.

"Rikard, I admire your passion but you make a lousy politician," she whispered. "You have no sense of who your friends are."

She unlocked his cell and swung open the door. With a wave of her arm she invited him to join them.

Rikard's face, at least, was unmarred, but his movements were stiff and she spared a moment to wonder what injuries were concealed beneath his clothes. If he was too badly hurt, he would not be able to keep up with them.

"What is this?" he asked.

"We are leaving," she said. "Come now; if we miss this opportunity, then we may never have the chance again."

"I do not know what game you are playing at," Rikard began.

"There is no time for debate. Are you with us? Or shall I leave you here?"

The door at the end of the corridor swung freely open at her touch, and she shook her head at this sign of laxity. A proper gaol would have a lock on that door, opened by a key that was different from the master key that opened the cell doors. She would have told them as much, if anyone had consulted her when they fitted up the dungeon.

Beyond the door were two lifeless bodies slumped on the floor, both wearing the uniform of the special detail that had been assigned to the dungeon. One lay on his back, and as she took in his features, her eyes widened in shock. With the toe of her boot she turned his companion's body over. After weeks of searching, she had finally found her two missing guards. But they were dead, and with them went any hope of discovering the role they had played in Devlin's disappearance.

It was disquieting to think that she had searched for them for weeks, only to find that they had been in the palace all along. She wondered what else had been going on under her very nose.

With a nod to Oluva, Drakken began stripping the weapons from the woman on the right, while Oluva took care of the man on the left. Drakken took the woman's sword for herself, but handed the belt-knife to Rikard.

"Don't use this unless you have to," she said. "Not all those we meet tonight will be unfriendly."

"Your arrest was a sham?" Rikard asked.

"No, the arrest was real. I told Embeth that I was planning on accusing the King of murder, and she promptly went off and informed him of my plan."

"But—" Rikard shook his head in confusion.

"But she also left the key to the cell doors in the straw and made sure I was assigned to that cell. And these two here are her work. I recognize her touch with a knife."

She wondered what had happened. The plan had been to disable the guards, not to kill them. One of them must have recognized Embeth and thus sealed their fates.

Captain Drakken led the way up the narrow staircase, through the wine cellar, then paused at the kitchen door. She sheathed her sword, and Oluva did the same. Quickly Drakken stripped off her cloak and wrapped it around Oluva, pulling the hood over her face. Hopefully no one would look at her too closely.

Rikard was another matter. His once-fine clothes were stained and ripped in places.

"Keep your head down and don't say anything," Drakken instructed him. "If luck is with us, word will not yet have spread about my arrest."

She and Oluva flanked Rikard, as if they were escorting him, then Drakken opened the door that led to the kitchen. At that hour it was quiet, save for the bakers laboring at their dough, who spared them barely a glance. It was not the first time that the guards had taken the shortcut through the kitchens when escorting a drunken or disorderly guest out of the palace.

As they stepped into the courtyard she could see that the stars had disappeared, and the sky was turning gray. She quickened her pace. They needed to be out of the city by dawn.

Everything depended on timing. She had waited an hour to make sure that Embeth had time to report the successful arrest to King Olafur, then to establish her own alibi for the escape. Ansgar would not be so lucky. He was to be drugged and made to disappear. Evidence would be discovered that he had fled the city, presumably after helping Drakken make her escape. Even if he did find the courage to come forward, once he was released, it was doubtful that King Olafur would believe any tale he might care to spin.

That is if Embeth let him live. Drakken had refused to countenance cold-blooded murder, but Embeth had already crossed that line.

Drakken led them to the prayer gate, a small door in the outer wall near the Royal Temple. Generations ago it had been carved into the wall so that devout worshipers could enter to pay their devotions at any hour of the day or night. Nowadays it was seldom used, but it was still functional.

Sergeant Lukas saluted as he caught sight of her. Wordlessly he handed each of them the brown cloaks of laborers, and to Drakken he gave a leather bag that she hung over her shoulder. The bag held her store of coins, as well as the maps she would need.

"Horses and provisions are waiting at the Drover's Inn, just beyond the East Gate. It's owned by Nifra's cousin. You'll be safe there."

Thirty years before, Lukas and Nifra had briefly been married. Their marriage had not survived, but their friendship had. Nifra had risked her life to carry messages between Didrik and Drakken. If Lukas trusted this cousin of hers, then Drakken would too.

"Thank you," she said. "Remember, follow Embeth's lead. I will return once I have found him."

"I'll keep things safe for you," Lukas replied, with a quick salute. "May the Gods watch over you, Captain."

"And over you as well," she replied. She was not a religious woman, but they would need all the help they could get.

No one challenged them as they made their way through the city, and as the dawn broke, the guards on duty looked the other way as Drakken and her companions slipped out of the eastern gate. She said nothing to them, so they could truthfully claim they had neither seen nor heard her.

It was humbling to realize how many people had risked their lives so that she could make her escape. From the moment Master Dreng had revealed that Devlin was alive, she had known that she could not remain in the city. But neither could she leave Kingsholm in the hands of Ansgar and his ilk. Together she and Embeth had hatched this plan, one that would bring Embeth into favor while eliminating the treacherous Ansgar.

War had been declared this night, though it was doubtful that anyone besides herself had realized it. Drakken might have been the first, but in time everyone would be forced to choose between serving a lawless King and their duty toward their country. Those slain tonight were but the first of the casualties that would come.

The horses were waiting at the Drover's Inn, as were Didrik and Stephen.

Didrik frowned at Oluva's appearance, but merely said, "The horses are saddled, and we are ready to leave as soon as you mount up."

"We are bound for Korinth, to rescue Devlin if we can. And once the Chosen One is in our hands, we plan to challenge King Olafur and his damned Selvarat friends," Drakken informed him.

Rikard's jaw dropped. "Devlin is alive? Are you certain?"

Stephen patted the great axe he wore slung over his back. "Yes, we have proof."

"Will you come with us?" Drakken asked.

Embeth had wanted to come, as had Lukas, and there were others who would have come if she had but asked. But it was a matter of balancing risks. Kingsholm needed the Guard to protect it, and to make sure that the city did not fall into anarchy. And a few more swords would make no difference. She was not planning on challenging the Selvarats to battle. She was planning on exercising stealth and cunning, and a small, swiftly moving group was of far more use to her.

Rikard shook his head. "My place is in Myrka," he said.

"Your province is under Selvarat rule, and you have been named traitor," she reminded him.

"My people will not accept the Selvarat yoke," he said confidently. "With me to lead them they will rise up and overthrow the invaders."

"You will get yourself killed."

"It is my life. Those are my lands, the very soil is in my blood. I can do no less."

"So be it," she said.

Didrik led a roan gelding out of its stall and held it as Rikard attempted to mount. It took him two tries, and when he finally succeeded Rikard's face was gray, and he held his right arm clamped firmly around his ribs. A brave man, but foolish. Riding alone and injured he would be easy prey for the patrols that the King would send out after the escaped prisoners.

"Didrik, do we have a spare sword?" she asked.

"Your fighting sword is on your saddle," he replied. "Lukas smuggled it out of the palace yesterday."

So absorbed had she been in her preparations that she had not even noticed one of her swords was missing. She wondered what else she had overlooked, then dismissed the thought as unimportant. What was done was done and there was no going back.

She unbuckled the borrowed sword from her waist and lashed the scabbard to Rikard's saddle. "If I were you, I'd not be taken alive," she advised.

"Give my respects to the Chosen One," he replied. Then he kneed his horse into a slow walk.

"Mount up," she said, as Didrik and Stephen led the remaining horses out from their stalls.

She watched as Rikard's figure disappeared from view.

"He will be lucky if he lasts a day on the road," Didrik said.

"So will we if we tarry any longer," she said sharply. "We'd best be going, as we will not find Devlin by standing around here talking."

As they rode, she resisted the urge to turn around, to take one final look at the walls of the city where she had served for over a quarter of a century. It felt as if she was abandoning her post, but she reminded herself that she was not running away. She was journeying toward a goal. They would find Devlin, and when they returned they would set the Kingdom to rights.

# Eleven

THREE DAYS PASSED, AND AS DEVLIN'S STRENGTH
returned, so too did his confusion and frustration. Prince
Arnaud had gone to great lengths to have Devlin brought
here, wherever this place was, yet now he ignored him.
And rather than being thrown in a dank cell, Devlin was
treated as if he were an honored guest. That is if one ignored the barred windows and the ever-present gaolers
who watched his every move.

Meals fit for Prince Arnaud himself were brought to
his chamber, far more than one man could do justice to,
though Devlin ate as much as he could. He had not
needed Master Justin's explanations to know that he had
lost weight during his captivity. His captors had kept him
so drugged that he could scarcely eat, and the flesh had
melted from his bones.

More, too, had been lost during the healing process.
Devlin had listened with only half an ear as Master Justin
had described how Devlin's mindless attempts to free
himself from his chains had torn his flesh, and the mangled shreds had begun to rot. Master Justin had healed

Devlin so that he bore only fading scars, but such healing had sapped his stamina. The healer had castigated Devlin for his recklessness, but Devlin had not seen fit to enlighten him. It had not been Devlin who had struggled long past the point of reason. It had been the Geas, which freed from Devlin's own reason knew only the mindless devotion to his oaths.

Protect Jorsk. Serve her King. The Geas spell was implacable. Even after King Olafur's betrayal, the Geas did not relent. Devlin must destroy Prince Arnaud so his evil could not threaten Jorsk. If he could find no way of destroying the Prince, then Devlin must escape. Or destroy himself, lest the Chosen One somehow be turned into a weapon against Jorsk.

Though how Prince Arnaud planned to use him, he did not know. Was Devlin's mere presence enough? Did he plan to use the Chosen One as a figurehead for an invasion of Jorsk? If so, he would be disappointed. The nobles had never loved Devlin, and with the exception of a few hotheads like Lord Rikard, no one would support him. The commoners had hailed Devlin as a champion, but before he could consolidate his power he had been sent out of the country, on a quest to retrieve the Sword of Light.

He paused a moment to wonder what had happened to the legendary weapon meant only to be wielded by the anointed Chosen One. Was it even now locked away within the King's vaults, awaiting the day when some other fool was named Chosen One?

"What place is this?" he asked.

His gaolers made no answer. There were always two of them. There were at least two more outside, who could be

seen whenever the door was opened. They were mercenaries, and their uniforms were as mismatched as their
features. But they were well-trained, for they stood their
watches without complaint and without visible sign of
boredom or fatigue. They did not speak to him except to
give him instructions, and they would not respond to his
taunts.

It would be difficult to take them off guard. And he had
not forgotten Prince Arnaud's threat. The consequences
of a failed escape attempt would be dire.

Devlin would have to be patient and await the right
opportunity to strike.

On the fourth day, Master Justin visited just after
breakfast and pronounced himself satisfied with Devlin's
progress.

"The sooner you cooperate with the Prince, the sooner
we will both be set free," Master Justin urged him. Apparently he still clung to his first impression that Devlin was
a witless fool.

Devlin smiled grimly. "The Chosen One serves no foreign master," he said. "Your future is your own to make."

It was possible that the healer might go free, but
doubtful. Prince Arnaud did not strike him as a man who
would relinquish any tool that came to hand.

Devlin's fate was even murkier. Prince Arnaud had informed him that he had great plans for him, but surely
the Prince must know that he could not expect Devlin's
cooperation.

Though it occurred to him to wonder what would have
happened if Olafur had simply commanded Devlin to go
with Karel and serve Prince Arnaud. Would the Geas have
compelled him to obey? Was the Chosen One a cur who

could be freely passed from one master to another? Or would his oath to protect the people of Jorsk have overridden the King's orders?

The Geas spell was a clumsy thing, meant to ensure the loyalty of the Chosen Ones. It had the relentless power of a bludgeon, and the finesse to match. A man might well go mad under its power, torn between obeying two conflicting oaths.

Had one of his predecessors ever faced such a dilemma? If Stephen were here, he would be able to answer Devlin's questions. But at this moment Devlin was glad that Stephen was far from this place, and safe.

With a few muttered imprecations, Master Justin took his leave.

Devlin began a slow walk around the perimeter of the room. As before, the mercenaries allowed him to approach within two paces before warning him away. He nodded, and altered his path. Perhaps given time they would grow less vigilant.

His head was bent, as if in thought, but his eyes took in every detail of the room, looking for something he might have overlooked in his previous circuits. Anything that could be used as a weapon.

But there was nothing. The bed had four tall posts, but the bed hangings and their cords had been removed. He could fashion a rope out of a torn sheet, but not while he was under constant observation. He had no belt, and he had been given a shirt with buttons rather than ties. His boots with their hidden knives were nowhere to be seen. Instead, they had given him soft leather shoes to wear. Even his meat was sliced before it was delivered, and his fork and spoon were carefully collected after each meal.

He gave a short laugh. It was flattering that they respected him so much, but for once he wouldn't have minded being misjudged.

Devlin halted midstride as the door swung open, and a woman wearing the uniform of a lieutenant in the Selvarat army entered. "The Viceroy wants to see him," she told his gaolers. "Bring him."

A rope had been brought and Devlin's hands were tied behind his back. The lieutenant led the way, flanked by two soldiers, while the mercenaries trailed a cautious pace behind. Devlin kept his eyes open, looking for a means of escape or any clue as to where he was. The corridor they traveled was wide, lined by the shocking extravagance of a carpeted runner, confirming his guess that this was the house of a nobleman or a wealthy merchant. The windows that lined one side were tall but narrow, too narrow for a man of his frame to pass through, hinting that the place had been built with an eye to defense, despite its opulence.

They escorted him to what appeared to be an office or library. There were bookcases on one wall, filled with bound books and racks of scrolls. Stacks of parchment and half-unrolled scrolls covered a massive heartwood desk, while a map of Jorsk was spread across a table and held down by leaden weights. Notations had been scribbled across the map in dark ink, but as Devlin leaned to take a closer look, his arms were grasped from behind, and he was jerked away.

There were five armed enemies and he was unarmed, so Devlin stood meekly as his arms were untied.

"Sit," the lieutenant said, as one of her men dragged a scarred wooden chair into the center of the room.

He did so, but when the soldier approached with a rope and grasped his left arm, Devlin withdrew it with a jerk.

"No," he said, preparing to rise.

"My orders are to break all the bones in your hands if you refuse to cooperate," the woman said politely. "Of course that means Elda and Renzo here will have to take over feeding you and wiping your ass. But it's your choice."

It was not her words that chilled him, but rather the absolute indifference in her tone. She truly did not care whether he was crippled or not.

He sat back down and allowed his arms and legs to be bound to the heavy chair. The lieutenant checked the bindings and only when she was satisfied that he could not move did she and the others leave.

As soon as the door closed behind them, the door on the far side of the room opened and Prince Arnaud entered. He wore boots and trousers, as if he had recently been riding or intended to ride soon.

"Chosen One," he said. Even wearing boots, his footsteps were nearly silent as he padded into the room and slowly circled around Devlin, studying his prisoner from every angle.

"I would offer you refreshment but in your condition . . ." The Prince waved his hand as Devlin's bonds.

"I would prefer a few answers instead," Devlin said. "Where am I? And why have you brought me here?"

"I apologize for ignoring you for so long. But other matters commanded my attention. Too, I thought it only fair to give you a chance to regain your strength before we spoke again."

Arnaud continued his wanderings around the room, forcing Devlin to crane his neck to keep him in view. He paused briefly by the map, his fingers tracing some feature that caught his interest. Then he moved over to his desk and picked up a wax tablet, seeming intent on its contents, as if he had forgotten all about his unwilling guest.

But Devlin knew his ploy for the game that it was and he did not react. Deliberately he turned his gaze back to the wall in front of him.

"Tell me, how does it feel to know you have given your loyalty to a coward and a fool?"

Devlin could not suppress a start, for Arnaud had come up behind him without his realizing it. His muscles clenched as Arnaud ran the fingers of one hand across Devlin's taut shoulders. Then the Prince circled around him, cupping Devlin's chin with one hand, forcing Devlin to meet his gaze.

"He betrayed you without a moment's hesitation, to save his own hide. Not twelve months ago you saved him from a conspiracy that would have cost him his throne, and this is how he repays you. He did not even ask why I wanted you, though surely the dullest of men could understand that I meant you no good," Arnaud said. "He is unfit to rule a dung heap, and yet this is the man you have sworn to serve. The man who will lead your country to its ruin."

There was something about Arnaud's voice that teased at the back of his memory. Something about the deliberate cadences of his speech.

"It's not my country," Devlin ground out.

Arnaud smiled as if Devlin were a particularly clever child, and released his hold on him.

"Yes, there's that. You are a living contradiction. King Olafur's father crushed your own folk under his heel, yet now you serve his son. Pledged to defend him and his kingdom until your death. Tell me, do your vows still bind you, now that you have been betrayed? Are you your own man? Or are you still Olafur's lapdog?"

"Other men may take and cast off oaths like a man changing his cloak. But I am the Chosen One," Devlin answered.

In the end, he had no choice. The Geas spell ensured as much. The Chosen One was compelled to remain faithful to his oaths. It would drive him to the very limits of human endurance, and beyond. It knew neither doubt nor pity, and under its control the Chosen One was both less and more than a man.

"And if you weren't ensorcelled?" the Prince asked. "What then would be your answer? Would you be free to join me?"

Devlin's skin crawled. It was as if the Prince had been inside his mind, seeing his very thoughts.

"I've dabbled in spells in my days, but the spell that binds the Chosen Ones is indeed a marvel. One such man is an asset, but an army of Chosen Ones? Soldiers who feel no fear, who cannot disobey, and who will fulfill my orders at all costs? With a thousand such I could rule the world," Arnaud said.

"You will never command me," Devlin said.

"But I already do. You belong to me."

The words echoed in Devlin's brain, calling to mind

the dark days of the past winter, and how a disembodied voice had nearly driven him mad.

"You," he breathed. "You are the one. The mind-sorcerer."

Arnaud gave a half bow, as if Devlin had just paid him a compliment. "Indeed, I was wondering when you would recognize me. You see we are old friends already. I have lived in your mind, and I know everything about you."

Devlin's heart quickened as he fought off the beginnings of panic. Last winter Arnaud had used mind-sorcery to attack him, nearly driving Devlin mad. And it had been done while Arnaud was several hundred leagues away. Who knew what such a mind-sorcerer could do, now that he had captured Devlin?

His arms jerked involuntarily, seeking escape. But as Arnaud's smile broadened, Devlin fought to bring himself under control. Witless panic would not serve him, and he would not give the man the satisfaction of seeing his fear. He slowed his breathing and deliberately relaxed his limbs.

"Twice now you have attacked me, and twice now you have failed," Devlin said. "Perhaps it is time you found a new obsession."

"I will have your help, willing or not," Arnaud said. "But you can spare yourself this ordeal. Swear to me that you will serve me, and I will set you free."

A cunning man would lie. Convince the Prince that he meant his new oath and wait his opportunity to strike.

Devlin opened his mouth, but his tongue was frozen. He could not lie, not even if it would save his life. After a long moment he closed his mouth and shook his head.

"Chosen One, you do not disappoint," Arnaud said. He

turned away from Devlin and walked over to a side table, where he selected a goblet and filled it with a pale yellow wine. He took a sip, then set the wine aside. Moving to the map table, he picked up one of the metal weights in his hand. He turned it over for a few moments, then moved to the fireplace. Each movement was deliberate as he grasped the weight with a pair of tongs and held it in the center of the flames.

It was not a forge fire, but merely one meant for warming a largish room. Still, it was enough for his purposes, and when the tongs were removed the metal glowed a sullen red.

Slowly, as if he were stretching each moment out, Arnaud crossed the few feet that separated him from Devlin. He held the glowing metal in front of Devlin's face, so close that Devlin could feel the heat rising from it.

"Remember you can end this at any moment. Swear to me your allegiance, and it will all be over."

"You know that it is not possible," Devlin said.

"So I intend to find out," Arnaud countered. "It should be a fascinating experiment."

With that he released the tongs, and the metal weight fell on Devlin's right thigh. The first impact was not unbearable, but then the metal burned through the leather and touched the skin beneath.

Sweat broke out on his forehead, and Devlin ground his teeth together as he struggled not to scream. The smell of seared flesh filled his nostrils, and his blood pounded in his ears. He twitched the muscles of his leg, but it was firmly bound and he could not shift the burning metal.

She had known this would happen, he realized. The lieutenant had not bound him in order to ensure that he would not try to attack Prince Arnaud. She had trussed him up like an animal awaiting the slaughter.

"Shall we try another?" Arnaud asked.

He did not wait for Devlin's response, and in far too short a time a second glowing chunk of iron was suspended over Devlin's body.

"You can burn the flesh from my bones," Devlin panted. "But my answer will be the same."

"You repeat yourself," Arnaud said. He walked behind Devlin and pressed the burning metal against the back of Devlin's neck.

Devlin gasped in pain and tears began to stream from his eyes. His body bore its share of burn scars from his days as a metalsmith. But the wounds caused by a splash of molten metal or a careless touch were far different from what he felt at the Prince's hand. This was a deliberate attempt to inflict the maximum amount of pain upon another human being.

"Tell me, Chosen One, whom do you hate more? Me for torturing you? Or your King for his betrayal?"

# Twelve

**"WHAT IS YOUR PLAN?"** DIDRIK ASKED.

Captain Drakken leaned forward and added another branch to the fire, which hissed as the rain-soaked wood was added, before settling down to a sullen burn. She adjusted the blanket wrapped around her shoulders, then stretched her hands out to the feeble warmth of the flames.

They had pushed themselves hard in the days since the four of them had fled Kingsholm, traveling the main roads when they must and taking the smaller country paths whenever they could. There had been no time for leisurely discussions. But just after dark they had reached this creek. Swollen with spring rains, it was too dangerous to ford in the dark, so reluctantly they had made camp for the night.

Her body craved sleep, but she ignored its demands, just as she ignored the other discomforts of the journey. Rest would come later, after she had accomplished her mission.

"What do you intend?" Didrik's tone was respectful, but it was clear that he expected an answer.

Didrik had changed. He still called her captain and looked to her for orders, but he no longer did so unquestioningly. In time he might make a decent captain himself. If he lived that long.

Seated on the opposite side of the campfire, Oluva and Stephen leaned forward, waiting to hear her answer.

"We will go to Korinth, or wherever the axe leads us," Captain Drakken said. "We will find Devlin, free him, then deal with the Selvarat invaders."

"That's it? That is your plan?" Didrik's voice rose in incredulity.

She grinned. "Do you have a better one?"

He shook his head. "For all we know, Devlin is surrounded by an army. What do you expect the four of us to do?"

"We will do what we must," she said.

"I wish you had recruited others. Behra, Signy, I can think of at least a dozen who would have begged to join us," Didrik said.

"The smaller the party, the greater our chance of passing unnoticed," Captain Drakken said. "The risk was not worth it. Four swords or twelve, we will do what must be done."

"We are not as friendless as you think," Oluva chimed in. "There are many in Korinth who know my face and will be willing to take up arms to free the Chosen One."

Didrik nodded grudgingly. "Any help is good, but if we had trained guards—"

"We have what we have," Drakken said sharply. "And Oluva's peasants may yet surprise you."

Korinth had long been troubled by sea raiders, and while the King had done nothing to protect them, Devlin had sent Oluva and Sergeant Henrik to travel among the coastal villages, teaching the natives the rudiments of defense. Such actions had shocked the King and his court, who feared that armed peasants would rise up against their overlords. King Olafur had forbid Devlin to train any more armies of the people, but in Korinth he could not undo what had been done. Hundreds of folk had been trained to defend themselves.

It was for this reason that Drakken had asked Oluva to accompany her when she left the city. Oluva had agreed, and had duly been arrested as Drakken's so-called accomplice. It was not till they had made their escape that Oluva had learned the true reason for the journey. She, along with those who had helped Drakken escape, only knew part of the truth—that the King no longer trusted Drakken to be Captain of the Guard, and that her life was in danger. Only Embeth had been told the full truth, that Devlin was still alive and Drakken intended to find and free him.

"The axe still calls us to Korinth?" she asked.

Stephen nodded. "I checked as we made camp. Still north and east. I fancy it has grown a little warmer, but that may be wishful thinking."

Within its leather coverings, the axe blade glowed faintly with a reddish light. Master Dreng had altered the spell, so the axe glowed strongest when it faced Devlin's location and grew darker when it was pointed away. A crude locating device compared to the elegance of the soul stone, but it would serve.

"Why Korinth? What use have the Selvarats for the Chosen One?" Oluva asked.

"They knew he would never agree to the protectorate," Didrik said.

"Then why not simply kill him? Why take him prisoner?" Oluva asked.

It was a question that Drakken had often asked herself in the past days. "I suppose they think he has value as a hostage, though the King's declaration that Devlin is dead would cast doubt on any claim they might make. Either that or they think they have some way to use him against us," she said.

In hindsight, she should have paid more attention to Lord Karel's departure. He had left the city on the very day that Devlin had disappeared, reportedly carrying messages from King Olafur and Marshal Olvarrson to the Selvarat commander in the east. He had left on horseback, with only a single servant to accompany him.

Such in itself was not suspicious, until it was added to the disappearance of the mercenaries who had arrived in Kingsholm aboard Ambassador Magaharan's ship and taken quarters in the old city. Only now was it apparent that while she had been searching for Devlin's body, he had been smuggled out of the city from under her very nose.

"Did the King order Devlin to leave? Or you think he was taken against his will?" Didrik asked.

"Devlin would not have left without warning, without speaking to anyone," Drakken replied. "Nor would he have left his axe behind."

"He would not have stood by and let Saskia be killed," Stephen added.

They sat in silence, lost in their own thoughts. Satisfied that she had dried out as much as she was going to, Drakken was ready to stretch out for sleep when Stephen's low voice caught her attention.

"I think I may know why they want him. Or rather not why, but who," he said.

"What do you mean?" she asked.

Stephen bit his lip and tugged the axe a bit closer, seeming to take comfort from its presence. "I think it is the same enemy who attacked him this winter."

"What enemy?" She had heard almost nothing of what had transpired during Devlin's return to his homeland, only that after much searching he had found the Sword of Light and had been bringing it back to the capital as proof that he was indeed the true Chosen One.

Didrik shook his head. "No. He was defeated. That witch in Duncaer destroyed him."

"Not destroyed. Cast out," Stephen argued.

She raised her voice to get their attention. "What enemy? What haven't you told me?"

Didrik shrugged. "It is his tale," he said, pointing to Stephen. "Let him tell it."

"Do you remember when Devlin and I were attacked by the creature of darkness? An elemental, Master Dreng called it, created by a sorcerer and sent to attack us?"

"I remember Devlin told me of it," she said cautiously. She had not witnessed the actual attack, but then again Devlin had no reason to lie. He had said it was a sorcerous creature, and she had believed him.

"This winter Devlin was attacked again. A mind-sorcerer cast a spell on him, causing him to hear voices and see things that weren't there. It nearly drove him mad."

"But the Chosen One is protected against direct magic," Drakken argued. "That's why the sorcerer had to send an elemental to do his bidding."

"Devlin performed a ritual of his people that inadvertently left his mind open for attack, and the mind-sorcerer seized the opening," Stephen said. "For a long time no one knew what was happening, but in the end we found a wizard woman who was able to cast out the invader. She told us the spell had been cast by a mind-sorcerer, someone who was a great distance away."

"It could have been anyone," Drakken said. "Even one of his own people."

Stephen shook his head. He had always been stubborn, and since being proven right about Devlin he had become even more so. "The Caerfolk are wizards, not sorcerers. And Ismenia said that whoever had cast the spell was not in Duncaer. It could have been one of our own, but who would have the skill for such? Master Dreng is only a mage of the second rank, and yet he is the Royal Mage. The best the King has at his command. But in Selvarat they teach mind-sorcery for its healing powers. If one of their sorcerers has studied the dark side of that talent, then he could well be Devlin's long sought enemy."

"But why take him? What do they intend to do with him?" Oluva asked the question that was on everyone's mind.

Drakken shivered, but not from the cold. It was bad enough to imagine Devlin a prisoner, held captive by his enemies. But the prisoner of a mind-sorcerer? Someone who could drive a man mad with his touch? There were no limits to the horrors that such a one could inflict.

Even if they succeeded in rescuing Devlin, would there be anything left of the man they had once known? Or would they arrive only to find a lifeless shell had taken his place?

"Enough," she said, rising to her feet. "It does no good for us to spend the night fretting over things that we cannot change. Didrik, you have first watch. The rest of us should sleep while we can. It may be a long time before we have another uninterrupted night."

"Aye, Captain," Didrik said.

Using their saddlebags as pillows, they wrapped themselves in bedrolls and pretended to fall asleep.

It took several hours before Prince Arnaud declared himself satisfied that Devlin would not break under torture. By the time his gaolers returned to unfasten him from the chair, Devlin was so weak he could not stand and they had to drag him back to his room.

He half stumbled, half fell onto the bed, then immediately groaned from the pressure on his burned back. The burns on his front were even worse, so he curled up on his right side, which had received the least amount of Arnaud's attentions. His breath came in short pants as he tried to cope with the pain. His head swam, but the mercy of unconsciousness was denied him.

Arnaud had enjoyed torturing him and had displayed an expert's touch. At times the pain had been so intense that Devlin thought his heart would burst, but each time Devlin felt he had reached the limits of his endurance,

Arnaud had pushed him one step further. The Prince had shown a perverse pride in Devlin's refusal to yield, caressing his head and praising him as if he were an obedient pet. Then he would begin again, promising Devlin that he could end the pain if he swore allegiance.

Devlin could not fathom his captor, nor the twisted game that he was playing. It was easy to say that the Prince was mad, that he was the embodiment of evil. But what about those around him? His soldiers had shown no surprise at Devlin's condition; indeed, they had prepared him for his ordeal. How often did one have to witness torture before it became simple routine? How many victims had they trussed up to await Arnaud's intentions?

"You stupid bloody fool," Master Justin said.

Devlin opened his eyes. His vision was blurry, but he could see the mage, accompanied by an older woman.

"Where are you injured?" the healer asked.

Devlin glared. It was a foolish question. After a moment, the healer seemed to realize his mistake. He turned to the woman and said, "It looks like burns, but may be more. Fetch springwater, the linen strips, and the salves in the blue jars. Both the jars, the large square one and the smaller round one, understood?"

The woman nodded and left to do his bidding.

Justin grasped Devlin's shoulder with one hand and rolled him onto his back. Devlin bit his tongue rather than cry out.

"Kanjti had better claim you, for no one else would have such a fool," Justin said. His tone was angry, as if Devlin were somehow responsible for his injuries.

"I did not ask for your help," Devlin spat out.

"I am not doing this for you," Justin countered. He

beckoned to one of the guards. "Come now, give me a hand. We've got to get these clothes off so I can clean out the wounds and see the damage."

Between the two of them they stripped off his clothes, showing little care for either his modesty or his comfort. By the time the woman returned with her supplies, Devlin's hands were clenched into fists, the nails biting into his palms to distract himself from the pain elsewhere in his body.

There were dozens of burn marks, each of which had to be cleaned and coated with a thick salve. Some were left to breathe, while the worst were wrapped in linen bandages. As he worked, Master Justin muttered under his breath, complaining about the impossibility of his task, the difficulty of working without properly trained apprentices, disparaging Devlin's faculties and his breeding.

His voice was angry, and his touch less than gentle, but under his care the throbbing aches of the wounds grew slowly numb. At last he pronounced himself satisfied, and with the old woman's help he loosely draped a quilted robe over Devlin before allowing him to lie back down on his side.

"I have done what I can," Master Justin informed him.

Devlin nodded. He would not offer the words of thanks. The healer had made it quite plain that he was here not to serve Devlin, but because Prince Arnaud required it of him. Strange to think that such a bitter man could have been called to Lady Geyra's service.

With a wave of his hand the healer dismissed the old woman, who left bearing the stained rags and filthy basin.

"You will not be so lucky next time," the healer declared.

"Next time?" Devlin's breath caught in his throat. Surely the prince didn't intend to repeat that day's work?

"Each healing places a strain on your vitality and robs me of my strength," Justin declared. "If I were well rested, I could have done more for you, but two major healings in the space of a week would be a challenge for even a healer of the first rank."

"I did not choose this," Devlin said.

"Of course you did." Justin crouched by the bed, so his eyes were level with Devlin's. "Just do what the Prince asks, whatever it is. Swear you will obey him and he will have no reason to harm you," he whispered, in a voice too low for the guards to overhear.

"I cannot."

"Look around you. The world has changed. This may once have been Korinth, but it is now ruled by Prince Arnaud in the name of the Selvarat empire. There are only two choices for those of us here. Cooperate or be killed."

So he was still in Jorsk, in the coastal province of Korinth. Devlin had suspected as much, from the few glimpses of scenery that he had seen outside his window.

"The Prince rules Korinth? But what of the alliance?"

King Olafur's message had spoken of the revival of the ancient alliance between Selvarat and Jorsk. Devlin had imagined the Selvarats supplying troops to help defend Jorsk's vulnerable coastline. But from what he had seen and heard, it seemed the results had been far different than anyone had imagined.

Justin chuckled mirthlessly. "Arnaud has proclaimed himself Viceroy of the Selvarat Protectorate. His rule stretches from Rosmaar down to Myrka."

"You are mad or deceived." Arnaud might have captured part or all of Korinth, but he could never have taken the eastern territories in such a short time. Mikkelson and his troops would have seen to that.

"You are the one who is mad," Justin replied, no longer bothering to keep his voice lowered. "King Olafur sent his orders. Our armies marched out of their encampments, and the Selvarats and their allies marched in. The King abandoned us to our fate."

"I cannot believe the King would have surrendered without a fight," Devlin said. "You may not have heard of it, but surely the Royal Army is preparing even now for an attack."

Even to himself the words sounded hollow. Olafur had never been a man of courage. And he had handed Devlin over to the Selvarats. Devlin, who was both Chosen One and the General of the Royal Army. Devlin, as bearer of the Sword of Light, could have rallied the Jorskian people in their own defense.

But it seemed Olafur did not want war. Olafur wanted to hold on to whatever shreds of his kingdom he could. But like a man who cut off his leg to escape a trap, Olafur might well find that he had inflicted a fatal blow upon himself. It was just a question of how long it would take him to bleed to death.

"You deceive yourself," Justin said. "There is no army, no rescue, no reprieve. Give in to Arnaud, and we will both be the better for it."

King Olafur's betrayal stung, and in other circumstances Devlin might have been tempted—if Arnaud had been a fair man instead of a monster. If Devlin's will had been his own, then who knew how he might have chosen.

But Arnaud was too evil to be allowed to rule, and the Geas would never permit Devlin a choice.

"You have a choice. You can choose to obey the Prince, or you can defy him. You have your free will. I do not. I am what your people made me. The Chosen One. I must obey my oaths until death."

Justin rocked back on his heels. For the first time he truly seemed to see Devlin as a person rather than as an inconvenience.

"Then we are both damned," he said.

It was a fair conclusion.

The healer rose to his feet. "I will send the woman up with a mixture of poppy seed," he said. "Drink it, and it will help you sleep."

Devlin supposed that was his way of apologizing for his earlier treatment. "Thank you," he said.

"I hope never to see you again," the healer said.

A kind thought. But it depended very much on what Prince Arnaud intended, and his treatment of Devlin so far had given little reason to hope that he might be merciful. Whatever happened, Devlin would simply have to endure. He had to survive until the day came that his captors thought him weak and tame. On that day he would be ready, and he would seize the opportunity to break free and destroy the evil creature that went by the name of Arnaud.

# Thirteen

THE MAPS DRAKKEN HAD BROUGHT PROVED
more valuable than coin, for the travelers were able to
make good time while sticking to the lesser known roads
and trails. Perhaps it was because they took these seldom
traveled ways, but they saw few other travelers. Most of
those they encountered were locals, walking on foot as
they journeyed between the tiny villages dotting that part
of the countryside. Thrice they heard hoofbeats, and each
time managed to conceal themselves in the forest before
being seen by a mounted patrol.

When their provisions had run low, they had risked
stopping in a village large enough to have shops catering
to travelers. She had given Didrik enough coin to buy half
the village and instructed him to return swiftly. He had
returned three hours later, burdened with provisions,
having spent only a small portion of her silver.

"I told you to be quick," she had groused.

"They would remember a man in a hurry who foolishly paid far more than the goods were worth. It was not
worth calling attention to us," Didrik had replied.

Indeed their small party had drawn few signs of interest. The farmers went about their business, working the small fields while pig herders supervised their charges in the forest. If they appeared somewhat grim, it could be the result of a hard winter rather than the prospect of imminent war. Indeed the others reported the countryside little changed from when they had journeyed here last summer, accompanying Devlin on his quest to expose the traitor Egeslic.

They followed the pull of the axe, northeast to begin with, and then north. She was surprised, for a part of her had assumed that the Selvarat general would have taken over the seat of the Baroness of Korinth. But the axe led them more north now, nearer where Rosmaar bordered Korinth.

Oluva reported that there were at least two fortified manors in the area, either of which would make a suitable base. And it was not far from where Major Mikkelson had stationed a substantial portion of his troops, to anchor the western end of his command. If Devlin was being held prisoner, she suspected it would be in one of those encampments. That is if he was still within the borders of Jorsk.

Even a child knew that Rosmaar was a coastal province, with numerous coves and small ports where a ship could drop anchor. In her darkest moments, Captain Drakken feared that Devlin had already been taken aboard ship for the voyage back to Selvarat, that the axe would show them a path that led over the waves, toward a place where they could not follow. But she kept these grim thoughts to herself, and if the others shared her worries, they did not speak them aloud.

Reluctantly they left the forest trail and emerged onto a

wide road that led north to the coast, and to where they hoped to find Devlin. During the night they had crossed into the territory that made up the Selvarat Protectorate, and they would need to be careful. She had no way of knowing how tightly the province was held in the Selvarats' grip.

They would pass a cursory inspection, she had seen to that. She had scoured their possessions, ensuring that there was nothing that could identify them. Their uniform tunics had been discarded, replaced by plainer gear. She still had her cloak, though she had laboriously unpicked the damning insignia. Didrik's and Stephen's wardrobes were even odder assortments, for they had bits from Duncaer and the southern lands mixed in with the gear they had purchased in Kingsholm. The very variety of their garb, along with the well-worn weapons they carried, would lend credence to their tale that they were a group of unemployed caravan guards, looking for work.

But the tale would not hold if someone recognized them. Oluva's face was known here, and anyone who had spent time in the capital might well recognize Drakken or Didrik. It was a risk, but it was a risk they had to take.

Their luck almost ran out on their very first day on the main road. As they rounded a curve, they came upon a patrol riding toward them. There was no time to hide, and fleeing would only confirm any suspicions the riders might have.

"Stick to our story," she cautioned. "Wait for my signal."

There were five of them, four dressed in the livery of provincial armsmen, trailed by a woman who wore the uniform of the Selvarat army. As they approached, Captain Drakken signaled her party to halt.

"Fair day to you," she said, as the patrol drew their horses to a halt. She noticed that the armsmen were careful not to bunch up, but rather fanned out to block the road. It would be difficult to take them, but they would if they had to.

Didrik and Oluva had resumed their practice with the throwing knives. They lacked Devlin's skill, but they were accurate enough. If she gave the signal, they would take down two of the armsmen before they had a chance to draw their weapons. That would make the odds four against three.

But there was no assurance of victory, and a missing patrol would call down attention they did not need. Best to try and bluff their way through this encounter.

"Who are you and where are you bound?" the senior armsman asked.

"We are travelers, bound for Selborg," she said. Selborg was a goodly sized town, about two days' travel from where they were. It was a reasonable destination, and yet not important enough to call attention to them.

The senior armsman held up his left hand, and she heard the sound of crossbows being cocked. The senior armsmen half drew his sword from its scabbard.

"Selborg is a half day's journey south from here. You are riding north," he said.

She swore silently to herself. The forest trails had twisted, and they had emerged far more to the north than she had expected.

"Of course, you are correct," she said swiftly. She called to mind the dozens of times she herself had interrogated travelers. Appearing too calm would raise their suspicions. She hoped they would think her flustered by their presence.

"I meant to say that we are bound *from* Selborg, where we spent the past night. We are making our way to—"

"Our affairs are none of your business," Stephen interrupted her. He nudged his horse forward a few paces.

The senior armsmen drew his sword, but Stephen seemed unconcerned. She glared at him, wondering what game he was playing at. He might think he was serving as a distraction, but all he was doing was making the armsmen even more nervous, which meant they had lost the element of surprise.

"I do not speak with lackeys," Stephen said. His voice dripped with disdain. Most times it was hard to remember that he was the son of a ruling Baron, but in this instance he was every inch the haughty noble's son.

He rose in his stirrups and called out a greeting in a language that she did not recognize.

The Selvarat officer nodded and rode forward.

Stephen gave a flourishing court bow, a remarkable feat for one on horseback. The officer gave a half bow in return. Still speaking in what she presumed was the Selvarat tongue, Stephen launched into some kind of explanation. He gestured to the party, apparently answering the woman's questions. After a few moments he beckoned for Oluva to come forward, and seemed to introduce Oluva to the officer.

Oluva had the sense to play along, smiling and nodding. Drakken, for her part, did her best to look bored, as if she had not a concern in the world. But inside she seethed. If they got out of this, she was going to strangle Stephen. Slowly, and with great pleasure.

Finally, after what seemed an eternity, another series of bows were exchanged.

"Let them pass," the woman commanded.

The armsmen sheathed their weapons and parted. Drakken and Didrik rode through, her spine prickling under their unfriendly regard.

"Ensign Romana has advised me that the roads ahead are in fine shape, and we should reach Dhrynes before nightfall. There is a decent inn there, which she has been kind enough to recommend," Stephen said.

"Safe journey to you," the Selvarat ensign said. At least this time she spoke in the trade tongue. "And remember, the regional proctor will know where your cousin is stationed."

"You are kindness indeed. I will remember you to my cousin," Stephen said.

With a final nod, he guided his horse forward, and the rest fell in behind him. They rode in silence until Captain Drakken was absolutely certain that they were not being pursued.

Then she nudged her horse beside Stephen's. "What did you think you were doing back there?"

She did not know whether to be furious over the risks he had taken or grateful that his ruse had worked.

"Saving our hides," Stephen said tersely.

"But what did you tell him?"

"I told him that I was Stephen, son of Gemma of the house of Narine, and that I had learned my cousin Hayden was stationed with the encampment. Naturally, I and my wife Oluva were going to pay our respects to my cousin and offer him our hospitality in this land of barbarians."

"Naturally," she said dryly. "And what if she hadn't believed you? What would you have done then?"

Stephen shrugged. "Whatever needed to be done."

"What if someone thinks to check your story?" Didrik asked. "They got a very good look at us. Once they find out there is no Stephen of the house Narine, they will have sketches of us plastered across the province."

"I am not stupid," Stephen said. "I did not lie. My mother Gemma is of the house Narine, a half-blood to be sure, but they acknowledge her lineage. And I have a distant cousin named Hayden, who last I heard was a lieutenant in Thania's army. For all I know he could indeed be among the invading troops. If he isn't, I could always claim to have been mistaken. Hayden is a common enough name among their folk."

"You did well," she said grudgingly. "But next time you think to take such a risk, tell me first. I do not like being surprised."

"I will if there is time," he said.

It was the best she could expect.

"Come now, pick up the pace," she said. "Now that you have announced our intentions, we had best be sure we reach Dhrynes by nightfall so we can stay in that damn inn. Just in case the ensign thinks to check on us."

There was one virtue of Stephen's improvisation. Till now they had avoided inns, for fear of being recognized. This one night, at least, they would have soft beds and fresh food. And a chance to listen to the other travelers, to find out what else was happening in the province. They had been lucky this time. They could not afford to make any mistakes.


Master Justin visited the next morning and pronounced himself satisfied, though he grumbled that he could have done a better job if he had been at his full strength. Yet even diminished, his skill was remarkable. Devlin had experienced his share of burns before, mostly due to his own carelessness as an apprentice. Back then he'd been too poor for a healer's care and had suffered through the blistering soreness, weeping rashes, and tender healing skin that split open at a touch. But now, after less than a day, his wounds were visibly smaller. And the pain, which should have been incapacitating, had softened into mere discomfort.

The healer's manner had improved, and if he was not particularly kind neither did he vent his anger upon his patient. Instead he was nearly civil, even going so far as to inform Devlin that Prince Arnaud had ridden out to consult with his commanders and was not expected back until late that day.

Devlin thanked him when he had finished his work. Master Justin was not much of an ally, but he was all that Devlin had. Even if he were not willing to help Devlin make his escape, he still had access to information that could prove vital. And, should Devlin continue to need his services, there might come a time when he could be convinced to slip Devlin a weapon. A scalpel or even a small knife could give Devlin the edge he needed to take down his guards.

And if Master Justin was unwilling to provide direct aid, he might well prove useful as a hostage or distraction. It was worth cultivating his forbearance.

Though for Master Justin to continue his visits, Devlin must be injured again. It was not a pleasant thought.

As sunset approached, a servant arrived with fresh clothing and Devlin was instructed to dress. Again he had a full escort as if he was a particularly savage animal who might attack at any moment. He grinned for a moment, wondering how they would react if he were suddenly to growl. His apparent cheerfulness seemed to make his escort nervous, so he continued to smile, even as they drew near the room where he had been tortured.

To his hidden relief they passed that room and instead descended to the ground floor. He was led into a well-lit dining room, where a table had been laid out with two places. Devlin was seated at the near side of the table, and this time they chained his left arm to the chair, along with both his legs. But his right arm was left free.

Not that he could do much with his arm, unless he intended to hurl his plate at Prince Arnaud, or perhaps stab him with a fork.

As if thinking of him conjured him up, the Prince entered the room, followed by a pair of servants in livery.

"Chosen One, I am glad to see you looking so well," he said. His face beamed with pleasure, as if he had somehow forgotten that he had been the author of Devlin's suffering.

A servant pulled back the chair and Prince Arnaud took the place opposite Devlin's. "I thought we might dine together and get a chance to become better acquainted," the Prince said.

It was all a piece of his madness, but Devlin had no choice except to play along.

"Master Justin is a treasure, is he not? I found him serving a noble's house. The noble did not deserve him, he had no idea how to make use of him. But I did. Just as I know how to make use of you," Arnaud said.

"I have always believed a man should choose his own path," Devlin said.

"Yes, but your path has hardly been of your own making, has it?"

The observation cut close to the bone, but before Devlin could think of a reply, the door swung open. A pair of servants brought out the first course, a clear fish broth and a plate of bread for each of them. Wine was poured for the Prince, but in front of Devlin was placed a tall tankard of what appeared to be ale.

He raised his eyebrows.

"Try it, and tell me what you think," the Prince urged him.

Devlin lifted the tankard and took a sip. It was indeed ale from Duncaer. A touch bitter from the long journey, but far more to his taste than the finest wine would ever be.

"Is it good?" the Prince asked.

"It is decent," Devlin said.

"Wonderful. My cook thought the cask spoiled and nearly threw it out, but I assured him you would like it."

This was insanity. The Prince was behaving as if Devlin were an honored guest rather than a prisoner. If he had just met him, Devlin might well have mistaken the Prince for a man of honor and breeding. That is until he looked into his eyes. The Prince could smile and feign affability, but his cold gaze told the true story of his soul.

"Quite a pleasant country, really," the Prince said, launching into an account of the day's activities.

Devlin listened, making murmuring noises where appropriate. The Prince was remarkably frank with him, revealing that he had traveled to his encampment to discuss the disposition of his troops and to settle a matter of precedence between the allies. From his comments Devlin surmised that the occupying forces were composed of two disparate groups. The first were regular troops from the Selvarat army. The second was a contingent of mercenaries, loyal to the Prince. That matched with what he had witnessed himself, in the strange mix of soldiers surrounding the Prince.

Even Devlin could see the difficulty of requiring the two units to work together. The disciplined troops of the army would despise the mercenaries, whom they saw as feckless opportunists who would cut and run if faced with real danger. The mercenaries, for their part, would resent any attempt by the army to control them.

It was a useful bit of information to have. If one could find a way to drive a wedge between the two groups, it would hinder any plans the Prince might have to extend his dominion. He wondered why the Prince was speaking so freely in front of him. Was it because he still expected somehow to win Devlin over to his side? Or was it because he planned on killing Devlin before he had a chance to make use of this information?

The fish soup was cleared away and replaced by roasted lamb. Devlin's portion had been neatly sliced into small pieces, as if he were a small child who could not be trusted with a knife. But while he had only two utensils, the Prince had the elaborate array of one eating a state dinner, including a set of three knives. Devlin glared at them. They were only a short distance away, but chained as he was they might as well have been in the next village.

Seeing the direction of Devlin's gaze, the Prince

smiled. He patted his mouth with a napkin and signaled to the servant, who refilled their glasses.

At last, the meal was over, and Devlin waved away the servant who had tried to set a sweet in front of him. He hadn't really been able to do justice to the food, in part because of the strangeness of eating with his captor. And, in part, because he was dreading what would happen when the meal was over and the Prince tired of his sport.

The ale had been a temptation, but he had limited himself to a single tankard. He would need his wits about him.

"Tell me about the Geas spell," the Prince said, after the plates had been cleared away and the last servant had left the room.

"You have been in my mind, and know what I know. You even know my taste for ale. Why should I tell you what you already know?"

"Indulge me."

He hesitated. The Prince must have a reason for asking. He knew the Prince had accessed at least some of Devlin's thoughts while their minds had been linked. But had that linkage been less complete than the Prince had implied? In which case it would be folly to give the Prince any information that could be used against him.

"Answer my questions and you will be allowed to return to your chamber to sleep. Undisturbed."

The alternative was unspoken. He had no doubt that the Prince had even more creative ways to make him suffer.

Devlin shrugged. There was no harm in telling the Prince that which was common knowledge in Jorsk.

"A candidate to be named Chosen One presents himself at the Royal Temple," Devlin began. "The priest prays and the mage chants the Geas spell. If the candidate is false, he is struck down and consumed by flames. If he is true, then he is named Chosen One."

Some held that the Gods themselves were responsible for choosing worthy candidates to hold the post. But the cynic in Devlin believed that it was the spells cast by the mage that destroyed those who were deemed unfit.

"A position of power, second only to the King in the old days," Arnaud mused.

"So I have been told." Indeed, Stephen had recounted the lore of the great Chosen Ones so often that, despite himself, Devlin had learned their stories by heart.

"Yet they are so frightened by that power that they bind the Chosen One to his duty, using a spell so that you cannot betray your oaths. A strange thing to do to one who is called the champion of the Gods."

"The Gods did not call me to champion. I volunteered for the reward," Devlin said. At the time he had been able to see no further than the ten golden disks that were given to the newly named Chosen One. Now, two years later, it was hard to believe that he was the same man.

"So you claim. But how many times have you wondered if the decision was ever truly yours to make?"

Devlin jerked back in his chair. This was an abomination! The damn sorcerer knew more about him than even his closest friends. The secrets of his soul had been laid bare to this man's prodding. And now the man was using that knowledge against him.

The violation outraged him, all the more because he was completely helpless. There was nothing he could do, no means to strike back at the Prince. He could only feign calm, and not give Arnaud the satisfaction of seeing how rattled he was.

"As for the Geas spell, I know not how it works," Devlin said, returning to the Prince's original question. "Not even Master Dreng understands it."

More the pity. Dreng had sworn he would lift the spell if it was in his power, but experiments had revealed that it was not. Devlin would bear the burden of the Geas until the day he died.

"I wouldn't expect your so-called mage to understand the spell. He can barely enchant a fire-starter," Prince Arnaud said, dismissing Dreng with a wave of his hand. "If he had studied a bit more, he would realize that Geas was based on mind-sorcery. A far different skill than the petty magic he practices."

The Prince toyed with his wineglass, seeming intrigued by the shifting patterns of light on the dark liquid.

"Unlike your petty mages and hedge wizards, I have true power. If I chose, I could free you from the Geas."

"Then why haven't you done so?" Arnaud had to be lying. It was a trick. It must be.

"It would require your cooperation," Arnaud said. He caught and held Devlin's gaze. "But think of it. Isn't that what you have wanted ever since you became Chosen One? I could give you your life back. Your free will. You would once again be your own man, free to make your own choices."

Devlin drew in a deep breath and exhaled slowly. The Prince could have found no better bait for his trap. And surely this was a trap of some sort, even if Devlin could not see the iron jaws waiting to close on him.

He was tempted. Even knowing what he did of the

Prince. Knowing his madness, his evil, and even with a body that still ached from the Prince's care, Devlin was tempted.

Ironically it was the Geas itself that saved him. Devlin's own wants were immaterial. The Geas understood only duty, and it would not allow itself to be destroyed.

"I must decline," Devlin said, as if he had been offered a great boon.

"Do not be hasty," the Prince said, rising from his chair. "Sleep on it and give me your answer tomorrow."

"My answer will be unchanged," Devlin said.

"I hope you are wrong. For both our sakes."

# Fourteen

STEPHEN PAUSED AT THE FOOT OF THE STAIRS, struck by a sudden fit of nerves. This should have been a familiar place, for in his travels as a minstrel he had been in dozens of such small country inns. But then his only concern had been whether or not the patrons would care for his music. Sometimes the audiences had been appreciative, giving him copper coins and buying him glasses of dark wine. Other times they had been less friendly, including one memorable night where they had thrown crockery and driven him into the street. Such was the life of a man trying to make a name for himself as a minstrel.

But these days he played a different kind of game. He had left his music behind in Kingsholm. And now if he failed to play his part, the stakes would not be a lost dinner, but their lives.

He forced himself to move forward until he stood on the threshold of the common room, peering around for an empty table. The room was crowded, for they had reached town on the weekly market day. He watched a group of drovers rise to their feet; Stephen made his way quickly through the crowd to claim the places they had left vacant.

A young boy appeared out of nowhere, pocketing the coppers left on the table, then picking up the empty glasses and giving the table a halfhearted wipe with a rag.

"Just you?" the boy asked.

"My wife will be joining me in a few moments, and I expect my guards will come once they have finished their business," Stephen said, keeping to the story they had agreed upon. "Bring a pitcher of wine and four glasses to start. And find out what the cook is serving for dinner."

"It's pork," the boy said with a grin. "It's always pork on market day. But I'll ask Ma if there's anything else."

Stephen shrugged. "Pork will do. But not now. Wait till the others have joined me."

The boy nodded and wandered off. He returned with the wine and the glasses just as Oluva arrived and took her seat. She frowned as she glanced around the room.

"Was everything to your satisfaction?" Stephen asked.

"Yes, quite a pleasant place. We must thank Ensign Romana for her recommendation," Oluva said. But her eyes continued to scan the patrons of the inn, looking for trouble.

Their table was practically in the center of the room. A good spot if one wanted to be seen but a poor one for defense. Devlin would never have sat here, but in his assumed role Stephen could hardly call attention to himself by refusing the only open table.

Around them he heard scraps of conversation. On the surface it was the usual chatter of a small town, talk of bargains made, a swindler who had gotten his comeuppance, and a whispered scandal that seemed to involve the local priestess, a young man, and the gift of a pig. Sadly the speaker lowered her voice before Stephen could figure out what part the pig had played in the affair.

He shook his head, realizing that he had allowed himself to become distracted. It was not what these folks were saying that was of interest. It was what they were not talking about. No one mentioned the Selvarat troops, or the newly announced protectorate. Nor did anyone mention the King's name. It was as if they were all trying very hard to pretend everything was normal. They were either deluding themselves, or they lived in fear of informers. If Stephen had to bet, he'd wager on the latter.

Folk continued to stream into the common room, pushing their way onto the few benches and standing when there was no room to be found. Stephen came in for his share of glares when he refused to give up the two empty chairs at his table, but no one challenged him. He'd heard at least one voice muttering the word half-breed, and so he knew that the tale he'd told the innkeeper had already begun to spread.

They were halfway through their second glass of heavily watered wine when Captain Drakken and Didrik made their appearance. Like Oluva they frowned when they saw the table, but there were no other places open and so they took their seats.

"I bought fresh grain for the horses, and the other provisions will be delivered tonight, sir," Didrik said.

In keeping with the story he had told the ensign, Stephen was posing as the distant connection of a Selvarat family, no doubt hoping to use his family ties to improve his fortunes. Oluva was his wife. Didrik and Drakken were two unemployed mercenaries whom

Stephen had hired as escort. The story would hold upon a cursory scrutiny. Stephen had his mother's brown hair and in appearance favored her side of the family. But if he met anyone from the house of Narine, or, Gods forbid, his cousin Hayden, then the game would be over. Stephen son of Gemma would be unmasked as Stephen son of Brynjolf, Baron of Esker, and a wanted fugitive.

Captain Drakken lifted the wine jug, and with a "By your leave," poured glasses for herself and Didrik.

"I made inquiries in the market. The first speaker tells me the regional proctor is riding circuit and is not expected back for several days," she said, pitching her voice so he could hear her over the babble of conversations around them. Of course doing so also meant that any listeners would hear confirmation that Stephen and his companions were just who they said they were.

"That is unfortunate," Stephen said. "I suppose we could wait—"

He let his voice trail into silence.

"The speaker was kind enough to tell me that the main encampment is a dozen leagues north of here. If your cousin is not there, they will have records of where he has been sent," Captain Drakken said. "Of course it is your choice, but it might be pleasant to rest in an inn for a few days."

The boy returned, balancing four trenchers on his thin arms. He set the dinners down before them, then returned a moment later with cutlery. It was indeed pork, garnished with dried apples, accompanied by slices of fresh bread.

Compared to their journey rations, this was a feast. Only good manners prevented them from falling upon their food. As it was, they made swift work of their portions, and Didrik summoned the boy over to bring him a second serving.

Only after they had satisfied their hunger did Captain Drakken return to the topic of their earlier conversation.

"Have you decided to stay and wait for the proctor? If so, I will inform the innkeeper and let the stable hand know that he needs to store our provisions," she said.

He wondered what she expected him to say.

"It seems a shame to travel and leave behind such fine fare," Didrik said. His face, at least, Stephen knew how to read. Didrik's words urged that they stay, but his eyes said otherwise.

"I see no reason to dally when my cousin may be so near to hand," Stephen said. "We will press on in the morning."

"As you wish," Captain Drakken said.

After a few moments he and Oluva excused themselves. Captain Drakken and Didrik stayed behind, to see what local gossip they could pick up. Normally that would have been a task that Stephen excelled at, but not now. Not when he had publicly declared his connections to the occupying forces.

Oluva pulled off her boots, then stretched out on the bed that dominated the tiny room, propping her head up on one hand. She patted the empty right side of the bed with one hand in invitation, but Stephen shook his head and began to pace.

Declaring Oluva his wife had seemed a brilliant inspiration this afternoon. Certainly the patrol had been convinced by the tale he had spun. But that had been on an open road, in the clear light of afternoon sun. Now, in this tiny room, lit only by lamplight, he was beginning to have second thoughts. Oluva was a fine-looking woman, and if she were anyone else, he might have seen this as an opportunity. But since the earliest days of their acquaintance Oluva had made it quite clear that she viewed him as if he were a younger brother. It was ironic that he was forced to pretend affection for the one woman who had made it quite plain that she wasn't interested in him.

He knew that Oluva could sense his nervousness, but fortunately she put it down to the strain of their mission.

"Relax, you did fine. There is nothing to worry about," she reassured him.

"There is everything to worry about," Stephen said. And the knowledge suddenly distracted him from Oluva's presence.

It had been weeks since Devlin had disappeared, and who knew what might have happened to him during his captivity? If the mind-sorcerer was indeed involved somehow in Devlin's disappearance, then what did that mean? Why had he chosen to capture Devlin rather than trying to destroy him as he had before?

Stephen glanced over at the corner where Devlin's great axe stood. The blade was covered now, but he had made a ritual of checking it every morning when he arose and every night before he retired. Assuring himself that Devlin was still alive.

And Devlin was not his only concern. Solveig had refused to leave Kingsholm, despite his entreaties. She'd promised that she would return to Esker when she felt the dangers outweighed the possible rewards of having a set of eyes and ears at the court, but it would be easy for her to misjudge the situation. The same mistake his mother might have made, when she and Madrene found themselves detained in Selvarat.

Stephen would never forgive himself if anything happened to his family while he was searching for Devlin. But he could not give up the search for the Chosen One. Didrik and the others were skilled warriors, it was true. But they did not have Stephen's faith. They had mourned Devlin as dead and would have abandoned him to his fate.

Stephen would never forsake his friend. No matter how dim the hope or how far the trail led. If he had to pursue Devlin on his own, he would. He would find Devlin and trust in the Gods and his own strength to free him. And then, let their enemies beware.

The Selvarat army had established an encampment on flat meadowland along the banks of the Floryn River. The river provided easy access to supplies and reinforcements from the sea, while the flat open plain provided perfect defensive conditions. It would be impossible to approach the encampment without being seen.

From the hillside overlooking the valley, they had observed what they could of the camp. It was laid out in a grid pattern, with neatly ordered rows of tents of various shapes and sizes. The smallest of the tents housed the soldiers, while the largest in the center were probably for the officers and the administration. Captain Drakken had estimated that there might be as many as five hundred soldiers in the encampment. Along with space for horses, wagons, provisions, and all the baggage of an army in the field.

It fell to Stephen actually to enter the camp. The sentry on duty had summoned a messenger to take him to see the camp commander. Oluva was not allowed within, so with promises to return swiftly, he left her and their horses at the camp entrance. Drakken and Didrik had been left two leagues back, concealed in the thin pine forest. Just in case entering the camp turned out to be a trap.

General Bertrand was too busy to see Stephen, but his aide proved the talkative type, and it was some time before Stephen could take his leave. The aide insisted on walking Stephen back to the camp entrance and being introduced to his wife.

Oluva's face brightened when Stephen appeared. No doubt she had been wondering if he had been taken prisoner or exposed as a fraud.

"Did you find him?" she asked.

"Alas, no. It seems we were misinformed. There is a Lieutenant Hayden who has since been dispatched to Myrka, but he is from Vrital," Stephen said. "Major Willem, may I present my wife Oluva? Oluva, this is Major Willem, who has been so gracious as to make time to answer my questions."

The Major bowed, and Oluva executed a credible curtsy. "It is an honor to meet you," she said.

"A pleasure to meet such a reasonable-minded pair," the Major said. He turned back to face Stephen. "Remember your cousin may well be en route here to assume his new posting. New troops are expected before fall, and he may well be among them. If he is, I will give him the scroll that you left."

"You are kindness itself," Stephen answered. "And, of course, should your duties take you to Rosmaar, you must promise to call upon me. I promise to show you the best that this land has to offer. Our home is near the town of Somerled, just over the border in Rosmaar. Ask anyone in Somerled, and they can direct you."

"Of course, we would welcome you and your friends. At any time," Oluva said. If her voice held a touch of hesitation, hopefully it would be put down to anxiety over whether or not their home was grand enough to receive such an important guest.

After another exchange of compliments they were finally able to depart. They rode slowly away, careful to give no sign of haste, nodding politely and drawing their horses to one side as a patrol rode in toward the camp. Gradually the road rose up into the hill, and the flat plain gave way to a few scrubby trees, which thickened almost imperceptibly into a pine forest. They waited until they were well out of sight of the camp and the road had curved behind them before turning off into the trees and backtracking to where they had agreed to meet their friends.

The campsite was empty when they came upon it. Stephen felt a moment's alarm, then Captain Drakken stepped forward from her hiding place.

"Were you followed?"

"No," Oluva said.

"Not that I can tell." Didrik's voice came from behind them. "All's quiet along their back trail."

"Good. Did you get what we needed?" Drakken asked.

Stephen nodded.

He and Oluva unsaddled their horses and picketed them with the others. Unwilling to risk giving away their position by a fire, they made a cold camp, eating dried meat and washing it down with the contents of their waterskins.

"What did you find out?" Captain Drakken asked.

"He's there," Stephen said.

"How can you be certain?" Didrik asked. "Did you see him?"

"No, I didn't. But there is one tent set apart from the others, guarded by two sentries. Major Willem did not name the prisoner, but he did say that Prince Arnaud had been there that morning to question him."

"It could be anyone," Drakken said.

"It is Devlin," Stephen insisted. "Major Willem did not refer to him as *a* prisoner. He called him *the* prisoner. There is only one who would warrant that distinction."

Captain Drakken appeared unconvinced.

"The axe led us here. And this is the only tent with guards. The only one," Stephen added. He did not understand why they did not share his excitement.

"You did not see the entire camp," Captain Drakken argued.

"I saw enough," he said. True it would have been helpful if the axe could have led them directly to Devlin, but he could hardly carry an enchanted weapon through the midst of the enemy camp. Still, where magic failed, reason prevailed. "Devlin is a valuable prize, and where better to keep him than in the very heart of their encampment?"

"I agree with Stephen," Oluva said. "But now that we have found Devlin, what do we do next?"

Captain Drakken sighed. "We have to enter the camp, make our way unseen to the very heart of the encampment, disable two sentries, free this prisoner, then make our way out of the camp, before any one of the five hundred hostile soldiers raises an alarm," she said.

"And we have to be prepared for the fact that Devlin may be unconscious or injured," Didrik added.

At least they had ceased denying that Devlin was there.

"If we stole a uniform and darkened his hair, Stephen could pass as one of their own," Oluva said. "And while I waited at the gate, I saw carters allowed to pass in and out of the camp, delivering goods. The cart would be searched, but as long as we had no visible weapons they should have no reason to be suspicious."

"So we need a uniform. A cart, and a load of goods that will pass inspection," Captain Drakken said. "Anything else?"

"The Gods' own luck," Didrik answered.

"Luck is for fools," Drakken counted. "I'll put my faith in ourselves."

It was just after dusk when Stephen made his way through the camp, Oluva at his side. His scalp itched from the coarse dye in his hair, and the pants of his borrowed uniform dragged on the ground, threatening to trip him unless he kept tugging his belt up. Still, in the darkness, with only widely spaced torches for illumination, he should be able to pass as one of their own.

Oluva had no such worries. Her costume deliberately showed all of her features, as befitted the role she was playing. Stephen blushed as he glanced over, then hastily averted his eyes.

They had chosen to attempt their rescue at dusk, when the camp would be lulled into quietness after the evening meal. It had taken three days to make the preparations for the rescue attempt—time Stephen spent torn between the desire to sneak off on his own to rescue Devlin and his desire to rage at Captain Drakken for her overcautious approach. He was all too conscious of the nearby river. At any hour a ship could arrive to transport Devlin to Selvarat, and they would have lost him. Yet even in his impatience, a part of him knew that she was wise to take such care. They would get only one chance at this, and they dared not fail.

Still, he could not help wondering what Devlin was enduring in these three days, while his friends plotted his rescue. Could he somehow sense that they were near? Or did he think himself friendless and abandoned?

After weeks of searching, in a few short moments he would come face-to-face with his friend. It was difficult to contain his excitement, but he forced himself to stroll casually. As he passed a pair of soldiers playing dice, he nodded in greeting.

"Care to share the riches? We'll gamble you for her," one called out.

"Let me find out what she's worth first," Stephen said.

Captain Drakken's gold had purchased the dress worn by the village speaker at her wedding. It was at least two sizes too small for Oluva, and the neckline had been altered with a dagger, but such only reinforced the impression of a whore aping her betters. He would never have dared suggest that she wear such a thing, but it seemed Oluva was determined to play her part to the fullest.

"She'd better be quick," the second soldier said, with a disapproving glare. "Remember the rule; the natives have to be out by sunset. If the general finds her here, you'll be digging latrines until you're old and gray."

Stephen tugged Oluva's arm. "Come now," he said in the trade tongue.

She grabbed his head and pulled it down for a surprisingly lusty kiss. After a moment's astonishment, he responded enthusiastically. Clearly this was no sisterly affection, and he had a moment's fleeting regret that he had not taken advantage of his earlier opportunities. He reached up to embrace her, but she broke the kiss and took his hand in hers, towing him away from the fire.

He was embarrassed at having forgotten himself, if only for a moment. He could feel himself blushing, the soldiers' laughter ringing in his ears as they continued onward, deeper into the camp.

As they approached their destination, he saw that there was just one sentry guarding the tent rather than the pair he had seen earlier. He tried to take that as a sign that luck was with them, but the churning of his stomach told of his own misgivings. His steps slowed, conscious that everything depended on what he did next. Why had he agreed to this? He was a minstrel, not a warrior. If he made a mistake, it could well cost Devlin his chance at freedom.

But there was no one else. And there was no time to change the plan. By now Drakken and Didrik should already be in the camp, having entered through the west side where the provisions were kept. They could not linger there without risking exposure. It was now or never.

Oluva squeezed his arm reassuringly.

He took a deep breath to steady his nerves. He gave her

backside a pat, then, hidden by her wide skirts, he reached his hand into the slit in his cloak and withdrew his dagger. He had not seen her move, but knew that she would already have her own knife at hand.

"Halt," the sentry said, as they approached.

Stephen gave Oluva a push away from him, watching as she pouted. She would have made a fine member of a players troupe. The sentry was so busy paying attention to her that he did not notice that Stephen had come up on his right side, while Oluva was now on his left.

"I've brought a treat for Major Willem. Compliments of the village headwoman or whatever she calls herself," Stephen said.

"His tent is over there," the sentry said, pointing off to his left. "Next to the general's, where it ought to be."

"Sorry," Stephen said easily.

Oluva smiled. "He's a handsome one. I'll take him on when the Major's done," she said.

The sentry took a step backward. "What did she say?"

Stephen obligingly translated.

The sentry shook his head. "I don't hold with such trash, and neither will the Major," he said.

Oblivious to the insult, Oluva leaned forward and ran one hand along the sentry's arm.

As he flinched, Stephen stepped forward and slid his knife between the sentry's ribs. His body jerked and he opened his mouth to cry out, but Oluva covered his mouth with her own, holding him in a grisly embrace.

Stephen twisted his dagger, then withdrew it. Blood gushed over his hand. Pocketing the dagger, he held open the tent flap as Oluva dragged the dying sentry within. Stephen closed the tent flap and took the sentry's place.

He wiped his right hand against the dark wool cloak, but he could still feel the man's blood on his hand.

An eternity passed before he heard the rustle of the tent flap behind him, and Oluva stepped out, followed by a tall figure wearing the spare cloak that she had concealed under her voluminous skirts.

"Hurry," Oluva said. "We've not much time."

Stephen turned and looked into the face of Major Mikkelson.

# Fifteen

AFTER A FITFUL NIGHT'S REST, DEVLIN WAS roused shortly after dawn and brought before the Prince. His heart quickened as his escort stopped in front of the room where he had been tortured. Through the open door he could see that Prince Arnaud was already within, sipping from a mug of kava while a servingwoman cleared away the remnants of his breakfast. As she carried the tray past Devlin, the smell made his stomach rumble. He had scarcely eaten last night, and had been given no food this morning.

The Prince glanced at Devlin, then turned his attention back to the scroll that lay partially unrolled on the table before him. It was the opportunity Devlin had been looking for. If he could catch the Prince unaware, he could break his neck or choke him to death before the guards had a chance to intervene. The Prince had the build of a duelist, but Devlin had the muscles that came from a lifetime of hard labor. In close quarters, with the Prince apparently unarmed, Devlin would have the advantage.

And even if Devlin failed in his attack on the Prince, the odds were good that the Prince's guards would be forced to kill Devlin to save the life of their liege. Either way, Devlin would win.

He knew his escort expected him to hesitate, so Devlin took three quick steps into the room. He gathered himself for a leap, only to find himself brought short as he was seized from behind by one of the guards.

"Careful, my friend," Prince Arnaud said. "Remember their orders."

Disappointment was bitter upon his tongue. If he had been a bit quicker . . .

Arnaud turned slowly to face him, seeming unconcerned by Devlin's aborted lunge.

"I suppose this means that you are refusing my offer? You'd rather die than experience life as a free man again?"

"I will not agree to help you. I cannot," Devlin said.

Prince Arnaud rose. "But you can. Or rather you did. You already invited me into your mind once, when you performed your quaint ritual. Then my power was limited by the distance between us. Now, if you reenact the ritual in my presence, I could enter and take apart the Geas spell strand by strand until you were once again free."

Devlin shivered. The Geas spell was an unclean magic, but what Arnaud proposed was even worse. It was a sign of his perversion that he could speak so lightly of violating Devlin's soul.

"My answer is unchanged. I will not help you build an army of spellbound warriors."

He would not wish the hell of the Geas on any other

living being. Nor could he give such a weapon into the hands of Jorsk's enemies.

Prince Arnaud shook his head in mock sorrow. "I had hoped to spare you this," he said.

He gestured to the men holding Devlin, who once again secured Devlin in the heavy wooden chair. They bound him tightly, as if to make up for their earlier misjudgment, and Devlin felt his hands begin to tingle from lack of blood.

Arnaud walked around Devlin, checking the security of his bonds, then stood once more in front of him. "Still, your resistance does provide one pleasure. I look forward to the day that my men are as loyal to me as you are to your treacherous King."

"And I look forward to the day that Haakon claims your rotted soul," Devlin replied.

The nearest guard scowled at Devlin, but Arnaud did not react. He dismissed the guards, who closed the door behind them.

Devlin deliberately relaxed his muscles and slowed his breathing, bracing himself for what was to come. Surely Arnaud already realized that he could not be broken by torture. Another round of torments would do nothing to change his mind.

Arnaud stretched his right hand out and placed the palm of his hand on the center of Devlin's forehead. Devlin jerked his head to the side, but with his free hand Arnaud held his skull steady. His gaze caught and held Devlin's, who stared back, locked in a contest of wills.

The third finger of Devlin's left hand began to burn, and Devlin looked down to see that his ring was glowing. A warning that sorcery was being practiced. But if so, it was no magic that Devlin had ever seen before. There was no invocation of the Gods, no ritual offerings, none of the paraphernalia that Devlin associated with magic. Just the feeling of power in the air, his skin tingling as if he stood outside in a lightning storm.

Arnaud jerked Devlin's hair, and his gaze once again rose to meet the Prince's dark eyes. Arnaud stared at Devlin as if he could somehow see inside him, and Devlin fought the urge to close his own eyes in superstitious dread. The tingling of his hands had now spread to his legs as well, and he could feel the numbness rising through his body. He could hear no sound except the harsh rasping of his own breath, and even that grew fainter. He could no longer feel any part of his body. His head swam, and Devlin's sight grew dim until he could see only blackness. All sound had fled. He screamed, or rather he tried to scream, but there was only silence.

With dawning horror, the full extent of his predicament sank in. Arnaud had sent him to hell.

The first thing he became aware of was the slow in-and-out motion of his breath. He focused on the sound, clinging to this proof that he still lived. Then sensation began to return to his limbs, a strange warmth that burned as it awakened nerves that had fallen silent. With agonizing slowness his body once more became his own, and at last he was able to open his eyes.

He raised his head, fighting weakened muscles that did not want to obey and the nausea that rose within him. Exhaustion warred with a lingering terror as he wondered just what changes Arnaud and his sorceries had wrought.

"Your mage is better than I thought," Prince Arnaud observed. He was seated at the table, a large tome propped open by his elbow. The Prince appeared fatigued, and there were shadows under his eyes, but his gaze was still hungry as he stared at Devlin. He regarded Devlin the way another man might look at a rare jewel or a beautiful companion. As something that he had to possess at all costs.

Devlin licked his dry lips, but said nothing. He would not give Arnaud any information that could be used against him.

"Will you open your mind to me and rid yourself of this spell?" Arnaud asked.

"No," Devlin said instinctively. Then he smiled grimly as he realized what he had done. He had not hesitated for even a moment in giving his response. It had not been Devlin who had spoken. It had been the Geas. For all Arnaud's efforts, the Geas was still intact.

Arnaud nodded to himself, as if unsurprised by Devlin's answer.

"The spell is well guarded, but I will destroy those protections in time," he said. "Each day I will chip away at them until the day when your mind is as open to me as this book."

Devlin shivered involuntarily, earning him another of Arnaud's mocking smiles. Rising from his seat, the Prince spared Devlin a final glance before leaving the room.

A short time later two mercenaries came in and untied Devlin from the chair. Weakened by his confinement and whatever the Prince had done to him, Devlin's legs buckled and refused to take his weight. His gaolers had to drag him back to the room that had become his cell, where they dumped him on his bed.

Earlier he had thought to feign weakness, to trick his captors into letting down their guard. But this was no act. His arm muscles quivered and his legs ached as if he had been at hard labor for days. Whatever magic Arnaud practiced, it seemed the price was paid for out of his victim's flesh.

Devlin slept for a time, then roused himself long enough to eat when a meal was brought. Grimly he exercised each limb in turn, until his body was once more his own to command. His gaolers watched, but did not interfere. Only then did he allow himself to fall asleep for the night.

When he rose the next day, he expected to be summoned once again to face the Prince. But as the day advanced and no summons came, Devlin's anxiety turned to frustration. He was no nearer to escaping now than he had been on the first day of his captivity. And every day that he remained Arnaud's captive only brought him closer to the day that Arnaud would succeed in his goal.

Devlin hurled insults at his captors, but they refused to respond to his taunts. When the watch changed, he tried his tactics on the new guards but they proved equally unflappable. Veterans, by the look of them, and too afraid of Prince Arnaud to risk incurring his wrath.

The next day, the Prince sent for Devlin. This time he knew what to expect, but he still felt fear when the world disappeared and he fell into the black and soundless void. This time Arnaud allowed him to retain the sensations of the world around him, but that turned out to be no mercy. Within moments he felt the first wave of crushing power, squeezing the very bones within him. As the pressure grew he wondered dimly why he was still alive. He knew he could not endure a moment longer, and then the pressure increased.

It was past noon when Devlin opened his eyes. He did not know if his torment had indeed lasted hours or if it had taken him that long to recover.

It was small consolation to see that Arnaud, too, appeared worn, with grim lines around his mouth. This time the Prince did not boast of his powers, but merely ordered Devlin taken away.

The next morning Devlin's body ached with exhaustion. He craved sleep, but instead forced himself to rise from his bed and eat the meal that his guards had brought. He needed to keep up his strength if he were to have any chance of escaping. Slowly, as the day wore on, the unnatural exhaustion left him. He felt almost himself when the Prince's men finally came for him at dusk.

Once again he was taken to the Prince's room, and bound to a chair, then left to await Arnaud's arrival. Long minutes ticked by, ensuring that Devlin had plenty of time to think about what awaited him. But he was too disciplined to give in to his fears, and when the Prince arrived, he was able to greet him with at least the outward appearance of calm.

"Do you know what mind-sorcery is?" Prince Arnaud asked.

"It is an abomination."

The Prince smiled, as if Devlin had just complimented him. He stepped closer, catching Devlin's gaze in his. "It is a matter of *will*"—the Prince brushed his right hand over Devlin's forehead—"and power," he concluded, placing his right hand over Devlin's heart.

Devlin flinched, certain that the Prince was about to invoke the mind spell that would plunge him into torment. But instead Prince Arnaud took a step backward.

"Mages rely upon tricks. Ancient runes, magical objects, garbled spells passed down for so long that their meaning has been lost. Most of them have no understanding of the words they chant or the true origins of the powers that they are invoking."

"And yet these so-called incompetents invented a spell that you cannot break," Devlin said.

"No, the Geas spell was crafted by a true mindsorcerer. One who understood how to focus will and intent, and distilled that knowledge into a ritual even an unranked mage could invoke."

Devlin shrugged. He did not care how the spell had been crafted. What did it matter if it were mind-sorcery or mere magery? However the Geas spell had been designed, it worked. Far too well, sometimes.

"You know that the spell draws its power from your own strength? That the chains that bind you are forged by your own will?"

Devlin kept silent. Even if he wished to cooperate, there was nothing that he could reveal. Master Dreng himself did not understand the workings of the Geas, though he had memorized it well enough to cast it.

He wondered how long it would take Arnaud to realize that he should have kidnapped Master Dreng instead. If the Prince had access to the text of the spell, along with whatever records the mage's predecessors had left behind, he might well be able to re-create the spell. With or without Devlin's help.

It was chilling to think that all of his efforts might be for naught. But there was no time for despair, as the Prince placed his right hand on top of Devlin's head. Devlin closed his eyes, but the Prince was prepared for this trick, and he gouged his thumb into the corner of Devlin's left eye socket. Instinctively, Devlin's eyes flew open, and his gaze was caught and held by the Prince's glittering gaze.

Unlike the previous interrogation, he did not sink into unconsciousness. Instead, he felt a steadily growing pressure, battering away at his resolve. *I will not give in*, Devlin thought. *I am the Chosen One and I surrender to no man.* He clung to these thoughts, but the pressure increased, and he felt his concentration slipping.

Cold blue eyes stared into his own, daring him with their defiance, even as their owner trembled from the force of the mind battle. He admired the prisoner's courage, even as he regretted the necessity of destroying such a fine weapon. But regrets had no place on the path to power, so he cleared his mind, and focused his will.

Then the world tilted, and he was staring back into the Prince's dark eyes. Devlin shuddered as he realized that he had briefly shared the Prince's thoughts. In his horror he lost his concentration, and the Prince swiftly pressed home his advantage.

Unbidden, the image of Devlin's Choosing Ceremony came to mind, and once again he heard Brother Arni invoking the blessing of the Gods upon the one who would be their champion.

Devlin held a knife against his arm, ready to embrace his death, only to be thwarted by the power of the Geas.

King Olafur appeared, asking Devlin to be his general and to lead the fight against their enemies.

Then he was in the distant past, a young apprentice as he first beheld the sword that would shape his future.

He struggled to regain his focus and close off his mind, but the Prince ruthlessly brushed aside his feeble efforts. Faster and faster the visions came, images of his past flickered by, some too swiftly to discern. He ceased trying to control the flood of thoughts, and new faces began to appear, intermixed with his own memories. A regal woman wearing a triple crown, who stirred in him feelings of loathing. An old man, coughing up blood. A fine-boned racing horse, grazing in a paddock. A young peasant boy, screaming as he was dragged away by his elders.

A cup of dark red wine, overturned on an oaken table.

He did not know what the images meant. He could no longer tell which memories were his and which were Arnaud's. Where his mind began and ended. At last he gave himself up to the pull of the darkness. When he awoke, the Prince was gone.

Devlin's days fell into a pattern. One day would pass or two, while he regained his strength under the watchful eyes of his guards. And then the Prince would summon him and subject him to another sorcerous attack.

Each time Devlin resisted as long as he could, but in the end, the Prince always succeeded in prying a piece of his mind open. But for all his searching Arnaud did not find what he was seeking. Devlin's will remained unbroken, and it pleased him to witness Arnaud's steadily grow-ing fury.

The brutal invasions of Devlin's mind had one strange benefit. Each time Arnaud probed Devlin's memories, a portion of his own thoughts and memories leaked across the linkage. Usually Devlin was in too much agony to take conscious advantage of the connection; but long after his interrogation sessions had ended, he would turn over the hard-won scraps of knowledge in his mind.

Arnaud was worried. Time was his enemy, for mid-summer approached and he had yet to create his army of spellbound soldiers. The people of Jorsk had seemingly accepted their so-called protectors, but Arnaud was con-vinced that it was only a matter of time before a leader arose who could unite them in rebellion.

The Selvarat troops were stretched thin, which ex-plained the presence of the mercenaries under Arnaud's banner. Rather than sending for reinforcements, Arnaud had gambled that he could make each of his soldiers do the work of ten, strengthened by the relentless drive of the Geas spell.

It was a strangely complicated plan. At first he'd won-dered why Arnaud hadn't summoned reinforcements. Selvarat was a mighty empire, and with no one to oppose their landings they could easily bring in enough troops to crush any opposition.

Unless there was some reason that the troops were not available. Was there civil unrest in Selvarat? Had Olafur and the rest fallen for an empty bluff that the Selvarats had no means to back up?

Was there some reason why Prince Arnaud did not want more Selvarat troops under his command? Was he concealing the weakness of his position from his enemies? Or from his own countrymen? What had brought the imperial consort here to Jorsk in the first place? Surely he had power enough in Selvarat, as well as plenty of opportunity to indulge his perversions.

Or did his ambition stretch further? Did he seek to be ruler in truth rather than merely a consort to power? On the day that Thania died, Arnaud would be expected to go into seclusion, pushed aside as Thania's daughter by her first husband inherited the throne.

Knowing Arnaud as he did, Devlin could not imagine him stepping aside for anyone. Instead, the Prince might be using the Selvarat occupation of Jorsk to strengthen his political position at home.

Or he could have decided to carve out his own kingdom. That would explain the presence of the mercenaries, whose only loyalty would be to their paymaster. And it would explain Arnaud's obsession with crafting an army that would be unable to disobey him.

It was an interesting theory. If there was even the slightest truth to Devlin's speculations, then it might well be possible to drive a wedge between the Selvarat regulars and the mercenary auxiliaries. That is if anyone would believe Devlin.

But first he had to make his escape.

# Sixteen

DEVLIN'S ROUTINE WAS BROKEN, FOR THIS TIME the guards insisted on blindfolding him and tying his hands behind his back before they led him from his room. He wondered what the change meant. Were they moving him? Had Prince Arnaud decided upon another tactic? Had he finally given up on sorcery after the previous six attempts?

Or had it been seven? Devlin cast his mind back, but the days and his torments seemed to blur together. He had been Arnaud's unwilling guest for at least a fortnight, but had it been longer? How long ago had it been that Arnaud had ordered the execution of his cousin Karel?

Why couldn't he remember? Was this a sign that Arnaud's spells were finally taking effect? But as soon as the doubts occurred, Devlin ruthlessly pushed them aside. It did not matter how long he had been Arnaud's captive. What mattered was that Devlin was still his own man, still free from the Prince's control. Every day that Devlin managed to defy him was a victory, and he had to believe that each day brought him closer to the time when he would be free.

He held firmly to this resolve, even as his captors led him into the torture room and once again secured him to the chair. *I will be free*, Devlin chanted silently. *Arnaud will not win. He cannot.*

He heard footsteps approach, then with nimble fingers the Prince untied Devlin's blindfold.

"I have a treat for you," Arnaud announced, with a broad grin.

Devlin's muscles tensed. Anything that pleased the Prince boded no good for his prisoner.

"I thought you might be lonely, so I brought you a friend," Arnaud said. He stepped aside, giving Devlin the chance to see what lay behind him.

"By Kanjti's left ball," Devlin swore.

The chair had been moved so that it was directly before the long table, which gave him a clear view of the man who was bound to it. If Devlin's hands were free, he could have reached out and touched him. But instead he could only look helplessly as Stephen turned his head when he heard Devlin's voice.

He was naked, with his face covered in bruises, and there was a blood-soaked bandage on his right arm. A gag prevented him from speaking, but his eyes spoke eloquently enough. Stephen was terrified.

"You know what I want," Prince Arnaud said, standing beside Devlin. "You will not cooperate to save yourself, but what about your friend's life? Is your oath to Olafur worth more to you than a man who has saved your life at least twice?"

Devlin cursed under his breath. Of all the ill luck. How

had Stephen fallen into Arnaud's hands? He should have been safe back in Kingsholm by now.

"Your friend thought to rescue you," Arnaud said, answering Devlin's unspoken question. "He fell into my trap instead."

Arnaud circled the table, so that he stood on the far side. With one hand he squeezed Stephen's bandaged arm. Stephen's body jerked, but the Prince's attention was entirely on Devlin.

"An interesting dilemma before you. Olafur betrayed you, but Stephen has proven loyal beyond measure. He is of Jorsk, one of those innocents whom you are bound to protect. Which way will the scales tip in your mind?"

Despair rose within him. From the moment he had seen Stephen, Devlin had known what the Prince intended. His mind cast about desperately, but he could think of no way to stop what was to come. He could not give in to the Prince's wishes, yet neither could he let Stephen be tortured.

Devlin's body strained against the bonds that held him to his chair.

"You said it yourself. He is innocent," Devlin said, though he knew it was folly to try and reason with this madman. Still, he had to try. "Nothing you do to me, to him, or to a hundred innocents will change my mind. I cannot yield to you."

Arnaud rubbed his chin thoughtfully. "A hundred innocents. Hmm. Perhaps that might be arranged. There are children enough in the villages around here . . ." His voice trailed off suggestively.

Rage rose within Devlin. His hatred for Arnaud was dwarfed by his anger at those who had placed Devlin in such an impossible position. King Olafur, who had betrayed him. Master Dreng, who had cast the damning spell. The Gods themselves, who had set Devlin's feet on the path that led to him becoming Chosen One.

No man should have to endure this. No man should be a slave to another's will. The Geas was the unyielding anvil upon which Devlin's soul would be broken.

"We can save such treats for another day," Arnaud said. "For now, I believe your friend has something to say."

Arnaud motioned to one of the guards, who untied the gag from Stephen's mouth.

"Sorry," Stephen said.

Was Stephen apologizing for having found himself in this predicament? For placing Devlin in an untenable position?

It did not matter. Stephen's regrets were nothing compared to his own. Devlin regretted every step that had led him to Jorsk, and every step he had taken since then, all leading him to this cursed place.

"Don't give in, no matter what he does," Stephen urged him. "Remember, you are the Chosen One. I believe in you."

His absurd faith would be the death of him.

"Believe in yourself," Devlin said, his voice roughened by anger and grief.

"Touching. Though I have found such faith is fleeting in the face of true suffering." The Prince picked up a slender knife and held it up so that Stephen had a good view of it. It was a skinning knife, sharp and flexible. "Remember, you can end this at any time," Arnaud said.

"I will kill you slowly," Devlin said. Bravado was all that he had left. "You and all those here who bear witness to this evil. When I am done with you, even Haakon will refuse to take your souls."

"Devlin always keeps his promises," Stephen informed Arnaud. He attempted a cocky grin, but his smile soon faded.

The first cut was along Stephen's left arm, a shallow cut that took long moments before it began to bleed. Arnaud then gave him a matching cut on his left arm, severing the bandage that had covered his wounded forearm.

Sweat sprang up on Stephen's brow, and he began to pant shallowly.

The next series of cuts was on his chest. They were deeper, and when he was finished Arnaud began to peel back Stephen's skin.

Stephen moaned.

Devlin struggled against his bonds. For the first time in years he prayed to the Gods. *I will do anything, anything you ask of me,* Devlin promised. *I will embrace the destiny that you laid out for me as Chosen One if you but spare Stephen from this torment.*

He prayed desperately, invoking Kanjti, who had been his patron when Devlin swore the oath as Chosen One. But the Gods had turned their faces from him. They cared not for mortal woes, nor for the man whose breaths now came in half-choked sobs as he writhed under the knife.

Devlin continued straining against his bonds, jerking his arms and legs. "Stop this," he said.

The Prince looked up from his work. "Have you changed your mind? Will you swear to give me access to your soul?"

Devlin opened his mouth, praying for the strength to lie, but no words would come out.

"I thought not," Arnaud said. "Think hard on what you value most. I can keep your friend alive for many days like this."

"Please," Stephen said.

Devlin forced himself to look at his friend.

"Please," Stephen repeated.

Was he asking for Devlin to save him? Stephen had always cast Devlin in the light of a mythical hero, but now he was paying for his naïveté.

Devlin should never have allowed him to become his friend. Never should have let another close to him. Hadn't he learned his lesson with his family? Devlin was tainted, and he brought death to those who loved him.

The Prince set down the skinning knife, and picked up another blade. He pressed it down over Stephen's right hand, and there was a sharp crack before Stephen screamed.

Arnaud held up Stephen's severed thumb. "He won't be a minstrel when I am through with him. Yet say the words and you can still save his life."

Stephen's face crumpled and he began sobbing uncontrollably.

Arnaud dropped the severed thumb on the table, as if it were so much trash, then walked around so he stood on the other side. The side closest to Devlin.

Arnaud picked up Stephen's left hand.

Devlin could endure no more. Arnaud had to be stopped. At any cost. He released the hold on his emotions, letting all of his rage and anger well up within him. Then he surrendered his will to the mindless urgings of the Geas.

The Geas channeled Devlin's rage into strength beyond that of mortal man. One foot broke free and, still bound to the chair, Devlin managed to half stand.

Arnaud's back was to him as Devlin lurched forward.

A guard called out a warning, but it was too late, as Devlin rammed into Arnaud. They fell to the floor with an ominous crack.

Arnaud lay still beneath him, crushed beneath Devlin's weight and that of the heavy chair, which weighed at least as much as a man. If luck were with him, the Prince had fallen upon his knife.

Devlin struggled and managed to pull his right arm free. He found Arnaud's neck and began to squeeze. His body jerked as the guards tried to move the heavy chair. He could feel Arnaud's pulse beneath his fingers as he tightened his grip. Nothing else mattered, not the shouts of the guards, nor the sharp pain that stabbed at Devlin's side. All his will was focused on crushing the life out of his tormentor.

But even as the Prince's pulse slowed, his prize was ripped from his grasp, and a sharp blow to Devlin's head sent him reeling into the darkness.

He awoke to the sound of rain falling upon the roof. It was a comforting sound, as it had been since his childhood, when he and his brother would listen to the falling rain from the safety of their bedchamber up under the eaves. He clung to the memory, and to the image of falling rain, feeling strangely reluctant to wake.

But when he opened his eyes, he found himself once again in a horror chamber.

It had not been rain that he heard, but rather the

sound of Stephen's blood dripping onto the floor. Devlin watched the slowly falling drops for a moment, mesmerized by the widening stain. Then he lifted his eyes.

Stephen was dead. His eyes stared sightlessly at the ceiling, and his chest was still. No more would he look to Devlin for his salvation.

It was a mercy of sorts. Devlin was too numb to feel anything. Not anger, not despair, just an overwhelming numbness.

"You killed your friend."

Devlin turned, and saw that the Prince was seated on a chair a short distance to his left. His robe was dusty and blood-speckled, and there were shadows that would soon blossom into bruises around his throat; but he was still very much alive and unharmed.

Devlin had failed.

"Your foolish charge jarred my hand. Instead of merely cutting your friend, I plunged the knife into his chest. He died before the healer could be summoned."

"He is free from you, at least," Devlin said. It was a small comfort.

He looked over at Stephen, and for a moment his vision swam and he saw two figures lying there, one imposed over the other. He blinked, and then when he looked again, the image had solidified.

The blow to his head must have addled his wits. Devlin's right arm began to throb and as he looked down he saw that his wrist was bent at an unnatural angle. He tried to move his fingers, but the swollen digits no longer obeyed.

"I warned you what would happen," Arnaud said. "That arm is only the beginning of your punishment. I wanted to save the rest for when you would be aware of what was happening to you."

He had gambled, and he had lost. Arnaud was still alive, and worse, Devlin had not been able to provoke the guards into giving him a mortal wound. He would spend his final days as Arnaud's prisoner, a helpless cripple unable to influence his fate.

Only death would save him now, but he knew better than to expect that he would be granted that mercy. Not until Arnaud finally unlocked the secrets of the Geas spell.

Until now, he had clung to the belief that somehow he would find a way out of this trap. If he was strong, if he kept his wits about him, if he kept himself ready to act when the opportunity presented itself. But now, with Stephen's death, Devlin realized that he had been fooling himself. There would be no miraculous escape. No chance to twist the ugliest of defeats into something that resembled victory.

Despair washed over him.

The door opened, and the female ensign entered, bearing a long slender object wrapped in leather. Prince Arnaud rose to his feet and accepted the object from her.

Devlin could feel it calling to him, tugging at him. Even before Arnaud unwrapped his prize, Devlin knew what it was. The Sword of Light. The weapon of the Chosen Ones, said to have been crafted by a descendant of the Forge God Egil. For centuries, it had been borne by men and women whose names were legends to the people of Jorsk.

The sword that had been lost during the Siege of Ynnis, when Devlin's people had been conquered by the armies of

Jorsk. But not before they had killed the Chosen One Saemund, and his sword had vanished. Lost for forty years, its power had lain dormant until the day that Devlin had first beheld it. Since then his destiny had been tied to the sword. Unwittingly it had led him to his doom, shaping the path that forced him to become Chosen One and later leading him back to Duncaer to reclaim this Jorskian treasure.

At great cost Devlin had brought the sword back to Kingsholm. And now, like himself, it had been handed over to the Kingdom's greatest enemy.

With this sword King Olafur could have named a new Chosen One, found a figure to rally his people in their own defense. But the King had relinquished this advantage, just as he had discarded Devlin himself. He had thrown away the very things that might have preserved his throne.

"It knows you," Arnaud said.

Indeed, the stone set in the pommel of the sword now glowed with a dull red fire, matching the glow within Devlin's ring. The fingers of Devlin's left hand scrabbled helplessly at the arm of his chair. Legend held that the sword would come when the Chosen One called it, but though Devlin bent all his will upon summoning the sword, it moved not a fraction.

Stephen had been wrong. He would have to tell him—

Grief rose up within him, as he recalled himself to the present. There would be no chance to gently chide his friend for believing in the most improbable of tales. No chance to remind him that Devlin was living flesh and not one of his pretty ballads brought to life.

No chance to make amends.

"Since you have proven immune to all other forms of persuasion, there is one more spell to try," Arnaud said. "It may leave you witless, but in your situation that would be a kindness."

Arnaud removed the sword from its scabbard and laid it flat on the end of the table, at the foot of Stephen's lifeless body. Dipping his fingers in Stephen's blood, he wrote runes along the length of the sword and upon the pommel. Then he turned it over and did the same on the other side. Coated with Stephen's blood, the glowing jewel gave off a ghastly light, pulsing like a beating heart.

Arnaud dipped his fingers in the pooled blood a final time, and then came over to Devlin. Devlin spat on the floor, but Arnaud ignored him as he marked Devlin's forehead and both cheeks. Lastly, he ripped open Devlin's tunic, and applied a final rune over his heart.

The two guards who had stood passively at attention while Stephen's flesh was cut from his body now looked distinctly uneasy. Their revulsion was matched by Devlin's own. Blood magic was a custom of his own people, but the ritual bloodletting was tied to the remembrance of the dead and sacrifices of atonement. And then it was only your own blood that you shed. Using the blood of another to fuel your ritual was an unthinkable abomination.

Returning to the sword, Arnaud placed both of his hands over the glowing stone. He closed his eyes and began a chant in his foreign tongue.

Devlin's head felt as if it were being squeezed in a vise. As Arnaud pressed down on the sword, it felt as if the weight of a thousand men bore down upon Devlin's mind. Arnaud's arms trembled with the strain and his voice shook, but still he continued his obscene rite. The pressure grew within Devlin until he knew that something must give way.

The stone in the sword brightened, its dull red glow giving way to bright red, then yellow, and finally a white light. The light filled the room, blinding Devlin until he could see nothing else.

His senses fled him. He no longer knew who he was or what was happening around him. All of his thoughts were consumed by the brilliant light that devoured him from within.

He heard a clap of thunder, then was plunged into darkness.

Sight returned to him, slowly, as did the knowledge of who he was. He was Devlin of Duncaer, the Chosen One. He blinked, and the room swam into focus around him.

Arnaud lay slumped over the table, his eyes wide and unseeing. The two guards had crumpled to the floor, their weapons beside them.

The spell must have gone wrong, somehow. Arnaud was dead or unconscious, while Devlin was still breathing. And in possession of his wits.

He would never get a better chance for escape. He flexed his hands, wondering if it was possible to free himself. His left hand was still trapped but his right . . .

He looked down. His right arm, which had been crushed, was now whole, and the three fingers of his hand were wrapped around the hilt of the Sword of Light. Burned clean of its obscene markings, the steel blade shone, while the stone in its pommel glowed, pulsing in time with his heartbeat.

It was the work of an instant to free himself. Crossing over to the fallen guards, he slit their throats in turn, ensuring they would raise no alarm.

Then he moved back to the Prince. He dragged Arnaud off the table and secured him to the wooden torture chair, using the same ropes that had once held him. He tore a strip off his tunic and used it to fashion a gag.

The sentries outside were apparently well used to the sound of a man screaming in agony, but should they hear their master's voice, they might feel compelled to investigate.

Returning to the table, Devlin examined the body of his friend. Stephen's face was oddly peaceful, showing no sign of his final torment.

Faint sounds alerted him that Arnaud had awakened.

Devlin turned to face his captive. A wise man would use the opportunity to flee. At any moment one of Arnaud's minions could step through the door and Devlin would be taken prisoner again. Logic urged him to kill the Prince swiftly and make his escape. It was his duty as the Chosen One.

He set aside the Sword of Light and picked up the skinning knife, which was still stained with Stephen's blood. Then he turned back to face his captive.

Arnaud blinked as Devlin stroked the side of the Prince's face, deliberating echoing how the Prince had treated him.

"I promised to kill you slowly," Devlin said. "And as Stephen told you, I always keep my promises."

# Seventeen

SOLVEIG STROLLED THROUGH THE MERCHANTS'
quarter, as she had done each third day since the bazaar
had reopened with the spring. Upon reaching the great
square with its myriad of small booths, she wandered as if
aimlessly, pausing first at a booth that sold gaily colored
necklaces, then allowing her eye to be caught by a display
of hair ornaments and elaborately carved wooden combs.
She lingered over a comb-and-brush set, made of rare
woods from the islands and inlaid with pearl, before re-
gretfully shaking her head and moving on.

At the edge of her vision she saw a woman abruptly
drop the belt she had been holding, then hurry to catch
up with her. It was an insult to be followed by such a one.
Then again, perhaps she should feel relieved that they
considered her so little a threat that they assigned someone so inept to watch her.

If that was her only watcher. For all she knew the
woman could be a diversion, while a more skillful comrade was assigned the task of watching every movement

she made and reporting the names of all those with whom she conversed.

These days there was no privacy to be had. Living in Kingsholm was like living in a place with no walls. Every word said, every movement made was duly noted and reported. Even some of King Olafur's most vocal supporters had developed nervous tics and the habit of looking around carefully before beginning a conversation. And it was little wonder. No one could be trusted. Anyone could be an informer. These days no proof was needed. A few whispered words of accusation, and the accused would find themselves confined to their apartments under guard. If they were lucky.

Others disappeared for a few days, to the dungeons that all knew were below the palace but no one spoke of aloud. When one of these unfortunates reappeared, he or she was suitably chastened.

Some disappeared and were never seen again.

Like Captain Drakken. Most believed she had been executed for treason, killed in secret before those loyal to her had a chance to react. Embeth was now acting Captain of the Guard, and she refused to answer any questions about her predecessor.

Solveig knew that Drakken had escaped, though it was hardly news that she could share. Drakken, her brother Stephen, and the others had last been seen at a stable just outside Kingsholm. Since then weeks had passed, and there had been no word.

She did not even know what she hoped for. If they rescued Devlin, what would he do? Would he raise a rebellion in the east? Or would he return to Kingsholm and confront the cowardly King who had betrayed them all?

Was it fair to place all of their hopes of deliverance upon the shoulders of a single man? Devlin had courage aplenty, along with a strong sense of justice. But he was also a man betrayed. Even if Devlin were freed, he might well decide to abandon Jorsk to its fate, just as the King had abandoned him.

And if he did, she would not blame him. She, at least, remembered that Devlin was more than the title of Chosen One, more than the reluctant hero they had forced him to be. He was also a man, one entitled to make his own path, wherever that might lead. She admired Devlin, but she would not wish to trade places with him.

She stopped for a moment to watch a juggler, who balanced precariously on stilts while tossing a half dozen brightly colored balls in the air. Children squealed in glee as one of the balls turned into a white bird that flew up into the air. Each ball in turn was transformed, until the final bird appeared, circling around him thrice before flying off.

Solveig joined the applause and as he doffed his hat she tossed two coppers in it.

"I had not thought such entertainment to your taste."

Solveig turned and saw that Councilor Arnulf had come to stand beside her while she had been absorbed in the juggler's performance.

"I admire all skilled artists," Solveig said. She turned to walk away, and Arnulf fell into step beside her.

Now this was an interesting development. The councilor was a pillar of the conservative faction of the court, well-known as King Olafur's man. He was only of the minor nobility, but his bloodline could be traced to the earliest days of the Kingdom. And his family holdings were west of the Kalla River, in the heartland of Jorsk that had yet to be threatened by the invaders.

Arnulf had opposed Devlin at every turn of the council, calling the Chosen One brash and impetuous. He had voted against allowing Devlin to send troops to defend the borderlands, insisting that they be kept in the garrisons, ready to defend the heart of the Kingdom. Of all people, she had expected Arnulf would be pleased with the status quo. Instead, he had seemed increasingly unhappy and distracted.

"What brings you to the market this day?" she asked.

"This and that," Arnulf said. "And yourself?"

"The Princess's birthday approaches and I must find a suitable gift," Solveig said. "As my father's representative in Kingsholm, it is up to me to find a gift worthy of the people of Esker."

Arnulf frowned. "Yes, of course. With all the, err, changes, I had nearly forgotten."

Now this was interesting. A veteran courtier like Arnulf should not have forgotten such an important occasion. The Princess's birthday was an opportunity to curry favor with the King. And with Ragenilda seemingly destined to be the wife of a Selvarat prince, any slight to her would be seen as a slight to their new masters.

"If you would be so kind, I would appreciate your advice on a gift I was considering," Solveig said, pitching her voice loudly enough to be heard by their watchers.

"I am at your service," Arnulf said. He extended his arm, and she placed her hand upon it. She guided him back to the cart where she had seen the brush-and-comb set.

Arnulf picked up the brush in his hand and turned it

over consideringly, tracing the pearl inlay with the tip of one finger. "My daughters would have liked such a thing. When they were younger," he said softly.

"And how are your daughters these days?" she asked, her voice equally low.

"I had word from Kallarne the other day. Lynnheid's troops returned to the garrison, but she was not with them," he said. He glanced around, before handing the brush to her. "She, along with a number of the other officers, was asked to remain behind to advise the Selvarat forces."

"I see," Solveig said.

So Junior Troop Captain Lynnheid Arnulfsdatter was a hostage. She was not the first that Solveig had heard of. Major Mikkelson had not returned with his troops, and there had been no word from him. Others of his key staff had failed to return as well. Solveig had mentioned their absence in passing to Marshal Olvarrson, who had explained that he had detached a small number of officers who would be advising their new allies.

Most of the court seemed to accept his explanation or knew better than to question it. No one mentioned the obvious. The officers chosen to stay behind had been selected not for their rank or knowledge but because of their bloodlines. Indeed the officer corps of the Royal Army was drawn from the noble families. Those who had no prospect of inheriting great wealth or noble titles, but who were nonetheless family. Which made them ideal hostages to ensure the compliance of their noble kin.

Like Lynnheid, Arnulf's youngest daughter.

"You must be proud of your daughter," Solveig said. "I am certain the Selvarats will value her advice."

Arnulf shook his head. "She is a child."

"She is a junior captain of troops," Selvarat countered. It was the next rank above an ensign, meaning that she had at least forty soldiers under her command. True, like most officers in the army she no doubt owed her position to her father's rank rather than her own skill, but that did not change her responsibilities. It was too late for her father to protect her.

"If you could speak to the ambassador, explain to him that Lynnheid is of more value at home, I would be in your debt."

"Have you pled your case to the count yourself?"

"He refused to grant me a private audience," Arnulf confessed. "But he will listen to you."

Solveig spread her hands. "I think you overestimate my influence with Count Magaharan," she said. Picking up the brush and comb, she gestured for the stall owner, who had been attending to other customers while they conversed.

"A silver latt, you said?"

"Three," the woman replied, with a smile, ready to bargain.

"They are fine but—" Solveig began.

"Done," Arnulf said. He pulled his purse from out of his belt and rooted through it till he found three silver latts, which he pressed into the hand of the merchant, who blinked with astonishment before closing her fist tightly around the coins.

The merchant wrapped the brush and comb set carefully in a scrap of velvet before placing them inside a carved wooden case. She tried to give the case to Arnulf but he waved his hand, so the trader gave it to Solveig instead.

As they moved away from the trader, Solveig chided Arnulf. "I cannot accept this. And what were you thinking to pay her so much?"

"They are yours," Arnulf said. "A token of my friendship."

So it was a bribe. A trifle clumsily done, but she could no longer doubt that he was genuinely concerned for his daughter's safety.

"I can make you no promises," Solveig said. She understood Arnulf's fear, but there was more at stake here than the life of one junior troop captain.

"Secure Lynnheid's release and you will have my gratitude—which is a thing worth having. Many in the old court owe me favors, and you may find yourself in need of such friends in the coming days," Arnulf said.

A veiled threat wrapped inside a promise. Now that was the courtier whom she had come to know.

As chance would have it, the very next day Solveig was invited to a private dinner with Count Magaharan. As ambassador the Count had a full suite of apartments within the royal palace, but he also maintained a separate residence in the city. It was here that he hosted lavish entertainments, and it was also here that he retired when he wished to be discreet. Some claimed that he maintained a mistress within, but it was more likely that he used the residence when he had matters to discuss away from the prying eyes and ears of the palace.

In the two years since she had been at the court, Solveig had cultivated a friendship with the ambassador. He had seemed to enjoy her company, or perhaps he merely enjoyed the pleasure of conversing with someone who spoke his native tongue. She had dined in private with him on several occasions, but this was the first such invitation she had received since the announcement of the so-called protectorate.

She dressed for the dinner with great care, choosing a dark blue silk gown that flattered her still-youthful figure. By contrast the only jewelry she wore was a gold pendant engraved with the seal of her father's house. Magaharan was intelligent enough to read her message. She did not need jewels to proclaim her wealth, for she was the next Baroness of Esker.

When she arrived, a servant led her to a garden courtyard within the residence, where a table for two had been laid. Magaharan handed her a glass of pale yellow wine from his homeland, and then they took a short stroll among the flowers.

She could play court games as well as anyone. Solveig admired the blossoms, including the rare white snowflower from Selvarat, and inquired whether he had brought the delicate plant from Selvarat or if he had grown it from seed. Over dinner they discussed the difference in climates between the two lands, and whether it would be possible to have a water garden in Selvarat, as was commonly done in the south lands of Jorsk. Solveig opined that it could be done, perhaps if the garden was protected during the winter by glass, while Magaharan demurred.

It was all very civil. But there seemed no reason for him to have summoned her, unless Magaharan's purpose was merely to call attention to the fact that he and Solveig had enjoyed a private dinner together. That would raise her standing in the court, and ensure that Councilor Arnulf wasn't the only one who would be begging her for favors. But she could see no reason why Count Magaharan would grant her such a boon, unless he was expecting something of equal value in return.

So far he had granted her few signs of favor. She had repeatedly pressed Magaharan for news of her mother and her sister Madrene; but each time he had politely brushed aside her requests, saying that as a new bride Madrene was no doubt occupied in learning the intricacies of her role and making the acquaintance of her husband's family. He assured her that in time Madrene would resume her correspondence and that her mother, the Lady Gemma, would return home in due course.

Solveig had taken the hint and stopped asking questions. When a brief letter from Madrene had arrived, she had made a point to mention it to the ambassador, and to tell him how Madrene had praised her new husband. She had not mentioned that Madrene had used the code phrases that indicated she was under duress and that her mail was being read.

Even the letters from her father were becoming more infrequent. She suspected that at least half of them were being intercepted before they reached her. Not that it mattered. The tone of them was the same. Lord Brynjolf, Baron of Esker, commended his daughter for her sense of duty but lamented her long absence from her own people. He urged her to return to her home.

Her father knew it was not safe for her in Kingsholm. No one here was safe. Solveig had her bags packed, and a steady horse stabled at an inn by the western gate, just in case she had to flee.

But if news came, it would come here first to Kingsholm. And so here she would stay, as long as she could.

Occupied by her thoughts, she was surprised to look down and see that the servants had cleared away the plate with her untouched dessert, leaving behind a cup of sweetened tea in the Selvarat style.

"Is there something on your mind?" Count Magaharan asked.

"It is a small matter, a trifle that I hardly feel is worth your time," she said, letting her voice trail off into silence.

"Please, whatever it is you must share it."

Solveig took a sip of her tea. As a rule she disliked sweetened drinks, but she made sure to smile as if in pleasure before setting the cup down. "I met Councilor Arnulf the other day in the market. He seemed quite anxious about his daughter, who is advising your forces in the east. I told him that he should be proud that his daughter is serving such a valuable role, but he seemed to think that she would be of more use to him back here." Solveig shrugged delicately. "Perhaps he has a marriage in mind for her, or perhaps it is just the fondness of an old man for his youngest daughter."

Magaharan was silent for a long moment, apparently in contemplation. "I suppose I could make inquiries," he said.

"If there is anything you can do, I would be in your debt," she said.

"And Arnulf would be in yours," he said with a thin smile.

"Precisely." She returned the smile with one of her

own. It was a pleasure to converse with one who knew how the games of court were played.

"Your friends have changed," Magaharan observed. "Arnulf is a member of the King's faction in the court, is he not? While not so long ago you had backed the Chosen One and his radical friends."

Magaharan was not the only one who wondered about her seeming change of heart.

"Esker needs a strong ally in the court. Devlin had potential. He rose from nothing to General of the Royal Army. There was power to be had, but he did not know how to use it. He squandered his political capital, then disappeared on another of his strange quests, taking my brother with him."

Her tone was angry, and she knew Magaharan would assume that she blamed Devlin for the loss of her brother, who was widely presumed to have been killed by the same thieves who had taken Devlin's life.

"In times of trouble, it is good to have powerful friends," Magaharan said. "Just as your King has seen the advantage of our alliance."

"The protectorate is a bold move. Prince Arnaud has secured the east, but there may be opportunities to extend your influence," Solveig said.

Count Magaharan raised one eyebrow.

"It has been said that Esker is the key to holding the northwestern lands. My father has not used his influence, but then again, he was never much for the court. I, on the other hand, can see quite clearly the advantages to be gained by forming a personal alliance."

"Your sister Madrene—"

"My sister is beautiful, but she is not my father's heir,"

Solveig said sharply. "Nor does she have the trust of our people. But I am known there—I have ridden border patrols, supervised the tax collection, and passed judgment in my father's name. When the time comes, may it be long hence, the people will accept me as their Baroness. And my husband."

"You have given this matter much thought," Count Magaharan said.

"An idle fancy, only, and hardly worth the breath to mention," Solveig said. The seed had been planted; now it was time to change the subject lest she appear too eager. "Come now, tell me what other news you have to share. Have you decided if your horse will run in the summer races? I hear that Lady Vendela's son has trained a fine colt, who he claims will astonish us all."

Count Magaharan followed her lead, and they spoke of trifles until it was time for her to take her leave.

She knew she had given him much to think about. Only the most foolish believed that the Selvarats would be satisfied with ruling the eastern provinces under their so-called protectorate. It seemed inevitable that once they consolidated their power, they would seek to extend their rule to the rest of Jorsk.

But wars could be drawn-out and costly affairs. If the northwestern provinces could be made to see the advantage of a Selvarat alliance, say if one of their leaders was married to a Selvarat noble, then the central kingdom would be surrounded on both sides. King Olafur would have no choice but to surrender.

Not that she had any intention of going through with such a match. But she had dangled the idea in front of the ambassador. It would be interesting to see how quickly he would rise to the bait. If he were anxious for the alliance, it would reveal much about the state of the Selvarat plans.

She knew it was a dangerous game she played. She should be safe as long as everyone believed that she was allied to the Selvarat cause. But the moment anyone saw through the deception, she would have to flee for her life. It was just a question of how long she could play the game and whether Devlin would return before she was forced to reveal her true allegiances.

And if Devlin did not return? If, after all, the rescuers arrived too late to save him? She prayed each night for his safety and that of her brother, but if her worst fears came true, then it would be up to her to do what must be done. She would find the strength within herself to do whatever was necessary, to secure the future of her people.

# Eighteen

As Devlin fed the fire a slender pine branch, it hissed and snapped before settling down to a sullen burn. It was a small fire, not large enough to provide any true warmth: But it was familiar, and comforting in its way. Fire was an old friend. Hearth fire, forge fire, or one of the countless campfires from his travels, they were all part of a thread that tied him to his past.

He held his hands out to the blaze. He had scrubbed them in a stream earlier, but they were still stained red with the Prince's blood. Arnaud had taken a long time to die. He'd held on to his defiance far longer than Devlin expected, but in the end he'd broken. He'd spilled his secrets, until Devlin could no longer think of any more questions to ask. Even then he did not stop. Consumed by his need for vengeance, Devlin had continued until each wound the Prince had inflicted upon Stephen had been repaid a dozen times over.

It should not have been an easy thing, to torture a man to death, but Devlin had done it without hesitation. A dark part of him had enjoyed seeing the Prince suffer, victim of the same torments he had so callously inflicted on others.

Some would call it justice; Devlin knew better. It had not been about justice. It had been revenge. A just man would have executed Arnaud for his crimes, leaving the judgment of his soul to Haakon, Lord of the Dread Realm. But Devlin had no faith in the Gods. He had executed his own judgment, ensuring that Arnaud's final hours were spent in agony and humiliation.

Devlin did not regret what he had done, but he wondered what he had become that he was capable of such a deed.

Two years ago a simple metalsmith, half-crazed with grief, had walked into Kingsholm and presented himself as candidate for Chosen One. A year later, after exposing the traitor Gerhard, the same man had been named General of the Royal Army and a trusted advisor to the King.

Now, he did not know who he was. Was he still the Chosen One? The King he had sworn to serve had betrayed him, handing him over to their enemies. He had forsaken any claim he might have on Devlin's loyalties. What honor was there to be found in obeying oaths given to one who had proven faithless?

Devlin leaned back against a tree, tucking his hands under the borrowed cloak. He stretched his legs out before him, wincing as his feet protested their too small boots.

After he had killed Arnaud, he had stripped the bodies of the Prince and the two guards, taking whatever he could use. He had ill-fitting boots, a slightly better fitting cloak, three daggers, and a pouch containing a generous handful of coins along with flint and steel.

And, of course, the Sword of Light. It was quiet, but earlier it had blazed with white fire as he had struck down the soldier who'd had the ill fortune to come across Devlin as he was making his escape. He'd expected to have to battle his way free, but luck had been with him. There'd been only one witness to his hasty departure, and Devlin had hidden his body where it would not soon be found.

By now someone among the Prince's followers would have summoned the courage to interrupt their lord at his sport and discovered his mutilated corpse. Devlin had a head start, but his advantage would not last. By dawn the woods might well be crawling with soldiers summoned from the nearby encampment.

By dawn he would have to have a plan. And a destination.

He could hunt for food, though that would slow him down. Or he could venture out of hiding and purchase food from a farmstead or village, weighing speed against the risk of discovery.

He had no maps, but he knew he was in Korinth, near the border with Rosmaar. These lands were held by the occupying troops, who controlled the Great Southern Road and all the territories that lay to the east. His pursuers would expect him to head west, to the safety of Rosmaar and of lands still controlled by Jorsk. They would concentrate their patrols along that border, fearful that Devlin would return to Kingsholm and rally an army against the invaders. They would be looking for a legend, a champion on horseback, making all haste to return to his duties.

They would not expect him to head south. He had traveled on foot before, and he knew how to set aside hunger, when needs must. A solitary traveler might well slip past their patrols. Even if he had to walk the entire way, he could be in Duncaer before the harvest.

It was up to Devlin to choose. It had taken him some time to realize that he had choices, once again. It was not until he had reached the relative safety of the forest and set camp for the night that he understood what he was missing. For two years the Geas had been a familiar presence in his mind. At times it slumbered, other times it called to him, urging him onward, letting him think of nothing but his duty and his oaths to his King.

Arnaud's final spell must have destroyed the Geas. Rather than mastering the spell, he had unleashed magics that rendered him unconscious, and Devlin had taken him prisoner before he had a chance to recover.

Now Devlin was free. Not simply free from his captor, but free for the first time in two years. He was once again a man, able to choose his own fate.

Devlin had served the people of Jorsk to the very limits of human endurance and beyond. He had battled monsters for them, brought justice to evildoers, and foiled a planned invasion. His maimed right hand bore testament to the duel which he had fought to expose Duke Gerhard as a traitor. Time and again Devlin had shed his blood for these people.

He owed them nothing. He could walk away and return to his homeland, where he had kin who would welcome him back. Not as the Chosen One but simply as a friend. He could no longer practice metalcraft, but he could still teach others. Or if his guild refused him, then surely he could find some work to turn his hand to. Honest work, which did not leave a bitter taste in his mouth or an emptiness in his soul.

There was nothing holding him in Jorsk. No reason to stay.

But there was one who would never understand why Devlin had resigned his post as Chosen One.

Stephen would expect better from him. Stephen, who even now, could be hunting for his friend.

After ripping out the Prince's heart, Devlin had crouched over Arnaud's body, watching as the life faded from him. Only when he was certain that Arnaud was truly dead had he risen. And then he had glimpsed the table where Stephen's body lay.

But it was not Stephen who lay there. The murdered youth bore a passing resemblance to Stephen, but his hair was blond instead of light brown, and what skin could be seen was the weathered tan of a farmer who worked bareback in the fields.

Somehow the Prince had enchanted him to resemble Stephen. He had used his knowledge of the minstrel, drawn from Devlin's own mind, to shape his form and his speech. Devlin had seen what he had expected to see and heard what he had expected to hear. Only with the Prince's death was the enchantment broken.

Robbed of his semblance, his voice, and even his ability to speak his own final words, the nameless youth had died. Devlin had closed his sightless eyes and covered him with the Prince's own robe, as a sign of respect. He could do no more. He doubted the Prince's servants would think to give the boy a decent burial. And somewhere a peasant family waited anxiously for a son who would never return.

Arnaud had been mad for power and heedless of the damage he inflicted upon others in his quest. Though these provinces had been occupied only a few short months, it was likely that the nameless youth was not the first victim of the Prince's madness. Devlin had come to know the people of this region last year, when he had traveled through Korinth. Downtrodden under an unjust lord and suffering from the so-called coastal raiders, at first they had appeared defeated. Sheep, waiting placidly for their slaughter.

Then he had met Magnilda, who had murdered a tax collector in a misguided attempt to protect her village. And her father, Magnus the village speaker, who had confessed to the deed and taken upon himself the death sentence that the law required. Magnus had been a brave man, and his daughter was equally brave, if hot-tempered.

He wondered what had happened to Magnilda and the village she now led. Had they accepted their new masters, uncaring whether they swore allegiance to an empress or a king? Or had they resisted the invaders, using the skills that Devlin had tried to teach them? How had they fared under Arnaud's rule? What would happen to them as the Selvarats brought in reinforcements and tightened their grip upon their newest possession? Would they be dispossessed from their lands as Arnaud had hinted?

The murdered youth could well be one of Magnilda's folk. It was a sobering thought, and Devlin regretted once again that he had no name to give the boy, no means to tell his kin of his fate. Arnaud might have wielded the blade, but Devlin felt responsible for his death.

Once he had known what it was to be an honorable man. Then his life had been simple. Duty to family and kin. Duty to craft and those tied by the bonds of friendship. Now, who was he? Where did his duty lie?

Could he return to Duncaer and be the man he had once been? Or were those the thoughts of a coward?

Devlin owed King Olafur nothing. Indeed, the King was as one dead to him. For weeks he had thought of returning to Kingsholm to seek revenge, but Devlin had burned out his taste for vengeance during the long hours in which he had made Prince Arnaud suffer.

But what did he owe to the people of Jorsk? Those who believed in him as Chosen One and looked to him for their protection? Folk like Lord Brynjolf, the Baron of Esker, battling against the anarchy of the northlands, protecting his people when the King had failed. Brynjolf, who held nothing back, sending even his own children into deadly danger. Or Magnilda, who was as far removed in rank and wealth from the Baron as one could be. In her own way, she also did all in her power to keep her people safe.

Devlin had made promises. To Brynjolf and Magnilda, to his friends, and to a host of others great and small. He had sworn he would do whatever was in his power to protect the folk of Jorsk and keep them safe.

Those words had not been in a formal oath, nor had they been prompted by the hellish spell. They had come from his heart. From a man who had found a new purpose for his life when he realized that he could use his strength and skills to protect those who could not defend themselves.

Olafur had rejected Devlin, spurning his efforts to serve. Arnaud had lifted the Geas spell. But as the long night wore on, Devlin realized that neither had changed who he was. He was still Devlin of Duncaer. He had a sword and the will to use it. It would have to be enough.

When dawn came, he began to head north.

"The village appears safe. We crept as close as we could and saw no sign of Selvarat troops," Didrik said.

Captain Drakken turned to Oluva. "And do you agree?"

Oluva nodded. "I saw no signs of trouble. There are people working the fields and tending their animals. Just what I'd expect to see at this time of year."

Captain Drakken hesitated. They needed information, but this small village was exposed—if this was a trap, there would be nowhere to run, nowhere they could hide.

"Oluva, you may go. Be cautious. Learn what you can, but tell them nothing of why you are here or who you are with. At the first sign of trouble, we'll split up and retreat to where we camped two nights ago. Understood?"

There was a ragged chorus of assent. Oluva saluted and began making her way back through the trees, in a direction opposite from the village. She would emerge some distance away, so as not to draw attention to the fringe of the pine forest where the others waited. From here, they could see a league of open meadow, and the village beyond. All appeared calm, but appearances could be deceptive.

A short time later, Oluva's figure appeared on the road. Drakken's skin prickled as a group of people gathered at the entrance to the village. Welcoming party? Prudent caution at the sight of a stranger? Or hostile forces? Whoever they were, they surrounded Oluva as she approached and led her deep into the village.

"I'll keep watch," Major Mikkelson said.

By rights Mikkelson could have challenged Drakken for leadership of this strange expedition, but he had deferred to her instead. Which was fortunate, for she had lost her taste for following any orders but her own. Still she was careful never to give him a direct order, but rather to phrase her commands as suggestions.

She rose, handing Mikkelson the transverse bow and a handful of bolts before retreating a few hundred paces deeper into the woods, to where they had set up their camp last night. All was ready for a hasty departure. Their horses were saddled, their packs on the ground nearby, ready to flee at the first sign of trouble. She could only hope it would be enough.

Stephen stood in the center of the small clearing, holding Devlin's axe before him. He turned slowly in a circle, three times, pausing finally as the axe pointed northeast.

"Put that away," she said crossly.

"It's changed direction again," Stephen said. "Yesterday it was more north, and now it is easterly. And I think the glow has brightened."

"It means nothing," Drakken said. "We followed the axe, once, remember? Now we need to temper hope with reason."

Stephen stubbornly shook his head. "We are wasting our time. Even now, Devlin could be moving farther away."

She was tired of these arguments. Had Stephen learned nothing from their earlier mistake? The axe was a crude tool at best. They had followed it to the army encampment, only to discover that Devlin was most likely being held on a nearby estate, where Prince Arnaud resided in luxury. Worse, Mikkelson's rescue had alerted the soldiers to their presence, and they had been forced to flee the numerous patrols that had combed the countryside. There'd been no chance to try for a second rescue.

Stephen had nearly driven her mad, insisting that he was going back to find Devlin. Alone, if the others were too cowardly to join him. At one point she'd threatened to gag him and tie him to his horse. It might have come to that, if the axe had not seemed to show that Devlin, too, was on the move.

Unlike Stephen, Captain Drakken had learned her lesson. Knowing that Devlin was in this region, they would do their best to find out where he might be held rather than charging blindly ahead. When their path took them near a village that Oluva knew, she had volunteered to speak with those she trusted and find out if there had been any troops passing through the area.

"We will do Devlin no good if we are captured ourselves," Drakken said. "Oluva will speak to her friends. Find out if they have seen any soldiers or where they might have set up their camp."

"And if Devlin is being taken to the sea? What then?"

The coast was less than a day's walk. As they had followed Devlin's trail north, the sea had never been far from her mind. If she were in command, she would have seen Major Mikkelson's rescue as a sign that her security was vulnerable. She might well have decided it was time to move her prisoner to safety—perhaps even to remove him from the country entirely.

But even if Devlin were being taken to a ship, he and those who guarded him would be vulnerable while they were on the move. It was a question of finding him in time, without their being discovered.

An hour passed. Stephen paced and grumbled under his breath. Didrik wandered off, obeying her caution to remain within earshot. He returned with handfuls of nearly ripe berries, which they shared among themselves. The scant mouthfuls did nothing to satisfy her hunger. Provisions were low, for there'd been no time for foraging, and they'd been unwilling to risk venturing into a village to buy what was needed.

"If she's not back in another hour, then we must assume the worst. We'll mount up and return to our previous camp," Drakken said.

"We can't abandon her," Stephen protested.

"Oluva knew the risks. Losing one of our number is better than losing all of us. And if we wait until sundown, it will be too dark to retreat safely."

The road would be a death trap if they were pursued by mounted soldiers. Moving along the game trails of the forest was possible—if one had enough light to see by. And with a waning moon, that meant travel was limited to daylight.

Stephen looked to Didrik for support, but Didrik wisely kept his mouth shut. He knew the risks, and in fact he had argued that he be the one to make the approach, not Oluva.

Stephen turned to face her, and she knew from the stubborn look on his face that he was not prepared to accept her judgment. Not for the first time, she wondered how Devlin had managed to travel so long with the minstrel without giving in to the urge to strangle him.

Before Stephen could launch into his argument, a low whistle sounded.

"Get ready," Drakken said.

She left Stephen and Didrik to see to their mounts, while she made her way to where Mikkelson kept watch.

"Oluva is returning. And she is not alone. There are two people with her," Mikkelson said.

His eyes were better than hers. She loosened her sword in her scabbard, waiting as the distant blur resolved itself into three people approaching on foot. Oluva was in the lead, flanked on either side. Sunlight glinted off the shoulders of one of her companions, indicating that he might be wearing a sword across his back, or possibly a steel bow.

The three approached swiftly, but without undue haste. There was no sign of pursuit from the village. It was possible Oluva was bringing back those who had news that could help Drakken and the others. It was also possible that Oluva was luring these two out to her friends, where they could be eliminated.

Mikkelson loaded a bolt in the transverse bow and cocked it. Drakken drew her sword.

The group paused, just outside of effective bowshot. Oluva appeared to be arguing with the man on her right. After a long moment she threw up her hands in apparent disgust, then walked forward until she was within shouting distance.

"Captain, I've brought a friend, but he will not reveal himself until you come out where we can see you," Oluva shouted.

"You've brought two of them," Drakken answered. She remained partially hidden behind a tree. From here she could see the woman carried a cudgel, while the man to whom Oluva had spoken did indeed have a sword across his back. A sword that he now drew and held loosely in his right hand. A prudent precaution in this troubled land. They had taken the risk of coming this far, it was up to her to cross the final distance.

"Stay hidden," Drakken told Mikkelson. "And at the first sign of trouble, take out the swordsman."

At this range it would take an expert shot. Mikkelson merely nodded.

Drakken stepped out of the woods. She held her sword in her right hand, point down, indicating that she was not an immediate threat.

The villagers waited, remaining just out of bowshot, as she approached Oluva.

Oluva grimaced and spread her hands wide. "He still seems to think this is a trap," she explained. "Maybe you can convince him otherwise."

Oluva turned and walked with Drakken toward the villagers. There was something familiar about the man's figure, though his face was hidden in the shadow of his hood. A suspicion grew in her. "Who is he?" she demanded.

Before Oluva could answer, with his free hand the man pulled back the hood of his cloak.

It was Devlin. After all these weeks of searching, he had been the one to find her.

"Devlin!" she exclaimed. She sheathed her sword in one fluid motion.

Ominously, Devlin made no move to do the same.

Drakken glanced at the woman villager, but if Devlin was worried about her, it did not show. Instead his attention was fixed upon the woods behind her, as if he expected an imminent attack.

"Captain Drakken," he said. He did not smile, nor was there any warmth to his greeting. "Who is with you?" he asked.

"Mikkelson is in the woods, with a bow. Stephen and Didrik are nearby."

"Is that all?" he asked.

"See, it is just as I told you," Oluva said.

They both ignored her.

"Call them out," Devlin ordered.

"You don't trust us," Drakken said, stung by the realization. She had given up her post, forsworn her oaths, and risked her life for a man who no longer trusted her word.

He favored her with a mirthless grin. "We will talk about trust later. Call them out, where I can see them."

It went against all her instincts. But the search for Devlin had already taken her far beyond what she knew. She could go this last distance.

"Oluva, tell Mikkelson to stand down and summon the others," she said.

Oluva took off at a lope. Drakken looped her thumbs in her sword belt and rocked back a bit on her heels. It had been more than half a year since she had seen Devlin. He was thinner than she recalled, and his hair was now more white than black. There were new lines carved into his face, and his expression was unyielding. She was surprised by the ease with which he held the long sword in his crippled hand. And then as her eyes traveled up the blade to its grip, she saw the dark stone set in its pommel.

"Is that it?"

Devlin nodded. "A trinket from my travels."

She wanted to demand explanations. What did it mean that she found Devlin a free man, carrying the legendary Sword of Light? Had he ever been a prisoner? Had she and the rest somehow misread the signs in Kingsholm? Had the gossips been right when they whispered that Devlin had gone rogue?

She saw Devlin's frame relax as she heard Stephen's shout. Stephen brushed by her, and Devlin barely had time to lower his sword before Stephen grabbed him in a fierce embrace.

"I never believed you were dead," Stephen declared. "I never gave up hope."

As Stephen released him, Devlin sheathed his sword. He named each of them in turn. "Didrik. Mikkelson. Drakken. Much has changed since I saw you last."

Gone was his earlier wariness. It seemed Stephen's presence had been enough to convince Devlin that they meant him no harm.

"We need to talk. And make plans," Devlin said. He gestured to the woman who had observed the proceedings in silence. "Magnilda is speaker of the village. She has offered us her home for the night. We'll be safe there."

"There are patrols on the roads," Drakken warned him.

"There are patrols everywhere since the Chosen One slew the foreign Prince," Magnilda declared. "My people are on watch. They will give us fair warning."

So Prince Arnaud was dead? It seemed they both had stories to tell.

"Oluva, Didrik, you break camp, then join us," Drakken said as she fell into step beside Devlin.

"What happened to you?" Stephen asked.

"I was betrayed by those I trusted." Devlin's voice was cold, and his gaze slid over Drakken.

"King Olafur declared you dead," she informed him, wanting to see his reaction.

A chill smile touched Devlin's lips. "That is not the first mistake Olafur has made, but it may well be his last."

She shivered, not at the threat, but by the matter-of-fact tone of voice in which he made it. Even Stephen was shocked into silence. Theirs should have been a joyous reunion, but instead it was a grim party indeed that made its way into the village.

# Nineteen

DEVLIN LOOKED UP AS MAGNILDA ENTERED.

"I've brought more kava," she said, setting a clay pitcher on the rough plank table that dominated the room.

"Thank you," he said. "All is quiet?"

He knew she would have warned him if there were any trouble, but it was a sign of how off-balance he felt that he needed to ask.

"All quiet," she repeated, with a patience that he had not expected from her.

"Join us. We need your thoughts."

Magnilda shrugged, then took a seat next to Mikkelson, who slid down the bench to make room for her. She was a stocky woman, broad-shouldered with hands strong enough to choke the life out of a man, as he well knew. Elected village speaker upon her father's death, the last year had smoothed the rough edges from her temper. She had no love for the nobles who ruled over her, but she had opened her home to Devlin and given him honest counsel. Though their tentative plans had been overset by the arrival of his friends and allies.

He lifted the jug of kava and refilled his mug, then passed the jug to Stephen, who sat on his left. By now Devlin had drunk so much kava that he would bleed brown not red, and yet it still brought no clarity to his thoughts.

Captain Drakken sat across from him at the table. She watched him with wary eyes, as did Mikkelson. He knew they had been dismayed by his coldness when they met, but he would not apologize for his caution. He remembered too well the night he had been taken. It had not been just King Olafur who had betrayed him. Marshal Olvarrson, head of the army in Devlin's absence, had stood alongside the King. And two of the Guard had been present as well. They were the ones who had killed Saskia and bludgeoned Devlin into insensibility.

His captivity had given him long hours to reflect and to wonder who else had chosen allegiance to the King. But his friends had proven themselves beyond measure. Drakken had challenged the King, resigning her post to search for him. Didrik and Oluva had risked their lives, leaving behind everything they knew on the faint hope that they could find him and rescue him. Stephen's unswerving loyalty was something he had come to expect. Less welcome was the hungry look in Stephen's eyes. He had come looking not just for a lost friend. He had journeyed here to find the Chosen One. A savior for his people.

What had seemed so simple only the day before was once again fraught with complications.

"Chosen One," Drakken began.

"Devlin," he said, interrupting her.

"Devlin, then. What are your plans? How do you intend to fight them?"

"With a sword. Or my axe, now that Stephen has returned it." Though he was not quite certain that he wanted the axe back, not after hearing what Master Dreng had done to it. The axe had led his friends to him, but he was bitter that yet another piece of his past had been tainted by sorcery.

Drakken favored him with a glare perfected through years of cowing errant recruits. "This is not the time for jests. What are your orders?"

"Orders? Whom do I command? You? Didrik and these others? Shall the seven of us declare war upon the Selvarat Protectorate? Upon Jorsk? Shall we split our forces and attack both at once?"

He had come here to see for himself how the villagers fared and whether they needed the help of a strong sword arm. But he had come here as Devlin, not as the Chosen One, and it was as Devlin that he was determined to remain.

"With the death of Prince Arnaud, there will be confusion and disorder among his forces. We must seize this opportunity, before they have a chance to regroup," Mikkelson said.

"I have no army," Devlin said. "Remember? King Olafur declared me dead, and the Marshal commands in my place. What is it you expect me to do?"

"We expect you to be who you are," Stephen said. "We expect you to be the Chosen One."

"No," Devlin said, cutting him off with an angry gesture. "I am not the Chosen One."

He began to rise to his feet, but Stephen gripped his arm, refusing to back down under Devlin's angry gaze. "You *are* the Chosen One. You know it as well as I. It is why the King feared you. If you give the word, the people will rise up."

He shook off Stephen's arm and walked a few paces away from the table, putting as much distance as he could between himself and the others. Stephen's words had angered him, because in his heart Devlin knew that Stephen had spoken the truth. There was power in the name of Devlin of Duncaer, and power in the legendary sword that he now bore. Those who barricaded themselves behind Kingsholm's walls might ignore him, but the folk of the occupied lands would rise up if they were given a leader.

But did he want to be that leader? It was one thing to fight alongside others to protect their kin and homes. It was only his own life he was risking, his own death if he failed. It was another to lead a rebellion, to know that people would die in his name. His soul was already bloodstained, and now they were asking him to bear the burden of countless deaths.

"We will have to fight one day, if what you told me is true," Magnilda said. "Better now, before they send over more troops, and the first batch of settlers arrives to claim our land."

Like most of the folk of Korinth, she and her village had cooperated with the protectorate. As long as they were allowed to live their lives unhindered, it did not matter whether they paid their taxes to their Baron or to the Viceroy. Life under the protectorate was not nearly as harsh as the rule of the late Baron Egeslic, and Prince Arnaud's cruelty was not widely known.

Only Devlin knew the true scope of the Selvarat plans, owing to his brutal interrogation of Arnaud. His dreams were still haunted by images of the Prince's mangled body, and the knowledge of what he had done. Yet whatever its source, the knowledge that Devlin possessed was invaluable. Unlike the blind fools at court, Devlin now knew that the Selvarat empire was in turmoil. Long-simmering resentments had led to a series of uprisings in the north, which had been brutally crushed, but not before thousands of refugees had fled south. Weary of the cycle of unrest, they refused to return to their homes, but neither were they welcome in the southern lands. A series of poor harvests added to the overall misery, creating a potentially explosive situation.

Faced with the threat of civil war, Empress Thania had taken a bold gamble. She would expand her empire, claiming the fertile lands of Jorsk. There she would settle her displaced subjects, rewarding her loyal supporters with land grants and titles once the Jorskians had been driven out.

Arnaud had planned to carve out his own kingdom, betraying his Empress. Thus he had brought over only troops whose loyalty could be assured and mercenaries who obeyed their paymaster. But the failure of his plans did not mean that Thania would give up her dream of an expanded empire. She would send reinforcements, and settlers to take possession of the newly claimed lands.

Magnilda and her people would not risk their lives for their lord. But like folk anywhere, they would fight for their homes.

"If we do this, there can be no half measures," Devlin said slowly. "No turning back."

"We understand," Drakken said.

"Do you? Are you prepared to teach children how to

smile at their enemies before stabbing them? To use the old as bait for an ambush, because you cannot risk the lives of your valuable fighters? To fight to the death—no quarter, no mercy? Because nothing less will serve. We must destroy their army utterly. We must terrify them so greatly that they will flee across the ocean rather than stand and face us."

The occupying forces were spread thin, but they were experienced, disciplined, and well armed. There were a few trained peasants, but for the most part the fighters would be inexperienced, with only the crudest of weapons. They would have to make up for their lacks by the sheer weight of their numbers.

And by their willingness to die.

Even then, he did not know if it would be enough. If he failed, they would have been killed for nothing.

"If we succeed in driving the invaders out, it will not stop there. Not as long as King Olafur sits on the throne of Jorsk. In victory I would be even more of a threat to him. It will mean civil war," he warned.

"The King didn't betray just you," Didrik said. "He betrayed us all when he handed you over to the Selvarats. I will follow you, here and to Kingsholm if you ask it."

"And I as well," Oluva said.

Magnilda shook her head. "I will fight for my land and my people, but nothing more," she said. It was as he had expected.

"I am yours," Drakken said. "And you have more friends in Kingsholm than you think. When the time comes, Embeth and our allies will fight on your side."

Supporting Devlin might earn them nothing except a swift death. From what Captain Drakken had revealed, it seemed that the Guard was split between those obedient to their Captain, and those receiving secret orders from the King. If Devlin returned, the factions would turn on each other, echoing the greater strife around them. It would mean civil war, friends turning upon one another.

"I will follow you, wherever you lead," Stephen said. His mouth twisted in a wry grin. "Whatever happens, it will make a fine song."

Devlin snorted, remembering Stephen's previous attempt at immortalizing the Chosen One. Still, there were worse fates that could befall a man.

"If we are both still alive at the end of this, I will let you make your songs," Devlin promised. "Just as long as I don't have to hear them."

Stephen's face brightened, his gaze turning inward. No doubt even now he was crafting lyrics in his mind, content to ignore the gravity of their situation. His optimism would not let him imagine any outcome other than victory.

Devlin turned to Mikkelson, who had remained silent. Unlike the others, Mikkelson was not here by choice. The others had already cast their lots, choosing friendship over duty when they left Kingsholm behind. Now it was Mikkelson's turn to decide where his loyalties lay.

"You ordered me to defend the eastern coast, against all enemies. That order still holds. I will follow you," Mikkelson said.

Devlin felt a grim resolve. For good or ill, he had made his choice. It had been foolish to think he could take on the role of a simple soldier and leave the responsibility for the coming war to another. Whether he willed it or no, the fates had destined him as a leader. It was not enough that he be willing to sacrifice his life for these people. He had to be willing to bear the burden of the war, however great the cost would ultimately prove to be. He prayed fervently that he would be worthy of their trust.

"Seven of us, plus the villagers that Oluva trained last summer. It is a start," he said.

"I will send runners to the other villages and ask them to spread the word. We can gather a hundred before the full moon, and more each day that follows," Magnilda added.

"There are five thousand armed soldiers who would follow you," Mikkelson said slowly.

"Kallarne," Devlin said, naming the central garrison where the army was based.

"Kallarne," Mikkelson agreed. "On the King's orders they were pulled out of this region and sent to Kallarne. But they will have no taste for the protectorate. If you called them, they would come."

"You have more faith in them than I," Devlin said. In his time in Jorsk he had developed a close relationship with the guards, which was why his betrayal at their hands had stung so deeply. The army was another matter. Mikkelson was the exception, handpicked by Devlin for his position. Most of the others had resented the foreign interloper who had been named to command them. They had been obedient, but they did not love him.

"I cannot speak for all the army, but my troops will follow you. If you could come with me to Kallarne—"

"No," Drakken said. "The risk is too great. And there is no time. We need him here."

Devlin had walked into a trap once. He had no intention of doing so again.

"The troops have been told the Chosen One is dead," Mikkelson retorted. "They will not follow on my word alone. They need proof."

"It is a fool's errand. Those loyal to Olvarrson will arrest you and execute you as a traitor," Devlin said.

"I will take my chances," Mikkelson said. "But I need proof of your survival. Something that cannot be questioned."

It was folly. And yet, it was not his life to risk. If Mikkelson could bring back even five hundred soldiers, that could well spell the difference between victory and defeat.

"I can give you proof," Devlin said. "Mark you so that all know you as my man. But once I have done so, it cannot be undone."

Mikkelson swallowed hard. "Let it be done," he said.

Devlin turned his ring so that it faced the palm of his hand, then walked over to Mikkelson.

"Give me your hand," Devlin said. He grasped Mikkelson's left hand so that his ring was centered in the palm of Mikkelson's hand.

"I am the Chosen One," Devlin said.

The ring responded to his invocation. It did not care that Olafur had repudiated him, or that Devlin had tried to renounce his title. The ring recognized its master and began to glow.

Devlin held the image of the ring in his mind, the solid gold of its curves, the crystal stone, and the runes around the stone that proclaimed its owner as the Chosen One. He imagined the metal heating, as if it were held in a forge fire.

Mikkelson sucked in a breath of air, but he did not

struggle as the ring seared his flesh. Devlin held the grip for three dozen long heartbeats before he relinquished his grasp.

Mikkelson turned over his hand to see that the seal of the Chosen One was branded into the center of his palm.

Devlin stripped off his ring, and dropped it in Mikkelson's outstretched hand.

"Put it on," he said.

Mikkelson slipped the ring over his finger.

"Now, concentrate on the ring, and say 'I serve the Chosen One.' "

"I serve the Chosen One," Mikkelson dutifully repeated.

The crystal of the ring brightened, and glowed with a white fire.

Stephen leaned across the table, staring at the glowing ring. "But how can he do that? Only the Chosen One can summon the power of the ring," he said.

The ring was sealed to its bearer during the Choosing Ceremony and used to identify him to others. A wise custom in the days when the Chosen Ones were killed so frequently that there was little time to remember their names or faces. The ring, along with the soul stone and the Geas, were all part of the customs of the Chosen Ones, handed down for generations, until even the mages who invoked the spell no longer understood what they did. And what they thought they knew was wrong.

"Arnaud knew more about sorcery than any ten of your mages," Devlin said. "Before I killed him, he taught me a few tricks."

His tone was even, giving no hint of what the knowledge had cost him. Arnaud's efforts to pry the secrets of the Geas spell from Devlin's mind had forged a strange link between the two. As Arnaud learned from him, Devlin learned from his captor. Some of the information was useful, such as the insights into the Empress's plans and how Arnaud had intended to thwart her. Other knowledge sickened him, tainting Devlin's soul.

It was Devlin's hand that had wielded the knife, but it had been the skills he learned from the Prince that had enabled him to keep Arnaud alive even as his body was being butchered.

He'd hoped he would never have to call upon such savagery again. But if Devlin truly launched a civil war, he might one day be grateful for what Arnaud had taught him.

The next morning, Mikkelson departed for Kallarne, with instructions to recruit as many troops as he could and begin the task of securing the Southern Road. Before his figure had dwindled in the distance, Devlin had already dismissed him from his mind. He could not afford to wait for Mikkelson to succeed or fail.

True to her word, Magnilda sent out runners to nearby villages, and summoned their leaders for a council. They listened gravely as Magnilda explained the reasons why they had to rise up against the forces of the protectorate, but their eyes were on Devlin, who sat off to one side, the Sword of Light propped in a chair next to him. On the first night of the council, a brash young man asked Devlin to prove that he was the Chosen One. Grimly Devlin had unsheathed the sword, invoking its power until it glowed so brightly that no one could bear to look at it. As the spots faded from his eyes, he looked around and saw their doubts had turned to awe. They looked at him and saw a legend. It was not a comfortable feeling.

Most but not all of the village representatives agreed on the need for action. Those who declined were dismissed. No doubt at least one of these would turn traitor and inform the invaders of Devlin's plans. In fact he was counting on it. News of his presence would dishearten his enemies, those who had seen Prince Arnaud's mutilated corpse and knew full well what Devlin was capable of. And it would bring hope to those who had not yet dared to oppose the conquerors.

But the possibility of traitors meant that Magnilda's village was certain to become a target. As a precaution Devlin ordered the smallest children evacuated to a temporary camp in the forest, while those who had stayed behind were organized into fighting bands. Thanks to the efforts of the previous summer, each of the coastal villages in this region boasted one or two trained fighters, who had in turn passed along what they knew to others. A few had bows, meant for hunting small game but capable of killing a man at close range. Others had wood axes, or crude spears, some tipped with metal, others merely sharpened stakes.

Each day that passed brought new recruits and increased the danger that the Selvarat army would discover their presence. A fortnight after the council meeting, Captain Drakken had finally had enough.

"The risk is too great. We can no longer stay here," she announced, as Devlin joined the others for a cup of weak kava and a stale biscuit. With nearly a hundred recruits billeted in the village or camped in the fields outside, food was growing scarce.

"I agree," Devlin said.

Drakken, who had opened her mouth to argue, abruptly closed it as she realized that she had won her point.

"Oluva, how many bands do we have ready? Seven?"

"Eight now. Waltyr Crippletongue arrived in the night, and I've assigned the newest band to him," Oluva answered.

Conventional warfare called for massing one's forces, but he and Captain Drakken had mapped out a far different strategy. The recruits were assigned to bands numbering no more than a dozen. Their small size would enable them to move swiftly and help avoid detection.

Each leader had been given a target area, ensuring that they would be widely scattered once they left the village. Even if the Selvarat army discovered one of the bands and destroyed it, the others would be able to fight on.

"I will want to meet this Waltyr, and make certain he understands what he is to do," Devlin said.

"I trained him myself last year," Oluva replied. "He knows what you want. He will pick his battles wisely, relying upon ambush and surprise. He brought with him a half dozen fighters, all of them armed with swords."

Devlin raised his eyebrows at that news. Six swords was a sign of unusual wealth. Or of initiative.

"Were these perhaps liberated from the Selvarat army?" he asked.

"A patrol of mercenaries had no further use for them," she said, smothering a grin.

"Good man," Captain Drakken observed.

"My compliments to his trainer," Drakken said.

Oluva had proven herself a good judge of character, and those she had trained last summer had been the first to volunteer. In her own way, she was as much a rallying point to these folk as Devlin was, and it was an advantage he intended to exploit.

"Magnilda, will you summon the leaders? I would speak with them one more time to give them their orders before we disperse," Devlin said.

He waited until Magnilda was out of earshot before turning his attention back to his friends.

"Didrik, Oluva, when Magnilda leaves for the east, I would have you accompany her," he said.

Didrik shook his head, his mouth set in a stubborn line. "I will not leave you unprotected."

"If we stay together, then we are too tempting a prize," Devlin said. The rebellion was still a fragile thing. If those present were to be killed, it was unlikely that other leaders would emerge to take their places.

"Oluva and Magnilda will head for the sea, gathering new recruits and establishing lines of communication," Devlin explained. "I need you with them to take charge of the east."

Unlike the Royal Army, Devlin did not have the advantage of being able to send orders that his troops would carry out. The scattered bands would be largely autonomous, organizing themselves and responding only to the overall strategies. There would be no clear chain of command, which meant that it would be harder for the Selvarats to defeat them. Each band would have to be dealt with separately. And just as the bands were scattered, it made sense to disperse the leadership to ensure they could not be taken out with a single blow.

"I cannot be everywhere at once, yet I need someone there I trust. You know what we have planned here, and you know how I think. You will be my voice in the east," he said.

"Oluva could do as much," Didrik protested.

"And if you are killed, I expect her to carry on. Likewise, if she is the first to die, then you will take her place. The two of you will guard each other," Devlin said. And if he were to be killed, either Oluva or Didrik might well be able to take his place as a rallying point.

"And I will watch over the Chosen One," Captain Drakken said.

He had already had this argument with Drakken and lost. Accustomed to command, her experience would have made her an invaluable leader in the field. But Drakken had argued that he needed someone to watch his back, and when that had not swayed him, she had added that he needed her knowledge of tactics.

"What of me?" Stephen asked.

"You will stay with me," Devlin said. It might not be the safest place, but ever since he had been reunited with Stephen, Devlin had been unwilling to let him out of his sight. The horrific image of Stephen's mangled corpse still haunted his dreams. He knew it had been a trick, but a part of him feared that it might come true unless he was there to prevent it.

There might well come a time when Stephen was called upon to give his life for the rebellion. But if that day came, it would be because Devlin himself had already fallen.

# Twenty

CAPTAIN DRAKKEN MOPPED THE SWEAT FROM her brow, and shaded her eyes with her hand as she scanned the fields where corn ripened under the blazing summer sun. Assured that the fighters were in position, ready to cut off possible retreat, she made her way along the eastern ditch until it rejoined the road.

Devlin waited there, along with two dozen fighters on horseback. She had selected them personally from among the recruits who arrived nearly every day. Only the best were allowed the privilege of guarding the Chosen One.

"Everything is ready," she said. "You are certain you wish to do this? No parley?"

"The assessor has chosen her lot," Devlin said.

Devlin's face was grim, as it often was these days, whether the news was good or ill. Looking at him, one would suppose the rebellion was on the verge of being crushed. Yet the opposite was true. Against all odds, they continued to survive, and each day they grew stronger.

The tactics that Devlin had outlined were simple, if brutal. They launched no full-scale attacks, but instead relied upon ambush and assassination. If a chance arose to kill one of the invaders it was taken, and the captured weapons were distributed to the ever-growing band of rebels.

The cost had been high, as inexperienced fighters found themselves swiftly outmatched. Trading one rebel life for that of an enemy was considered a success. Sometimes they lost two, three, or four for each soldier they managed to kill.

But Devlin had the weight of numbers on his side, and as the summer wore on, his fighters grew more cunning and experienced. No longer did the enemy send out four-person patrols. Now they traveled in groups of twelve or twenty, and the rebel bands had grown in size to match.

At first they'd offered no quarter to the enemy, but then Devlin had suggested that when possible, a single survivor would be left for questioning. When they had learned what they could from him, the rebels would amputate his sword hand and then set him free as a warning to the others as to what they could expect.

General Bertrand, who had assumed command upon Prince Arnaud's death, did his best to hold his troops together, but spies in the larger towns reported that there were obvious signs of strain and poor morale among the soldiers. Using captured uniforms, Didrik had disguised his band as a mercenary unit and boldly attacked an army encampment, looting it of valuables. He'd repeated the same trick a week later. Other bands copied his tactics, as word spread through the informal network they had established. The change in tactics, from ambushes to wanton looting seemed to convince the army that they were now facing renegade mercenary bands as well, which served to increase the tension between the two presumptive allies.

As the weeks passed, the enemy casualties mounted, but so did the tally of fallen rebels. New recruits came each day, but the majority of folk in the occupied territories remained neutral. Some would offer the rebels food or shelter for a night, others offered only their silence. If Devlin was to succeed, he would need to convince these to join him.

And now, against Drakken's advice, Devlin had chosen to escalate the fighting to a new level. It remained to be seen if his new tactics would garner him more supporters or would drive a wedge between him and those who followed him.

"Burn it," Devlin said.

Drakken stood in her stirrups and raised her fist high. The fighters she had positioned around the field repeated the signal, as they touched their torches to the glowing coals that they carried, then tossed the burning torches in among the grain.

As the first wisps of smoke rose above the fields, Devlin rode forward, and his escort followed. They moved swiftly down the gravel lane that led to the manor house where the Assessor Emiliana and her family resided. The troops scattered around the house, surrounding it, their bows cocked and ready.

Devlin positioned himself at the front of the house, his transverse bow dangling casually from one hand.

Those who worked the fields had already been taken prisoner, so it took a few moments for the alarm to be raised. The door swung open and a young man dashed out of the house calling "Fire," only to be brought up short as he saw those who waited outside.

The young man rocked back on his heels, nearly falling over.

"What? Who are you?" he asked.

"Fetch your mistress," Devlin said.

"But the fields—"

"The fields are burning on my command. Fetch your mistress," Devlin repeated.

The young man backed up slowly, never taking his eyes from Devlin. He disappeared into the house.

A few moments later, a woman emerged. The Assessor Emiliana was diminutive in stature, but her eyes blazed with anger.

"What is the meaning of this?" she asked.

"Emiliana, you have been condemned as a traitor for your support of the invaders," Devlin said.

Previous attacks had been confined to the Selvarat army and their mercenary troops. As far as she knew, this was the first time that a band had targeted one of the Jorskians who was collaborating with the enemy. Emiliana had made a name for herself in these parts as the first to pledge her loyalty to the invaders. The Selvarats had rewarded her by allowing her to keep her lucrative post as tax collector, but now her own people would judge her sins.

"By what right do you do this?" Emiliana asked.

"By right of arms, and in the name of the people of Jorsk," Devlin said.

Drakken glanced over her shoulder and saw that the smoke was growing thicker as hungry red flames devoured the crops.

Emiliana's estate was surrounded by fields, bordered by a small stream on one side and a road on another. The fire they had set would utterly destroy her possessions, but there was little risk that it would spread. The blaze was meant as an object lesson, to show that only those who cooperated with the invaders need fear their neighbor's wrath.

"So, you mean to kill me?" Emiliana said. "Will you murder an unarmed woman and her children? Is this the famed justice of the Chosen One?"

"You may leave here, with the clothes on your back, and a waterskin each," Devlin said. "Nothing more."

"But—" Emiliana protested.

"I would hurry, if I were you," Captain Drakken advised. "The flames are getting closer."

Indeed, the wind was already pushing the heat toward them. The wide tree-lined lane would provide an escape route to the open road, but only if they left before the flames reached it.

After one last look, Emiliana disappeared back into the house.

A few moments later, the young man they had seen before emerged, accompanied by an older woman. After a brief search, the servants were allowed to leave. Others swiftly followed. Finally, just as wind-whipped embers began to land on the wooden shingles of the roof, Emiliana emerged. A young boy clutched one of her hands, while she held a baby in her other arm. A pair of waterskins were hung around the boy's neck.

Drakken swung down from the saddle and walked toward Emiliana. The boy's face turned white with fear, and not for the first time, she wondered if they had gone too far. What did it mean when even a child was afraid of her? But there was nothing she could do to reassure him. After all, it was by her command that his home was being destroyed and his family impoverished. She could not expect a child to understand. Some days she did not understand herself.

"Let me see the baby," Drakken ordered.

Emiliana clutched the child to her breast. "I will not let you harm her."

It was a fine show of devotion, but Drakken was not swayed by such tactics.

"You have little time," Drakken warned. "And I will not let you leave until I am certain that you have complied with our demands. Unwrap her blanket, and hold the child up."

The thick smoke surrounded them, making it difficult to breathe.

"Loathsome bitch," Emiliana cursed. As she unwrapped the blanket a leather purse fell to the ground with a solid clink of metal.

It was as Drakken had expected. It was probably not the only purse. The boy's loose tunic might well hide treasure, as could the bodice of Emiliana's dress. But time was indeed running out, and they needed the assessor alive and humiliated, rather than dead and a victim.

"Go," Drakken ordered.

Emiliana hurried past. Drakken walked back to her horse and swung herself back in the saddle, giving a piercing whistle to summon those fighters who had surrounded the manor house to prevent any from escaping with the assessor's treasure. As the band re-formed, it followed the assessor and her family down the lane. The servants were waiting at the crossroads, and she watched until the assessor had joined them.

She wondered how long they would have to travel before they found someone willing to take them in.

"I still don't know if this was for good or ill," Drakken said. "I never thought I would make war upon children."

Indeed this entire affair went against her very nature. She had just destroyed acres of valuable crops, which would have fed hungry souls throughout the winter. And even now she could see the manor house ablaze, the fire consuming all within. Coins, jewels, clothes, provisions, foodstuffs. The accumulated wealth of the assessor's lifetime, destroyed in a few short hours. Such wanton destruction went against everything Drakken believed.

Yet, despite her misgivings, she had obeyed the orders given her and put her faith in Devlin. If the act marked her as unclean, then so be it. Though she felt a moment of resentment as she thought of Stephen, who had been left behind in the base camp. Devlin still protected the minstrel from the worst of the war, finding reasons for Stephen to keep his hands free of the killings. He did not seem to realize that none of them were innocent. All those who followed Devlin bore their share of responsibility for the deeds done in the name of the rebellion, and one day it would fall to history to judge them.

"Come now, what is done is done," Devlin said, breaking into her grim musings. "If there is a Selvarat patrol within a half dozen leagues, the smoke will draw them here, and we had best be gone before they arrive."

"We ride," she called, and the fighters fell into a ragged line, six ahead and the remainder trailing behind.

As they rode, one part of her kept her eyes open,

searching for any threat. But another was wondering just what it was that she would be called upon to do next, and if there were any lines left that she was not prepared to cross.

They took a circuitous route to avoid being followed, and it was nearly sunset by the time Devlin and the raiding party rejoined the others in the latest of their forest camps. Drakken saw to the care of those injured, while Devlin sought out the leader of the scouts. She reported that all seemed quiet, but that her instincts warned her of trouble coming. Devlin, whose own instincts for danger had saved them on more than one occasion, listened gravely, then instructed her to double the watch on this night. They would leave in the morning.

At last he made his way back to his tent, where he accepted a basin of water and a rough woolen towel from a round-faced girl who looked to be all of twelve years of age. Someone's sister or daughter, brought along because her home was no longer safe. He sighed, even as he thanked her. This was no place for a child. But there was no place in Korinth, or indeed anywhere in the occupied lands that could truly be called safe these days.

He scrubbed away the soot from his face and arms, then rinsed out his mouth with a cup of watered wine. When he looked up, he found Stephen watching him.

"What is it?" he asked.

"We've news from Sarna," Stephen said.

The speaker of the nearest village was one of the links on the informal chain of communications that bound the rebels together. Messages were seldom committed to paper, but instead passed from one trusted soul to another. Knowing that Stephen would be disturbed by witnessing the eviction of the traitor Emiliana, Devlin had sent him instead to the village, to see if there were any messages for him.

"And?" Devlin prompted, as he began walking toward the cookfires. The hunters must have had success today, for the remnants of a boar were on a spit by the fire. Small knots of people, many of whom had accompanied Devlin on the raid today, sat around the fire. He nodded in acknowledgment of their greetings, pausing as he saw Turla, one of his rebels, sitting by herself.

"How is your daughter?" he asked.

"She is resting. But her wound is healing, and she is fit to journey," she hastened to assure him.

"Good." Turla was barely competent with a spear, but her daughter had shown a flair for the sword. Unfortunately, her daughter had taken a deep slash in a skirmish two days ago. With no true healers, there'd been nothing to do but bandage her wounds and hope for the best. Anyone who could not travel with the band was left behind. It was considered a kindness to slit their throats rather than leaving them to die a slow death.

The cook picked up a wooden trencher and piled a generous portion on top before handing it to Devlin.

"Eat hearty, it will not keep," the cook advised him. "And we may not see meat again for a while."

"We're moving on tomorrow," Devlin informed him. "You may pass the word."

With over fifty fighters in this group, they needed to keep moving both to avoid the enemy and to forage for food. No village could afford to feed them for more than a day or two, and venturing into a larger town to buy provisions had its own risks. Perhaps it was time to look at raiding another Selvarat supply caravan.

Devlin ate swiftly, not even tasting the food.

"What of this Sarna?" he asked Stephen, as he handed the trencher back to the cook. It was rare that Stephen had to be prompted twice to answer a question.

"Let us find Captain Drakken, so I only have to tell the tale once," Stephen said.

Devlin shrugged. He made his way over to the small clearing where Captain Drakken sat on a flat rock near the tent that held their gear. As she saw him approach she lifted her wineskin and took a long swallow.

"To our success," she said. Her words were light, but she grimaced as she spoke.

He had known that Drakken did not like what she had been asked to do. They would be lucky if this was the worst of it.

"The raid went well?" Stephen asked.

Devlin accepted the wineskin from Drakken and drank before sitting down on the ground, his folded cloak under him to protect him from the chill earth.

"Success," Devlin said. "Emiliana's holdings were destroyed, and she walked out of there with only what she could hide under her cloak, muttering curses upon us all."

"Did we lose any of ours?" Stephen asked.

"Nothing serious," Drakken reported. "Thom burned his left hand, and the baker woman was singed when the fire took an unexpected turn."

"Anna. The baker is Anna Karlswife," Stephen said. He had a gift for names and faces.

"It was a useful tactic, and a valuable lesson taught to

any who might think of casting their lot with the invaders," Devlin said. "We should pass the word to the other bands."

"We must tell them to be careful," Drakken said.

"Yes, if the wind turned, the fire could easily have gotten out of hand and turned back on the forest," Devlin agreed.

Drakken glared at him. "Tell the bands to be careful in their choice of targets as well. I understand the need to make an example out of traitors, but the innocent should not be made to suffer."

"You may draft the message," Devlin said. It was as much of a concession as he was prepared to make. He turned his attention to Stephen. "And what is the news of this Sarna?"

He did not even know if Sarna was a person or a place.

"Sarna is a town in the east, just past where Egeslic had his keep. Didrik has had some success in that zone, and so the local commander finally decided to take action. He went to Sarna, chose three dozen folk at random, and executed them in retaliation." Stephen's voice was flat, but his eyes glittered with suppressed emotion.

Devlin held out his hand, and after a moment Drakken handed him the wineskin. He took another swallow, though he knew that there was not enough wine in the entire camp to drown his anger.

"Have you nothing to say?" Stephen's voice rose. "Those were our people. There were three children among those killed."

"I heard you," Devlin said, letting the anger creep into his voice. "What would you have me do? I regret their deaths, but they are not the first innocents to die, nor will they be the last. And at least their deaths may yet be turned to good."

"How can any good come out of this?" Stephen asked.

"There are no innocents," Devlin said. "Not anymore. Bertrand has forced them to make a choice. They support the protectorate or they join us as rebels. There is no longer any middle ground."

"But—" Stephen began.

He was surprised by Stephen's outrage. The Jorskian army had long executed hostages as a means of controlling the population in Duncaer. Now they had the first taste of what they had doled out to others.

"Have you already forgotten how Kollinar keeps order in Duncaer? Or is it different when it is your own people who are dying?"

Devlin tossed the wineskin to Stephen, who caught it awkwardly in his left hand but refused to drink.

"If you remember, I protested against those killings as well. Wrong is wrong, regardless of who does the deed," Stephen said.

Devlin bit back a curse. He had known this day would come, and yet he was too tired for a confrontation. It would have been better if Stephen had accompanied the raiding party today and the news of Sarna had been left for another time. At least that way he could have preserved his illusions. For at least a little while longer.

"This is what you asked for when you asked me to lead you," Devlin said. "You were the one who told me that I was the Chosen One. You were the one who said you would follow me, as I did whatever it took to drive out the invaders."

He knew his words were harsh, but they masked his

anger. Stephen had grieved for the folk of Sarna for only a few hours. For weeks Devlin had grieved for them, along with all those who would perish before he was done. He had known from the moment he accepted the leadership of the rebellion that there would be innocents killed, and that their blood would be on his hands.

He grieved for them, but he would not allow his grief to blind him to what must be done.

"I did not think it would come to this," Stephen said.

"Then you are a fool." Drakken's judgment was harsh, but he knew she condemned herself as well as Stephen. She, too, had not reckoned on the price that they would all have to pay.

"I did not ask to be your leader," Devlin said. "But having started down this road, we must continue to the bitter end. Each hostage executed will bring a dozen new fighters to our side. Every act of terror that he commits will be repaid thrice before I am done."

The Jorskians had no experience in civil war, but the Caerfolk had long memories and the tradition of blood feud to call upon. He was not simply teaching the people to defend their homes, he was turning them into an army of assassins. The consequences of his actions would echo for generations, and plague the next ruler of Jorsk.

"How else will we win this war? We must be harder than they are. More cunning, more brutal, and more willing to die. We cannot stop to count the cost," Drakken said. It was strange to hear the words he had often said coming from her lips.

"But surely when Mikkelson returns with his troops—" Stephen said.

"Mikkelson is most likely dead, and the army will not

come. False hope will get us all killed. There is no one to protect us, nothing that we can count on except ourselves. This is what I have been trying to teach you. One man can do nothing on his own; but if we band together, we will be invincible."

The enemy was the anvil upon which they would either break themselves or he would forge an army the likes of which Jorsk had never seen. Whether he led them to victory or to defeat, his soul was already damned for what he had done, and what he was prepared to do, to win the war.

From the look on Stephen's face, it was clear that he was coming to the same realization. The Stephen of old might have cursed Devlin, or pled with him to find some other way to win the war. But the man he was becoming simply sighed and lifted the wineskin to his lips.

"I hope you know what you're doing," Stephen said.

"So do I."

# Twenty-one

MIKKELSON'S HEART QUICKENED AS THE RAM-
parts around Kallarne came into view. The palm of his
left hand itched, reminding him of the mark he now bore.
The brand had healed cleanly, without infection, but it
was not an easy thing to bear. A small part of him was always aware of it, and of the matching weight of the
Chosen One's ring.

The journey from Esker had been difficult; but with
the help of Captain Drakken's coin and borrowed clothing, he had managed to avoid the roving patrols, crossing
back into Arkilde, which was still under King Olafur's
rule. Even there he had not let down his guard, continuing his disguise until he knew he was only a few hours'
ride from Kallarne.

Last night he had taken shelter at an inn, scrubbing a
fortnight of travel grime from his body. This morning
he'd shaved his beard, braided his hair, and donned the
uniform he had carefully packed away. The inn-wife's
eyes had opened wide at the transformation in her guest,
but she'd taken his coins and asked no questions.

He'd given much thought to how he should approach Kallarne. By some measures, he could be considered a deserter. After all, his orders had been to remain in Esker and assist their Selvarat allies. Orders signed by Marshal Olvarrson, under the seal of King Olafur. Dutifully he had obeyed those orders, until it became clear that the allies were occupying troops. Before he'd been able to act, he'd been disarmed and confined as an unwilling guest of the Selvarat army.

Helpless to influence his fate, he had dismissed Prince Arnaud's tales of the new protectorate as lies, meant to weaken his morale. He'd known that the Prince was lying, just as he'd known that the orders he'd been shown must have been forged. He'd clung firmly to that belief, until Captain Drakken had rescued him and told him the truth. That King Olafur had betrayed them all, sacrificing the eastern provinces so he could retain his grip on the rest of his kingdom.

Mikkelson knew that there were others in the army who must feel equally betrayed. They—not to mention those who came from the lands that now comprised the protectorate—had sworn to defend Jorsk, not to step tamely aside as their lands were taken from them. Those were the troops he hoped to win to Devlin's cause.

If he could reach them. The garrison of Kallarne was the largest of the four army garrisons, dating back to the time of Queen Reginleifar. It was from here that he had drawn the troops to shore up Esker's defenses, and it was to here that they would have returned. As soon as he approached, he was bound to be recognized.

He contemplated trying to send a message in to one of the officers he trusted, but such a scheme seemed chancy.

He was not the only hostage the Selvarats had held, and he had no way of knowing who was or was not in the garrison. Sending messages to those who were absent might do nothing but reveal his presence, ensuring that he would be captured before he could spread the news of Devlin's uprising.

If Devlin were here, he would ride boldly through the main gate, trusting in his luck and that the Gods who watched over him were not finished with him yet. Mikkelson was not Gods-touched. He was not a legendary hero. But he bore the Chosen One's mark, and his seal. It was time to see if he held a bit of his luck as well.

As he approached the main gate through the rampart, he was surprised to see that the wooden doors were shut even though it was the middle of the day. Two soldiers stood at attention outside the gate, and archers were visible in the towers that flanked each side of the gate. It seemed that the garrison commander was taking nothing for granted.

Mikkelson slowed his horse and came to a halt a short distance from the sentries.

"Major Mikkelson, reporting to the garrison commander," he said.

Both sentries saluted, then the senior stepped forward. "Major, may I see your orders?" she asked.

The last time he had been here, the sentries had merely saluted as he passed.

"My orders are for those within," Mikkelson said.

"Sir, my orders are—"

"My orders come from the commander in the east," he said, interrupting her. "Summon your watch officer, if must be, but you delay me at your peril."

Her eyes swept over him and she apparently decided that a single man was no great threat. She gave a hand sign, and the second sentry called an order to those in the gate tower. Slowly the right hand gate was pulled back.

"Thank you, Sergeant," he said.

"The sentries inside will escort you to the watch commander," she said.

He nodded.

As Mikkelson guided his horse through the open gate, he was surrounded by a half dozen soldiers. One of them grabbed the bridle of his horse. "I'll take him for you," the man said.

Mikkelson dismounted, watching as the wooden gate was swung closed behind him. He was well and firmly trapped. But it would be worth it, if he could convince even a handful of soldiers that Devlin was alive, and that there was a chance to take back the east. Such news could not be kept secret for long. And he knew there would be those who would join Devlin's ranks, whether Mikkelson was alive to lead them or not.

Rumors of Devlin's survival might have already reached the garrison, but without a living witness, they would be put down as wishful thinking. But Mikkelson had known the Chosen One and bore his mark. His testimony could not be lightly dismissed.

His escort led him through the broad grassy field behind the rampart, which served as a training ground for the mounted troops in peacetime. In time of war it would form a killing ground for anyone foolish enough to attack Kallarne, as those protected by the stone walls of the main garrison could rain arrows down upon the exposed invaders.

The inner gate into the stone fortress was open. Just beyond the inner gate he could see two squads practicing formation drills. Luck was with him indeed, for not only did he know one of the soldiers on watch, but Private Jonas knew him very well indeed. Jonas had not only been part of Mikkelson's troops in the east, he had also been one of the band of twelve who had accompanied Devlin on their journey to oust Baron Egeslic.

Mikkelson took that as a sign. He could not allow himself to be whisked away into the deeper fortress, where he could be conveniently made to disappear. Whatever he did, it had to be public. And loud.

And it had to be now.

He nodded at Jonas as he passed, then stopped just past the gate, so swiftly that one of his escort bumped into him.

"Jonas, I bring news from a friend," Mikkelson said.

Jonas's head turned. It went against all custom for an officer to speak so casually to a mere private, especially when that private was on duty.

Mikkelson held up his left hand so that the ring was clearly visible.

"Devlin sends his greetings," Mikkelson said.

Jonas took two steps forward.

"Private, back to your post," one of his escorts ordered.

Jonas ignored him, coming closer.

Someone shoved Mikkelson. "Do not speak. You will go to the commander. Now."

Mikkelson stumbled and righted himself. Once again he lifted his hand. He glanced around swiftly. Attracted by the commotion, a number of the drill squad had broken formation to see what was happening.

Mikkelson spoke, in a voice trained to carry over a parade ground.

"I am Major Mikkelson, and I serve the Chosen One, Devlin of Duncaer. He is raising an army in the east, and he calls on all true Jorskians to join with him to drive out the invaders. This I swear in his name, and with the seal of the Chosen One as my proof."

The ring, which had begun to glow as he spoke, now brightened until one could no longer stare at it directly. He heard startled exclamations, and a few muttered curses.

Hope warred with doubt on Jonas's face. "They told us he was dead," he said.

"I swear to you he is alive, and . . ."

The rest of his speech was lost as a blow to the back of his head sent him crashing to the ground. His senses swam, and he could barely resist as he was picked up and half-dragged away.

But they had silenced him too late. There had been at least two dozen witnesses to his return, and to the news that Devlin still lived. The garrison commander could not silence all of them. Whatever else ensued, Mikkelson had done his duty.

The sight of a Major being dragged through the garrison was not a common one, especially when said Major had a gag in his mouth and a cloak hastily wrapped around his left hand. Folk drew to a halt as they passed, their jaws dropping in astonishment before they hastily averted their eyes. He heard his name whispered. Despite his pain, Mikkelson grinned. If the leader of his escort had any sense, he would have stashed Mikkelson away and merely informed the garrison commander of what had transpired. Instead, by publicly displaying Mikkelson, he ensured that the news of Mikkelson's return would spread like wildfire.

Finally, the odd procession reached the offices of the garrison commander. The commander's aide rose to her feet as they entered her office.

"What is the meaning of this?" she demanded.

Once they had stopped, Mikkelson was able to get his feet under him. He recognized the aide—Senior Troop Captain Rika Linasdatter. From an old family, she had been a junior ensign under his command ten years ago. With her family connections, she had swiftly risen to the rank of ensign, then junior captain, all the while he had languished as a mere ensign until Devlin had plucked him out of obscurity.

She was unlikely to be an ally.

"He claimed he had a message for the commander, but then as soon as he entered the fortress he began speaking all sorts of subversive nonsense," the sergeant explained. "I knew my orders, so I brought him here."

"May I assume no one saw him in this condition?" Her tone was frosty.

"Well, err, that is . . ."

She sighed heavily. "Sergeant, you will be dealt with later. Leave these two here and take the rest of your squad and wait outside."

The soldiers saluted and left.

The sergeant and most of his squad withdrew, leaving Mikkelson still held between two soldiers.

Captain Linasdatter turned on her heel and went

through the connecting door that led to the commander's private office. When she returned, Commander Gregorson was at her side. It seemed Marshal Olvarrson had replaced the previous commander with one who was bound to him by ties of blood. That did not bode well for Mikkelson's mission.

At Gregorson's command, the remaining two soldiers were dismissed. Only then was the gag taken from Mikkelson's mouth. Impatiently, he shook the cloak off his left hand, revealing the ring, which still shone with a faint light.

"Your presence here, against all orders, condemns you," Commander Gregorson said. "Marshal Olvarrson—"

"I serve the Chosen One, Devlin of Duncaer," Mikkelson said. "It is in his name I come, to bring word of a rebellion in the east."

He held up his left hand, revealing the still-glowing ring. "Devlin is assembling an army in the east, and he orders the garrison to be emptied and the troops sent to join his efforts. He gave me the ring of his office as proof of what I say."

"Devlin is dead," Gregorson said.

"He is very much alive. And he wields the Sword of Light."

"Lies, traitorous lies." Gregorson spat out the words, his face turning red with anger. "I do not know what your purpose is, but I will not allow you to disrupt my command. Your treason will cost you your life."

It was no more than Mikkelson had expected.

"Whether you kill me or not, you cannot silence the truth. At least I will die with honor, having fulfilled my oaths."

Gregorson shook his head in apparent disgust, before turning to his aide. "See how he infected them all with his madness. Devlin was a menace, and we are well rid of him."

"But if there is a chance he is telling the truth—"

"It does not matter. We take our orders from King Olafur, not from the Chosen One. Olafur has approved the protectorate, and it is not our place to question him. If the Chosen One himself were to appear in this office, I would tell him the same. We must follow the King's orders, or we will all be lost."

Blind fool. If Gregorson had argued that he needed his troops to be ready to defend central Jorsk, then Mikkelson would have understood. He would not have agreed with his decision, but he would have understood that Gregorson was preparing to fight a defensive war rather than an offensive one. But Gregorson lacked even that much foresight. He was not preparing for defense. Instead, he would sit here, tamely waiting for orders, until the day that the Selvarat armies overran the garrison.

"Remember the oaths we swore," Gregorson reminded his aide.

"I do, Commander," Captain Linasdatter replied. "I will see to this disturbance and make certain you are not troubled any further."

Gregorson turned on his heel, heading for his own office. As he passed his aide, she struck him solidly in the back of the head. His body crumpled, and she caught him before he hit the floor.

"Don't stand there, help me," she said.

Mikkelson shook off his astonishment. Picking up the discarded gag, he shoved it in Gregorson's mouth. Together they dragged the commander into his office, where they bound him to a chair.

"We will both be hanged for this, so you had better be telling the truth," Linasdatter said.

"I swear to you upon my life that every word I said was true. And before they can hang us, they must first catch us."

She grinned. "True enough."

"How many others are likely to follow us?"

"Your old command will follow you even without orders," she said. "We've had trouble with them ever since they returned to the garrison. A number of the officers are still held by the invaders, but you should be able to fill in the holes."

He nodded. He'd caught glimpses of the other prisoners in the early days of his captivity, before they had been moved to another camp.

"Why are you doing this?"

"Because I swore an oath to defend Jorsk. I refuse to sit in a garrison while the Kingdom crumbles around me. There are a number of others who feel the same, and we'd been planning our strategy. Your arrival just moved things forward a bit. When I give the order, the royalists will be detained. It will take us at least a day to organize, but we should be able to take nearly all of the garrison with us."

"We'll need them. Devlin has asked that we try and take a portion of the Southern Road. If we can hold it, we will cut the Selvarat supply lines."

If they succeeded, they would drive a wedge into the occupied territory, forcing the Selvarats to go far out of their way along the lesser roads to move supplies and troops between the northern end and southern ends of the occupied territories. Of course doing so would also mean that Mikkelson's forces would be exposed, subject to attack along both flanks. And if he was defeated, only the headquarters regiment in Kingsholm's own garrison would stand between the invaders and the capital.

It was a dangerous gamble. But it was a risk they had to take.

# Twenty-two

IT WAS NOT EASY TO LURK UNOBTRUSIVELY outside the council chamber. To start with, when it was in session, two sentries stood outside, so that the deliberations would not be disturbed. Nor could one casually stroll past the chamber, since beyond it lay the entrance to the private wing reserved for the royal family. Fortunately, the chancellor's office was adjacent to the council chamber. Knowing that the council was meeting that morning, Solveig had descended upon the chancellor's office. Esker, she'd declared, had not received proper credit for supplying armsmen to fill the King's levy, and she had been instructed by her father to take up his claim.

With the chancellor occupied in the council, it fell to his hapless assistant to answer Solveig's questions. In a rare burst of efficiency he'd produced a detailed listing of the tax credits allotted to each of the Barons who had answered the King's call. As it was a summary only, she sent him to find the actual muster records, so she could confirm the count of those enrolled. He'd protested that those files were stored elsewhere, but she'd fixed him with her best glare until he mumbled that he supposed he could fetch them.

At least she was able to intimidate a petty clerk. She'd never had to stoop to such tricks when Lord Rikard had been on the council. But nowadays all she could do was wait and hope she could glean a few scraps of information before the rest of the court heard the tale. Whatever had happened, it was urgent enough that King Olafur had summoned his councilors to an early-morning meeting, rather than waiting till their regular weekly session.

As she waited for the clerk to return, she heard raised voices from the direction of the council chamber, though she could not make out their words. The argument, if that was what it was, lasted for several minutes. Then the voices quieted. At last she heard the squeal of hinges as the massive doors were opened.

Fortunately, the clerk had still not returned from his errand. He would be surprised to find her gone, but she could always come back later and explain she had grown tired of waiting. Solveig stepped out of the chancellor's office just as the first of the departing councilors passed by.

Marshal Olvarrson was the first to appear, his shoulders slumped and his gaze fixed downward. As if separating themselves from the hapless Marshal, the other councilors appeared a few paces back, Lady Vendela in the lead, her lips pressed firmly together. Whatever had happened, she was most displeased.

"Lord Arnulf," Solveig said, as he drew near.

He barely glanced at her. "Mad, the world has gone mad," he muttered.

She fell into step beside him. "I was wondering if there was news of your daughter Lynnheid," she said. It would do no harm to remind Arnulf that he owed her a favor for bringing the matter to Count Magaharan's attention.

Arnulf stopped so abruptly that Baron Martell bumped into him, before apologizing and walking around them. "Lynnheid's lost to me, and you had better look to your own affairs," Arnulf said. "Whatever agreements we thought we had are gone. The garrison at Kallarne has deserted."

That was grave news indeed. Kallarne was the bulwark that protected the eastern approaches to Kingsholm. If the garrison were truly empty, then there would be little to stop a hostile force.

Solveig placed her hand on Arnulf's arm. "Walk with me," she said, not wishing to draw further attention to them.

"What did you mean when you said the garrison deserted?" she asked, when they had strolled far enough away from the others so there was no risk of being overheard.

"A messenger found Commander Gregorson and a handful of loyalists locked in the punishment quarters. There were a few dozen soldiers manning the walls; but the rest—numbering in the thousands—have marched east and declared war upon the protectorate."

A fierce joy rose up in her, even as she tried to feign horrified disbelief. So the soldiers of Kallarne had the courage to face what the King and his councilors did not. Now they were fighting a war, whether Olafur willed it or no.

"Madness," she said, echoing his earlier comment. And it was indeed madness. One garrison, on its own, could inflict damage upon the enemy, but they would not be sufficient to drive the invaders from Jorsk. The best they could hope for was that they would harass the enemy, throwing them into confusion, thus giving her father and his allies in the north more time to prepare to meet the ultimate challenge. Every enemy soldier they killed was one fewer who would face her father's troops.

"I am told Major Mikkelson broke his parole and secretly journeyed to Kallarne. When he whistled, they came. King Olafur explained that Mikkelson was acting on his own, but the Ambassador did not believe him."

"Would you, if you were in his place?"

Arnulf shrugged. "The Ambassador has informed King Olafur that the treaty is broken and warned that we face the most dire of consequences."

Troop Captain Lynnheid Arnulfsdatter would not be returning to join her father, nor would any of the other hostages that the Selvarats held. Not in light of what Mikkelson had done. It was tempting to see Devlin's shadow behind Mikkelson's daring; but if there had been news of Devlin, then Arnulf would surely have blamed him rather than Mikkelson.

"I did not see the Count leaving the chambers," she said.

"Wasn't there. He'd heard of Kallarne, of course. But Olafur wanted to keep the latest news quiet, though he is foolish to think that there are any secrets in this court. My fellow councilors are no doubt racing across the palace grounds, hoping to be the first to inform the ambassador." Arnulf gave her a sidelong glance. "Messenger birds brought word from Lord Kollinar. He has emptied the garrisons in Duncaer and is marching north."

"Why? Is he bringing his troops as reinforcements?"

That was even more astonishing than the news that the garrison had deserted.

"Against his orders? I'd wager he merely wishes to take advantage of the confusion and grab what land he can for himself and his followers. Duncaer is a bleak and poor place, but there are richer lands to be found."

Mikkelson had learned his tactics and courage from the Chosen One, so his bold actions did not surprise her. But Kollinar was a conservative, who had spent over a decade as the Royal Governor of Duncaer, seemingly content to preserve the status quo. She could not imagine why he would have deserted his post, or what would have drawn him north.

True, the uneasy occupation of Duncaer had meant that large numbers of soldiers were required to maintain Jorskian rule—troops that would be invaluable in shoring up the Kingdom's defenses. But King Olafur had refused to consider recalling those troops, even when faced with probable invasion of his Kingdom. If Kollinar had indeed taken all of the occupying forces with him, something which she doubted, then he had also ceded the territory of Duncaer back to the natives. And that would be treason, something for which King Olafur would see him hanged.

It seemed Kollinar no longer feared King Olafur's wrath or the justice of his peers. She did not know who led the army these days, but it was assuredly not King Olafur or Marshal Olvarrson.

"What will you do?" she asked.

"See what can be salvaged from this disaster," Arnulf said. "There are still alliances to be formed, though you may find the ambassador far less friendly than he was a few days ago."

"Of course," she said.

She bade Arnulf good-bye and left the palace to stroll outside in the courtyard, trying to gather her thoughts.

Arnulf was an experienced courtier, but he was wrong in his assessment of the situation. With King Olafur's authority being eroded, the Selvarats would be even more anxious to secure agreements with those who still held power. Like her father, whose influence extended far beyond his own province of Esker, thus her bargaining position strengthened as Olafur's weakened. She could obtain much from the ambassador if her father could be convinced to form an alliance with the Selvarat Protectorate, or even simply to sign a treaty pledging neutrality.

If the situation worsened, they would have no choice. She and her father would have to do whatever it took to preserve Esker. But for now, she still had hope. Stephen had surprised her before. He and his friends might still find the Chosen One and bring Devlin back so he could lead the armies of Jorsk in throwing out the enemy. It was a slender hope, but it was all she had.

It might be time to return to Esker, to inform her father of the latest news, and to find out his wishes. Such matters could not be put down on a scroll, nor was there anyone in Kingsholm that she trusted with such a vital task. And it was clear that Kingsholm was no longer safe.

It was well enough for Arnulf to stay in Kingsholm, working to form alliances with his neighbors in the face of the new threat. But those whom she might seek as allies had already left the court or were in detention. Here she was vulnerable. In Esker, she would be negotiating from a position of strength.

Her musings were cut short by the arrival of Lieutenant Embeth, accompanied by a pair of guards.

"Lady Solveig, the King has requested your presence. If you please." Lieutenant Embeth's words were studiously polite, but the escort signaled that she would not take no for an answer.

Solveig eyed the escort, noting that they wore the short swords of city patrol rather than carrying the spears that were used in strictly ceremonial guard duties. She could run, but in the long skirts and thin sandals of her court garb she would not get far. And it had been too many months since she had last carried a weapon.

It seemed she had stayed in Kingsholm one day too long.

"I am at the King's service," Solveig replied.

Lieutenant Embeth walked ahead, and the escort followed carefully behind, as she was led through the courtyard, into the Queen's garden, and then through the private entryway into the royal family's private apartments. Few people saw her pass, and those who did hastily averted their eyes.

As a member of the court, she had occasionally been invited to visit the King in his private chambers, so she recognized the small sitting room into which she was taken. But she did not recognize the man inside. The King had aged, nearly overnight. She knew him to be younger than her father, but at the moment he appeared old enough to be her grandsire.

"Leave us," the King said, dismissing her escort.

Solveig curtsied deeply. "Your Majesty, how may I serve you?"

She thought of all those courtiers who had simply disappeared, vanished into the dungeons that were never spoken of, yet somehow all knew existed. And those few who had reappeared, weeks later, pale and wan, loudly proclaiming their loyalty to the King even as they were stripped of their lands and possessions. At least Embeth knew where Solveig was. Before she'd left, Captain Drakken had told her that Embeth could be trusted but that Solveig was only to contact her as a last resort.

It might well be that time.

Solveig held the curtsy until the King acknowledged her with a jerk of his head. Only then did she straighten up.

"Whom do you serve?" King Olafur stood, his hands clasped behind his back.

"I do not understand your question," she said, playing for time. "I am Your Majesty's loyal subject, of course."

Olafur glared at her. "None of those empty court flatteries; I haven't time for such tripe. Tell me, whom do you serve these days? Where do your loyalties lie?"

He began walking around her, inspecting her as if she was a particularly valuable piece of bloodstock. She forced herself not to react.

"Kollinar betrayed me, may the Gods curse his line. Abandoned Duncaer to go haring off on his own fool quest," Olafur said.

Solveig remained quiet. Surely the King could not blame her for Kollinar's deed. She had never met the man; nor were their houses connected by ties of blood or alliance.

"You've no doubt heard that the garrison at Kallarne is gone. Kingsholm is left defenseless."

He paused in front of her, seeming to expect an answer. She chose her words carefully. "So I had heard. But surely we are not completely defenseless. There is the headquarters garrison, not to mention the City Guard. Though I hope that the fighting will not reach the walls of Kingsholm."

Olafur snorted. "This is all Devlin's fault," he said.

"I thought he was dead," she said, then bit her tongue before her next words landed her in one of the dungeon cells.

"His followers keep his cult alive. The report from Kallarne says that Mikkelson committed his treason in the name of the Chosen One, and the fools who followed him believed his lies."

Joy rose in her at his words. So Devlin was alive. Alive, and free. And he was raising an army in the east, to throw off the invaders. The news from Kallarne would spread like wildfire. It was only a matter of time before the people of Kingsholm learned of the Chosen One's miraculous survival.

Now she could read the emotion in Olafur's quick movements, and his inability to stay still. It was not anger. It was fear.

He must be desperate indeed. Even his councilors did not know the full extent of the crisis, which made it all the more puzzling that he would confide in her. Unless, of course, he knew he was taking no risks, since she would be in no position to tell anyone what she had learned.

"You never answered my question. Where do your loyalties lie?"

Did he expect her to condemn herself by proclaiming her loyalty to the Chosen One? Did he think her a half-wit?

"My duty is to Esker. To my father and to the people that I will one day rule over," Solveig said. Her voice was calm, for she had spoken nothing less than the truth. It did not matter if she had to bargain with Olafur, with the Chosen One, or with the representatives of Prince Arnaud. Solveig would do whatever it took to secure the peace and prosperity of her province.

"And the rest?" he prompted.

"Beyond Esker, I owe my allegiance to Jorsk. My father and I are your vassals," she said.

She'd expected him to challenge her, but instead he simply nodded. Then he took a few steps over to the window, which overlooked the Queen's garden.

"Come," he said.

She walked to stand beside him.

"You're a fighter as well, I am told."

"My father insisted that all of his children be trained, and I've spent my time riding with the armsmen on patrol," she said, though it had been nearly two years since she had held a sword in her hand for anything except a practice bout.

"Ragenilda loves the gardens," Olafur said. "They were her mother's favorites, and so she feels close to her when she spends time in them."

Solveig made an encouraging noise, even as she wondered at the strange turn the conversation had taken. The King had nearly accused her of treason and now he wished to confide in her? Perhaps the events of these last days had indeed unsettled his mind.

"She will be loath to leave them," Olafur said.

"Indeed?"

"Empress Thania has invited Ragenilda to visit her court. She feels the Princess would benefit from an extended stay in Selvarat and the opportunity to get to know Prince Nathan, her future consort."

"I see," Solveig said. It had long been rumored that Ragenilda would be married off to a Selvarat prince, and Nathan had been the name most often mentioned. The marriage would be some time off, the Princess having just turned eleven. But spending a few years in a Selvarat court, dependent on her future in-laws, would shape the Princess into the kind of ruler who would accede to Empress Thania's demands. And she would make an excellent hostage to guarantee her father's good behavior.

"My daughter is a gentle soul. I protected her too much. Perhaps I should have been like your father and trained her in the arts of war. But now it is too late."

It was hard not to feel sympathy for him. To see him, not as a king, but as a bewildered father who was desperate to protect his daughter.

"What do you plan to do?" she asked. She knew what her father would do in this situation, but her father had five children to carry the burden of his hopes and obligations. Olafur had only one daughter, and a frail reed she was to bear the weight of the Kingdom.

"I want you to return to Esker. To consult with your father," Olafur said.

She blinked in astonishment. Surely this was a trap of some sort. Perhaps he feared having her disappear publicly, and so had made arrangements that she would be taken while on the road, thus making sure no one in the court knew of her fate.

But even that did not make sense.

"Do you have a message for my father?"

"He will know the message when he sees you. You will travel in a small party, and you will take along your maid."

"But—" Solveig did not have a personal maid, relying upon the palace servants for those tasks she did not perform herself.

Olafur touched her arm. "You will leave as soon as possible. You may take a small escort of those you trust with your life, but not large enough to draw attention to yourself. And you will take along a young girl, one whom you will tell others you are training to be your maid."

She drew a deep breath as she realized the implications of what he was asking. "I think it would best if she were my niece. My brother Marten's daughter, traveling from Tyoga to spend the season with her cousins in Esker."

Marten had a daughter of the right age. It would fit if no one examined her story too closely. They would have to keep Ragenilda well hidden until they were some distance from Kingsholm, but once they were beyond its walls, it was unlikely anyone would see through their deception. Ragenilda was too young for her face to be on coins, and few outside the court would recognize her.

"Are you certain you wish to do this? I will guard the Princess with my life, but is there not another you would trust more?"

There were those in the court who were tied to the King by blood or decades of political alliance. Surely it made more sense that he would turn to one of them as someone he could trust to protect Ragenilda while not abusing the power that she represented.

"I cannot risk her being taken to Selvarat. Even if the rest of the Kingdom falls, Esker and the northwestern provinces may yet endure," Olafur said. "If the worst comes to it, I trust your father will protect Ragenilda until the day she is able to reclaim her inheritance."

"That he will," Solveig said.

She could taste the irony in the situation. For years, Lord Brynjolf and the other Barons in the northwestern borderlands had been abandoned by the King, forced to rely upon each other for protection from the border raiders. They had built up their defenses, recruited armsmen, and—with Devlin's help—prepared themselves to defend against an invasion. Of all the provinces in Jorsk, they were the ones who were most ready for a war. And now King Olafur was forced to turn to those he had once ignored and beg them for their help.

"Swear to me that you will keep her safe," Olafur said.

She took his right hand and clasped it between her own. "I pledge to do all in my power to deliver her safely to Esker. As Baron, my father will protect the Princess. And as a father, he will treat her as one of his own daughters."

Which was not to say that Ragenilda would be coddled. Far from it. Instead, Brynjolf would do his best to see that Ragenilda was fit to lead a kingdom at war, or to survive in the Selvarat court, if such was to be her ultimate fate.

It was the best that the Princess could hope for. It was the best that any of them could hope for.

# Twenty-three

OLUVA DREW HER HORSE ALONGSIDE DIDRIK'S as the walls of the keep came into view. "I keep looking around for the Chosen One, wondering why his litter bearers have wandered off."

Didrik kept his silence. The same thought had occurred to him, more than once on this journey, not that he would admit it to her.

"Do you suppose the Gods are punishing us? It doesn't seem right that we have to bluff our way into the same keep twice. Surely once was enough for a lifetime."

Didrik nodded in reluctant agreement. He had never thought to return to this place. The previous spring, he, Devlin, and Oluva, along with a handful of others, had deceived their way into the keep and arrested the Baron Egeslic as a traitor. It seemed a lifetime ago, back when his only concerns had been ensuring Devlin's safety and deciding whether Mikkelson and his soldiers were to be trusted.

"At least this time we won't have to clean vomit off our

boots," she added, referring to Devlin's impersonation of a dying man.

Her constant cheerfulness grated on his nerves. It was nearly as bad as traveling with Stephen. Well it was for her to jest and make light of their situation. She was not the one in command. Having taken the keep once by stealth, he now must do it again. And this time there was no Chosen One to lead. This time their success or failure would rest squarely on Didrik's shoulders.

"Drop back along the lines and remind the others of their orders. They are to look bored, but alert. While we are gone, Arvid is in charge, and he is the only one to speak."

"They know that," she said.

"Then remind them again."

She glared at him before giving him an irregular salute. "Yes, sir," she said.

She slowed her horse and he could hear her speaking to the first of the riders that followed. Knowing that he could be observed from the walls of the keep, Didrik fought the urge to turn around for a final check on his company.

He knew what the watchers would see. A band of two dozen mercenaries, openly approaching the keep, with no attempt to conceal themselves. Those who accompanied him today had been chosen not so much for their fighting skills as for the fact that they fit into one of the uniforms that had been taken during their raids.

Didrik's own tunic had been hastily cleaned and a large gash in the back sewn shut. Fortunately, the short cape of a mercenary captain covered the repair. His skin itched from the wrongness of wearing a dead man's clothes. He hardly recognized himself. It was not just the strange garb or the fact that he had cut his warrior's braid and instead sported the short-cropped hair of a barbarian. Those were merely the outside changes.

The man inside had changed as well. From the time he was a boy, he had wanted nothing more than to join the Guard. He had enlisted on his sixteenth birthday and quickly learned that it was not merely weapons skill that made the Guard such an effective force. It was discipline and order, held together by adherence to regulations and the long traditions of service. He had taken his lessons to heart, and he had risen from private to sergeant, then to lieutenant.

He had never imagined that he would be called on to leave Kingsholm, and the carefully ordered world of the Guard. Even when he had followed Devlin to Duncaer, he had done so as a lieutenant of the Guard, obedient to his duty as Devlin's aide. He had never imagined he would find himself called upon to lead others in a new kind of warfare. A war without rules or command structure, where there were no customs, no regulations to fall back upon. Everything he did was new, and there was never a second chance to get things right.

It was a heavy burden to bear, and he knew he was not the only one whose outward appearance hinted at the changes that had taken place within his or her soul.

Oluva had used tanner's dye to turn her hair and skin deep brown, and braided colorful beads in her hair. She could be taken for a savage from the Green Isles, and she had developed a casual disregard for protocol that went well with her persona as a mercenary. Others in their band had affected similar disguises. There were two trained armsmen, the tanner who had helped Oluva with her disguise, a wine seller, and a groom. The rest were farmers of one sort or another. Yet looking at them, it was impossible to tell the armsmen from the others. All bore their weapons with the ease of experience and had the hard edge that came from seeing battle. They might not understand the discipline of the Guard, and he doubted any of them could stand motionless for hours at a time as was required when one stood ceremonial guard duty. But they knew how to fight, and they were prepared to die for their cause.

Too many of them had died already, some before he had a chance to learn their names. More might die today, if his gamble proved unsuccessful. But the risks were worth it.

After glancing at Didrik's orders, the sentries on duty allowed them to enter the keep. The band dismounted, and in rough patois Didrik ordered Arvid to see that the horses were watered and that the troops did not wander off.

Arvid gave a lazy salute and rattled off a reply. Didrik assumed it was an agreement, since of them only Arvid spoke the bastardized version of the trade tongue that was used by the mercenaries. Didrik had memorized a few phrases, but that was the extent of his knowledge. Still, it should be enough to fool a casual observer.

As the escort led him to the commander's officer, Didrik glanced around as if casually, noticing the changes that had occurred since he had last been here. On his previous visit, this had been the Baron's keep, serving both as the seat of his government and as a barracks for his armsmen. Now it was occupied by Selvarat troops, who had stripped aside all pretensions to gentility. Soldiers were everywhere; they had even pitched tents in the courtyard because there was no room for them within the keep. With such numbers, they must be confident that no enemy would dare approach. And it was that very confidence that would make Didrik's plan succeed.

Familiar with the layout of the keep, he nearly turned down the corridor to where the Baron's offices had been, only to realize at the last moment that his escort was continuing straight ahead. Fortunately, no one appeared to have noticed his misstep.

They passed the great hall, which had been converted into a barracks room, with some soldiers standing around the perimeter, while others sat or lay on pallets strewn across the floor. It took a moment for him to realize that those who sat on the floor wore the uniforms of the Royal Army, while their guards were indeed Selvarat soldiers. They were the ones he had come to find, and yet he spared them no more than a glance before he continued onward.

At last they reached the commander of the keep. A Major in the Selvarat army, he scowled at the sight of two presumed mercenaries before reluctantly accepting the scroll that Didrik held out.

Didrik did not bother to salute. Without waiting for an invitation, he took a seat in a chair, his long legs stretched before him. Oluva leaned back against one wall, her arms crossed.

The Major said something in Selvarat, to which Didrik shrugged. With a muttered imprecation, he tried again in the trade tongue. "Do you know what this says?" the Major asked.

Didrik nodded. "Orders from General Bertrand. Says

your hostages aren't safe here, and wants them moved. There's a ship waiting in the cove, will take them to Selvarat."

The Major peered at the signature and the General's seal, rubbing the parchment carefully between his fingers. But there would be nothing for him to find. The orders were genuine, captured from a courier. Only those sent to carry out the orders were false.

"Why would he send you?" the Major asked.

Didrik shrugged. "The General pays; we go where he says. He have hostage escape, not want have this happen again. Safer if prisoners in Selvarat." He hesitated as he spoke, as if he were searching for unfamiliar words.

"But how do you expect to guard so many with only a small group? There are nearly three dozen hostages."

Didrik had hoped for more. Accounts had said that there were over fifty officers being held here. Perhaps some had been transferred to other places. Or perhaps they had been killed.

"Only need two men to guard three dozen," Didrik said. "Tie rope around necks. One fall, all fall. Simple. But General not take risks, so I have company outside, waiting to form escort."

The Major pursed his lips in disgust, and Didrik worried that he had pushed him too far.

"I cannot countenance this," he said. "I understand the General's concern, but he entrusted these hostages to me. My men will take them to the waiting ship."

"No," Didrik said.

"Who do you think you are?" the Major barked. "You will do as I say."

Didrik thought furiously, as he felt the opportunity

slipping from his grasp. He had to find a valid reason for his refusal, yet he could not let the Major see how important taking the prisoners was to him.

"General Bertrand gave me orders too," Didrik said at last. "Your men can be in charge of the prisoners, but we will go with them, keep General happy."

He could see the struggle in the Major's face, his dislike of the mercenaries warring with the ingrained obedience to orders from a superior. After all, despite the rumors of renegade mercenary bands, officially the mercenaries and the regular army were allies in this venture, serving a common leader. They still trusted each other. It was Didrik's task to break that trust.

At last the Major sighed and nodded. "You and your band accompany the escort. But you are to take your orders from my lieutenant and not interfere in any way, understood?"

"Yes, Major, sir. Your soldiers do the work, and my band gets paid."

Oluva chuckled, then at the Major's glare she lazily straightened and gave her own salute.

With obvious distaste the Major gave orders that Didrik and his band were to be allowed to draw the supplies they needed from stores. They were then to wait in the courtyard while the prisoners and their escort were assembled. It was only a short two hours' ride to the shore, so they would be able to leave shortly and complete their errand before nightfall.

Didrik and Oluva returned to the courtyard. Finding a shady spot, they played an idle game of dice while the rest of their band lounged nearby. He had never realized how hard it was to pretend to be relaxed.

He counted as a detail of three dozen soldiers was assembled to form an escort for the prisoners. It was more than he hoped for, but he and his troops would not be too badly outnumbered. And they would have the advantage of surprise.

Finally, the prisoners were brought out. Thirty-one in all, each wearing leg shackles, their hands bound with rope and then secured to a long chain. It was an efficient method of securing the prisoners, but did not fit with his plans. Didrik wandered over, and pointed out to the Captain in charge of the detail that the prisoners wouldn't be able to manage better than a slow crawl in the heavy shackles. It would take them more than a day to make their way to the shore. Of course it didn't matter to him if they were forced to camp out overnight.

The Captain glared at Didrik, and then retreated inside to consult with his superior. Didrik took advantage of his absence to stroll around the captives, looking for familiar faces while ostensibly checking to see how they were secured. His dealings with the army had been limited, so he was not surprised that he didn't recognize anyone, although one woman's eyes widened and it seemed she recognized him. Fortunately, she had the sense to keep her mouth shut.

He leaned in close, and tugged on the rope that bound her to the chain. "Wait for my signal. When we are well clear of this place, I will give the word, and I want you to fall to the ground. Take as many with you as you can, understand?" he whispered.

"Since when did you become a mercenary?"

"Never," he answered.

He could see a thousand questions in her eyes, but he

moved on, rather than draw attention to her. He repeated the rope check on four other officers, none of whom appeared to recognize him. A young ensign spat at him, for which Didrik repaid him with a causal backhand that knocked him to the ground, taking his two neighbors with him.

At least that part of the plan would work.

The Captain returned and supervised the removal of the leg shackles. Satisfied, Didrik returned to his band, ordering them to saddle their horses and prepare to leave. It was an odd procession that finally rode out of the keep. Thirty-one prisoners on foot, flanked on both sides by mounted Selvarat soldiers. Trailing the band was Didrik's own mercenary company. The size of the force suggested that they were guarding priceless treasure.

Devlin's irregular bands would think thrice before attacking such a large force. And the path to the shore led them over a wide plain that offered no chance for ambush. The Captain should have every reason to feel safe.

It was a slow procession, for the officers could not move swiftly, their weeks of captivity showing as their unused muscles protested the exercise. A few of them were limping, accustomed to riding rather than walking.

Didrik waited until an hour had passed before he gave Oluva the hand sign. Behind him, the mercenaries who had been riding in a ragged group gradually quickened their pace so they began to surround the rear portion of the column. Didrik rode forward, and as he caught the eye of his confederate, he nodded slowly to her. He had just reached the Selvarat captain when he heard a curse, followed by shouting.

The woman had done a splendid job, for nearly a third

of the prisoners were on the ground or struggling to get up. The soldiers had drawn their horses to a halt, and looked down in disgust, while one of their lieutenants shouted orders. Several of the prisoners regained their feet, only to be brought back down as one of them stumbled.

It was the perfect moment. All eyes were on the prisoners.

Didrik laughed, drawing the Captain's attention to him.

The Selvarat officer muttered something that was probably a curse in his native tongue.

"Wasting time," Didrik said. He called out one of the phrases he had memorized, instructing his band to help the prisoners. Four of them dismounted, and moved over to the prisoners. They reached down, appearing to help them up, but their orders were to cut them loose from the chain. Just as the first prisoner was free, a Selvarat soldier screamed and slipped from his horse.

Unnoticed by the soldiers, the rear contingent of Didrik's band had loaded their crossbows, which they now unleashed with devastating effect. Before the Selvarats could recover from the surprise, Didrik's fighters were among them, slashing at them with their swords, and driving them away from the prisoners.

Didrik plunged his dagger into the back of the Selvarat Captain. He slumped forward and his horse carried him a few paces away before he fell from the saddle. He landed on his back, driving the dagger even deeper into his lung.

Didrik whirled his horse and took aim at the nearest Selvarat. She'd had time to draw her sword and was experienced in fighting on horseback, a skill he'd never needed as a Guard. He took a glancing blow to his arm and a deeper slash in his side, while she parried each of his blows. Swiftly he changed tactics, and slashed the tendons of her horse's foreleg. The horse screamed as it fell. Pinned under the bulk of her horse, she was an easy kill.

She was replaced by another, even as he glanced around, trying to get some sense of how the battle was going. Newly freed prisoners united to drag one soldier from his horse, overwhelming him with sheer numbers. Those prisoners they had not been able to free hunkered on the ground, wary of the flashing hooves of friend and foe alike.

There were far too many bodies on the ground, some dead, some groaning in pain from their wounds. But the Selvarats were retreating.

"Protect the prisoners," he called in the trade tongue. "Remember we get paid for each one we bring back alive."

From some distance he heard Oluva take up the cry.

He dispatched four of the enemy, chasing the last one some distance before finally cutting him down. He turned, looking for a new opponent, but there was only empty grassland around him. Cursing his inattention, he rode back to the knot of people still visible. A few Selvarat soldiers could be seen fleeing westward; the rest were dead. As he rejoined the band, the last wounded fighter was taken prisoner.

It was over. The skirmish had lasted no more than a half hour, but he was as weary as if he had fought for days. He dismounted, wincing as he felt the wound in his side open. His stolen tunic was wet with blood, but he judged the wound annoying rather than serious. He pressed his left hand to his side to stop the bleeding, then walked over to where Oluva and two others stood guard over the three prisoners they had taken—two young Selvarat soldiers and a lieutenant, all showing signs of minor injuries.

Oluva had the beginnings of a black eye, and blood dripped down her face from a cut over her eyebrow, but she grinned as she caught sight of him.

"Four got away. Shall I order a pursuit?" she asked.

"There's no profit in it," he said. It was important that they preserve the illusion that they were a renegade mercenary band.

"What of these?" Idly she kicked one of the Selvarats in the leg.

"Search them for hidden weapons, take their boots, and let them walk back," he said.

Oluva repeated the orders, and two of the band made quick work of stripping the captives. They showed little enthusiasm for walking barefoot over the stony ground and had to be encouraged at the point of a sword.

"What is our toll?" he asked, once the prisoners were out of earshot.

"Seven killed, four gravely wounded. And we lost five of the prisoners."

It was victory of a sorts. Without the element of surprise, his band would have been no match for soldiers trained to fight on horseback. He knew the toll could have been much higher. But even if their entire band had been destroyed, it would have been worth it. The hostages had been only the secondary goal. Their primary aim was to drive a wedge between the mercenaries and the Selvarat army. As news of this apparent treachery spread, the army commanders would think twice about trusting any of the mercenary units. And since the mercenaries comprised nearly half of the occupying force, their loss would severely cripple General Bertrand's plans.

But the price of victory had been high. Seven already dead, and with no healer it was unlikely any of the gravely wounded would survive the forced march they must now make.

"We'll leave as soon as we've rounded up enough horses," Didrik said.

They could not stay here. The fleeing soldiers would soon return, bringing reinforcements.

He walked around the bodies of the fallen, nodding at those who were stripping friend and foe alike of anything of value. As he reached the line of prisoners he saw that most of them had been freed. The woman who had helped him now wielded a dagger as she cut the last of them free.

"I am Troop Captain Arnulfsdatter," she said. "You were the Chosen One's aide, weren't you? I recognized you from court."

"Lieutenant Didrik, late of the Guard. Now of the Army of the People," he said.

"The what?" In her surprise she paused with her dagger stuck in the middle of its stroke. A protest from her comrade recalled her to her task.

"The Army of the People," he repeated. Stephen had come up with a number of more lofty titles, but none of them had stuck. He'd been fond of Drakken's suggestion: "Those too stupid to know when they're beaten," which was accurate enough but too much of a mouthful.

"You soldiers, come here, gather round," he called. After a few moments he was surrounded by the former prisoners. More than a few regarded him with suspicion, as if they still believed him to be a mercenary. And not one of them uttered a word of thanks for their rescue.

He'd always known the Royal Army was an ungrateful lot.

"I'll make this quick, because there's not much time. We need to be long gone before the Selvarat army returns."

"We're not going anywhere with your lot," a man said.

Didrik glared. "I am Lieutenant Nils Didrik, aide to the Chosen One. Captain Arnulfsdatter will vouch for my identity."

"He speaks the truth," she said.

"Devlin is alive. He is in Esker, raising an army of the people to destroy the invaders," Didrik explained.

"Then he is a fool. What chance have peasants against the Selvarat army?" It was the same man who had complained before.

"Those peasants rescued your ungrateful hides. Seven of them died for you and more will die before this day is through," Didrik said.

A few of the others had the grace to look ashamed.

"But what of the King's orders?" Captain Arnulfsdatter asked.

"The King may have been cowed by Selvarat threats, but we refuse to be defeated. We have sworn to fight on, until the last of the invaders is killed. Once we are free from pursuit, each of you will be asked to make a choice. You can continue riding north with us, and join Devlin's army. Ride west, and you will meet up with Major Mikkelson and the troops that are seeking to take control of the Southern Road. Or you may take the coward's way, and ride back to Kingsholm to hide behind its walls."

"Obedience to orders is not cowardice," an older woman said.

"Neither is it bravery to hide while others fight your battles for you. Each one of you must decide for yourself. I have pledged to defend Jorsk. All of it. And so I will, with my last drop of blood."

As he paused to catch his breath, he looked over the former prisoners, among whom a few heads nodded in agreement. Perhaps he had swayed them. Devlin could use experienced officers. Or, if Mikkelson had indeed managed to bring troops from Kallarne, perhaps they would join up with his forces, seeking the familiarity of serving in an ordered regiment. In the end it did not matter. The twenty-six surviving officers were not enough to tip the balance of the fighting one way or another. They had been rescued as a symbol rather than for their military value.

He felt chilled, despite the heat of the day and his exertions. He longed suddenly for a place to rest and a chance to turn over his burdens to someone else. But there would be no rest, not for long hours yet.

"You don't have to decide now," Didrik said. "But prepare yourselves to leave. Each of you will be given a weapon, though some of you will have to share horses. Anyone who falls behind will be left behind, understood?"

"I am not taking your orders," the man said.

Didrik's temper snapped. "Then I'll leave you here. But first I'll cut your tongue out so you can spread no tales."

The threat shocked the others into silence. There were no more objections.

"Captain Arnulfsdatter, see Oluva over there, the one

dressed as an islander? Go to her, and she'll give you weapons to hand out."

"I'm not senior," the Captain protested.

"You are today," he rejoined. He did not have time to figure out the intricacies of the army command. With his luck, the man who had challenged him would turn out to be the senior officer. "Welcome to the Army of the People."

"I liked the old ways better," she said. But she did as she was bade, and in a short while each of the freed prisoners had at least a dagger to defend themselves with and they mounted up.

There were not enough horses for everyone. The gravely wounded members of Didrik's band each rode with a comrade to steady them, and most of the soldiers were forced to ride double. They headed north, toward the distant fringe of the forest. They should reach it by nightfall.

If all went as planned, friendly eyes would be looking for their approach, ready to guide them along the game trails, deep into the forest. It would be dark before the Selvarat army reached this spot, and even if they followed their hoofprints to the forest, their pursuers would not be able to enter the woods until daylight. By that time, Didrik and his band would have an insurmountable lead.

Unfortunately, Didrik's mare proved fractious. It took him three tries to heave himself into the saddle, and by then he was covered with sweat. He breathed shallowly, trying not to disturb the wound in his side.

He'd taken a deeper slash than he'd guessed, but he could not waste the precious time it would take to bandage it. He'd underestimated how long it would take to round up the horses and free the soldiers from the chain. Even now, the first of the fleeing soldiers was undoubtedly telling the Major of the mercenaries' treacherous attack.

He bit his lip, concentrating simply on staying erect and making certain that his horse followed the one in front of it.

"Are you all right?" Oluva's voice came from his right side.

"I can ride," he said.

They had few standing orders in this new army, but there was one that was sacrosanct. No one was left behind alive.

If he could not keep up, it would fall to Oluva to slit his throat.

Although they pushed the horses and themselves as hard as they dared, it was twilight by the time they reached the trees. Didrik had grown steadily numb; but he held himself erect through sheer force of will until he recognized Maalvo, the first of those who had come to greet them. Swiftly the scouts lit torches, ready to guide them through the forest paths.

"Good hunting today," Maalvo greeted him, as the first to arrive dismounted and filed into the woods.

Didrik watched until the last of the band had entered the forest. He squinted at the plain behind him. There was a dark blur, but whether it was a pursuing army or the approaching dusk he could not tell.

"Come now, we've a long night ahead of us," Maalvo said.

Didrik mumbled his agreement. He tried to kick his right foot free of the stirrup, ready to dismount, but it did not obey him. The reins slipped from his clumsy hands, as he slumped forward in the saddle.

It was darkest night when he hit the ground. And cold, so cold that it seemed he was standing on the castle battlements in the depths of winter.

*Devlin is never going to forgive me for this*, he thought as he died.

# Twenty-four

DEVLIN DISMOUNTED, HANDING THE REINS OF his horse to one of the archers who led the horse over to join the others at the wooden trough. The young boy pumping water for the horses gaped as he caught sight of Devlin, his hands slowing at their tasks. A quick word from the archer recalled the boy to his duty and he ducked his head, pumping as if his life depended upon it.

Devlin bit back a curse. It would not take long for news of the Chosen One's arrival to spread through the village. And it was not only the children who would stare, following him around and hoping for a word of acknowledgment. He called himself General, but as the weeks had passed, he grew to realize that he was not the leader of these people so much as he was their talisman. A living symbol of defiance. His presence inspired those to fight who might otherwise have stayed in safety. Where he journeyed, farmers walked away from their crops, craftsmen abandoned their trades, and parents left their children.

King Olafur had issued a decree denouncing the False

Chosen One and branding all those who followed him as traitors, but this did nothing to slow the tide of recruits. Those who could not join one of the roving bands found other ways to serve, providing safe havens in the villages and towns. They shared information and provisions with the rebel bands, and learned the value of a well-placed knife.

That was not to say that everyone was pleased with his efforts. Some folk bitterly resented the new kind of war he had brought to the region, convinced that the struggle was doomed. Others blamed Devlin for their losses. One woman had pledged her loyalty, then that very night she'd tried to kill Devlin. She'd had passion, but no skill. He still remembered the astonished look on her face as his throwing knife lodged in her throat. Later he'd learned that the woman's husband had been one of the hostages executed by the Selvarat army.

Wary of another such incident, Devlin's followers had created an unofficial escort comprised of their most trusted members. One of them was always at hand, so that he was never left alone. He felt trapped, like an animal in a cage, a rare exotic beast brought forth to awe the crowds.

Apparently Captain Drakken was his watcher that morning, for after leading her horse to the trough, she limped across the small square to join Devlin. Her left foot had been broken a fortnight ago, but she'd not let that slow her down.

"What is the name of this place?" she asked.

Devlin shrugged. "Does it matter?"

They wouldn't be there long, and one part of Korinth looked very much like any other to him. He and his band had ranged throughout the province and its southern neighbor of Ausland, and west nearly to the Southern Road. Now they were heading back north through Korinth, planning on joining up with other scattered bands to harass the Selvarat supply lines near the port of Trelleborg.

A frail elder, his back bent with age, limped toward them, his right arm slung over the shoulders of a sturdy girl child. As he drew near, the elder stopped, drawing himself upright, and raised his right hand in a pitiable attempt at a salute.

"General Chosen One, I have come to make my report," he said. He held the pose until Devlin nodded his acknowledgment.

"And your name is?" Devlin asked.

"I am Ulmer, and this is my granddaughter Leyza. Her father leads the village fighters, while I have the honor of being the message keeper," the old man said proudly. "I have much news to relate."

As he began to sway, Leyza slipped her grandfather's right arm back over her shoulders. He was an odd choice for a message keeper, so frail that a single blow would crush the life out of him. Yet perhaps that was the very reason why he had been chosen. If he were captured by the enemy, Ulmer would not live long enough to betray their secrets.

His granddaughter was another matter. She appeared to be ten or eleven years of age, old enough to understand what was being said around her and young enough to be too curious for her own good.

"Let us find somewhere in private where we can sit and I will hear what you have to say."

He summoned Stephen to join them, and they followed the old man to the house of the village speaker, who seemed more than pleased to have the Chosen One take over her home. Leyza was dismissed, with orders to wait outside until her grandfather needed her.

"What news have you?" Drakken asked.

Ulmer closed his eyes for a long moment, as if trying to recall what he had been told.

"As of the new moon, the Major and his troops now control the Southern Road from Trond down to the bridge at Ljusdal. He continues to sustain losses, but he reports that they are holding their own."

"Ljusdal is near the border with Ausland," Captain Drakken explained, seeing the blank look on Devlin's face. "Mikkelson has pushed south at least a dozen leagues since our last report."

That was good news. They now controlled a large stretch of the main road that linked the northern provinces of Korinth and Rosmaar with their neighbors to the south.

"Last week, my son observed a small group of mercenaries being attacked by Selvarat soldiers. He and his band remained hidden until the fight was decided. Those mercenaries who escaped were allowed to continue along the road north, while all save one of the soldiers were executed."

"That was well done," Devlin said. His plan to drive a wedge between the mercenaries and the regular Selvarat army had succeeded beyond his wildest hopes. There had been a number of reports of the two groups skirmishing. One mercenary captain had apparently decided that she had had enough, so she had seized a Selvarat supply ship, commandeering it to take her and her troops back to their homes in the Green Isles. He could only hope that others would follow her lead and join the growing ranks of deserters.

"Five new bands have formed in the last month," Ulmer said.

Devlin listened closely as Ulmer described each of the bands, who led them, what successes or failures they had had, and where they were most likely to be found. He dare not commit any of this intelligence to paper, which was why Stephen's presence was so valuable. He had a minstrel's recall and could be counted on to remember anything Devlin or Drakken might miss.

Some of the news was old, and Devlin had already heard of two of the bands that Ulmer named; but such often occurred, when messages were passed from one trusted soul to another. It was better to hear the same message several times than to risk never hearing it at all.

Unless, of course, the news was ill.

"The one called Didrik sends news that he believes there are hostages being held in the keep belonging to the former Baron of Korinth. He and his band plan a raid there as soon as they are able," Ulmer continued.

Devlin clenched his left fist, digging his fingernails into the palm of his hand, as he fought to quell the grief that rose up within him.

Ulmer's eyes darted from him to Captain Drakken, then back again.

"Is there something wrong?" Ulmer asked.

"Your message is old. We have already heard that the hostages were successfully rescued," Drakken explained.

Ulmer smiled. "Then that is good news indeed, that I will pass on to my brethren."

"Tell them also that Nils Didrik died in freeing the hostages," Devlin added.

"I am sorry for his loss," Ulmer said, showing unusual sensitivity. The messenger who had first brought the news of Didrik's fate had called it a glorious death. His callous dismissal of Didrik's sacrifice had enraged Devlin. Only Stephen's hand on Devlin's sword arm had prevented the messenger from being struck down.

"Is there any other news to share?" Drakken asked, breaking into the silence that had fallen over them.

"That is all I have been entrusted with. What messages have you for me?"

"Tell your son and the other leaders that our aim is twofold. First, to drive the enemy back toward the coast, wherever possible. Let the mercenaries pass unhindered, if they agree to surrender their bows and swords. And second, we must cut off the Selvarat supply lines. As the harvest begins, they will seek to provision themselves for the winter. We must not let that happen. Any crops that cannot be secured for our own folk must be destroyed," Drakken said. "Do you understand?"

"It is a hard thing you ask," Ulmer said.

Many of Devlin's followers would have said yes, without stopping to reckon the cost. But no doubt in his lifetime the old man had seen his share of famine and hungry winters.

"Starving men cannot fight," Devlin said. "They will be forced to bottle themselves up in their fortresses, and then we can surround them."

"I will pass the word as you have given it to me," Ulmer said.

"I thank you," Devlin replied.

With that, Ulmer summoned his granddaughter and took his leave.

In theory, all of the bands had sworn allegiance to Devlin as the General of the Army. But with only the loosest of command structure, it was up to the band leaders to make their own decisions. In the beginning a few had scorned Devlin's tactics, likening them to those of bandits rather than soldiers. One reckless youth with a head for glory had taken on a full company of the enemy. On open ground, with nearly equal numbers, the result had been a slaughter. Those few of the band who had surrendered had been spared only to face public execution.

It had been a brutal lesson, and one Devlin was swift to hammer home. The rebel bands were never to fight a pitched battle. They were to attack only on their terms, using the elements of surprise and of overwhelming numbers. If faced with a larger force, they were to retreat and wait for the opportunity to attack the force from cover, or from positions that offered a quick escape. Strike when the enemy was least expecting it.

Assassination was their tool of choice. Even killing a single soldier could be a victory, if the killer vanished and was never found. Anyone could be the enemy. Handsome young men and women flirted with the Selvarat officers, then wrapped garrotes around their necks when they leaned in for a kiss. Stooped elders still had enough strength to wield deadly daggers, and even young children could be taught to lure the enemy into a trap.

It was a fine thing he had done, when in his name the folk of Jorsk taught their children to be killers.

No one among them had ever conceived of this kind of warfare. Even Stephen, with his vast knowledge of the history of Jorsk, could bring to mind no comparisons with the past. There was not a single song in either Jorskian or the Selvarat tongue that told of such a brutal war.

But there were plenty of ballads in the Caer tongue from which Devlin drew his inspiration, tales of blood feuds and kinwars that lasted generations. Entire families destroyed, down to the least member. He alone of the fighters knew what he had unleashed and how high the price would be. For now the Jorskians had eyes only for the immediate future and for driving out the invaders. But even if they should prove victorious, they would not find it easy to set aside the memories of what they had done and the new skills they had acquired. The echoes of their rebellion would shape Jorsk for decades to come.

Would future generations hail him as a deliverer? Or curse him as a destroyer?

He could not afford such grim self-indulgence. It did not matter what they thought of him. It did not matter what the far-off future held. Only the present mattered, and the conviction that each day, each victory led them closer to their ultimate triumph.

For now his tactics were working. The Jorskians were new to this kind of warfare, but they learned swiftly, and their unconventional tactics baffled the Selvarat invaders. Devlin's forces were more than holding their own, despite the cost.

Didrik was just one of the many who had fallen in the weeks since Devlin had declared war against the Selvarats.

More than one had died at his own hand, when they'd been forced to execute those who were too wounded to continue. Every victory or defeat brought a tally of those who had been lost.

He had grieved for Didrik, who surely had never expected that he would die so far from Kingsholm and the Guard to which he had dedicated his life. Didrik had been one of the first friends he made in this land. Yet even as he mourned Didrik's loss, Devlin's grief was touched with guilt. What of those others who'd died, those whose faces and names he'd never known? Was he any less responsible for their deaths, and were they any less deserving of his sorrow?

And how many more would be killed, friends and strangers alike, before he finished this bloody quest? It was a daunting thought, but he pushed it aside, just as he pushed aside his grief over those he had lost. He could not afford the weakness of mourning his dead. He could not stop to count their losses. He had to rediscover within himself the single-minded dedication that the Geas had provided. The ability to think of nothing but the task at hand and to conceive of no other outcome than ultimate victory.

It was ironic that he had spent two years desperately seeking to be free of the Geas, only to find that freedom brought its own burdens. It had been easier when he had had no choice, was able to blame his decisions on the consuming power of his duty. Freed of the Geas, he had no such shield. The consequences of his actions would rest squarely on his own head.

Devlin blinked as he left the dim house for the bright sunshine outside. A small crowd had gathered in the lane, children mostly, and he pushed impatiently through them as he returned to the square where the horses were being tended. There was so much to do, and he was conscious of time slipping away. Already they had lingered there too long. Trelleborg was still several days away, and his forces had to be in position before the first shipments of the confiscated harvest began to arrive.

The archer who had taken his horse earlier now approached Devlin, handing him a cup of water and a cloth-wrapped bundle that proved to be a chunk of cheese and a small loaf of bread, gifts of their hosts, no doubt.

"Is there enough for everyone?" Devlin asked.

Most days the band that traveled with him was relatively small, numbering fewer than fifty. That enabled him to travel swiftly and ensured that they would not place too heavy a burden on the villages and towns where they foraged for supplies. New recruits were swiftly assigned to one of the roaming bands, but a few stayed, replacing those who had been killed. This particular archer had been with them at least a fortnight, but Devlin had not yet learned his name.

He tried very hard not to learn any of their names, nor, indeed, to grow fond of any of them. His nights were haunted enough, he did not need to add to the tally of those who reproached him for their deaths.

"Yes, General, the rest of the band has been fed, and Lirna is paying for the supplies," the archer replied.

"Good."

When they could, they paid for the supplies they needed, to assure that the folk here would be well-disposed toward them should they need to return. There had been some lean days, but for the most part they had not lacked for food. That, too, would soon change, for the harvest was upon them. At each village where they stopped, Devlin had given the same orders that he had given to Ulmer. Any crops that could not be secured for the rebellion were to be destroyed. Nothing was to fall into the hands of the invaders, not so much as a single mouthful of grain.

Cut off from their supply lines, and unable to feed themselves from the land, the invaders would be forced to surrender or risk starvation.

It was a bold plan, but one that would bring privation and suffering to the very people that he was trying to save. The smaller bands might be able to survive off forest game, but the coming winter would be one of hardship for everyone.

# Twenty-five

TINY SNOWFLAKES FELL FROM THE LEADEN GRAY sky, dusting Stephen's cloak briefly with a sprinkling of white before melting away. The stone cobbles underneath their horses' hooves were wet from melted snow, and there were icy patches that required care. But it was not full winter, not yet.

Stephen shivered as much from apprehension as from the cold. He looked to his left, where Devlin rode, bareheaded despite the weather. Even without the snow, Devlin's hair was more white than black these days, a visible reminder of the time he had spent as Prince Arnaud's captive. The other changes were no less profound, even if they were not visible to the casual observer.

Stephen still did not know what had happened during Devlin's captivity. Devlin, as was his nature, had been remarkably silent about his ordeal. It was left to his friends to piece together his story from the few clues that Devlin had let slip. They knew that Arnaud had been a mindsorcerer, the same one who had previously tried to kill Devlin or drive him mad. There was no doubt that he had used his skills to torture Devlin, yet Devlin had somehow defeated him and emerged sane from his ordeal.

Or as sane as one could expect. There were those who would argue that Devlin's decision to launch the rebellion was a sign that his wits had been badly damaged. Yet if madness it was, it was a peculiar kind, for against all odds, Devlin and the army he led were winning the war. A war in which Stephen had played no small part, though his actions were far from the heroic deeds he had once imagined.

When he had joined with the others in urging Devlin to lead the rebellion to throw out the Selvarat invaders four months ago, he had not understood what it was that he was asking. Devlin had warned him of the horrors they would unleash, but Stephen had dismissed his concerns. He had not realized that the cost of victory might be nearly as high as the cost of defeat.

If he were to be faced with the same choice today, he did not know what he would do. Would he still urge Devlin to launch this people's war? Could he still blithely urge untrained peasants to join the fight, now that he knew how many of them would be killed? Old, young, men, women, veteran army soldiers and peasants who barely knew one end of a spear from another . . . He no longer knew how many deaths he had witnessed. Hundreds perhaps.

He had killed as well, dispatching at least a dozen of the enemy to join Lord Haakon's realm. Others had done more, but Devlin had guarded Stephen closely, refusing to allow him to take any of the dangerous scouting missions, or indeed to venture far from Devlin's sight. And Stephen had never been called upon to deliver the final mercy, that of dispatching wounded comrades so they did not fall into the hands of the enemy.

He knew that Devlin was attempting to protect him and to spare what remained of his innocence. He had not the heart to tell him that there was no innocence left to protect. Stephen's hands were as bloodstained as anyone else's. He may not have been the one to give the orders, but that made him no less responsible for what was done in the name of the rebellion.

His nights were haunted by memories of what he had seen, and the knowledge that it might still come to naught if Devlin was not able to secure the concessions he needed.

"What will you do?" he asked.

Devlin glanced over at him, then fixed his gaze at the walls of Kingsholm, which loomed before him. "What needs to be done," he replied.

It was not a comforting answer. In the past Stephen had ascribed Devlin's single-minded ruthlessness to the force of the Geas spell. Now, with the spell removed, it was disquieting to realize how much of that ruthless focus was an intrinsic part of Devlin's nature.

Devlin would do as he saw fit, with only his own sense of honor to limit his actions. Ordinarily it would have been enough. Stephen trusted Devlin. He would trust him with his life and the lives of all those he cared about. Devlin had demonstrated on numerous occasions that he could put the welfare of others and of the Kingdom ahead of his own concerns. But he was still a man, and more important, he was a man who had been betrayed. There was no telling how he would react when he came face-to-face with King Olafur.

At least this time Devlin would not face the King alone. Stephen rode on Devlin's right, while Captain Drakken rode on his left. Behind them were two hundred fighters, mostly drawn from the ranks of Devlin's volunteers, with a few of Mikkelson's regular troops to leaven the mix. Hardened veterans, all of them, who had personally pledged their loyalty to the Chosen One. The force was not enough to take the city, but it would make those within Kingsholm think twice about trifling with Devlin.

"We need King Olafur," Captain Drakken chimed in.

Devlin shook his head. "We do not need him. We need what he has. Troops. Supplies."

"We do not need a civil war. Not now," Drakken added. It was an oft-repeated argument.

"And that is why I sent in Arnulfsdatter under a seal of truce. I will treat with Olafur civilly, if he is willing to do the same. We can set aside our differences. For now."

Devlin did not make any promises about what he would do if the King refused to support the rebellion. It was clear that the final reckoning was merely postponed. Though Stephen did not believe that Devlin meant to depose King Olafur and start a civil war, he was sickened by the killings, as they all were.

And it would be difficult to explain the reasons for Devlin's anger against King Olafur. Only a handful knew that the King had betrayed Devlin, handing the Chosen One over to the Selvarat invaders to face certain death. The rest merely saw Devlin as a disobedient hero, one who had gone against the King's orders, finding victory where the King had seen only the certainty of defeat.

Not that they had won. Not yet. But they were close. The Southern Road was firmly under their control, as were the territories in the south where the improbable alliance of Lord Rikard and Marshal Kollinar had succeeded in liberating Myrka and burning the Selvarat fleet docked in the harbor. Most of the mercenaries had deserted, seizing the ships that had brought resupplies so they could return to their bases in the Green Isles. The surviving Selvarat invaders were now cut off, confined to a narrow ring of territory around the port of Trelleborg and the fortifications they had built along the southern coast of Esker.

Winter had begun. Soon the harbors would freeze, making it impossible for the Selvarat armies to receive reinforcements or supplies. If they did not starve before spring, they would emerge greatly weakened.

But Devlin's irregular forces also needed supplies, as did the thousands of refugees who had been displaced from their homes. And they needed access to the arms and soldiers contained within the other royal garrisons, those who had remained in barracks obedient to Marshal Olvarrson's commands. Jorsk had shown that it was not easy prey, but it was possible that Empress Thania might try a full-scale attack come spring, and they needed to be ready to defend themselves.

There were few folk abroad on this dreary morning, and those who were quickly drew aside as Devlin's party came into sight. They recognized the Chosen One at once. Devlin's features were clearly visible, as was the hilt of the Sword of Light, which he wore in a baldric across his back. Some cheered and called out his name, while others bowed their heads. Devlin did not acknowledge their greetings, but the stone in the sword's hilt began to glow, as it did when the Chosen One was preparing to wield it.

Captain Drakken drew her horse closer to Devlin, and Stephen did the same. He felt an itch between his shoulder blades and resisted the urge to look behind him. He knew well the risks that they were taking. A single archer could put an end to all their hopes. Devlin believed that the rebellion would survive his death, but Stephen was not as sanguine.

The gate ahead of them was open, and Stephen tried to take that as a good sign. Had it been barred against them, they would have been forced to abandon their mission or try to fight their way in.

A half dozen guards were at the gate, and as Devlin approached, one of them stepped forward. He recognized Lieutenant Embeth, though she wore the two gold cords of a Captain.

"My Lord Chosen One," Captain Embeth said, thumping her right shoulder in the formal salute. Then she did something unexpected, sinking to one knee and bowing her head. The guards behind her did the same.

Stephen's skin crawled as he witnessed the formal obeisance given only to the ruler of Jorsk. It was a shocking departure from custom, but it left no doubt where Embeth's loyalties lay.

"Rise. Report," Devlin growled.

Embeth rose to her feet. "Kingsholm is secure, General Devlin. Those who supported the Selvarat occupation have been rounded up and await your judgment."

"And what does the King say to all this?"

Embeth drew closer, pitching her voice so it could be heard only by those who were closest to Devlin. "King Olafur is dead," she said. "We found his body just before midnight."

Devlin began cursing in his own tongue.

"Have you arrested the assassin?" Drakken asked.

"The King took his own life," Embeth said.

Stephen shook his head, certain that he had misheard her. It must be a mistake of some kind. What reason could Olafur have to kill himself?

"What are your orders?" Embeth asked.

"Assign someone to find lodging for my troops, then I want to see his body," Devlin said.

The body of Olafur, son of Thorvald, was laid out upon his bed. A pair of guards stood vigil, and at Devlin's command they drew down the silk shroud that covered the King's body. From his contorted features it was clear that Olafur had not died an easy death. There were traces of dried vomit on his face and clothes, and his tongue was bloodied from where he had nearly bitten it in two.

Devlin forced his gaze lower, to the King's belly, where a gaping wound revealed how the King had nearly disemboweled himself. A loop of intestine could be seen, still threatening to spill forth. And the room held the sickly-sweet stench that he had become all too familiar with, for it was the stench of death.

"Coward," he said, reaching down to grasp the King's chin in his hand. He turned Olafur's head, but the King's lifeless gaze held neither secrets nor apologies. Devlin's anger, which had carried him through the long months, rose up, and it was only with great effort that he resisted the urge to strike the King's lifeless body. How dare Olafur have done this? What right had he to take the coward's way, abandoning his people in their time of need? He had deserted them. And he had robbed Devlin of his chance for justice.

He had spent months dreaming of the moment when he would see Olafur, when he would force the King to acknowledge his errors and demand satisfaction for the wrongs that had been done to him. And now that, too, would be denied him.

"You stupid bloody fool," Devlin proclaimed.

One of his watchers hissed at the insult, as Devlin relinquished his grasp upon Olafur, letting his head loll to one side.

"Cover him," he ordered, then turned to face Lieutenant, no Captain, Embeth.

"Tell me again what happened," he said.

"The King met with his councilors last night, after receiving your message. He ordered that the city be prepared to welcome you. Then he retired to his private sitting room. We found a bottle of poison by his side. It appears that it did not act swiftly enough, so he turned to the knife."

"And no one heard anything? No one heard him cry out?"

"The guards were outside the entrance to the royal suites. They heard nothing. A chamberman found the King's body as he was preparing to bank the fires for the night," Embeth reported.

Indeed the thick walls of the sitting room and its interior location could mask a multitude of sins, from an illicit liaison to a horror like Devlin's betrayal. There was a grim symmetry in the fact that Olafur's blood stained the floor not far from where Saskia had spilled her own life.

But why had he killed himself? Had he really feared

Devlin so much? Had he thought that Devlin intended to murder him? It only showed how little Olafur had understood him. Devlin had sought satisfaction, yes, but he would not have murdered Olafur.

Strange how the King's cowardice proved to be his final undoing. Terrified by the thought of Devlin's revenge, he had chosen for himself a far harsher punishment than Devlin would ever have inflicted.

And now it was up to Devlin to clean up the mess that the King had left behind.

"Who knows of this?" he asked.

"Only a handful of us know. The chamberman who found the body is in seclusion along with the guards who were on duty when the body was discovered. These two have kept watch over the King's body, while the guards outside were told nothing except that the King was not to be disturbed. Although Lady Ingeleth may suspect something is awry. She was quite angry when I refused her admittance earlier," Embeth reported.

Her quick thinking had preserved the calm, but it would not last long. Knowing that Devlin was arriving in the city that morning, Embeth had implemented the plans she had made long ago with Captain Drakken. Before dawn trusted members of the Guard had rounded up those of their number who were suspected traitors, confining them to the goal before seeking out the members of the court who were equally suspect. Over a dozen courtiers were either confined to their chambers or guests of the Guard, including Baron Martell, whose armsmen had betrayed Devlin, and Count Magaharan, the Selvarat ambassador.

Even if all those sworn to secrecy held their tongues, it

would soon become obvious that Olafur was no longer in charge of Kingsholm.

"Fetch Lady Ingeleth. And Marshal Olvarrson, if he can be found," Devlin ordered. "And send messages to the rest of the King's Council that they are to meet in one hour."

Embeth saluted again. She had developed an odd taste for formality, but Devlin was too tired to correct her. She disappeared for a moment, speaking softly to those outside before returning.

Devlin noticed that she was careful not to glance at the shrouded body. Indeed, all present had turned their heads away. Even the sentries on either side of the bed faced outward, guarding against threat. He glanced at Stephen, who had remained unusually quiet; but if Stephen was troubled, he gave no sign. Strangely, that disturbed Devlin more than it would have if Stephen had appeared ill. Once such a sight would have sent the minstrel stumbling from the room. Now Stephen had grown hardened to such horrors, as indeed, they all had.

Devlin ran the fingers of his good hand through his hair, noticing that it was still chill and damp from the melted snow. The room was cold—no fire had been lit in deference to the King's body.

Olafur's death had shocked him, but as Devlin gathered his wits, he realized that his purpose in coming was unchanged. He still needed the same things—provisions, arms, and troops to reinforce those who had grown weary with battle. His goals had not changed, only the means by which he must achieve them.

Lady Ingeleth arrived swiftly, before his panic overwhelmed him. Hard on her heels was Marshal Olvarrson.

Both were dressed in their court finery, but the effect was ruined, for they arrived out of breath, as if they had run the length of the palace. And, indeed, perhaps they had.

"What is the meaning of this?" Lady Ingeleth asked as she crossed the threshold.

Devlin stepped aside so she could see the King's body.

"What have you done?" she demanded, striding swiftly into the room.

The chief councilor was elderly, but she did not lack for courage. She had practically accused Devlin of murder, even though she could see that he was surrounded by those loyal to him.

"Uncover his face," he ordered.

Lady Ingeleth's steps slowed as she approached the bed, and the guard drew down the coverlet to reveal Olafur's tormented visage.

"As you can see, this was done last night. Long before I arrived," Devlin said.

Lady Ingeleth swallowed convulsively, but she stood her ground. Marshal Olvarrson fared less well, for he turned pale as he beheld the King's body.

"He took his own life rather than face me," Devlin said. His eyes caught and held Olvarrson's. "The King killed himself in his private sitting room, surrounded by reminders of his betrayal."

The Marshal took two hasty steps back, only to find his retreat blocked by Captain Drakken. His eyes widened as he caught sight of one who had been proclaimed a traitor.

"You cannot blame me. I was acting under orders from my King," Olvarrson began. His face was dotted with perspiration.

"You had a choice," Captain Drakken said. She drew

her sword from its scabbard, holding it lightly in her right hand, as if she were preparing to duel. "We all had a choice. Olafur chose the path of dishonor and betrayal, but you did not have to follow him."

Lady Ingeleth's eyes widened as she observed this interplay. She had not been present on the fateful night when Devlin was betrayed, although surely she must have had her suspicions about what had occurred.

"Olafur has already paid his debt. Will you?" Captain Drakken asked, raising the point of her sword so that it was aimed at Olvarrson's heart.

"Please, my lord, I beg your mercy." Olvarrson's voice broke.

Suddenly Devlin had had enough. He understood Drakken's anger, but Olvarrson was merely a contemptible worm. A feeble target for their wrath, since they had been deprived of their rightful prey. Olvarrson's fault was that he had been blindly loyal to a bad king, and though he was dishonored, he did not deserve a cold-blooded execution. "Hold. Drakken put back your sword," he said.

Drakken muttered, but did as she was ordered.

"Thank you, my lord," Olvarrson began, but then, seeing Devlin's face, had the good sense to shut up.

"Where is Princess Ragenilda? Has she been told of her father's death?"

"Ragenilda is not in Kingsholm," Embeth said. "She was preparing to leave on a journey to Selvarat, but instead she was spirited out of the city by Solveig, who took Ragenilda to join her father in Esker."

"King Olafur professed himself most aggrieved by the kidnapping, but in truth he seemed rather relieved that the girl was safe from the intrigues of the court," Lady Ingeleth added. "It is rumored that he had spoken with Solveig Brynjolfsdatter only a few days before she conceived her mad plan."

Devlin breathed a sigh of relief. He owed much to Solveig for keeping Ragenilda safe. If the Princess had been taken to Selvarat, then the King's death would have been a disaster indeed. As it was, perhaps something could be salvaged from the mess he had left behind.

"Stephen, I need you to go to Esker and bring back the Princess. Take as many of the Guard as you need, but bring her here swiftly."

It would be a hard journey, but Brynjolf was unlikely to release his prize to any messenger other than his own son.

"What should I tell her?"

"Tell her she is needed here and must return."

"I mean what should I tell her about this?" Stephen waved his hand in the direction of the bed.

Devlin hesitated. "Tell her that her father is dead," he said. He would not let the girl travel here in false hopes of a reunion. Better that she hear the news from Stephen than from some chance gossip on the road.

"And what do you intend to do with the Princess?" Lady Ingeleth asked.

"Guard her. She will be the next Queen of Jorsk. That is if you and your fellow councilors can be persuaded to put aside your petty quarrels and join with me in saving the Kingdom."

# Twenty-six

IN THE END, IT WAS NEARLY TWO HOURS before Devlin was ready to meet with the remaining councilors. It was not deliberate discourtesy on his part, though he knew that some would see it as such. Rather it was that there were suddenly a hundred demands upon his attention.

After leaving the King's chamber, he had reviewed with Embeth the list of those she had taken into protective custody. Nearly a quarter of the Guard, and all of the newest recruits, had been gaoled, until their loyalties could be proven one way or another. Embeth had erred on the side of caution, but it was troubling to learn that some of those who had not previously been suspected had chosen to desert once they saw what was happening to their comrades. In time, they too would have to be hunted down.

The city was calm, but Embeth had suggested extra patrols to keep order when the news of the King's death was announced. The defections and the need to watch their newly acquired prisoners had stretched the Guard thin, so he authorized Embeth to draw upon the members of his escort and delegated Captain Drakken to make the necessary arrangements. Embeth, he noticed, was quick to defer to Captain Drakken, but after serving as Captain of the City Guard for these past months, it would be difficult for her to be demoted to a mere lieutenant again. Not to mention a poor reward for her loyal service. Nor could he slight Drakken. That was just one of the problems that he would have to solve in the coming days.

Brother Arni had been summoned to take charge of the King's body. Lady Ingeleth had asked what Devlin intended for funeral arrangements, to which Devlin had replied that he cared naught, as long as it was swift, as befit a country at war. He would not pretend to mourn for Olafur, but neither was he so petty that he would deny those who had served the king the chance to pay their final respects. Let Olafur be buried with his ancestors in the royal tomb. History would pass its own judgment upon the failed King.

He had written a letter to Baron Brynjolf, and a separate one to Solveig, which Stephen would carry with him. Then he had left Stephen to make his preparations for the journey, along with Oluva, who was personally selecting those of the Guard who would form the escort.

And that was another matter. The Guard was being pulled in a dozen different directions, forced to bear the burden of responsibilities far beyond its scope. Yet for now, it was the only effective fighting force in Kingsholm. The royal garrison was nearby, but whether its officers could be trusted was a matter for another day.

For the present he had a roomful of council members, who were impatiently awaiting his presence. As he approached the council chamber, he saw Captain Drakken waiting outside, along with a pair of guards who were there for more than mere ceremony. She had found time to change into her dress uniform, which one of the Guard must have saved for her all these long months.

Devlin had no time for such niceties. Expecting to meet with the King, he had dressed in a clean tunic and leggings that morning, but it was a far cry from the formal uniform of the Chosen One. Only the Sword of Light, which he still wore in its harness, proclaimed his rank. It would have to be enough.

He nodded, and at his signal the nearest guard swung open the door of the council chamber. He could hear the murmur of conversation, which fell silent as he entered, followed by Captain Drakken. A few appeared surprised to see him, and even more surprised when the doors were swiftly swung shut.

Devlin strode to the head of the table, where there were two empty chairs—the center chair that belonged to King Olafur, and the seat immediately to its left. Once, during a brief period of amicability, that seat had belonged to Devlin as the Chosen One, before Olafur's scheming had driven Devlin away from Kingsholm and his rightful place on the council.

Devlin was the center of all eyes, yet no one greeted him or expressed their gratitude for his miraculous survival. Instead, a few frowned at his unkempt appearance, while more than one regarded the Sword of Light with a thoughtful expression.

One did not bear arms in the council chamber. Ever. Yet here was the Chosen One, wearing a sword, and the supposed traitor Captain Drakken, now in uniform and clearly armed as well. It was a powerful message to those who had learned to read the shifting alliances of the court from the subtlest of clues.

"Has the King been delayed?" Lord Sygmund asked. It seemed the others had deferred to him to speak. As one of the few neutral members of the council, he was not Devlin's friend, but neither was he his foe.

"Olafur is dead, killed by his own hand during the night," Devlin said bluntly.

There were a few gasps, and Councilor Arnulf blanched.

"May the Gods have mercy," Lord Baldur said, making the sign for ill luck.

With the exception of Lady Ingeleth and Marshal Olvarrson, the council members appeared genuinely surprised. Apparently the pair had held their tongues, which argued that they saw the value of cooperating with him. At least for the present.

"Is there anyone who can vouch for how he died?" Councilor Arnulf asked.

"I have seen the King's body, and it appears that he did indeed perish during the night," Lady Ingeleth said. "The Guards were informed of his death and chose to keep the news quiet until the Chosen One arrived."

Her words were carefully phrased. Devlin might not have killed the King by his own hand, but there would be those who would assume that the King had been murdered by someone acting under Devlin's orders. Even Lady Ingeleth might well believe him capable of such a deed, and there was no way to prove his innocence.

But either way, they would have to work with him. Either because they trusted in his honor and believed in his cause, or because they feared sharing Olafur's fate. It did not matter why they obeyed him, only that they did so.

Devlin, who had remained standing, took his seat at the head of the table, in the chair that had once belonged to Olafur. He motioned for Captain Drakken to take the seat next to him, but she shook her head and instead stood directly behind him, so she could direct the full force of her attention upon the council members.

"Do we now call you King?" Lady Ingeleth's expression was sour, but he could only admire her courage. Here was a woman who was not afraid to speak the hard truths. It was a wonder she had lasted as long in Olafur's court as she had.

"I am what I have been. Devlin of Duncaer. Chosen One, General of the Royal Army," he said.

"And leader of a ragtag mob," Councilor Arnulf added.

"And leader of the Army of the People, whose ranks include your own daughter. A woman of courage and conviction, you may be justly proud to call her your own," Devlin said.

Arnulf frowned as if searching for some hidden meaning, but Devlin had meant the praise honestly. Troop Captain Arnulfsdatter had indeed acquitted herself well, once she had gotten over the shock of commanding irregular forces rather than the highly disciplined troops of the Royal Army. She was one of the many whose service would have to be rewarded.

"Princess Ragenilda will be brought from Esker," Devlin said. "In time, she will rule here as Queen."

"With you as consort?" Lord Baldur asked.

Devlin stared at him, wondering how anyone could

imagine him capable of such a foul deed. "She is a child," he said.

"Not too young to be pledged," Lady Ingeleth pointed out.

Ragenilda was all of eleven summers, while Devlin himself was rapidly approaching his thirtieth year. He was old enough to be her father. He knew that such dynastic matches were not unheard of among the members of the nobility, but he could not comprehend how a grown man could contemplate taking a child to his bed. Even if he waited until she was of age, she would still be a youthful maiden, while he would remain a man grown old before his time, scarred by what he had done and the horrors he had witnessed.

Not that he had any wish to be King, either in name or as the power behind the Queen. Though there were few present who would believe him. Power was the game of the court, and ambition the language spoken by all. They would not understand one who had no interest in their games.

"In five years, Ragenilda will be old enough to assume the throne, then she may make what alliance she chooses. Until that day I will act as Regent. With the blessings of the council, of course."

"Of course," Councilor Arnulf echoed.

"What do you want?" Lord Baldur asked.

What he wanted was to walk out of the room and take himself far from these people. He had given them two years of his life, and now the task ahead of him would consume him for years to come. Yet he stayed, knowing that there was no one else who could take his place. To name any other as regent was to risk civil war. Only the

Chosen One could command the obedience of the common people and the nobles alike. The people's army that he had raised would not lightly lay down its arms, nor would it follow any save Devlin or his chosen successor. And only by becoming Regent could he fulfill the oath he had made, to ensure that the people of Jorsk had the chance to live in peace.

"By the time Ragenilda assumes the throne, I intend to hand over to her a Kingdom that is peaceful, its borders secure," Devlin said.

No one sneered openly, but a few wore expressions of mild disbelief. They did not worry him. It was those whose faces he could not read who would bear the most watching in the coming days.

"And there is one thing you will give me. I want Duncaer."

"You want what?" Baldur's voice rose.

"I want Duncaer," Devlin repeated. "Mine, to dispose of as I see fit."

Councilor Arnulf smiled, apparently pleased that Devlin had finally said something he understood. "So you disdain our throne for kingship over your own people?"

"It costs you nothing to give it to me," Devlin said. "Kollinar emptied the garrisons when he took his troops to fight the invaders. Attempting to reconquer Duncaer would cost you treasure and lives, neither of which you have to waste."

"I see no harm in doing so. Though we cannot force your people to acknowledge you as ruler," Lady Ingeleth cautioned.

That was unimportant, since Devlin had no intention of trying to rule over Duncaer. Still, it was the price of his cooperation, and it would make the councilors feel that they had negotiated with him. Even grudging allies were better than those who must be subdued by force.

"Shall we put it to the vote? I agree to serve as Regent for no more than five years, and in return Duncaer will be given into my care."

"I recommend that the council accept your proposal," Lady Ingeleth said. "Stability must be preserved, and there are no other suitable candidates for Regent."

Lady Ingeleth, at least, could read the shifting winds of fortune and power. No doubt she wished to serve as chief councilor of the new Regent's Council. Devlin had already assigned her such role, for the continuity would reassure the nervous members of the court. But he had said nothing to her of his decision, for he intended to see that she worked hard to earn the position.

Lady Ingeleth turned to her right, fixing her gaze on Lord Baldur. Like herself, Baldur was a longtime courtier, having served both Olafur and his father Thorvald. Baldur was a traditionalist who bore no love for the Chosen One, but he would favor any arrangement that preserved Ragenilda's claim to the throne.

"I concur," Baldur said in a clear voice. "Devlin of Duncaer shall serve as Regent until the Princess reaches her sixteenth birthday."

Devlin watched impassively as each councilor in turn cast his or her vote in favor of his Regency. Some were more enthusiastic than others, but there were no dissents.

Only Marshal Olvarrson was silent, for he had a seat on the council but no vote.

"It seems we are in agreement. Lady Ingeleth, may I ask you to draft a proclamation of the King's death and the announcement of the Regency? It would be best if the people heard the news from the palace rather than from gossip."

"Of course," Lady Ingeleth replied.

"And now, for the next matter of business before this council. Given my post as Regent, I must relinquish the generalship of the Royal Army," Devlin said. He noticed a few surprised looks at his willingness to relinquish at least some of the power he now held. Of course the same fools had little notion of what was truly involved in leading the army, while at the same time trying to govern a realm. A man could answer one challenge or the other, but not both. Not successfully. And it was best that he begin as he meant to go on.

"Marshal Olvarrson has expressed a wish to retire from service," Devlin continued. Olvarrson had actually said a great deal more, including pleading for his life. Devlin had agreed to let him retire quietly, without retribution. He felt nothing but contempt for Olvarrson, but Devlin realized that he himself bore part of the blame. He had been the one to elevate Olvarrson to the rank of Marshal. He should have known the man was not fit for the post he held. It was a lesson that Devlin would not soon forget. "A messenger has been sent to Kollinar, Earl of Tiernach, summoning him to take leadership of the Royal Army," Devlin announced.

"An interesting choice," Councilor Arnulf observed. "I am certain he will serve you well."

"Lord Kollinar has shown initiative and the ability to put the needs of Jorsk ahead of personal concerns. Would that all could say the same," Devlin replied.

He and Kollinar had had a tense relationship during

his sojourn in Jorsk, but Kollinar had proven his mettle when the crisis came. And as one long exiled from the machinations of the court, he owed no allegiance to any of the factions that would be maneuvering for power.

Not to mention that, as Earl of Tiernach, Kollinar came from one of the old noble families. His bloodlines would appeal to the conservative factions of the court, those most likely to take umbrage at the declaration that they must pay homage to the foreign-born metalsmith who ruled as Regent.

Devlin had been tempted to name Mikkelson as General, but Mikkelson was still too young for the post. Instead he planned to name him a Marshal, placing him in charge of the defense of the east. As it was, Mikkelson would have gone from ensign to Marshal in less than two years, a feat no doubt unparalleled in the ranks of the Royal Army.

"And now, for the next matter of business, what message do you intend to give the Selvarat ambassador?" Lady Ingeleth asked.

"Leave him to me," Devlin replied.

Count Magaharan bowed low, his left arm tucked behind him, his right hand sweeping forward in the flourishing gesture he used for the most formal of occasions. He held the pose for a half dozen heartbeats before straightening.

"Lord Devlin, this is an unexpected honor," the ambassador said. Only the faintest glint in his eyes indicated that he was aware of the irony of his words. Indeed, he looked remarkably composed for a man who had been roused from his bed in the dark hours of the night and brought under guard to the palace. Erring on the side of caution, Embeth had confined the ambassador in the small suite of rooms that was set aside for his use when he chose to stay in the palace rather than in his personal residence. It was more diplomatic than a gaol cell, but the message was the same.

"Surely you must have known this day would come," Devlin said. "Once you learned that I had escaped Arnaud's custody."

"I expected we would meet again, though confidentially I thought it would be later rather than sooner," Magaharan said. With his free hand he gestured to the chairs that flanked the fireplace. "Shall we sit and discuss affairs as civilized men?"

Devlin shrugged and took the nearest seat, one which gave him full view of the door. There was a guard stationed outside, but it did no harm to be careful. He had left the Sword of Light in his chambers, knowing that the legendary weapon of Jorsk would hold little meaning for a foreigner. But he had his throwing knives in their forearm sheathes, and two daggers openly displayed in his boot tops. Just in case.

He had not forgotten that Magaharan had been one of the witnesses to his betrayal.

"Shall I summon a servant to bring us wine? There are a few bottles of my private stock still here that I would offer. I know that your people place a great store upon hospitality."

So he had studied the ways of the Caerfolk. If he had taken time to study their history as well, he might have had some inkling of the forces that Devlin could unleash.

"I do not accept gifts from my enemies," Devlin said.

Count Magaharan leaned back in his seat, the relaxed pose of a man who had no serious worries. "But are we enemies? There is a peasant uprising in the east, or so it is rumored, but our countries remain firm allies. Your wise King and my gracious Empress have pledged their eternal friendship."

"Olafur is dead. Killed by his own hand, last night."

Magaharan's head jerked, startled by the news or perhaps merely by Devlin's blunt statement. No doubt one of the King's councilors would have taken a quarter hour to broach such a sensitive topic.

But Devlin was not a courtier, and it was well that Magaharan he reminded of that fact.

"An hour ago, Lady Ingeleth sent out the proclamation of the King's death and announced that I had been chosen as Regent for Princess Ragenilda," Devlin said. "And my first act as Regent was to dissolve the alliance with Selvarat."

Magaharan stroked his narrow chin with the fingers of his right hand. "Certainly I would be willing to discuss a few changes in the terms of the protectorate," he said slowly. "Subject to the agreement of my Empress, of course."

He was a bold one, acting as if the Selvarats were still a force to be reckoned with. Olafur might have fallen for such deception, but Devlin would not be taken in by such trickery.

"There will be no negotiations. The protectorate is finished."

"You will not find it so easy to be rid of us. Our troops—"

"Your troops are beaten. Arnaud's mercenaries deserted

when it became clear that their master's promises would not be fulfilled. As for your army, the bodies of your soldiers can be found scattered across the eastern provinces. Those few who survived have retreated to their fortresses, where they are licking their wounds and hoping that winter ends before they starve."

"You lie." Anger turned Magaharan's face red as the veteran diplomat lost hold of his temper.

"I have no reason to lie," Devlin said. "Your army in Myrka was destroyed and the survivors retreated north, to a handful of fortifications on the coast of Esker. The forces in the north were forced to retreat to the port of Trelleborg. Less than a third of those who set foot in Jorsk remain alive today, and many of their number will not last the winter."

Count Magaharan stared at Devlin as if trying to judge the truth of his words. He must have suspected that the war was not going well, for news of the uprising and Devlin's victories had been trickling into Kingsholm for weeks. But it seemed the ambassador had not realized the full extent of the Selvarat losses.

Since the beginning, the Selvarat threat had been a bluff. They'd gambled by sending every soldier they could spare from their internecine struggles to take part in Prince Arnaud's scheme, going so far as to hire mercenaries to supplement their own troops. It was unlikely they could find enough to launch a serious invasion against an enemy that was prepared to defend its shores.

"What is it you want from me?" Magaharan asked.

"Tomorrow you will be escorted to a river boat, to journey to the port of Bezek. There you will find a ship to take you to Selvarat, and you will bear my personal messages to the Empress Thania."

It was late, but there was still time for one last crossing before winter came and the Bay of Storms again demonstrated how it had earned its name.

"In spring I expect two things. First, the Lady Gemma of Esker and her daughter Madrene are to receive safe passage to their home. I expect to hear of their arrival with the first ships in the spring."

"That can be arranged."

What would happen next would depend on how they had fared during their captivity. Stephen's mother and sister had been held hostage by the Selvarats for over a year now, and Madrene had reportedly married one of the Selvarat nobles. If she had indeed been forced into the alliance, Lord Brynjolf might well demand retribution, and Devlin saw no reason to deny him.

"And you may send ships to evacuate your soldiers from Trelleborg, and from Sunrise Bay in Esker. We will be watching carefully. If there is any trickery, any attempt to land more troops, my soldiers will slaughter your forces. There will be no quarter given. And once we have destroyed the invaders, I will raise an army to conquer Selvarat. Tell Thania that if it is war she wants, then I will teach her the true meaning of the word."

"Bold words from a country that only months ago was begging for our aid. You could never defeat us," Magaharan said.

Devlin leaned forward and held out his left hand. "Do not presume to tell me what I can and cannot do. Prince Arnaud made that mistake. He thought me weak and helpless, bound by his chains. He thought he could control me. But the last thing he saw was his beating heart, clenched in my fist."

For a moment Devlin remembered how it had felt to grasp the Prince's heart, warm blood dripping down his arm as he squeezed the quivering muscle. Magaharan stared in fascination at Devlin's hand, swallowing hard as Devlin closed his fist.

"You are a madman," Magaharan declared.

It was not that simple. Devlin was not mad, though Prince Arnaud's tortures had driven him to the brink. But rather Devlin was the sum of his experiences. Every step he had trod had led him to this place, and to who he was now. His family's death at the hands of the banecats. The exiled wanderings that had led him to the post of Chosen One. His discovery of a new purpose for his life, as the champion of those who had no other to turn to.

All culminating in his betrayal at the hands of King Olafur. Had King Olafur welcomed Devlin's return, then he would have spent these last months in Kingsholm, held prisoner to the King's will by the power of the Geas spell. There would have been no rebellion, no liberation for those whose lands were intended for the Selvarat settlers. Instead, Olafur had unwittingly delivered Devlin into the hands of a mind-sorcerer, one of the few who had the power to break the Geas spell. Devlin had emerged from his ordeal with fresh scars, but with a soul he could finally call his own.

"I am what I have to be," Devlin said finally. "Loyal to my friends, and the most ruthless foe that you will ever face. Go and tell your Empress that she does not wish to be my enemy. She has one chance for peace."

Magaharan nodded slowly, as if he realized that this was no diplomatic game. Devlin was not posturing; nor was he uttering empty threats. He was merely making promises.

"I will tell her of your message. And for my part, I will urge her to accept your terms."

"Then I wish you safe journey," Devlin said. "You and your escort will leave at first light."

Devlin hoped Thania would see reason and accept his offers. He had seen and done enough killing for a lifetime. But if Thania wanted war, he would not rest until he had made sure that she and her empire no longer had the power to threaten Jorsk. He had vowed to bring lasting peace to these lands, and he would keep his promise. Whatever it took.

# Twenty-seven

WINTER CAME TO KINGSHOLM WITH A DECI-
sive flourish, beginning with a snowfall that lasted three
days and nights. When the sun finally appeared the city
glittered under the white blanket that decorated the finest
mansions and wooden hovels alike. From his perch on the
palace walls, the snow gave the illusion of a city united.

But Devlin knew that for the illusion that it was.
Kingsholm was calm, but it was a waiting watchfulness.
Nobles and commoners alike were wary of the new
Regent, wondering if he would be able to fulfill his prom-
ises and bring peace to the realm.

At least the people would not starve. Food shortages
had seemed certain, until one of the local merchants confessed that he had hidden stores away to prevent them
from being confiscated by the King. After suitable encouragement was applied, other merchants came forward
as well. Those who volunteered their caches were allowed
to place them in open warehouses and profit from their
sale. After that, Devlin's guards had searched the city,
seeking other hidden stores. Those who had not come

forward on their own were condemned to suffer the very fate they had feared, for Devlin seized their goods in the name of the absent Princess, to be held in reserve.

The refugees in the eastern provinces faced a more uncertain future, though Devlin had done what he could before the deepening winter made it impossible to send further shipments of provisions. He would have to wait for spring and trust that those he had placed in command would ensure no catastrophe befell those under their charge. It seemed all he did these days was wait, and it chafed at his nerves. He was a man of action, used to doing things. As Chosen One, it had been his duty to journey to wherever he was needed and set things right.

But as Regent he was trapped in Kingsholm. He had to place his faith in others, trusting that they would carry out his orders. No longer could he lead men by his presence. Now he had to command them through a few lines scribbled on a scroll. He had gone from warrior to clerk. Even more irksome, most of the courtiers had chosen to winter over in Kingsholm, to ensure they could ingratiate themselves with the new Regent. He, who had never cared for court politics, found himself at their very center.

As the weeks passed, frustration often threatened to overwhelm him. He confessed to Drakken that he would far rather face another Duke Gerhard on the dueling floor. She had offered him scant sympathy. Her own role as his chief advisor had been intended as a reward, but it carried its own burdens.

At noon on the first day of the New Year, a guard finally brought the news he had been waiting for. Lord Brynjolf's party had passed through the western gate. Devlin sent a messenger to the chamberlain, then hurried down to the courtyard, reaching it just as the travelers arrived.

Stephen threw back the hood of his cloak as he caught sight of Devlin. His face was white with cold, but he managed a rueful smile as he slid off his horse.

"This is the last time I travel in winter. I'm going to find a room with a fire and stay there till spring," Stephen said.

Devlin grasped his hand. "You may stay as long as you like," he said.

He would have said more, but mere friendship had to be set aside for duty. His eyes had already found Lord Brynjolf, who was mounted on an enormous bay, large enough to accommodate both him and the girl perched on the saddle before him.

The Princess's eyes widened as Devlin approached, and she leaned back a bit into Brynjolf's arms. It was to be expected. All she knew of Devlin was that he was the Chosen One and a thorn in her father's side. It would take time for her to learn to trust him.

"Lord Brynjolf, thank you for guarding this treasure, and bringing her safely home," Devlin said.

Brynjolf merely nodded. There would be time for them to talk once they were in private.

Devlin hesitated. For the first time it occurred to him that he did not know how he was expected to greet the Princess. Was there a protocol on how one dealt with the heir to the Kingdom? No doubt Lady Ingeleth was well versed on the customs and ceremonies that governed how one dealt with the heir to the throne. Was he expected to bow? To pledge his loyalty to her? The few times he had seen her and her father together, he had been struck by the formality of their manners. Surely she would not expect him to behave in the same way.

Princess Ragenilda opened her mouth and yawned, and Devlin realized his foolishness. She was not only a Princess, she was also an eleven-year-old girl—one who had just endured a long and difficult journey.

"Princess Ragenilda, welcome home," he said, holding up his arms to help her dismount.

After a moment's hesitation she nodded, and he lifted her down from the saddle.

Grooms held the horses as the others dismounted. He caught a brief glimpse of Solveig before the shifting figures blocked his view.

"There is much news to share, but now is not the time," Devlin said, pitching his voice so the entire party could hear. "Servants will show you to your rooms, where you may rest and refresh yourselves. I will meet with you later."

He turned his attention to Princess Ragenilda, finding he still held her right hand in his own. "Your maid Marja has missed you. She is waiting in your chambers," he said.

Ragenilda smiled at this news, and Devlin was glad that she would have at least that much of a link to her past. The world that Ragenilda was returning to had changed greatly in the brief months she had been gone.

He escorted Ragenilda to her rooms and turned her over to her former nurse, who clucked over her charge, promising that she would be warm and well fed in no time.

Having seen Ragenilda settled, he then spoke with the servants, who confirmed that Lord Brynjolf and his family had been shown to the rooms prepared for them in the palace, while their escorts had been given rooms with the guards. Devlin's feet carried him toward the rooms he had assigned to Brynjolf, but he found his steps slowing, and he turned away before he reached them.

It was simple courtesy, he told himself. The travelers were cold and tired, and they needed to rest, not to answer his questions. He gave them their peace out of consideration. Not because he had anything to fear.

Still it felt like an act of cowardice when he retreated to his offices. To placate himself he arranged for dinner to be served in the smallest of the royal dining rooms and sent a servant with the message that those who wished to join him could do so.

He spent the rest of the afternoon working in his offices, reviewing the tax rolls. A few weeks previously the Royal Steward had sent over a list of those who were delinquent in their taxes, urging immediate action. Several of the names on the list had been familiar to him, including the Baron of Esker. It had not taken him long to realize that the royal steward had prepared a list that included only the names of his political enemies, while failing to include others who had been supporters of King Olafur. When confronted, the steward had claimed these were honest errors. Hopefully, he'd learned better than to try such a petty trick again. In the meantime, Devlin had had the complete tax rolls sent over to his offices, and with the help of his aide was slowly going through them, putting together his own lists.

Some, like Brynjolf, would be excused. The Baron of Esker had not hoarded his treasure for his own gain. Instead he had spent his personal fortune on training and equipping a force of armsmen. Without his troops, the northwestern territories would have fallen to the border raiders. It was the crown that owed a debt to Brynjolf, not the other way around.

Few cases were as clear. Some tax payments had never reached the capital, falling victim to robbers or pirates. Devlin doubted that all the nobles who claimed such were telling the truth, but it was a hard thing to prove, and he knew better than to utter accusations that he could not back up. He needed their taxes to rebuild the kingdom, but he also needed their support. It was a tricky balancing act, and while his aide combed through the files and prepared recommendations, each case ultimately had to be decided by Devlin.

He looked up, as a soft knock interrupted his thoughts.

Jasen, his aide, stood in the doorway. "Lord Devlin, you have a visitor," he said.

Not for the first time, Devlin realized how much he missed Didrik. Jasen was more than competent, but he would never be the friend that Didrik had been. Burdened with a strict sense of propriety, he had spent weeks addressing Devlin as "Your Excellency," and it was only with great reluctance that he had finally adopted the less formal address of Lord Devlin.

"Show him in," Devlin said, then he hastily rose to his feet as Solveig entered.

His palms began to sweat. He had expected that Stephen would be the first to seek him out, or perhaps Lord Brynjolf. But not Solveig.

Devlin jerked his head and Jasen closed the door behind Solveig, granting them privacy.

"Please sit," Devlin said, pulling out the chair he kept

for visitors. "Shall I have Jasen fetch you wine? Kava? Citrine?"

He knew he was babbling, but he could not help himself.

Solveig took a seat, but Devlin leaned back against his desk, too nervous to sit.

"You look well for a man whose funeral I attended," she said. He noted that she had taken the time to change from her traveling clothes into an embroidered tunic of undyed wool, worn over darker leggings and high boots. It was casual attire, rather than the formal garb worn when the court was in session.

"I am as surprised as any by my survival," Devlin said.

It had been over a year since he had last seen Solveig. On the day he had left for Duncaer she had embraced him, urging him to come back safely, though he had known that her concern was for the Chosen One as much as it was for the man her brother called friend. Since that time he had changed greatly, but it was comforting to see that Solveig looked the same.

"I owe you a debt," he said. "For protecting Princess Ragenilda and keeping her out of the hands of the Selvarats."

Solveig shook her head. "I did not do it for you. I did it at King Olafur's request. Toward the end, even he could see the trap that he had fallen into."

"Nonetheless, you have my gratitude."

If Ragenilda had been taken, then Jorsk would have been lost in bloody civil war, for there was no other suitable heir. And if Devlin had tried to claim the throne by force, the quarreling noble factions would have united against him, while between them Nerikaat and Selvarat would have picked the bones of the Kingdom clean.

"The Princess seems no worse for her experiences," he said, as the silence stretched on between them.

"She understands her duty. And she grew fond of my father, and he of her," Solveig said.

Her gaze fixed on him, and he fought the urge to squirm. "My father plans to speak to you this evening, to tell you that he has decided to accept your offer," she said.

"Good."

When he had written to Brynjolf, he had offered the Baron a seat on the Regent's Council. It was in part as a reward for his past valor, and in part to ensure that the borderlands, which had suffered the most in the past years, had a strong voice in the deliberations of the council. He had known that Brynjolf would be reluctant to leave his lands, but Devlin had urged him to look to the greater duty.

"And what of you?" he asked.

As her father's heir, it would have been logical for Solveig to stay behind in Esker, to rule in her father's name. Instead she had made the long and difficult journey. Perhaps she had done so out of respect for the Princess, so the girl would have a familiar companion. But Devlin wondered if her presence was a sign that she was willing to consider the offer he had made in his letter to her.

"Why me?" she asked bluntly. It was one of the things that he admired about her. When she set her mind to it, Solveig could play the games of court, speaking in riddles and innuendo to shade her meaning. But she could also be as plainspoken as any farmer.

"Ragenilda is still a child. She needs a woman in her life, someone who can teach her to be strong. I could think of no better example for her to follow," he said.

Solveig pursed her lips, as if his answer had displeased her. She rose to her feet, and as she stood in front of him, he noticed that they were nearly of a height. He did not have to bend his head to meet her eyes.

"And what do you need?" she asked.

He needed a wife, to reassure all those who still thought that he coveted the crown and would marry Ragenilda to get it. But he knew enough of the workings of a woman's mind not to state his case so baldly.

"I need a friend. Someone I can trust."

He spoke no words of love. He respected Solveig and admired her strength of character. Her skills as a courtier would be invaluable, serving as a counterweight to his own blunt tactics. And he had hopes that in time their friendship would deepen into affection. But he was not capable of passion. Cerrie had been his soul mate, the love of his youth, and he would never love another in the same way.

"I will not promise love. But I can offer friendship and respect, and promise that I will be faithful to you," he said.

They both stood to gain from an alliance. As a future Baroness, Solveig had always been destined for a political marriage. He tried to tell himself that she might have done far worse for herself than one who bore the titles of Regent and Chosen One.

"And what shall we do when Ragenilda comes of age? Shall we go our separate ways? Do you expect me to follow you to Duncaer?"

It would be years before he could return to Duncaer.

Devlin the man would be welcome by his kin, but the Lord Regent would not be. His people were still recovering from the decades of Jorskian occupation. No doubt they had been shocked when Devlin's messenger arrived, instructing the Lawgiver Peredur that the Kingdom of Jorsk was prepared to recognize as sovereign whomever the six families should elect to rule. It would take time for the two kingdoms to learn to live in peace with each other, and Devlin's presence would only upset that balance.

"I plan to leave Kingsholm, and we can make our home in Esker. If you will have me," he said.

His heart quickened, which was strange. He was a man proposing a political alliance, not a callow youth proposing to his sweetheart. If Solveig rejected him, she would be rejecting the alliance, not spurning his heart. Yet, despite all logic, he held his breath as he awaited her answer.

"I accept."

His chest eased as he finally drew a breath.

"Thank you," he said, taking her hands in his. "We can ask your father for his consent this evening."

An ordinary woman could marry whom she pleased, but the heir to a barony had fewer freedoms. Not that he expected Lord Brynjolf to raise any objections, but it would be discourteous not to ask his consent.

Solveig grinned. "No need. He gave his blessing before we left Esker."

Devlin allowed Princess Ragenilda a day to rest, then early the next morning he made his way to her quarters. Three rooms were set aside for her personal use, including a bedchamber, a private sitting room for entertaining those few guests who were deemed suitable companions for the royal heir, and a small room where her maid resided. The Princess's rooms were part of the much larger royal suite, vacant since the death of her father. As he passed the sentry who guarded the corridor that led to the royal suite, Devlin was stuck by the silence, and he realized that this would be a lonely place to be. Not that he had any intention of taking residence in the royal suite. Such a move would only provide fodder for his enemies. Nor had he any wish to discover if Olafur's restless ghost haunted the site of his suicide.

But perhaps Ragenilda would like a change.

He knocked thrice on the door. After a brief delay it was opened by the Princess's maid Marja.

"Your Excellency! We did not expect you. You should have sent word so we could prepare," she scolded him, as if he were one of her charges.

"Is Ragenilda awake? Dressed?" he asked.

"Of course." Marja drew herself stiffly erect, which meant that her glare was focused somewhere in the middle of his chest.

"Then what is your concern?"

He brushed by her, and as he entered the sitting room, Ragenilda rose, and made a brief curtsy. Devlin gave a short bow in return.

"Good morning, Your Excellency," she said.

He grimaced. "There is no need for this ceremony. You may call me Devlin."

"It would not be proper," Ragenilda said, in dry tones that sounded as if her nurse had repeated this lesson often.

Devlin realized that he would have to rethink the wisdom of allowing Marja so much influence over her charge. Fortunately, the girl would have Solveig's example to follow.

"You called the Baron Lord Brynjolf, did you not? You may call me Lord Devlin, if you wish."

The noble title was an honorific, given to the Chosen One.

"Lord Devlin," she repeated.

He waited as she took a seat, daintily arranging her wide skirts around her, then took his own seat.

"You may leave us, Marja," he said, when the maid showed a tendency to hover.

The maid sniffed, then retreated to the Princess's bedroom, shutting the door behind her.

"You know I have been named Regent for you, is that right?"

She nodded.

"And do you know what that means?"

"It means you now rule, instead of a king," she said solemnly.

Her features were composed, giving no trace of her inner thoughts. It seemed impossible to think of her as a child, for surely no child could sit so still, without even a hint of fidgeting. But appearances were deceptive. She was still a child, and one in mourning for her father. He had to remember this and treat her accordingly.

"Being Regent means I will rule, yes," he said. "But it means that I am a protector. As Chosen One I protected the people of Jorsk. Do you remember when I slew the lake monster?"

She gave him a shy smile. "You told the funniest story.

But then one of the guards said you were a true hero, and he taught me a song about it."

The Princess had insisted upon meeting Devlin after his defeat of the giant skrimsal, and King Olafur had indulged his daughter's wishes. She had been amused by Devlin's tale of accidental heroics, though the Gods only knew what kind of song she had been taught. For a few months afterward there had been some truly awful ballads circulating. He still remembered Stephen's attempt. . . .

He forced his mind back to the matter at hand. "Now I have a new duty. As Regent I am to protect you, until the day you are ready to assume the throne and rule as Queen. And I am to protect your inheritance, ensuring that you have a prosperous Kingdom to rule over."

It would not be the same Kingdom her father had governed. Too much had changed and would continue to change. Turning peasants into warriors had enabled Devlin to defeat the Selvarat armies, but it had also changed the balance of power between the commoners and the nobles who ruled them. Abusive and incompetent landholders would no longer be tolerated by a people who had learned what it was to defend themselves.

It would take time to sort out the changes, and for both sides to come to a new understanding of their rights and duties. Time to restore prosperity to those areas that had suffered most under the invaders. Time to build new alliances and ensure that the Kingdom's safety was not threatened again.

"And what will you do when I become Queen?" she asked.

He realized that she needed more from him than a

promise that he would see to her political future. He was not just the guardian of the realm, he was also the guardian of a child, one who had no nearkin to care for her.

"As Queen you will be able to choose your own councilors, though you may always call upon me at need," he said. "I cannot replace your father, but I swear to you that I will care for you as if you were my own. As will Solveig Brynjolfsdatter, who has agreed to become my wife."

Ragenilda considered this for a moment, before switching topics. "You did not like my father."

"We did not agree," Devlin said. He hesitated, before deciding that plain speaking was best. "In the days and years to come you will hear many things about your father. Some good, some bad. From what I knew of him, he was not a brave man, nor was he wise. But he loved you, and that is how you should remember him."

It was a fine epitaph for a man, but a poor one for a King. Ragenilda would have to work hard to overcome her father's legacy. Still, they had time to teach her what it meant to be a wise ruler and to show her what was possible when power was allied with justice.

"Very well. I accept you as my Regent, Lord Devlin," Ragenilda said, in the tones of one granting a royal favor.

Her dignity was such that he did not point out that she had no choice in the matter.

"I thank you for your confidence," he said.

# Epilogue

——————➤

DEVLIN PULLED THE HOOD OF HIS CLOAK forward, hiding his distinctive features. The gray sky above whispered of the approach of dawn, but the streets were still dark, and the guttering torches served more as signposts than actual illumination. The streets were quiet, and he encountered only a handful of other souls—lovers or drunkards seeking their own beds and those whose labors began before the sun. None spared him a glance. And why should they? Who would believe that the man in his tattered cloak was in fact the Lord Regent of the Kingdom?

Such anonymity was a rare gift these days. Captain Embeth had assigned personal guards to him, over his objections, and few indeed were the times when he was allowed to appear in public without one of her watchful shadows. A faint smile touched his lips as he thought of how she would react when she learned that he had disappeared. Those assigned to watch him would be roundly castigated, and Embeth would berate him for his folly, then demand to know just how he had managed to slip away unnoticed so she could plug the holes in her security.

He might even tell her, if he was in the mood. Though by now she should have learned to expect the unexpected from him. The other nobles she had guarded were content to stay in the places assigned to them, but Devlin was not above a bit of subterfuge. Nor was he too dignified to crawl out a window, as he had done this morning.

He reached the tavern known as the Singing Fish just as the sky turned pink with the dawn. Even at that hour he saw a light burning in the common room, and as he made his way around the tavern to the stables behind, he saw a solitary figure saddling his horse.

"A fine day for a journey," he said.

The saddlebag slipped from Stephen's hands, falling to the ground. Stephen whirled around and stared at Devlin, his mouth open. At that moment he bore a striking resemblance to the carved wooden fish that had given the tavern its name.

Devlin reached down and picked up the saddlebag, then began to tie it to the rings on the saddle.

Stephen finally found his voice. "What are you doing here?"

"I have come to see you off, and wish you well. Is that not what friends do?"

"But how did you know?"

Devlin finished the last tie, then tugged the bag, testing to make sure that it would not shift as Stephen rode.

"I've been expecting this for some time now," he said. "And then last night, I knew you were saying good-bye."

"But I didn't say anything."

"You didn't need to."

It had been obvious to any who knew him well that Stephen was not happy in Kingsholm. Yet he had stayed, as winter passed and turned to spring. He had stood witness at the quiet ceremony that bound Devlin and his sister Solveig in marriage. He had been proud as his father was named councilor, watching as those who had once scorned Lord Brynjolf now paid heed to his words and asked his advice. But the games of politics had never interested Stephen, and as his family was cast into greater prominence, Stephen more and more often sought the shadows.

Still he had stayed until he was certain that Devlin no longer needed him. The coming of spring had seen the arrival of a new ambassador from Selvarat, one who offered Empress Thania's regrets for the recent misunderstandings. Those flowery sentiments were accompanied by a complete capitulation to Devlin's demands, as the Selvarat troops who had survived the winter embarked upon ships and sailed back to their homelands. Lady Gemma of Esker and her daughter Madrene had journeyed with the ambassador, and Stephen's pleasure in seeing his family reunited had kept him in Kingsholm weeks after Devlin had thought he would leave.

But now, as summer drew near, he had decided to go.

"Where are you bound?" Devlin asked.

Stephen shrugged. "I will wander where the roads take me. You will hear from me from time to time. Or perhaps you will hear one of my songs."

He would be glad indeed to hear one of Stephen's songs. Music had always been a part of Stephen, so much so that Devlin had taken it for granted, until the day he realized that Stephen no longer played at the campfire at night, nor did he quiz strangers trying to learn new songs from them. Devlin had cast his mind back, and had realized that sometime during the rebellion, Stephen's voice had grown silent and his hands had gone still. He had asked about it once, but Stephen had said only that he had no heart for playing. His tone had been so bleak that Devlin had not asked again.

It was ironic. Once he had forbidden Stephen to make any songs about the Chosen One, feeling that it was somehow indecent that strangers would sing of his struggles and despair. Yet now Devlin would be well pleased even to hear the atrocious ballad of his battle with the lake monster. Anything that would put the light of enthusiasm back in Stephen's face.

Stephen's had been the greatest innocence, so perhaps it was no wonder that he was the most scarred by what they had seen and done. Still there was a part of Devlin that wished he had been able to protect him. If he had been a better friend to Stephen, he would have never let him accompany him on his adventures.

"I promised that you could sing whatever you pleased, if we both survived this," Devlin said, trying for a light tone.

Stephen smiled, and this time it nearly reached his eyes. "And what would you have me sing of you?"

"Say that I ruled well, and retired to live a peaceful life, surrounded by my friends," Devlin said.

"If that is what you wish," he said. "Though I think they would rather hear about the Sword—"

Devlin pulled Stephen into a rough embrace, cutting off his musings. "Remember, there is a place for you whenever you wish to return. No matter what happens, you will always be my friend."

He released Stephen from his grasp. A small part of him wanted to tell Stephen to wait, that Devlin would find a horse and join him, traveling the roads together as they had done in the early days of their friendship. But duty bound Devlin to this place. He could not leave, and he was not selfish enough to keep Stephen here.

"Safe journey, Stephen of Esker," he said.

"I've trusted you with my sister and my kingdom," Stephen said. "Take care of them both, Devlin of Duncaer."

"That I will," he vowed. "That I will."

# About the Author

Patricia Bray inherited her love of books from her parents, both of whom were fine storytellers in the Irish tradition. She has always enjoyed spinning tales, and turned to writing as a chance to share her stories with a wider audience. Patricia holds a masters degree in Information Technology, and combines her writing with a full-time career as an I-T Project Manager. Patricia began her career as an author of historical romances, and currently has six novels out with Kensington Zebra (*A London Season*, October 1997; *An Unlikely Alliance*, October 1998; *Lord Freddie's First Love*, September 1999; *The Irish Earl*, March 2000; *A Most Suitable Duchess*, December 2001; *The Wrong Mr. Wright*, March 2002.) She resides in upstate New York. For more information on her books, visit her website at: www.sff.net/people/patriciabray.